THE
Oddity
A Novel

V.B. PRICE

UNIVERSITY OF NEW MEXICO PRESS
ALBUQUERQUE

Library of Congress Cataloging-in-Publication Data

Price, V. B. (Vincent Barrett)
The oddity / V. B. Price.—1st ed.
p. cm.
ISBN 0-8263-3303-6 (cloth : alk. paper)
1. Eccentrics and eccentricities—Fiction.
2. Women—New Mexico—Fiction.
3. Albuquerque (N. M.)—Fiction.
4. Loss(Psychology)—Fiction.
5. Friendship—Fiction.
6. Death—Fiction.
I. Title.
PS3566.R548O33 2004
813'.54—dc22

2003026971

Typeset in Janson Text 10.5/13.5
Display type set in Centaur Family and Love Letter Typewriter
Design and composition: Maya Allen-Gallegos
Jacket illustration: Rini Price

For Rini and Wendy

In Memoriam:
Clifford Brook
Roland Francis Dickey
R. W. Buddington
Patrick Chester Henderson
Sandra Rae Greenwald
James Michael Jenkinson
Warren Russell Martin
Edith Barrett Price
Marjorie H. Rini
Helen K. Herman
Dudley Wynn
Vincent Leonard Price, Jr.
Anne Seymour
Mildred and John Gifford
Mark Douglass Acuff
Katherine G. Simons
Kenneth Peterson
Milas Hurley
Florence and Bev Watts
Mary Grant Price
Dick Forbes
Susie Henderson
Paula Hocks
George Clayton Pearl

"Books lie, even those that are the most sincere."
—Marguerite Yourcenar, *The Memoirs of Hadrian*

Author's Note

The following story is an exercise in the fictionalization of everything. It is a *Rashomon*. Its author and characters bend reality to perspective. Their truths are fictions of viewpoint. I have written a book by somebody else about a world she almost invented, described by people who could exist, and who are, like all of us, confused. Reality exists. But here, only the emotions are real.

—V. B. Price
Albuquerque, 1999

Polishing the Mountain

by Helen Contreras-Robles

For Morris Wolf and The Moose

* * *

*Heaven and hell are of this world. They coexist here.
One can be seen through the other. But they are not
equal. Hell is an intrusion. It bursts through any context, but always subsides. Heaven is shy, though it always
comes first. It unfolds, but is never subdued. Our duty is
to find it and reclaim it every day, to dedicate ourselves
to its unfolding in our lives.*

—Hana Nicholas
Albuquerque, 1949

* * *

Polishing the Mountain is Helen Contreras-Robles's first published
novel. She is a journalist, poet, and immigration activist living in
San Diego, California. Dr. Contreras-Robles's Ph.D. is from the
University of New Mexico's American Studies Program. Her disser-
tation is entitled "Marija Gimbutas and the Civilizing Power of the
Goddess: An Existential Study of American Women and the
Subculture of Service."

Contents

Introduction 5

PART ONE: Diabolical Murder 7

PART TWO: Myths of Guilt 55

PART THREE: Mask of Horror 99

PART FOUR: Sticking to the Shadows 133

PART FIVE: The Disappeared 175

PART SIX: The Turning 215

PART SEVEN: The Hat of Hermes 253

PART EIGHT: The Starry Mire 293

Postscript 359

Introduction

This is a novel about meaning and the spiritual sickness that comes from searching for meaning and finding nothing that makes any sense. I have written this book under the spiritual mentorship of Dr. Viktor Frankl, the founder of logotherapy and survivor of the Nazi death camps. His book *Man's Search for Meaning* changed my life and empowered me to move beyond my chronic despair and horror of the absurdity of the world.

The frustration of what Frankl calls "the will to meaning" is what this account of the lives of Hana Claude Nicholas and Lowell Patrick Briscoe is about. It is written in the form of a novel—or, as it could be called, a literary docudrama—because so much of what took place between them in the late 1940s must always remain a fiction. Hana Nicholas could best be described as a sage, social pioneer, and eccentric who served her community in the North Valley of Albuquerque, New Mexico, with tireless and inspired devotion for more than quarter of a century. Lowell Briscoe was, of course, a world-renowned children's advocate, author, and social activist who gained quite a bit more than his fifteen minutes of fame in the 1992 multi-race riots in Los Angeles. I have compiled, edited, and creatively reconstructed the story of Nicholas's and Briscoe's remarkable relationship and personal tragedies from materials made available to me by the Lowell Patrick Briscoe Archives at the Center for Southwest Research at the University of New Mexico in Albuquerque. These include fragments of Lowell Briscoe's unpublished novel entitled "A Nest of Hells," portions of his beloved Christmas fable "The Witch and the Star," and journal entries, letters, and news accounts of the lives of the real people he fictionalized in his novel. This literary docudrama of mine is interlarded with my own fictional speculations derived from these sources and from my personal experiences and introspections as a feminist scholar and journalist working in the last half of the twentieth century searching for role models that abolish gender stereotypes in my culture. I have attempted without much success to substantiate some of the most disturbing allegations made by Dr. Briscoe and have commented briefly on my findings in the Postscript.

My ultimate goal with this novel could be described as an effort to fictionally represent the modern and, to some extent, postmodern struggle to maintain personal integrity in a philosophically unstable world. Ours is an open-ended moment in history, which demands the individual find her own way through social, religious, and psychological upheavals, but one that is also still dominated by a rigid emphasis on conformity to the power principle of what I shall call "nice appearance," or non-troubling appearance. This power principle is characteristic of decadent societies and takes the form of extreme conformism in which competing bigotries directed at women and ethnic minorities as troublesome classes, and at eccentricity as an unpredictable and unsettling tendency, create forces that crush the initiative and terminate the independence of those who think for themselves. Hana Nicholas and Lowell Briscoe were such people.

The action in the novel spreads out over seven decades, beginning in 1925 when Hana Nicholas first moved to Albuquerque, focusing on the post-war era from 1948 to 1949 and on the events surrounding the 1992 riots in Los Angeles. Although this is a thoroughly fictionalized account, I have composed it as a jigsaw puzzle of different kinds of texts, written by different characters. So as not to encumber the flow of the novel, I have used the device of footnotes to identify the "author" and "source" and date of each chapter entry. If no footnote appears, the text is purely my own informed invention.

—Helen Contreras-Robles
Albuquerque, N. Mex. 1998

PART ONE

Diabolical Murder

The April 29, 1992 Los Angeles Riot

Lowell Briscoe was listening to the news of the verdict on his car radio, thinking to himself "They walked. Those damn cops walked. And just 'cause they were cops. How could the jury do that? Everybody in the whole world saw what those bastards did. How could the jury get talked out of it? Wasn't the video absolute evidence? How could they rationalize a savage beating they saw over and over again with their own eyes? The sophistry of lawyers. Racism, racism, racism, racism. It's just horribly true, a poor black man in this country isn't worth the wood on a gallows."

The suburban jury had found six Los Angeles police officers not guilty of beating Rodney King half to death. The jurors concluded the officers had used "reasonable force" to subdue the ex-con after a high-speed auto chase. Lowell Briscoe could feel the cold rot of cynicism creeping relentlessly through him. "This is how it must feel to find that your neighbors were dragged out of their house and carted off to a gulag while you were at a movie matinee," he thought. "This is a bit of how Hana must have felt when she was taken away."

Lowell was in shirt sleeves, windows rolled down, cruising through South Central L.A. on the way to the University of Southern California from the coast. He was looking forward to teaching his seminar on Racism and Xenophobia in the Ancient World. It was a hot, breezy late April day. His anger was political and abstract. He felt in no personal danger. Traffic was moderate. Slowing to a stop behind three other cars at the intersection of Florence and Normandy, he became aware of people milling around in the street, of shouting and the sound of breaking glass. It took him a few moments to change focus from his angry musings to realize that a number of young men were running toward his car, shouting, "There's one, get him, get that fucker, break his fuckin' head."

Panic overcame him. Lowell was jolted by dizziness. "What!? They're coming after ME. Wait! Wait! Wait! Me!? God no, not me. No. . . ." As he tried to roll up his window, nightmare slow motion seized his muscles. The window wouldn't go up. He shifted gears, grinding into reverse, smashed into the car behind him, trying to turn out into another lane. Then a rock exploded through the driver's-side window, hitting him just below the left eye, driving glass into his cheek. "Fuckers, fuckers, fuckers, not me, you fucking idiots. Who do you think I am? Fuckers! I'll kill you, kill you for this, kill you, kill you, cut your fucking hearts out. Mother fuckers. Mother fuckers. . . ." The rush of adrenaline made his whole body shake. He gunned the engine, trying to run over his attackers. He smashed into the car ahead of him, backed up again into the car behind him, screaming and swearing at the top of his lungs, "Fuckers, fuckers, fuckers. . . ." Then hands grabbed his arms, tore his grip from the steering wheel; fists cracked his nose, his glasses were smashed into his face. His car was pushing the car behind out of its path when the hands finally hauled him out of the car and onto the street. Shoes hit his mouth and nose. Someone kicked him in the chest and stomach. "Sack a shit!" More foot blows landed on his lower back and spine. His face was grinding into the asphalt. "Jesus god, I'm dying. . . . I can't breathe. I can't . . . mob's too heavy, mobbed, mass . . . minded . . . too heavy, too heavy to breathe."

He tried to curl up and cover his head with his arms, when a shoe caught him on the shin and another battered him several times between the legs from behind. Someone hauled him to his feet; others hit him in the face, ribs, and stomach. Hands searched his back pockets and took his wallet; someone put a gun to his head. (Images of his mother's silk dress on his cheek; Joel's howls in the hospital; Juliet's milky belly; La Boheme by the pool; Singapore slings on the beach in the morning; pine smell and Christmas candles in Hana's Kiva; the back of Mark Spindle's head when the jury found him guilty of Juliet's murder; screaming at Nola, "You killed her. You did it. You did it.") He heard a young, squeaky voice say, "No guns. Too fast. Use this." A claw hammer cracked into Lowell's left jaw. He fell; the hammer came down toward his head again, it glanced off his skull down his ear, practically ripping it off. "Leave this sucker. Over there, over there." The beaters ran to another car across the intersection. Lowell rolled on the pavement, bloody-mouthed, aching, his heart pumping so fast he could feel the blood spurting from cuts on his face and where his teeth used to be. "Can't think; I'm burning up; I'll kill 'em, torch 'em, torch 'em. I'm dying, aren't I? . . . You're dying, you're dying."

He pulled himself up to open the door of his car. Another shoe crunched into his ribs and kidneys like a sledge hammer. He fell again, the hot front of the left tire smudging down his cheek.

"No, no! In Jesus' name, leave him alone; go home, go home, now," the big woman shouted. "Don't do this anymore; go home. Go away. Stop it, stop it." Hands picked him up, a face stared kindly into his. "You poor thing. What have they done to you? You're OK now. You're OK. . . ." Another voice, "Hurry, hurry, Marjorie! They're coming back!" Lowell felt himself being half dragged and carried to another car. "Hurry! You're OK, you're OK."

"I'm dying," he thought. And then he blacked out.

June 23, 1949

"All things counter, original, spare, and strange," Gerard Manley Hopkins wrote. Hana read and nodded in agreement, as she transcribed his words in her notebook. "You either are that way or you are not," she wrote. "I trust people like that. They have to know who they are. They can't glide along. They can't live by rote. It's too dangerous; it's too boring. They know what it means to pay attention and polish the mountain no matter what."

Hana was dreamy and comforted that morning with the living room curtains drawn, secluded in her wing-backed reading chair, safe among her books. For the first time in months she felt protected and invisible. Her camouflage worked, even though she could never quite believe it. Hopkins's words gave her the feeling of being known. She was still a little sleepy and her mind wandered among images and associations that surprised and repulsed her. "All things counter . . . think of all the old women, all the 'spare and strange' old crones carted off by the Inquisition. Three hundred years of burning women, gray hair blazing. Three hundred years of shrieking and horror and unspeakable pain. What does age and being a woman have to do with heresy? What would they have done to me?" Hana shook herself, trying to focus again on her reading. She leafed through her notebook and found Dostoyevsky's admonition in the *Brothers Karamozov*, "I think you should love life above everything in the world . . . love it regardless of logic . . . it must be regardless of logic, and it's only then one will understand the meaning of it." She had quoted those words for years, to herself and to others, in church and at board meetings. She knew it was the truth.

Hana read like this for two hours every morning, taking notes on as many as five books at a time. This morning, along with Hopkins, she was reading again in Eliot's *Four Quartets*, comparing the maxims of the Epictetus and Epicurus, and savoring Colette's novella *Bella Vista*.

Her living room at Gloriamaris also served as her study, her "thinking room." Years ago she had painted the walls hunter green, and the floor-to-ceiling bookcases were stained a dark Edwardian brown. Her lamps had 40-watt bulbs in them and gave off a "deep woods kind of yellow light," she wrote once in her journals. The thinking room is cave-like with the curtains closed, she admitted. "Why does that annoy people so much? I never draw the curtains when they're here. Why would they find my seclusion so threatening?" she wondered for the hundredth time. "It's been my habit for years." After she read each morning, she practiced her piano for an hour, playing mostly the Mozart, Beethoven, Bach, and Debussy she still knew by heart.

The cats and dogs and horses were hungry for breakfast when they heard the music stop. The turtles, rabbits, and various fowl needed feeding, and she had to patch the leak in the carp pond this morning before biking to the grocery. "Time to rise and shine," she thought. "This isn't the fourteenth century. Why do I think it is?"

She piled her music and books neatly on the side table and carefully capped her fountain pen. As she rose to change from her robe to her overalls, someone knocked forcefully at the front door.

The sound sent a shock of adrenaline burning through her. "God, who could that be? This is preposterous. Everyone knows better than to come in the morning. Maybe they'll go away. No, I'd better see if it's Lowell. Maybe he's in trouble." She moved to the door slowly, stepping lightly so whoever it was wouldn't hear her. She gingerly drew aside the edge of the front curtain and saw two sheriff's officers, one about to knock again.

She froze in horror, paralyzed as if she'd just witnessed a premonition come to life. She could barely breathe and then abruptly began to pant violently and sank to the floor of the little entrance alcove, sliding on the throw rug so her feet thumped against the door.

"Miss Nicholas, Miss Nicholas, this is the sheriff's office. Please open the door."

Hana stopped just short of hyperventilating. She was beginning to feel tingly, and she knew what that meant. She cupped her hands over her nose and tried to breathe slowly. "What is going on here?" she thought. "Pull yourself together, child. Pull yourself together. Get up, get up. Straighten up. There's nothing wrong. This is not a dream. It's all right. It's all right."

"I'll be right there, officers. I'm still in my night things. Let me change."

"What could possibly be going on? I've got to keep myself calm. Be alert. Relax. Stay calm." She changed into a work shirt and overalls. There was much to be done in the garden today. So many happy chores.

Some of the dogs and cats outside had begun to get nervous. Much barking and pacing was going on under the back portal. She thought for the slightest moment about bolting out the back door, as she had when she was a little girl, breaking free and riding away into the forest, disappearing forever. But the horses were of no use for escape anymore. And the mountains here were too far away.

"There's nothing wrong. Look strong," she said to herself.

A harder knock at the door. "I'm coming, officers," Hana said in a firm voice as she strode across her living room, pausing briefly to open the curtains.

She unlatched the door, turned the knob, and as she did an officer unexpectedly nudged it open, stepping into the alcove before she could graciously open the door. The other officer stepped inside too, and Hana back-pedaled into the living room.

"What can I do for you gentlemen?"

"Are you Hana Claude Nicholas?"

"Yes, I am. What's happened?"

"Don't be alarmed, Miss Nicholas. We're not here to hurt you. We want to make this easy for you, so don't worry. We have a court order here. We're authorized to take you into protective custody. You're going to be just fine."

"What on earth do you mean, take me into protective custody!? Why? Who are you protecting me from?"

"Yourself, ma'am."

"Myself?"

"Yes, Miss Nicholas."

"Why? What for? Tell me, for heaven sakes. For what reason? What have I done?" She felt like she was about to faint. Her voice had raised to a frenzied pitch.

"Please, Miss Nicholas, ma'am, don't give us any trouble. We don't want to have to cuff you. You're going to be just fine. You'll see. This isn't going to hurt at all."

"Mrs. Dasheller, would you come in now, please," the other officer called out in the direction of the front door.

"Nola, Nola, what's going on here? Who are these people? Why do they want to arrest me? What's going on?"

"They're sheriff's officers, dear. Can't you see? They don't want to arrest you, honey. They just want to help you, take you where you can get some rest for a while."

"Take me for a rest?! What do you mean? What do you mean rest? What is this!? Why are you here, Nola? What is this?" Hana said with a livid fury in her voice.

"Honey, don't worry."

"Don't call me honey. What on God's good earth is going on?"

"Don't worry. It's all going to be just fine. Just stay calm," Nola said like a pediatrician. "Do you see what I mean, officers? Just do your job, please, before this gets worse."

"That's what we're trying to do, ma'am," the bigger deputy said as he took Hana rudely by the arm.

"Let go of me. Who do you think you are? Are you out of your mind? I said let go. This isn't Russia. . . . What have I done? Why are you doing this? What IS going on?" Hana's indignation was getting hard as cement. She was enraged, terrified. "I feel like a dog being dragged off to the pound," she yelled. "Let go of me, let go right now!"

"Miss Nicholas, we're authorized to take you with us under state statutes regarding the involuntary referral and hospitalization of the mentally ill," one of the deputies said in an official voice. "Do you understand? A written application has been filed with the district court by Mrs. Dasheller accompanied, as the law requires, by a certificate of a licensed physician, you can see right there," the deputy said, showing her the document, "signed by Dr. Harold Barrows, here, that he is of the opinion that you are mentally ill."

"Mentally ill! Mentally ill! What on earth are you talking about," Hana screamed into the officer's face.

"Hana, my darling, calm yourself, dear, calm yourself. It's all right. It's going to be all right. I'll be with you. Hal will examine you again very soon, and you'll probably be fine. I'll be with you all the way. Just stay calm. Remember yourself. Stay calm, be at peace. This is what you need, darling one. A little rest. . . . Hurry officers! I can't keep her passive for long."

The deputies pulled and pushed Hana out the front door of Gloriamaris. Nola locked it with her own set of keys.

"This is not happening. This is not happening," Hana heard herself scream inside her head. "This is a dream. I'm going to shrivel up like a snail hit with salt. How can they do this? It's insane, it's insane! I can't stand it! I don't understand. . . . The babies. . . . I've got to feed the babies. They're going to kill the babies!"

"The babies," Hana screamed. "My babies! . . . I must feed my babies!"

"Come on, ma'am. Come on, come on. There you go. . . ."

"Don't worry, dear. I'll take care of them. I'll take care of them, darling. I'll feed them while you're gone," Nola said through the squad car window.

"Aren't you coming, Nola?" Hana asked like a child.

"Not yet, dear."

— —

Adapted from Lowell Briscoe's unpublished novel "A Nest of Hells."

"Diabolical Murder"
Christmas 1964

Juliet's old body was still cloud white and cool as fruit, Lowell thought as he tried to comfort her and calm her down. She was sixty and her arms were firm as a dancer's. Her ribs and the curve of her breast were a milky blue. He could see them through the folds of her nightgown as she lay sobbing on the bed, her eyes puffed up and leaking mascara.

"'Diabolical murder.' That's what Hana said to me, Lowell. 'This is diabolical murder.' Then she grabbed me like a child would, begging me not to leave, pulling at my arms, moaning like an animal dying of homesickness and grief."

Juliet turned stern. She got that hawkish look on her face that used to terrify Lowell as a child. She dabbed the tears from her cheeks and sat on the edge of the bed. Her long, red hair looked like Rita Hayworth's.

"Nothing in my life has been so horrible as that moment watching Hana struggle against her fate," Juliet said with a melodramatic shudder. "I couldn't bear it. I was all alone. I felt like a traitor, but I turned from her, turned my face, tried to walk away but she wouldn't let me go. She held on to me and I thought for a moment she was going to fall on her knees and beg."

Juliet crossed her legs and ran her fingers through her hair. "It was so terrible, Lowell, I wanted to take her in my arms and whisk her away, but then the attendants came and pulled her off. It was all I could do to slip through the jail door before she could get at me again. Once I was on the other side, Hana went limp, didn't make a sound. I watched her through the white bars as the attendants helped her back down the hall to the stale little holding cell." Juliet paused, mulling details. "She didn't sag, exactly, but her head hung down; the fight went out of her; and her bigness, that wonderful Clydesdale poise of hers—it was utterly gone. She looked as if she'd had a lobotomy. She scraped her feet as she walked. Her joy was drained; the hope, the optimism, the great shine of her life was gone. When they rounded the corner at the end of the hallway, Hana turned her head and looked at me. Oh, God," Juliet shuddered. "I saw that beautiful weathered face, that dear, innocent Joan of Arc look, those wise philosopher's eyes. But she'd been transformed, Lowell," she said with a strange harshness. "Her face looked monkey-like, like a chimp's. She seemed to snarl silently like a beloved pet I'd betrayed and sent to the vacuum chamber. That's exactly what she was like. It was like I'd left her at the pound to be put to sleep. I felt so ashamed, so ashamed," she said, staring into the room. "I could do nothing, nothing. I was helpless. I was the only one of us who went there, the only one who saw her before they took her to the state hospital, the sanitarium, or whatever you call it. Nola was there at the hearing, of course, so was Dr. Barrows, but I was the only one in that jail, in that hideous place."

"What do you mean by *jail?* Was she in jail? That doesn't seem right."

"After the hearing, Lowell, after the hearing in the County Courthouse," Juliet said with annoyance. "They kept her in the cells above the courtrooms . . . before they took her away."

"God, how terrible."

Juliet covered her face and shook her head, mumbling furiously, "The hearing. A sanity hearing! Can you imagine that? Is that the craziest thing you could think of? What were we doing? A sanity hearing for Hana! That's insane!"

Juliet started sobbing again. The hawk scowl faded. Lowell watched the familiar metamorphosis of her face, from Medusa to Aphrodite to Little Nell. She curled up on the bed and looked at him as if she were going to suck her thumb. She wept so bitterly she could hardly catch her breath. Her lipstick and spittle stained the peach-tinted satin pillow case. She smelled of gin and White Shoulders cologne and yesterday's vomit. Her bedroom was hot with dusty afternoon light. It filtered through the blinds and soiled yellow drapes. Hers was a sickroom now, an invalid's nest, no longer the refuge, the chamber of fantasy and escape that it was when Lowell came to live with her. It was a boudoir then, lacy and sweet-smelling and dark. In 1948, when Lowell was ten, this room was like he imagined a harem to be in the Arabian Nights, "a private harem, fresh and motherly, voluptuously sanitary—just plain glamorous, designed by the ad departments of Sears and Saks Fifth Avenue," he'd written in his journal more than forty years later. Now, in the Christmas season of 1964, it seemed like "a secret room in somebody's attic, a place to die or hide out, in shabby luxury, from the Nazis or the thought police. It was haunted with the stink of illness and old shoes and with the chill of lost delight."

Juliet is Lowell's half-sister. In 1964, Lowell was twenty-six years old. Adapted from Lowell Briscoe's "A Nest of Hells."

Religious Skirmishing

22 October 1934—Gloriamaris

The locust trees turned into great geysers of yellow leaves again. This morning a warm wind is blowing through the garden, quite ferociously at times. When I looked out my window a moment ago, the garden air was tempestuous with leaves, golden cottonwood, locust, dark red Virginia creeper leaves. Magnificent. Nothing like Gloriamaris in late autumn. Nine sublime winters here. Another one coming. I'm completely inconspicuous, despite knowing and being known by almost everyone in this part of the Valley. People here are so delicate about other people's business. I've said this so many times before. But I'm still astonished at their tact and civility. It's especially true in the winter. We all 'hole up,' as the mountain men used to say. And the next great burrowing is just ahead. And Thanksgiving again, Los Pastores, "the" play again—I've got to start writing it now—Christmas eve, Santo Domingo dances. What a fine time to snuggle in and be Mr. Badger in his housecoat.

All kinds of little tempests around here. I've been reading Jane Ellen Harrison's wonderful but long-out-of-print book *Themis: A Study of the Origins of Greek Religion*—1912, I believe. Fascinating to think of a world nurtured and defended by a Great Goddess long before old Zeus and old Jehovah. I mentioned to Nola Miss Harrison's view of Themis as the guardian of "right living," the keeper of the pre-Olympian idealism, the goddess of the social order, and Nola became quite distant, almost irritably impatient, implying—if not directly saying so—that there is no past before the God of the Bible, that "He" is all, and has always been "All," and that all the rest is silly and, I believe she used these words, "dangerous conjecture," when she really meant to say "nonsense." I was stunned and put out. What a strange and disagreeable close-mindedness for a scholar and university professor! We've spoken of religion many times before—especially Pueblo Indian religion. I remember how she was tolerant of the Pueblos because they had "plowed under paganism" in favor of "the

Christ." They have done no such thing, of course. And Nola should know better, even if she is a relative newcomer. Well, I suppose this will be a fruitful difference between us. Though I feel the subject has been almost sealed off and has become a wall between us. Is there a whole part of my life that Nola not only can't make any sense of, but thinks she disagrees with too? Certainly there is. I no more want Nola to know everything about me than I want to bare my soul to my mother and father, the cold, deaf demigods of childhood, or even to the great Nanna, grandmother of winter, who now talks to herself in a little room and wouldn't remember anything I said to her anyway. Freedom from forced candor. Freedom from arctic tortures. That's why I'm in New Mexico. So I don't have to disclose. What does it matter that Nola, good friend that she is, knows only a part of me and can know no more? Thanks to God, though, for Thea and George. They might not share my enthusiasms, but at least they don't slam doors of awareness in my face. . . . It's not unusual for someone like me, an outsider everywhere I go, to have no foolproof confidant, no one to completely trust . . . does anyone? Is there anything, in the last analysis, but prayer?

＿ ＿

This journal entry was written roughly nine years after Hana Nicholas's arrival in New Mexico.

Juliet's Purging
Christmas 1964

"What do you mean, exactly, by 'diabolical murder'? What on earth are you talking about?" Lowell asked Juliet with the high whine of an irritated child. Lowell could be gaggingly self-important and high-handed with Juliet. It was one of his more miserable qualities.

"You know, you know," she whimpered accusingly. "Thank God you've come. I want to tell you everything I can remember. I cannot bear to hold it in any longer. I'm the last one left, the last one. I just want you to listen to me, Lowell, just listen. Just be my therapist again for a while, will you Lowell?"

Lowell had expected something uncomfortable when she'd made those endless long-distance phone calls to Los Angeles, pleading with him to come home that Christmas, but nothing like this. He'd put his suitcase in his old bedroom, which Juliet kept pretty much the way it had been when he was a boy, poured himself a large brandy, sat himself down in a stuffed chair opposite her bed, and tried to appear detached. Juliet still had such a strong effect on him. The scars were deep, like the jagged edges of a half geode, and Juliet was the other half.

Juliet finished unburdening herself about the dreadful encounter she had with Hana at the County Courthouse and then asked him, "Do you understand what I'm saying, Lowell? Hana was judged insane, or incompetent, or something. The sanest person I have ever known was judged unable to care for herself and a danger to others. She was consigned to a rest home for a while and then transferred to the nut hatch in Las Vegas, that hideous place where you saw her before you left this house and left me to go to Yale. It was Yale, wasn't it? Yes, it was. Anyway, she never raised a finger in her own defense. Those ghastly words— 'diabolical murder'—were her only comment on the whole brutal travesty, and she never uttered them at the hearing."

This was the part of the puzzle Lowell had been looking for since he had been told Hana had died after the Christmas play of 1948. Through great efforts and heroic feats as a boy he'd learned that Hana had not died but had, as one adult told him, lost her mind. He knew many bits and pieces of the story, but didn't remember ever hearing anything about a sanity hearing other than Thea Pound's blithering tale, or anything about the torture Hana endured. Why didn't she defend herself? Why didn't she take the stand and prove to everyone how infallibly wise and savvy she was? Why didn't she demonstrate her clear-headed humor and intelligence? It was inconceivable to Lowell that someone as self-reliant as Hana could be cowed into silence. It must have been a nightmare for her. She was stunned, he was sure. And she was in agony. Lowell understood that clearly when he saw her in Las Vegas, sitting in a wicker chair with that monstrous grimace frozen on her face, her mouth gaping as if to make a demonic scream.

—

From Lowell Briscoe's "A Nest of Hells."

"Et In Arcadia Ego"

[JOURNAL OF HANA NICHOLAS]
2 June 1944—Gloriamaris

The war will never stop. Millions of people are being murdered, and we are rationing tires and sugar, safe in our little fortress America, our little paradise, our Arcadia where everyone in the world wants to come, where I came nearly twenty years ago, escaping reality and facts and God knows what, only to find the facts of paradise to be quite different from the facts of hope. All over the world, people are being driven from their homes, slaughtered, left destitute, mangled. And I am about to put on my overalls, my big boots, take my shovel, and let water out of my side ditch into my corn rows and victory cabbage patch. I have seen so many young men in the last three years in hospitals with terrible wounds and mental deformities. I've read them so many stories. I've talked to the German POWs tending the milk cows up Rio Grande at Los Poblanos farm. I've sat some nights like Whitman holding the hands of those who wish they were dying, so terribly do they hurt, so crippled will they always be. Here I am in Gloriamaris, in Albuquerque, in New Mexico, in Paradise, in the American Arcadia, in America's Arcadia itself, in this divine backwater wilderness of the way the world used to be, of the way it will never be again. And even Arcadia itself is dying and changing. Even the present paradise is becoming a thing of the past. When I moved here from my paradise, from my Arcadia as a child to this one, I changed it myself. Gloriamaris has changed it, no matter how respectful I am of it. Most of my neighbors still speak Spanish first. Most of them still sweep their yards so the dirt is immaculate. Most of them do a little farming, work at the jobs downtown or on the railroad or in hotels. Many, many of them are in the war; many in the war remember Los Griegos and the North Valley as their heaven on earth, aching to return to what will never be the same. Most of my neighbors are so courteous that they have never said they thought my big house and all the land I have is outlandish and arrogant and way too rico. They treat me not with deference but with kindness and respect, like a nice guest they don't want to embarrass and can put up with for as long as they need to because she's trying hard not to get in the way and to help out as much she can. Everyone is so poor here and so generous. So careful with each other, by and large. The only thief in the whole area is an Anglo woman over in Los Candelarias. And they excuse her because she lost her husband and drinks.

Et in Arcadia Ego. Even I am in Arcadia. This green island of courtly poverty, of Virgilian solitude, these fields full of corn and oats and apples and Pan. Even I am in Arcadia, companion of beavers and muskrats and kestrels and cranes. Hermes is here, too, in the cool of the shade, in the clarity of the water, in the deceptive grandeur of the shadows. Most of the world wants to live in America, and most of America doesn't know New Mexico exists. And I live in the place that nobody knows and everyone yearns for. And what have I done to it? I have changed it, delicately I admit. But as much as I love it now, I don't totally live here myself. I live part of my life in the long ago, in my dark forests and secret meadows, my streams of light. I am a refugee from paradise hiding in another paradise. And no one can know who I am. I live now in a place that I am reinventing because I love it, so it becomes for me a lovely dream, as lovely as the dream of the past. So I am that person who lives in two dreams and who still walks upon the earth, which is real, and lets water out into her fields, and shops at the little store down the way and passes on gossip about crops and animals and tiny human follies. And all around me, people walk in dreams different from mine. And the world all around us, the great world ocean all around us is on fire, oil burning on its waters, a hurricane of fire everywhere but here. For now.

— —

This entry was written three days before D Day, nineteen years after Hana Nicholas arrived in New Mexico.

Juliet's Purging, Continued
Christmas 1964

Juliet tried to answer Lowell's questions about the hearing, but as usual she was maddeningly vague and theatrical.

"I don't know how it worked. But we all agreed that Hana was in deep, deep trouble . . . psychologically, and that she needed a long rest, and was not about to take care of herself. It was Nola's idea more than anyone's but we all agreed. We all signed on. I don't think any of us, though, thought for a moment that Hana would be committed, exiled to a madhouse for the rest of her life."

"You don't think Nola thought that?" Lowell asked her as calmly as he could.

"You've always hated Nola, haven't you? It *was* her idea, but I don't honestly think for a moment that Nola thought Hana would clam up like she did, become spitefully catatonic, put on that ghastly face, and never budge again. I mean, she just seized up. When the sheriff came to her house, Nola said Hana froze, began to shake and rave, and eventually had to be carried bodily to the squad car," Juliet said with a familiar tone of defensiveness in her voice.

"Jesus, are you telling me the sheriff came to get her, dragged her from Gloriamaris, and carted her off? For God's sake, why? What possible reason could there have been for that?"

"I don't know, I don't know, I don't know!" Juliet yelled. She caught herself, gathered what poise she had, and continued. "Nola said that Hana had become a danger to herself, and to others . . . and that Hal Barrows, you remember Dr. Hal? that Hal Barrows said she was mentally ill. I mean, he was a doctor. . . . It all happened so fast. I feel so impotent, still. One moment we were all reveling in the sweetness and sentiment of Hana's Christmas play and the next moment Hana had collapsed, had to stay in bed for three weeks. And then you got sick, had one of your famous breakdowns. . . ."

"'Famous breakdowns'? Thanks a lot, Juliet, you sweet bitch . . . you always have to find something, don't you, some snideness to spice things up. . . . Isn't this ever going to stop?"

"Oh honey, don't, don't. I didn't meant it that way, really. I know you couldn't help it. It was a terrible time with terrible things going on. And Dr. Barrows explained it all to me," said Juliet, backpedaling with the savvy of a wounded boxer. "But you did collapse and so did she. And Nola . . . I don't know if you ever knew this . . . Nola thought that you and Hana weren't good for each other."

"Of course I knew. That God damn meddler! Who the fuck did she think she was?! What business was it of hers? Hana and I were friends! Best friends! Best friends! *Nothing* more or less than that," he screeched. "And that God damn Dr. Barrows, Dr. Hal, don't deny that he had both of us hooked on speed!"

"What are you talking about, young man?" said Juliet rising to her feet like a deranged school marm.

"God, Juliet, don't 'young man' me. You can't deny that Dr. Hal had hooked everyone in the crowd, but Hana, on amphetamines. Isn't that right? Isn't it? And what the hell did he do to me when I was down and out? Did he drug me? Did you let him?"

"You foul, foul, foul little bastard! You are shameless. You have no respect, none, absolutely none, none."

Lowell was about to lose all control. But when he looked at Juliet he saw her slump into herself, momentarily dejected or exhausted. It was just enough to make him pause and regain his composure. He didn't want to dredge up his feelings for Hana. He didn't need that now. He had too much going on in his life. And he'd always had a nagging guilt he might have been a cause of Hana's tragedy—or at least a last straw. He didn't want to admit it, but he could never let go of the idea. And he could feel it starting to eat into him again. And he had to put a stop to it.

— —

At this time in Hollywood and Washington, and other power centers, physicians, jokingly referred to as "Doctor Feelgoods," routinely prescribed amphetamines for their busy patients. Adapted from Lowell Briscoe's "A Nest of Hells."

Not To Be Lonely

[Diary of Nola Dasheller]
Sunday

I have resolved to do everything in my power not to be lonely. I was lonely with Boris. I don't need to be lonely without him. How can love and loneliness exist in the same person? I feel ashamed of that. But surely God understands, don't You? You know that I loved him. You know what I put up with. You know that in my heart of hearts I forgave him everything. Even though I still feel resentment. And he's dead! Surely forgiveness and resentment can coexist. They do in me. But am I truly forgiving, truly?

Hana took my hand during the eulogies.

This house is so big, so much to do. Thank God. I'm so tired. I don't mind sleeping alone. I have for months and months. Poor Boris and his enuresis. Is that what it's called, or is it incontinence when you're an adult? What a silly question.

> *"Look on everyone that is proud*
> *and bring him low;*
> *and tread down the wicked where*
> *they stand.*
> *Shall a faultfinder contend*
> *with the Almighty?"*

I'm always surprised there's not much comfort in Job. Just duck and keep low. That's the message, unless you have God in your heart, unless He is listening inside your mind.

This diary entry was written in August 1935.

"Boyish and Gallant"

[JOURNAL OF LOWELL BRISCOE]

I still can't shake the thought that I might have been to blame for what happened. But how can a kid of ten or eleven be culpable? It's not fair for me to blame him; I wouldn't do that to someone else his age. But I can't get rid of the idea. It's not exactly an idea; it's a shadow, a chill. It might be *the* obsessive guilt, if there is one, at the center of my life. But why would I feel guilty for love, and not for deceit, or manipulation, or venal self-indulgence? Why should I feel guilt for love? I did love Hana. I love Hana now. It's the kind of love you have for your deepest and truest childhood friend; a complete comfort, a giddiness, an awed happiness. Why should I feel guilty for that? Or even for expressing that? Is it because I suspect myself of having ulterior motives, sexual or possessive motives? So what if I did? They would have been based on true feeling, not on conquest or exploitation. But I didn't. I know, rationally and intuitively, that my love for Hana was boyish and gallant, and nothing like the steamy mire that kept Juliet and me in a stew.

These journals were written mostly in the summer of 1992 at the request of Melinda Tuttle, M.D., Lowell's psychiatrist, in the aftermath of the Los Angeles riot.

Juliet's Purging, Continued
Christmas 1964

Lowell backed off his anger about Nola and Dr. Hal, apologized, and calmed down. He and Juliet sat silently for many minutes. Then he asked her again to tell him about the hearing.

"I don't remember much. I really don't, Lowell, really, really. . . . I was there, yes. So were the others. We 'testified' about Hana's mental health, in the spirit of friendship. It didn't take half a day. It was all over so fast. And Hana didn't say a word. Her face was stony. She looked gray and disbelieving. . . . God, I feel so terrible. . . . Why didn't she say something, why didn't she respond when the judge asked her if she had anything to say in her own behalf? Nola said Hana just shut her eyes and pressed her lips tight."

"Didn't you see her yourself?"

"No, I couldn't look."

"Did you testify?"

"I told you I did."

"What did you say?"

"I can't really remember. I can't. I just can't. I'm sure I told the judge how wonderful Hana was, how wise and smart she was, and what a good friend I thought she was. I don't know what else I might have said. Nola wanted me to say something about Hana's relationship with you. I do remember telling the judge that I thought she'd been a very good influence, but that perhaps she loved you too much."

"What do you mean 'too much'?" Lowell asked irritably.

"I don't know what I meant. I meant perhaps that you spent too much time together. Maybe you were too much for her; maybe she bit off more than she could chew with you."

"You said *that* to the judge?!" Lowell yelled in disgusted disbelief.

"I don't know. I don't know. I must have said something like that. Nola was glaring at me. I can't remember. I can't. . . ."

"What else did you say about me?"

"Nothing. How could I?"

They sat quietly again. Juliet cried and coughed and sniffed. Lowell crossed and recrossed his legs, trying to think things through.

"How could someone be snatched from their house like that? What kind of law was at work?" he asked incredulously.

"I don't know."

"Is that all you can say?"

"Well, I don't know. You could do that in New Mexico back then and in California, too."

"If you don't know, how do you know about California?"

"Nit, nit, nit, nit. That's all you do. Listen to me, just listen. . . . I heard it somewhere. A person makes a complaint. A doctor concurs, the court holds a hearing, someone is appointed legal guardian, like Nola was. . . . And if you were having a little trouble upstairs you could be taken care of until you got better. But Hana never got better."

Then she said in a weary, wet little voice, "To tell you the honest to God truth, Lowell, I'm not sure she ever really was sick at all. . . . I never have been sure."

"You mean she was set up, framed? . . . But then why did you help put her away? If you weren't sure, how could you do it?"

"Don't you remember anything, Lowell? Don't you remember how fraught everything was back then, how frayed, how close to the edge, how crazy it was? You stupid, stupid boy," she said with a snide frown.

"How *could* I forget?" Lowell mumbled.

Juliet marched on. "Nola hinted, Lowell, that she knew about us, hinted that she thought you were an evil force, a 'bad seed,' she said. That you and Hana were. . . ."

"Now wait a God damn minute. . . . I'm sick of this," Lowell seethed, releasing a torrent of expletives. "For God's sake, it was the only clean thing in my whole life!"

Juliet gazed off around the room. It was an old tactic of hers. She appeared not to have heard a word Lowell said. Then she told him with a world-weary sigh, "The worst part, of course, Lowell, was when they came to take her animals away. They took them all to the pound . . . that's what Nola said . . . put them all to sleep. It took several trucks to get them all there. We all watched from the street. You, thank God, were still sleeping almost twenty-four hours a day. They took all the animals. All the dogs, all the cats, the birds, the turtles, the fawn, the fish, the horses, the cows, the chickens, the raccoon, the rabbits, the whole menagerie. I don't know if Hana ever found out. She must have known, though. I don't know why any of us didn't take some of them as pets . . . at least old Oberon."

"They'd be living proof of complicity, or is it conspiracy?" Lowell said. The malice slipped right past her. The mention of old Oberon, the black Labrador, "the king of the fairies and master of the gardens" as Hana called him, swamped Lowell for an instant with maudlin softness. For all his ambition and cold-bloodedness, all his frozen detachment, Lowell was prone to sentimentality about almost everything in his childhood. The death of Hana's "babies" was as outrageous as anything he could imagine.

"Was there some sort of court decree about the animals?" Lowell asked, shaking his head. "Who got Hana's property? Were there any relatives? Who benefited? Who subdivided the land? Who got the money? Who? None of this makes any sense, Juliet. It just sounds unbelievable."

"I know nothing about the legalities, Lowell. People told me, but I don't remember a thing. I never remember things like that. You know how bad I am with formalities and numbers, dear."

"But who got the land? Wasn't there at least five or six acres? It was a great hunk of property. A big, beautiful old adobe, ancient cottonwoods—the garden alone was worth a museum. When it was subdivided before I left for college, somebody must have made a killing. Pardon the pun. Was it Nola? Was it Thea or the Devons? Did you get some of it? Was it Dr. Barrows?"

Juliet put down the gin and tonic she'd been nursing. "Don't be absurd," she said around the ice cube in her mouth. "We've never needed money. You know that. What a mean, cruel question to ask of me! Joel took care of everything. He took care of you. He took care of me. Wonderful Joel, wonderful daddy." She took another slurp from her glass.

"Yeah, wonderful Joel," Lowell replied. "Dear, sweet, wonderful man. Such a wonder. Such a viper. Such a . . ." Lowell could never find enough sarcasm for his feelings about his father.

But then Juliet looked up at him and said, "You look so much like him today, Lowell, more so than ever. So much like him. It's uncanny."

"Please, Juliet. Don't start that again. Not now. I can't stand it. Really." Lowell was trying to be businesslike and cold. He got up from the chair and moved past the bed to the door. But before he could get by, Juliet's bare foot reached out and touched his shin.

"Don't go, sweetie. Come here," she said, patting the bed. "Sit down next to me. Just for a minute. Come on. Please."

"No, Juliet. Don't. It just can't happen. It just can't," Lowell said with pleading severity.

"Joel, I know, I know."

"Don't call me Joel. Don't do it."

"Lowellie, just sit down. Let's be safe together again for a while, Lowell. Just a little while. Here, sit down. Come here, honey. It's safe. Come here, oh please. Cuddle up. It's safe now, Lowell. No one can hurt us. No one will know."

He turned his head. It was all too much.

"I'll be back in a while, Juliet. Get some sleep," he said as he brushed past her foot and moved into the living room. "I'm just going for a drive to clear my head. Get some sleep. I'll be back."

From Lowell Briscoe's "A Nest of Hells."

Prudence, Ethics, and Desire

"It's really the only prudent thing to do, Hana. If you want to make sense of your portfolio."

"Look, Nola, I really appreciate all your thinking about these matters and all your research, but I do not want to spend my money buying stocks in companies that make war planes and tanks. I simply won't do it."

"I think you're just being a silly fool about this, I really do."

"Nola, don't you ever call me a silly fool again! Who do you think you are? How dare you! These are my stocks, my investments, my land. Who do you think you are?"

"Hana, please. Don't raise your voice to me like that. I can't stand it when you get emotional. I'm sorry. I'm sorry."

"Oh, Nola," said Hana taking a deep breath. "I'm sorry too. I didn't mean to get angry. But I will not be insulted, even by you, dear one."

"I would never insult you, but I do think that your financial decisions are insulting to your intelligence and common sense. I want you in solid American companies. It's the right thing to do, it's the sensible thing to do, it helps your assets grow and it helps our country grow."

"I'm not interested in helping our country grow, Nola. I'm not interested in such things. I want to make enough money to live on, to care for my farm, and to give to people who our country's government doesn't take care of."

"That's another thing. Who are these people who need your money? Why do you take out so much cash from your account every month? Is somebody blackmailing you? Is something wrong?"

"Nola . . . where is your mind? What I do with my money is my business. And you know as well as I do who needs it. I am not being 'blackmailed,'" Hana said with contempt. "I am feeding people! Feeding them! In whatever way I can. But I will not feed them with food that comes from investments in munitions. Do you understand? You know, maybe it's time for me to take back my own affairs. When I asked you and Boris for investment advice so long ago, I meant just that—advice—not this kind of meddling."

"Whatever you say, dear. But I still think this is perverse. This country takes care of your interests with its army and you won't contribute to the companies that keep our army strong."

"Nola, please, please. Stop this. I pay my taxes. That's all they can expect of me."

"Perhaps if you were born here, you'd understand. You're cutting off your nose to spite your face."

"What on earth do you mean by *that*? This is impossible, impossible. I don't want to talk about it anymore. I've made up my mind. Case closed."

"You're being silly, just. . . ."

"If you ever use that word to describe me or my decisions again, Nola. . . ."

"Just foolish pride, foolish pride," she muttered.

"I'm going to change the subject now, Nola. I'm not going to refer to this again. Do you understand?"

Hana ran her fingers through her hair repeatedly, close to exploding in fury. She turned her back on Nola, walked to the kitchen, and stood in silence for what seemed like an hour. Then she took a deep breath and said, "Nola, do you want some tea?"

"That would be fine, dear," Nola replied as she strolled comfortably through the Thinking Room. "It's a fine day for a walk through your garden. Could I see your corn and rhubarb and that big tomato plant by the east wall?"

"Of course. And then I want to show you the lilac by the ditch. I'd forgotten it entirely. . . ."

— —

The early fall of 1948.

Christmas 1948

[JOURNAL OF LOWELL BRISCOE]

I remember Hana standing in front of the altar literally wreathed in light from the candles on her Santa Lucia crown. Her smile was both girlish and motherly. She wore a flowing, sky-blue gown covered with sewn-on stars. Her arms were wide open and her palms upraised. The audience seemed to breathe in unison as the big doors closed behind me. Her Kiva smelled of scented wax and hay and piñon sap. Christmas balls and tinsel glistened from the santos and kachinas in their nichos. Pine bows decked the vigas. The cold air from the opened door clung to the brick floor, but the room was warm with bodies like the inside of a burrow. I marched down the aisle, an evergreen sprig held in my hand, the "Ode to Joy" rolling like the sea from Hana's Victrola behind the altar, and turned to the audience and proclaimed with preposterous solemnity, "My name is Odysseus, Kachina of joys and journeys. I have come to rescue Christmas."

The picture of that momentous December afternoon when I was eleven was never clearer to me than when I stepped from Juliet's front porch sixteen years later at Christmastime in 1964 and looked across the street to the pseudo-adobe subdivision where Hana's house— "Gloriamaris," as she called it, Glory of the Sea—used to stand in that "rustic mystery." A sprinkling of Christmas lights cheered the neighborhood. But her great pueblo castle with the giant star on its roof was missing and the thrill of Bethlehem had vanished with it. I could still feel, though, with intense clarity, what it was like to be on that stage. Some memories have the simplicity and permanence of great art. My body remembered the rush of power and calm that overcame me when I entered Hana's chapel. I wore rows of rattling cowrie shells on my ankles, Pueblo moccasins on my feet, and hawk feathers down my arms and back. I was energized by the strange liberty of having been freed from myself by wearing a mask. I was transformed, momentarily no longer terrified and morbidly self-conscious. The mask made me look like a cross between a smiling boy and a bird of prey. Was it a symbol of the real creature I was fated to become? As I stood there, ready to speak my lines, I could see Juliet in the audience, and Thea, Nola, and the Devons too. Juliet looked so beautiful, so full of angel smiles and wily contentments. In 1948 when the play was performed, Joel, our father, had been dead for three years and Alice, my mother, for two. Juliet and I had gotten used to each other by then. Our wars and pleasures had become quite mythologic.

It wasn't until much later that I could remember very much of the actual play itself, except for those first moments. But there's no question about that Christmas in 1948: it was the definitive moment of my life. It was always a sweet memory, but until the beating this year, I've never thought of it as a threshold. When I strode through the door into the candlelight of Hana's shrine, I was beginning a process of liberation that I have only now come to understand embodies the purpose of my life. I have always felt that I had in me a great capacity for happiness, and even a talent for helping others find happiness within themselves. As sick and bruised and spoiled as I was then, I could sense that drive in me to rejoice, to give thanks, even before I met Hana. But it was she who gave real form and life to that feeling of gladness, made it tangible, more than just a wordless, spiritual itch. Hana set me free before I knew I was a prisoner. And her Christmas play was the key. I remember Hana telling me that the Three Graces— Splendor, Mirth, and Good Cheer—would preside over our performance. They were the essence of that Christmas season. The graces hovered over our lives for weeks, protecting us from cynicism and suspicion, from everything that was too sophisticated and weary for the energy and clarity of innocence. I'd never been a part of anything so beautiful, so simple, so sincerely kind before—or since. It was really like being an orphan who had just discovered that the fairy godmother was his real mother, and that all her powers, and all her love, were his by right of birth.

— —

This refers to Hana's last Christmas play in the winter of 1948.

Like Father, Like Daughter, Like Son

How different it was that Christmas eve in 1964, and yet how normal. The wind had a grimy coldness to it as Lowell stepped from the porch and walked to his car. He had to get away from Juliet and clear his head. Her room was like a sponge cake soaked with too much brandy—heady, sweet, and smothering. He could barely breathe in there. The night air outside had revived him. He was feeling both angry and ashamed that Juliet had made a pass at him. It had been eight years since he had left her. And this winter, more than ever, he was repulsed by her and hated to be reminded of those early years. He could feel a generic guilt seeping up under his scalp. It was pure superstition, since he had no conscious belief in sin. It wasn't Juliet's fault or his. It was the best they could do for each other at the time. But the idea that outsiders would think it wrong, even monstrous, or that God, a notion he otherwise never considered, might condemn him for it, made him burn behind the eyes with a static heat not unlike the flush of horror people feel after realizing they've just missed running over a bicyclist or a small child in the street. The acid of guilt had obscured his memory of Hana before he'd reached the car. He unlocked the door and was about to slip inside when he heard Juliet calling out to him, loudly so everyone in the neighborhood could hear. He looked up and saw her standing under the porch light, stark naked in the cold. She was weaving and swaying, and looked on the verge of passing out. At one point she danced clumsily and shouted, "See, daddy, see. I'm such a good girl, aren't I?" Then she crouched down and moaned, "Oh, Joel, oh Joel, oh Lowell, don't go. I need you daddy. Don't go, don't go."

Lowell was horrified. He imagined everyone behind their curtains looking at him. He didn't care what they made of Juliet. He ran to the porch and herded her back into the house, and then pushed and lugged her into the bedroom. She was almost unconscious, and fell at the side of the bed. He had to pick her up like a corpse. She drooled on his shoulder and felt deathly thin. This was his half-sister, his surrogate mother, his comforter, his rescuer. She was naked in his arms. He didn't know how to interpret his feelings exactly, but he looked at her and felt something not unlike nostalgia.

He got her into bed, put an extra quilt over her, and tried to tiptoe out of the room. But she caught him. "Joel, Joel, Joel," she moaned. "Why me? Aren't I a good girl? Aren't I, aren't I good?" she said with what seemed like a grin forming around her words. Lowell was about to plead with her to be quiet, but he saw that she had passed out. He couldn't leave her even though he despised her—not for her addictions, not for her booze or pills or sentimental lust. He wasn't a hypocrite. He hated her for what she had done to Hana, or for what he imagined she had done. The child in him loathed her. And he still hated that child, doubted him, damned him for a fool and an unwitting accomplice.

Juliet was snoring. The room was thick and dark, filled with drowsy white noise and the faint, stale smell of hot dust coming from the wall heater. Lowell dozed off in the big chair by her bed. He must have been asleep for an hour when Juliet's whispered voice woke him. "I want to tell you everything, Lowell. Everything I've never told you. Everything. You mustn't hate me. We were such pals, such pals. You never betrayed me. Such chums, we were. Such chums. What would I have done without you? Be patient with me. Let me tell you, please?"

Lowell's head felt as if it were covered with lead. He could hardly hold it up. He whispered back, "Sure, go ahead." And closed his eyes. She'd done this sort of thing many times before. He knew her confessions would not be about Hana this time. It was the old story of Joel that bothered her now. Joel had been on her mind most of her life.

"Joel did things to me, did things, did things, did things," Juliet said compulsively. "And I was eleven. I felt proud when he asked me. He said it would ease his pain, that mother had failed him, that he was in misery, suffering horribly, and that it would help him. And if I loved him, I'd sit on his lap. . . ."

"Juliet, do you really want me to hear this now, again? I don't really want to be your priest. . . ."

"He did things, Lowell. Daddy did things, did things, did things," her voice hummed on, "some of my fav-o-rite things. Daddy did, Daddy did. . . ."

Joel was a narcissistic and destructive man. When Lowell was a boy living with Juliet, she used to tell him how Joel would wheel himself into her room late at night and "savor me, just like you do now." What a strange verb to use, Lowell thought. He was suspicious now to think that she compared him to Joel. It was almost too pat. "But that must be what happened," he wrote in his journal in 1964. "When she got drunk, she'd confuse me with our father, or at least put a fantasy mask over my life and turn what was perhaps with Joel a nightmare into a neurotic retreat with me. It's too macabre to think that she was getting revenge on her father by fucking up his son. But there wasn't all that much mind fucking. I wanted it, too. . . ."

Joel Briscoe died when Lowell was almost eight. Their faces did share a strong resemblance, especially the hairline. In one photo Lowell had of Joel, he looked like a young Howard Hughes, his hair slicked back, with a boyish but pompous grin. Lowell thought Joel must have had a terrible life, despite his role as the Zeus figure in the family. He controlled the emotional weather of their lives. The climate around their house in Santa Monica was a great fog of whimpering and fear. It was so palpable at times you could sense it moving through the tall pines like sea clouds in the morning. Joel must have made beating and berating Alice, Lowell's mother, a daily event. Alice had been his student, had idolized him, and decided to devote her life to nursing him and helping him with his work. But his drinking, the professional failures, the pain and humiliation of his wounds turned him into a beast. He even hit Lowell once. Alice was using him as a shield, at least that's what it felt like to Lowell, and his father grabbed her arm and was pulling her toward him in the chair, when he punched Lowell in the side of the head. Lowell literally saw stars.

"Even now I get a metallic taste in my mouth when I think of him. He was a domestic terrorist," Lowell wrote in his journals. "The whole house throbbed with his anger. He moved around in that wheelchair like a mutant crab, with menacing agility. He brooded, he pouted, he threw dishes, he yelled for help then damned the helper. He always smelled dirty to me. And I was in awe of his size, his animalness, the power of his grip, his huge shoulders, and the pincer-like action of his awful feet. One morning I found myself in his office at the back of the house, a vast cathedral-like room, filled with books and manuscripts. He suddenly wheeled in like a tank, snarling at me, trying to catch me and scoop me up in one of his arms. I dodged him, scooted under the table and made it to the door and into Alice's embrace before he could get me. I can still feel his spit on the back of my neck as he yelled at her to get me out of his way."

When Joel was dying in the hospital, he became a very different person. It was 1945, not long after the end of the war. Joel's bed was in a ward full of dying people. The scene reminded Lowell of the casualties piled in hospital tents in *Gone With the Wind*. Eight-year-old Lowell didn't want to see Joel. He didn't want to get anywhere near him. Lowell was afraid Joel would grab him, twist his arm, try to kiss him, bite him. But Alice kept pushing him toward his father's bed. Joel was on a heavy dose of morphine but still in mental agony. The cancer gouged him beneath the drug. He did grab Lowell's arm, as it turned out, and pulled the boy to him. His beard hurt Lowell's cheek. Joel squeezed him so hard that Alice tried gently to pull Lowell back until he stopped resisting as he heard his father whisper in his ear, "You're the apple of my eye, little man, my prince. I'm proud you're my son. Don't forget it." The stab of his whiskers, the sweetness of those words, the warmth of his breath—this was the first moment of intimacy and trust Lowell had ever had with his father. Joel ran his hand over Lowell's hair. The boy burst into tears. He wanted to hear more, feel more, but by then Alice had him in her arms. And he never saw Joel again.

"You know, Lowell, when daddy was dying, he tried to make peace with me," Juliet said with sudden seriousness and sobriety in her voice. "He held my hand one afternoon for the longest time. He told me I had 'a genius' in me and that I shouldn't waste my life on men and kitchens. . . . Maybe he was jealous of other guys getting me. . . . That's not nice."

A year and a half later, in December of 1947, Lowell's mother Alice Briscoe, who is Juliet's stepmother, died. From Lowell Briscoe's "A Nest of Hells."

Another "Fascinating Conversation"

"I love to see the snow on the black bark of cottonwoods," Nola told Hana as they chopped cedar for kindling on the shadowed north side of Gloriamaris. A harsh, wet wind gusted from the south. The temperature was well below freezing. It had been snowing off and on for two weeks. The whole valley was white. Roads were icy. Everyone was burrowed in. The air was smoky with piñon and cedar. The occasional car sounded like an avalanche. Holed up in this wild weather, New Mexico seemed more than ever isolated from the rest of the world, a Shangri-la, flourishing but forgotten, impenetrable and safe as the comfort of a warm bed with heavy covers. Winter inspired both Hana and Nola to make the most of New Mexico's feeling of a lost place, never to be found. They cooked, they baked, they laid up firewood for each other's houses, they had long coffees and teas by big fires, usually at Gloriamaris, wrapped up in blankets and shawls in Hana's oversized wing-backed leather chairs.

"What could be better than a bowl of Santo Domingo beans with brimstone red chile on a day like this," Hana said, interrupting the intensity of their discussion about politics, sniffing lunch simmering in the kitchen.

"Not to be contrary, but I should have thought a pot roast with potatoes and peas," Nola replied with mock seriousness. "We came right to the edge of all-out war on that one, didn't we?" she added.

"Well, it's an issue with intensely practical day-to-day realities that could have consequences even in our lives here," Hana said, modulating her seriousness. "It's something that gets to the very heart and soul of our way of life."

"Of course it is. I never said it wasn't. It's just that it's on the other side of the moon. Why would you think the House Un-American Activities Committee would come to New Mexico when it has Hollywood to muck out?" Nola asked with a tiny edge in her voice.

"We really are talking at cross purposes here. I never implied that the committee would actually come here, though I don't think it's unreasonable with so many atomic secrets in New Mexico. This state is a tinderbox when it comes to loose talking starting fires," Hana said with a smile. "But that's not the point."

"Well, spies are everywhere, aren't they?"

"I don't mean that. What I do mean is that when a witch hunt is allowed to go crazy as it is in Hollywood—all witch hunts are crazy anyway, mob rule—there's a chance it could spread, move from town to town like cholera or the Black Death. It infects the souls of all who touch it. They become righteous, authoritarian, intolerant."

"Hana, that's paranoid, isn't it? I mean there are communists in the movie industry, aren't there? And they are working against us. That seems clear, very clear. They want to undermine our country, undermine our freedoms. Don't they? We don't want to live in Russia, do we?"

"Nola, Nola, Nola. You're sounding like Hedda Hopper. What if someone accused you of being a communist just because they didn't like you? Or accused me of being subversive because they didn't like the way I lived my life, or because they thought I was too rich or too poor or 'strange'? After a while, when the Mob takes over, nothing has meaning anymore. People are denounced for the most personally malicious and irrelevant reasons. The French revolution, the Russian revolution, the Chinese revolution all show that's so."

"Are you implying that the House Un-American Activities Committee is a revolutionary tribunal, Hana?" Nola said with grave authority. "What revolution would they be in support of, the American revolution? Is that so terrible in America?"

"You really don't understand, do you?"

"Don't understand what?" Nola shot back. "I get so tired of it when you take the high ground like that, Hana; it just enrages me. You know it all. I'm always wrong. Well, I'm not wrong this time. The Congress of the United States of America has sent one of its legal committees to California to investigate if there are un-American activities going on in the movie industry. Any American would back them."

"Are *you* now implying that I'm un-American, Nola, because I don't like what the committee is doing? Is that what you're saying? If it is, then you've proved my point," Hana said looking into the fire with detached exasperation.

"What point? What point? I'm not accusing you of anything. I know you're as American as I am."

"But I'm not, you know. I'm a naturalized American. I'm foreign."

"So is Adolphe Menjou," Nola rejoined, fearful of Hana's obvious lack of good humor.

"And he's a turncoat, an informer, according to what I read in the paper."

"How on earth can he be a turncoat if he's cooperating with the committee, Hana? He's doing what every American should do: cooperate with their duly elected representatives in Congress. That's what the constitution is all about. That's what *our* revolution was all about. A nation of laws, not of despots."

"Is there any law that says an American person can't believe anything, anything he wants to believe, if it doesn't directly harm others? No. There is not. Is there any law that says a citizen of these United States can be accused without confronting his accuser? No, there is not. Is there any law, Nola, any law at all, which says that a person may be deprived of employment, may be starved out and humiliated and professionally destroyed because he is politically eccentric, a nonconformist? No, there is not."

"Hana, please, let's forget this. You're upset."

"I am not 'upset,' Nola. This is more important than you think."

"More important than friendship? Let's have some posole, please."

"Of course, you're right," Hana said with embarrassment. She started to add, "let talk about this later," but she stopped herself and smiled, "It really is too beautiful a winter's noon to squabble about idiots doing idiot things."

"I wouldn't say they're idiots, Hana."

"Come on, Nola. Let's put this aside."

"Yes, yes, let's do that."

The two women moved to the kitchen with deliberate slowness and in silence. Their conversation over lunch was redirected toward animals in the bosque, especially the ravens and the coyote family that Hana had seen on her ride through the woods that morning.

Nola was attentive, but very quiet, almost motionless. Anger for her was a slow boil and a long, long steam.

— ~

The winter of 1947.

A Danger to Herself?

[DIARY OF NOLA DASHELLER]
Sunday

Would I be doing the right thing. Am I imagining all this, or is she really a danger to herself? And in need of some time to cool off? Would I be doing the right thing? Is there anything else to be done? . . . It's so painful, so frightening. But the evidence seems clear. I'm not making this up. Suicide is a possibility. How many times has she quoted her Stoics: "The door is always open"? What a terrifying phrase! But wasn't she just speaking philosophically, as she said? But there's more to it than that. A deep instability. We all see it. Terrible danger. Withdrawal. Raging at McCarthy. Raging about "the bomb." Withdrawal, coldness, distance—even from me. I can see it in her eyes, this almost nastiness, this foggy, even fiery aloofness. She cannot be civil. She cannot control herself. She's locked us out. It's not me who's making this up. . . . But would I be doing the loving thing? Would I want someone to do this for me, to me? Will she thank me when she's rested and comes to her senses? I pray she will. But maybe she'll hate me and never speak to me again. Maybe she will never come to her senses. I'm terrified, but I must not be intimidated. . . . The folly of the strong. When giants crumble. . . . God help me, am I just jealous, just green, green with spite about being pushed aside, locked out, physically locked out, actually locked out of her house, her life? Am I a monster here, cruel only to be kind? That's what she said to me the other day when she threw me out. And that's how I feel now. Exactly. Exactly. I will call Dr. Barrows. I will do it. I will ask his advice. I'm sure he'll concur. I'm sure he'll help us. . . . She looks so disheveled. So vacant. Have I waited too long? No, this is absurd. Hana Nicholas is mentally fatigued. A nervous breakdown is one thing, going insane is another. She is not insane. But she does need help. I don't know what to do! Call Dr. Barrows? I will.

Early spring of 1949.

Notes on the
Children's Christmas Play

[JOURNAL OF HANA NICHOLAS]
4 March 1948

I think I finally have something to work with. It's not too zany, I hope.

Title: "With The Christmas Star To Guide You."

Lowell plays Odysseus the Kachina. A Hermes figure, a wily guide who navigates by the Christmas star, leading other Kachinas to find their way home, across the Wild Ocean of Desert and through the Dark Woods of Atomic Bomb Mountain.

I will play the Great Star Mother, Athena the Weaver of Light. Perhaps Anthony Lucero will play Telemachus, the Son Kachina and Slayer of Monsters. How old is he now? Eight?

The Plot: Odysseus and several Kachinas have been captured and kept in a Great Captivity in the Region of Los Alamos by terrible One-Eyed, Closed-Minded Monsters who are making horrible devices to blow up the world on Christmas Eve. Odysseus figures a way to trick the Atomic Cyclopes by being kind to them so they let down their guard. Odysseus guides the other Kachinas down the terrible Atomic Bomb Mountain by the Christmas Star, but becomes lost in the Desert. The Great Star Mother Athena finds him, shows him behind which cloud the Star is hiding, and tells him that he must not only take the Kachinas home, but warn everyone about the what the Atomic Cyclopes are doing. Odysseus finds his way home on Christmas Eve amid great rejoicing. He and his son, Telemachus, return to the Atomic Bomb Mountain after Christmas Eve mass, and through images of Christmas kindness and warmth, convince the Atomic Cyclopes to abandon their bombs, and join the Kachinas in a festival of light and rebirth.

Key ideas: Odysseus tricks monsters the first time by kindness, by sweet lies, like Hermes, that compliment the monsters not for what they are but for what they might be, wise, well-focused healers. Odysseus convinces them the second time, with the Star Mother's help, that the world is really beautiful and at peace on Christmas, not ugly and deformed as they think. If they stop making their bombs, he tells them, they can join the Kachinas to help make sure the world remained at peace.

Music: "Joy to the World."

Costumes and Sets: Kachina masks, candle stars, pine trees, mountain sheets, wind fans, alarm clock "bombs."

This isn't too political is it? No. Christmas is about peace. And peace is political.

— —

The "Children's Christmas Play" of 1948 was the last in a series stretching back to 1929 or 1930. All had starred children of the Los Griegos neighborhood.

Warm as Feathers

[JOURNALS OF LOWELL BRISCOE]
November 12, 1970

The audience in Hana's Kiva that Christmas Eve afternoon in 1948 was rigid and sinister. Everyone—maybe thirty people—seemed to be in a cryogenic stupor. As I looked out through the eye holes of the kachina mask I'd built from cardboard and feathers, with its fierce hawk bill and upraised eyebrows, I saw Nola and Thea looking strangely at each other, as if a character on stage had just farted or had told a dingy, off-color joke. Juliet and the Devons spent much of the performance exchanging worried expressions and making little exasperated sighs. Their hostility and lack of attention unsettled me until Hana caught my eye, Athena-like, and redirected my attention toward her and the lines she fed me while I composed myself to remember the rest. "The Hyenas of Science won't destroy the earth," she whispered as I repeated after her and then said on my own, "if we can only tame them with the magic of the Star, the treasure at the end of the path of light."

The Kiva itself was divided by a tiny stage and a dark blue backdrop covered with a comical competition of symbols cut from gold and silver paper. Stars, masks, lightning, and cloud forms clashed with atomic signs and bomb shelter insignias, effigies of the Fat Boy bomb, the sign for uranium, and huge mushroom clouds. All around and above the stage, in the darkness of the Kiva's rafters, were the ever-present wings, a veritable forest of them, wings Hana had liberated from road kills, or removed over the years from dead birds in the bosque. The whole ceiling of the Kiva was alive with feathers and wing bones that Hana had carefully kept glued together. Every now and then, despite her efforts, a feather would release itself and spiral through the air—an omen of movement or change in direction, she'd say. A feather fell from the ceiling that Christmas Eve. Just as I had spoken the lines, "Release the world from your terrible thunder," a feather, large enough to be a pelican's, drifted heavily onto the lap of a woman in the front row. Hana was so poised and attentive, she picked it up, waved it over the woman's head, and said in perfect timing with my next line, "and we will all be blessed with lives soft and warm as feathers."

I have such a hard time describing that afternoon to people, how it felt and what it looked like. The sky had a hazy luminescence that comes with clouds just before a late afternoon snow storm across the Rio Grande Valley. That winter afternoon I felt awakened and exquisitely more powerful than I had ever imagined was possible. Hana was the wizard who infused me with confidence. And it was all quite preposterous: wearing a huge mask, mouthing those—oh I hate to say this—those corny lines. But she was right about masks: they turn you into themselves, they transform you. I felt like Odysseus the Kachina. She knew that I would. She had told me to trust the mask and trust the performance. And she gave me the knowledge to attempt that, including a summer-long mutual reading of the Odyssey. The play, of course, was part of Hana's undoing, and both marked the highpoint and signaled the nadir of my young life.

What gave Hana so much energy and generosity? I think some of it came from having the freedom of mind to create the Kiva in the first place. It was as if it were a part of the landscape itself, a place that Hana had found in the earth, the interior of a huge nodule she had excavated. Nothing in it, not even the audience, was out of place, just as nothing can be out of place in an open field, a beach, or a desert where humans have never been. The candlelight (she never put in electricity) illumined faintly the far edges of the room, making the middle feel like the inside of a kaleidoscope of shadows. Hana's huge collection of Pueblo Indian pottery, shells, minerals, and Hispanic religious art in the Kiva's nichos and on its shelves seemed as natural as moss and wild flowers in a twilight woods.

◂ ▸

After Lowell Briscoe's "nervous breakdown" in 1969 and 1970, he became increasingly obsessed with the early years of his life.

Old Crank and Recluse

[JOURNAL OF HANA NICHOLAS]
10 December 1948

Lowell is doing much better than I'd hoped for. He has learned his lines flawlessly. He has a real feeling for the stubborn, adventuresome bravado of his character, Odysseus the Kachina. It still tickles me to pieces to have put those two words together. And to have Athena be the Christmas angel. Not bad for an "old crank and recluse"—those are the exact words that Nola used on the phone to describe me the other day. My, my, I'm dealing with a monster. I wonder if she's going completely mad, metaphorically speaking of course. One thing is certain: Lowell is not mad. Crazy and imaginative, yes. Full to bursting with pent-up fury, yes. Brilliant, yes. Devious and malign when pushed, yes, indeed. An eleven-year-old boy, of course; he's that first and foremost. When he was rehearsing yesterday, he just melted from the effort after an hour. I needed to revive him with Christmas candy, which he gobbled down like a beggar. There's something wily about him, Odysseus-like, innocent and lonely too, a Calypso's darling, desperate for a home . . . desperate is the word. And Juliet, bless her heart, is definitely not that home. She did her duty when her parents died. But she has no idea of how to be a mother, and I actually think she hates him, along with loving him, too. I know Lowell must have fantasies about her; she seems like his cyclops. He wants to get free, but isn't up to the fatal deed, thank God.

What a strange Christmas this is! All around the country, people are trembling, people who think like I do are becoming suspects, are having dossiers made on them. The war has left the world ragged. I wonder if Hedda Hopper and other "commie hunters" in Hollywood would think Odysseus the Kachina was a "dupe" of the Communist Party? So much tension, so much fear, so many people missing the mark, so many of my friends gone bad in the brain! And poor Juliet on the edge of it, her script-writing days apparently over, seemingly safe, but terrified even in Albuquerque, far away from the Hollywood Ten and HUAC, far away from being blackballed, or called to testify and name names, and financially secure enough, it seems, not to really care. Is this the source of her drinking, I wonder, this political ambivalence of hers? Is it an echo of a moral ambivalence? Has she become the reverse of what Nola seems to be verging on—hysterical political rigidity?

Walter and Auntie Ana

[JOURNALS OF LOWELL BRISCOE]
November 27, 1970

I was so frustrated. I tried to explain the significance of "The Play" to my so-called good friend Harry who's confessed his troubles to me since I moved to L.A. When I told him something that was important to me, he didn't get it at all. It made me feel so isolated. But it wasn't really his fault. I'm sure I just couldn't get the description straight. And Hana's mentoring of my childhood made no sense to him either. Maybe it's not something that adults *can* understand. Only kids—even a deceptive, cunning kid like I was—are guileless enough to be influenced by the power of goodness without doubting it for a moment. The power of goodness. What an expression! That's certainly what Hana had.

I took my usual beach walk to cool down. The Topanga Canyon coast line was clear, cold, and breezy. I watched the pelicans dive for at least an hour. Just what I needed to clear my head. And then it came to me. The whole idea. I need to write a Christmas story, a fable for kids that doesn't deal directly with Hana, but embodies her principles. The only way I'll be able to explain her in my life is to go at it Hermes-like, with indirection. Luck was with me today. As I started to feel the evening chill coming off the waves, I remembered a story Hana told me. It was the start, I think, of one of her earlier Christmas plays, which she for some reason abandoned during the war. Hana used it to explain, I believe, something of her feelings about our relationship, about the dangers of the world, and about the cruelty of judging people by the color of their skin or the strangeness of their birth. The basic elements were these:

A half-breed old woman, a sage who is, off and on in her pueblo, suspected of being a witch, is burdened with raising a delinquent nephew who's about twelve years old. The kid's a little crazy (Hana would not have described me as "crazy" to my face), a trouble maker and something of a rogue. One day around Christmas time during World War II, the kid (Walter Tafoya, I'll call him) is out roaming and comes across a barbed-wired compound in the foothills of the Jemez Mountains down from the bomb labs in Los Alamos. It was an internment camp for Japanese Americans. He sees children there, and catches the eye of one of them. He sneaks up to the fence and is told by one of the Japanese-American kids what is going on and how miserable some of them are without their parents at Christmas. Where are their parents? Walter asks. Many of them are sick or too depressed to celebrate Christmas. Walter runs back to his Aunt—Auntie Ana— and tells her about the children and where they are kept. Auntie Ana knew about the internment camps, but like everyone had felt helpless. Walter's agitation, however, gives her an inspiration. She has been having trouble with her neighbors because they think Walter is a bad influence on their children. Auntie Ana devises a slightly nutty scheme to channel Walter's energies and the rambunctiousness of her neighbors' kids in a positive way. They're to dig a small tunnel under the barbed-wire fence and help a few Japanese children escape for Christmas Eve. Then they will take them to a campfire prepared by Auntie Ana in the woods of the Jemez Mountains. Auntie Ana decorates the trees around the campfire with ornaments and makes presents for everyone. The Japanese kids escape, and all the children follow Walter, who is guided to Auntie Ana's campfire by a huge star, as his aunt promised they would be. The village priest and some of Auntie Ana's neighbors grow worried when their children turn up missing. They think the worst of Auntie Ana and suspect her of being a witch. The priest and some village elders follow Auntie Ana's trail into the Jemez, terrified they'll discover the children offered up in some Satanic sacrifice. But what they find, instead, are children dancing and laughing, singing carols, radiant with Christmas joy. There's a little scene where the priest approaches the campfire and all the children run to Auntie Ana and huddle around her. But once the priest steps from the shadows, he's seen to be full of smiles and the Christmas spirit, relieved to find the children safe and engrossed in such innocent merriment. He even offers to help smuggle the Japanese kids back into the camp later that night so they won't get into trouble. Auntie Ana sends them all off, telling them they will encounter along the way miracles of kindness and enlightenment that will prove to them once and for all that anything is possible at Christmas time when "love fills the sky with light."

I wonder if I can write this for children, say, around Walter's age, keeping it about twenty-five to thirty pages or less? I think I must try. I'll start this Christmas.

— —

As far as I can tell, this entry sets the exact date for the conception of Lowell Briscoe's "The Witch and the Star."

PART TWO

Myths of Guilt

The 1992 Los Angeles Riot
The Hospitals All Run Together

Lowell couldn't imagine what had happened. It was preposterous that he was suddenly in a hospital, feeling near death, aching everywhere, unable to move, falling in and out of deep sleeps, drugged and nauseated and tormented by stabs of blinding pain. One minute he was on the way to teach a seminar and the next he found himself in hell. He'd been in a disoriented semi-coma for weeks. When his head began to clear, he remembered seeing men run at his car, screaming obscenities. The memories triggered streaks of terror. Early on he had no direct memories of the beating, nor of his neighborhood rescuers. But he was filled with rage; he trembled with it; it gave him molten headaches. He'd grind his teeth, tense his body as if he were having a leg sawed off without anesthetic, and dream up the most terrible retributions, pounding his attacker's heads to mush with big stones, pouring gas on them and setting them aflame, locking them in a small room with a truckload of fire ants. He became obsessed with getting even. But he wanted to do it himself, all by himself. He didn't want the cops to get them. He wanted to remember them, each one, and kill them, one by one, on his own terms, in his own sweet way—catching them in bed at night with a chain saw; killing their mothers in the supermarket; putting a gun to their heads in their cars when they least expected it.

He didn't know which pain was worse, the torment of his body, or the furious frustration he felt at being a prisoner in the hospital. When a handful of young men were arrested for his beating on the strength of videotape evidence, he was furious and ground his few remaining teeth so hard he broke one of them. The more the haze lifted and his mind cleared, the more violently his imagination intruded itself and the more pesky his conscience became. Inevitably, old questions about Juliet, Nola, the Devons, Thea, and Hana resurfaced. His anger plagued him, and his shame and self-doubt nettled him without distraction.

His recuperation was marked by spells of claustrophobic hallucinations. As he told his psychiatrist, Dr. Tuttle, later, "It was like being jailed in a Chinese box. Every time I broke out of one, I'd find myself right in the middle of another. All the hospital rooms I'd ever been in were contained in this one. I couldn't escape. Talk about panic and desperation! I felt like I was going mad, and maybe I was. I've been close to madness enough times in my life to know what it feels like."

"What *does* it feel like?" Dr. Tuttle asked.

"It feels as if . . . it's hard to say. It feels as if you're on the verge of losing control. By that I mean observing yourself feeling things you don't want to feel and doing things you don't want to do and being unable to stop yourself. It would be sort of like screaming at yourself through a soundproof window."

"Good metaphor."

"Thank you."

"Tell me about the hospital rooms, if you like," she said.

"I could tell you a lot about them. I know them by heart, inch by inch, but it would take too long."

"We'll make the time."

"Some other time . . . well, let me give you a little picture. I'm lying in bed, in the middle of my stay in the Santa Monica Hospital, bandaged head to foot almost, trying one more time to remember the faces of those bastards, when I doze off again and find myself sneaking out of my room, armed with some kind of weapon, setting out to find my attackers. I open my door and step out, not into the hall, but into my room at the sanitarium, with its nice wicker furniture and lovely open windows."

"Which sanitarium was this, Dr. Briscoe?"

"Later, later. . . . Let me finish this. I look out the window at the Sandia Mountains, take in the delicious golden light of late afternoon, and tiptoe to the door, open it, and step past a wide shadow into Nola's room, for God's sake."

"Who's Nola again? I'll get these names straight in a bit."

"I haven't told you yet. She's the villain of the piece. That's a little melodramatic and now utterly beside the point. But there she was in her hospital bed, looking like a pumpkin, bloated, orangish, near death, and I'm sneaking around in my bandages trying to find the way out, terrified of waking her. She stirs a bit. I crouch down out of her line of vision and scoot my way to the door, open it slowly and snake around into, for God's sake, Hana's room in Las Vegas."

"Las Vegas?"

"Las Vegas, New Mexico. The state mental hospital there."

"Who's Hana?"

"I'll tell you later. But there she is, in her rocker, her back to me, gazing out her window. I'm stunned, flabbergasted to see her. Remember, I'm trying to escape to kill the fuckers who beat me up. Suddenly, I'm standing behind her, wanting to touch her shoulder, but not daring to—because I couldn't bear to have to see her face again, her awful, hideous face again."

Dr. Tuttle looked blandly puzzled as usual. "Do you want to tell me about that?"

"Not yet."

"Go on, then. Did you ever get out of the room?"

"No. I woke up while I was still with her. But I had waking dreams later—hallucinations, I guess—that I could hear her breathing in the next room in the real hospital."

"I mean, did you ever get out and find your attackers, in those dreams I mean?"

"Well, not in the room dreams. But I had several other dreams that I guess you could say were about revenge. They're all sort of embarrassing . . . crudely violent, childishly cruel. Once I dreamed I was the warden in what you might say was a dry-land jail for sharks. The sharks had to wear little masks and had to have hoses and fans in their cells that swooshed water over their bodies. The worst thing the state could do to one of these shark convicts was to remove their water masks so they could eat. Starve or breathe. Eat and suffocate."

"What did you do?"

"I woke up. I had other dreams, too. Fairly obvious ones. I was in a jungle, wearing military garb, carrying a machete. Men were tied up and lying on the ground, each wearing a hood. I'd stoop down, lift up the hood. The heads either had faces or no faces. The heads of the people with no faces I cleaved with the machete. And walked to the next body. I think the bodies were alive. I had one silly recurring dream, a little thing. I'm in an old part of an old city, in an alley, hiding in a sort of indentation in a tall brick wall. I hear gunfire around me. But I feel safe, even relieved. Then to my horror, a head pops up from the ground between my feet, screaming, 'There's one, there's one.' I kick at the head, knocking it off its body, sending it down the alley, singing some sweet song about falling in love. . . ."

"You certainly have good recall of your dreams, Dr. Briscoe," Dr. Tuttle said.

"I make it a point to keep track of myself. I write everything down in journals. I've done it for years."

"It might be a good idea to keep a journal about this experience—the riot, your beating, and our sessions, I mean."

"Naturally, I already am."

What neither doctor nor patient talked much about was the pain Lowell suffered in the hospital, the straitjacket agony of being in traction and casts, and falling in and out of sleep with no hope of exerting control. There was no talk either, of course, of the catheters, the partial blindness, the terrors of temporary paralysis, the torture of being unable to move to get comfortable. They did, however, speak at length about the pain Lowell suffered during the attack itself, trying to find a clue that might stimulate Lowell's memory so he could identify the faces of his attackers.

But Lowell would say after each effort, "All I can really remember was the act, the kick or the punch itself, not the pain it caused. I remember hands and feet, not faces."

"Well it's not unusual to blank something like that out. It really might be that you're just trying too hard to remember."

"You're probably right. The D.A., Mr.—uh . . . I can't remember his name—it's Cates. Anyway, he's putting a lot of pressure on me. I think he thinks I'm a nut case."

"Why do you think that?"

"Don't you think so?"

"Not at all, Dr. Briscoe," Melinda Tuttle said with sincere emphasis.

"No kidding?"

"No kidding!"

"Thank you. I've been feeling a little awkward—How would you say it?—a little victimized, victimized by the system, if you know what I mean. I *am* the victim, after all.

Portions of Lowell Briscoe's remarks have been adapted from his journals.

My Secret Life

[JOURNALS OF HANA NICHOLAS]
13 December 1942—Gloriamaris

Just back from Zuni and Shalako. War rages all over the world but not south of the Zuni Mountains and around the sacred Salt Lake. Many Zuni men in the army. Many dead already. Great emotion there this season. Perhaps the most beautiful and passionate Shalako ceremony I've ever witnessed. The Luceros had me to lunch, and the supper in the communal house of consecration was a feast. Very few Anglos there. An odd anthropologist or two. Very cold. Absolutely bitter; snow everywhere, highway deadly slick. Terrible wind. The gods of the world feel abandoned. War replaces them. And they return the insult with ice and hurricanes.

As well as I know my friends at Zuni now, my women friends and their splendidly kept houses and industrious lives, I realize I know nothing about them, despite all the ethnographies I've read. We like each other. We sympathize. We have a certain feminine affinity. We know what it means to be women, to be powerful, to be open, to be strong. We even look a bit like each other, now that I'm spreading out a little. But our cultures are utterly different. They own the land, they are the matriarchal authority, it's their pueblo. Their husbands are essentially visitors, from what I can tell. Women at Zuni have absolute authority over material existence. Nothing like my world. I have had to commit to a nearly celibate life—no husband, no children, no patriarchal presence of any kind—to keep my autonomy. I am like the Zuni women in that I own everything that is mine, my land, my house, my car, my books, my animals, everything. I sign all the papers. We are like each other in another respect as well, in our relationship to the so-called dominant culture. Pueblo women and men lead double lives and have essentially two cultures. One they show to the European world, the other they keep as secret as they can, shrouded in their own inexplicable language, safe behind their solidarity and impenetrable reserve. I have two lives as well. I realized that again while driving home. I stopped for breakfast in Gallup and the men in the cafe thought it was odd that a woman would be alone at that early time of the morning, dressed as if she were a rancher or a farmer coming in from morning chores. I bantered with them, said the right things, ate my bacon and eggs with relish, read yesterday's paper, drank tanks of coffee, and went on my way. I don't know what they thought of me, but after I left they knew nothing more about me than when I came in. But I had observed them very closely. The same is true with most of my friends and acquaintances. I spend so much time studying by myself—at the university in Zimmerman Library, writing in my study, or working in my garden—that I'm almost invisible anyway. The old stalwarts know more than the others, but I keep pretty much everything important secluded even from them, except Thea and Nola, and I really don't trust them very much either. As a consequence, I know much more about them than they suspect about me. I like it that way. The Pueblos have preserved themselves against the Europeans because they keep who they really are completely to themselves, and who they really are as people is immensely complicated, rich, and satisfying. They don't need anything else. And they don't want anything else. Even though I've let Boris and then Nola help me with my finances— she's sort of like my Bureau of Indian Affairs, my BIA; I need her for certain practicalities—she's irritated when she sees how much cash I withdraw every month, irritated because she doesn't know how I spend it. If she discovered that I have another entire set of books based on that money, and my own careful reckoning of my investments separate from theirs, she'd be in something of a bureaucratic rage. I enjoy, deeply and sweetly enjoy, living a secret life inside my public life.

Hana Nicholas published at least two brief ethnographic observations on Zuni, one communiqué on Hopi kivas, and several articles on Santo Domingo healing practices in *The Journal of Southwestern Anthropology* during the mid-1940s.

She Was Insane
Christmas 1964

"Why don't you do what you said you were going to do? Come clean, Juliet. Why did Hana say it was diabolical murder if it wasn't? Tell me that! Just tell me that!" Lowell demanded in an arrogant voice through the gloom of her bedroom.

"She was insane, Joel," Juliet said with snappish irritation.

"Uh, it's Lowell here."

"You . . . ," she growled, "you brat, she was insane!"

"But you just said she wasn't. Her tragedy, you said, was that she was *not* insane, Juliet, not insane. You called her the sanest person you ever met. Good God, did you summon me all the way out here just to tease me, just to fuck around with my mind again?! Come clean. Say what you have to say. There's something on your mind. Just say it. Don't back off. Say it!"

The silence that followed was like waiting for a mistake to happen.

Then Juliet, who was getting belligerent with fatigue, said in an annoyed but rational voice, "No, no, no . . . listen to me. Listen! I want release," she said dramatically. "Release, that's all. Release. I'm bursting with it, with grief, can't you understand?"

Her tone of voice changed again, more serious now than at any time since Lowell arrived. "Can't you see? I need to clean this out. Just listen to me, please. You're the only one who can. Just listen. I won't 'tempt' you anymore, if that's what you think. I was joking. It was always just for fun. But no more games. Just listen, that's all I ask."

Lowell gave up the fight. He settled deeper into his chair.

"It all runs together, Lowell. It always does at Christmas. I can remember you in Hana's play like it was yesterday. Hana looking like an angel of judgment one moment and a huge cherub the next. You were adorable. The play was enchanting, if a bit eccentric. A magic time, magic, magic."

"Go on, get to it," he said in a disrespectful whisper.

"Shut up."

Their words were empty and brittle, like stale birthday cake roses.

"You want me to confess something, don't you? Well, there's nothing to confess. . . . Of course there is, of course . . . but what? What will get this feeling out of my body, out of my heart?"

"What do you need to purge?"

"It wasn't us, Lowell. I don't feel guilt about that. We're Briscoes. Something's in the blood, a hormonal catastrophe like fate. That's not it. It isn't Joel either. I knew what he needed. He trusted me. After a while, it was charity. . . . I'm a good girl."

Juliet was dozing off.

"Juliet, wake up."

"I am awake."

"Well, go on. It wasn't Joel. It wasn't me. But. . . ."

"Why did I get you out here? What did I have to say that was so important?"

"Diabolical murder, maybe?"

"Yes, yes. But that's not it. I have so many regrets, so many regrets. . . . It's love, Lowell. Love betrayed. That's the reason. . . . I loved her. . . . I loved Hana more than anyone in my life. More than you, more than anyone. That sounds strange, but it's true. Not a romantic love, no sex; something closer to hero worship, like idolizing a saint. We were so much alike, like twins. Except I was the dark one, the deformed one, the shadow, incomplete and dangerous. She was so pure, so perfectly happy. And my guilts betrayed her. Reflex guilts for Joel, for you, for everyone, everyone. Nola got to them without really knowing it, I think. If you didn't tell. . . . If you didn't, then she just guessed, just said the right words without knowing what they meant. But she was so indignant, so outraged, so sure, so sure, so sure."

"Just exactly what are you saying?" Lowell asked with renewed interest.

"It's like I'd been leading a double life, a triple life. And suddenly someone put it all together. I can't explain it. But imagine if someone said something to you that made it seem, somehow, that she knew all your secrets. All of them. Wouldn't that scare the wits out of you?"

"Of course. Go on."

"What I'm saying, damn it," Juliet sobbed, "is that I knew there was nothing wrong with Hana. She wasn't crazy. She was just neurotic, had spells of depression, that's all. Just spells, like the rest of us. But I didn't fight it. I didn't, I didn't. I didn't fight it, Lowell. I went slack.

That's what I've done all my life. The Nazis came to the door, and I gave them Anne Frank. I went slack. I went slack with Nola, with Daddy, with you, and with my work, my dreams. I didn't oppose them. None of us did."

"Them?"

"Nola . . . and . . . Dr. Hal—you know."

"No, I don't."

"Yes you do. Hal, Hal. Doc Barrows. . . . None of us opposed her. Nola had a spell over us. I've always been a coward. I could never say no. Never. I've let everything have its way with me. Booze, pills, men, pleasure . . . escape . . . Nola. . . ."

"And Dr. Hal."

"Nola. I thought she knew, would turn me in. I panicked, then went slack, let her roll right over me. I just did it again. But this time, someone got hurt."

"'I' didn't get hurt? 'You' didn't?" Lowell asked in a whisper.

"We're alive, Lowell. We're tough. We're survivors, after a fashion. We're Joel's kids. We were hurt. Damaged even. But that goes with the genes. But Hana . . . she's dead."

"What are we, Juliet, genetic masochists?"

"We've had too much fun for that, Lowell. But Nola had no notion of fun, not the vaguest idea. I could smell her righteousness the moment I met her. You did too. Remember when you first saw her?"

"I did sense something, you're right. I hated her guts from the start," Lowell agreed. "And I didn't like 'Dr. Hal' any better. Tell me more about Hal."

"They seemed like the force of law. I was convinced she'd turn me in or something, that she'd found me out, that I'd been betrayed," Juliet countered, a squeak of hysteria in her voice. "I was on a paranoid rush, it was like dope, an opium descent. And, then, when you collapsed and Dr. Barrows had to medicate you, you were almost unconscious for two or three weeks. . . ."

"Medicate me?"

"When you had one of your fits, I thought you thought she knew, too. But you always denied it, always."

"Of course I did. She didn't know."

"But why was Hal so solicitous of me? He gave me all the shots I wanted. Took care of me, took care of you."

"What do you mean exactly."

"What?"

"About Dr. Hal?"

"Never mind him. Do you think I can ever trust *you*? How could anyone ever trust you?"

"You never have, that's for sure. You were the God-damned adult," Lowell said with childish malice.

"And you were some kind of satyr," she shouted, furious, half joking.

"All right. You want to start calling names? I'll call names, you fucking bottomless pit, you. . . ." Lowell stopped short.

Juliet made no response. It was as though a phone had gone dead. Lowell could hear her breathing. He felt guilty; she could always make him feel guilty. Her silence was the nastiest weapon. "I don't blame you for not trusting me," Lowell said. "But I never told anyone anything. I never told on you. Certainly not Hana. I loved Hana, too."

"I know you did," Juliet's voice said through the gloom. "But you and she didn't. . . . Did you?"

"I've already told you. No, absolutely no. How could you think that of her? You have such a dirty mind. It wasn't like that at all. You must know that, Juliet, you must."

"What was it then, and don't tell me it was spiritual."

"You sound like a cuckolded wife." Lowell didn't want to tell her anything. He had no need to release *his* burdens. As a dazzling young Ph.D. with promise and solid publications, he didn't think he had any. He evaded her, saying, "You betrayed Hana, didn't you Juliet? I see that now."

"Don't say it that way!" she shouted.

"Isn't that it?"

"Yes," came a whispered reply.

"I always thought all of you did. Was it some kind of plot? Who got her land? Did you do it for the land?" Lowell sounded like a prosecutor.

Juliet became indignant. "Haven't you heard a word I've said? I told you, land had nothing to do with it. You idiot! You brutal little shit! There was no plot, no plot, you bastard. I'm telling you everything, baring my heart, and you're smearing it with some shitty little crime and scummy innuendo. I hate you, you little swine! I hate you!" she shrieked. "There was no crime." Then quietly and steadily she said, "I just could not do what I knew was right. I told you that. I just couldn't say no. And before I knew it, it was all over. It was as if something had pushed one reality aside and replaced it with another, and when I tried to return to the old reality, it was gone. I simply didn't resist. I chose to please the wrong people. I went slack. I hope you never find yourself in a situation where you prove to yourself who you really are under pressure. If you ever do, remember me."

Lowell had nothing to say. Juliet lay back in the darkness and soon began to breathe deeply. He felt they would never speak of Hana again. It was all over between them, just like that. He settled into the big chair, closed his eyes, and felt a Christmas languor overcome him. The lights from the little tree on the piano blinked pale colors on the enamel of the bathroom door. He was almost asleep when an idea sliced into his consciousness, an old idea that always made him sweat. What if he hadn't told Hana he loved her? What if he hadn't gone to her house that afternoon to dance for her? What if Nola hadn't spied on them? Was he the cause, the trigger? Did he spring the trap?

He knew he couldn't spend the night in Juliet's house, not in his old room. It was late, he'd go for a drive. The moon was full. He'd go down to the bosque and walked the dirt roads along the irrigation ditches, or find some place for eggs and bacon.

— —

From Lowell Briscoe's "A Nest of Hells."

Campo Fiori

[JOURNALS OF HANA NICHOLAS]
6 August 1946—Gloriamaris

Why did they burn you, dear Bruno? Stuff a wedge in your mouth so you couldn't even scream? You believed in God, you believed that God was everywhere, in everything, in all the beauty and bounty of the world. The universe itself was divine to you and everything in it. Of course that's why they burned you. If the universe was divine, then it couldn't be exploited, its poor people tortured, its infidels, heretics, unbelievers destroyed, its landscape raped for money. Of course, the Pope and his Inquisition wanted you to recant. It didn't want even a simpleton like me three hundred years later to fall to the hideous truth, that the rock of the church was a den of thieves, built by thieves to further the ends of thieves. How could you operate a single gold mine, cut down a single forest, allow a single person to go unfed if the world and everything in it was filled with God? You were right, my dear Bruno, to be afraid, to give up, and then to recant your confession and submit to the fate of your thoughts. How could you have lived if you'd subverted your true faith? Your logic made enough sense to you that you had no choice but to choose the fire. Oh, dear God, I feel your terror, I feel your helplessness. You had to be who you are; for you there was no ambiguity; you were what you thought, and everyone knew what you thought. You gave them every chance to save you. You told them you'd be a good church man, you'd perform and believe all the sacraments; you'd do all that with perfect faith and reverence if they didn't make you deny what you knew to be true—that the dualistic world of Plato is a flaw, and such a terrible flaw that it spawned the murderous illusions of otherworldliness. You met them half way, and they dragged you off to the stake. God *is* everywhere. Pascal knew it too: "God is the circle, the perfect circle, whose center is everywhere and circumference nowhere." God was even in your fires, Bruno; that you must have known. Oh, I hope you felt Her when the fire first touched your skin; I hope She gave you visions, and the ecstasy of union with Her destroying form.

. . . We have no choice but to be who we are. No choice.

———

The Dominican monk Giordano Bruno was burned to death in the
Campo Fiori, Rome, in 1600, for holding that God both transcended the
world and yet was the world.

The Christmas of 1964, Continued

Snow had soaked into his shoes and Lowell was about a mile from his car. He turned back and started to jog. It must have been near midnight on the cusp of Christmas morning. He had tried not to think too much about Hana since she died in 1956. And his years as a scholar and a public intellectual in New Haven and Los Angeles had done much to distract him from the morbid and convoluted context of his upbringing. But during the Christmas of 1964 in Albuquerque, his memory wouldn't let him alone. It started to bombard him with images and realizations, with waking nightmares from his childhood, an assault that continued into the 1990s. Memory, for Lowell, resembled stepping through the looking glass. His consciousness simply flipped into the past. This odd ability asserted itself for the first time during that late-night walk on the snowy ditch. The looking glass was practically spinning on the cold jog back to the car. He could remember verbatim, or so he thought, Hana's remarks about joy distinguishing us from the herd, her loathing for what she called the "mass mind," and her devotion to the "sacredness of exceptions." His memory wasn't altogether playing tricks on him, though it did express itself in his flamboyant style.

— —

Adapted from Lowell Briscoe's "A Nest of Hells."

Memories of Kivas and Moths

[JOURNALS OF LOWELL BRISCOE]

We were rehearsing for the Christmas play in the little chapel behind Gloriamaris, which Hana had built years before to honor, she said, the world's lost religions. She called it the Kiva, referring to the religious structures of the Pueblo people and their ancestors the Anasazi. "In the Kiva," I remember her saying, "the old mysteries are revealed. This is the chapel of the world unfallen, a world unburdened by original sin. Paradise still thrives. Holiness doesn't hate the world. Holiness is health, is curiosity, is survival; it is the custom of the earth. Faith is nothing more than a vote of confidence for what is, an act of loyalty to the universe." Everything Hana did and said in the Kiva seemed stylized. The tone of her voice took on a theatrical air. Her posture was stiff and she walked as if dancing to a processional beat. The Kiva was always lit by candles, so it was dark and cool, and its shadows could be frightening, though the general atmosphere was wholesome and benign. Still, it was an environment that commanded respect. You could not be your normal self inside Hana's Kiva. As the doors closed behind you, all the noise of the outside world vanished. The big room was either utterly silent or ringing with Beethoven's Seventh or Ninth symphonies, or full of records of Indian drummers or Buddhist chanting. The ritual of entrance helped to sanctify the interior. Beside the chapel doorway was a tall yucca staff, which Hana would use to knock three times, each knock saying "attention, simplicity, calm." When the doors opened, she and I would bow our heads, and Hana would say, "We have a choice. Let us choose joy." Then we would lift our heads and enter the darkness and safety of the Kiva.

If one's friendship with God is to have any reality, Hana told me with one of her serious smiles, one cannot judge any of "Her" creatures. One must agree with all faiths, all people, all natural events, all myths everywhere. She asked me to imagine what religions might be on other planets. And she insisted that we must be spokesmen for "everything that is," even the wildest variations and the oddest of facts. She admonished me again and again that when any dispute arose, I was to "take both sides, believe in both sides, defend both sides," be "crushed" by both sides and "not whimper." Then she said to me with a regal serenity, "the universe does not take sides." I've thought of that phrase so many times. I didn't really attribute it to her, until now. "Try to treat your own life and everything else as a sanctuary to be defended against the profanity of the mass mind that seeks to impose one truth, a single truth, on the truthless flux and multitude of holy forms. The mass mind is the enemy of reality," she used to say. "Yet even it has the right to exist. One cannot oppose it, only absorb and redefine it with one's life."

Am I remembering her words or making them up, or is it a combination of both? It's like I'm uncovering my own unconscious cache of scrolls, long-forgotten parables, and pronouncements. Did Hana really think like this, or am I doing a fancy version of an evangelical translation of my own? It all seems tremendously real to me, though. I was an actual witness, not some disciple or scholar removed by the centuries. I saw the saint with my own eyes. That's the way she must have seemed to me. She still does, I guess. Some of my memories really are in parables.

Earlier in the spring of 1948, for instance, I remember Hana and I had something of a revelation together about moths, and their relationship to the mass mind. In particularly wet springs, Albuquerque can be flooded by miller moths that cascade from car windows, darken back-door lights at night, swarm madly into kitchens, and keep everyone awake as they crash into lamp shades or screens or whir around the bedroom like a million demons. Moth hordes used to bring out the worst in me. I would have gladly killed them all. We were in Hana's kitchen one night during the infestation that spring. We'd just fought our way through a mob of moths battering themselves on the back-door screen when we saw on the white enamel surface of the refrigerator a single moth isolated from the rest. The moth's body, which I would normally have considered to be a drab brown, or, in moments of hysteria, a sinister furry gray, had an arrestingly elegant, shiny black art nouveau pattern on the lustrous, silver-brown background of its wings. I had never seen an individual miller moth before. I had never stopped to look.

"Now, there's a message," Hana said to me. "The mass mind outside the door is dying to kill itself against the screen. The more individuals there are together, the less each is worth and valued, its singular virtues absorbed by the demonic qualities of the group. But look! Will you ever be able to kill a miller moth again without pain, without pausing, without wishing you weren't going to kill it? Look how sublime it is alone, how utterly beautiful, how important." Then Hana's face shone. "We should become friends of the moths. Let's go outside right now and learn to be their friends. Let's stand in the middle of the swarm and let them flutter all over us."

I'm sure I cringed in disgust. "I wouldn't have the guts either, right now," Hana told me reassuringly. "But one day, Lowell, I'm going to go out there and become a singular moth, tall and straight, and calm them down, smooth them out, and send them on their ways, not as a mob, but as separate moth souls each in their own beautiful body."

Written in the late summer of 1992.

The Christmases of 1964 and 1948, Continued

Jogging through the snow, very tired now, the last vestiges of alcohol burning off, Lowell flashed on Juliet's description of Hana at her sanity hearing: Hana's refusal to defend herself, her angry silence, her defeatism. It seemed so utterly out of character at first. Lowell tried to imagine how her face looked. He tried to read her emotions behind the expressions he imagined. It made no sense. But, then, he thought he saw the possibilities. Maybe she was standing still in a mob of moths. Maybe she'd just gone slack like Juliet, had frozen in panic. Maybe she couldn't believe that the mass mind had gotten hold of her, and she was just struck dumb by it. Maybe she was that moth on the icebox that the others just crushed. Where was "holy joy" in her response? Why didn't she protect the principle of the individual in her own person? Was she really insane? Or had fear just wiped away her choices? Was she just stunned, in a daze, like Poles herded into trains by the SS? "I can't stand it! It's monstrous!" Lowell screamed inside his head. "I've got to make sense of it." Why would she do that? Why didn't she resist? She wasn't doing a Socrates, was she? What principle was she defending? Did she get caught in her own paradoxes? Was she trying to manifest the universe by not taking sides? That would be a sublime martyrdom and triumph, if she hadn't told Juliet that what happened to her was "diabolical murder." Maybe her circle of friends did scapegoat her for some awful crime, some mortal folly of greed, spurred on by that pudgy New Yorker, Dr. Hal. How could she give up like that?

Such thoughts swarmed though Lowell's mind without ceasing. By the time he reached his car, his feet were sticky cold and he was utterly exhausted. Only the adrenaline that arose to the call of his memories had kept him jogging. Inside the car, the windows soon fogged up. The heater and tobacco smoke made him drowsy. He was going to find an all-night cafe, but he had to close his eyes, he was so tired. Images of a huge, hot room came back to him. It was Christmas Eve 1947 and Hana and Juliet and Lowell were in a middle pew in the packed church of San Felipe Pueblo for midnight mass. The nave was full of local people and onlookers. Incense and candle smoke were intoxicating. The snow was deep and icy outside and the wind gusted dangerously. Hana and her new friends were dressed in heavy layers and were damp with sweat. The priest had just finished giving communion and had moved swiftly to depart through the sacristy, when the front doors of the church burst open and a line of buffalo dancers thundered down the aisle, with drummers and chanters just behind. Hana clapped once with glee, turned to Lowell and Juliet, taking pleasure in their surprise, and then closed her eyes to focus on the mixture of foot beats, drum patterns, and holy songs. What moments before had been a hushed, melodious European rite, drained utterly of the ancient and releasing presence of Dionysus, became suddenly an ocean of rhythms and meanings, engulfing them in music that exchanged itself with the beat of their pulse. Lowell closed his eyes, too.

The car was so hot and comfortable that Lowell couldn't keep from dozing again. And then he heard the "Ode to Joy" and Hana saying, "Now it is time for us to visit our theater, what I call the Kiva." It was the first time Lowell had been invited into the holy of holies. He had never been within ten steps of it before, and he walked as fast as he could behind her. She seemed like a Moses, consuming the desert in full stride, like some giant Assyrian goddess with knees and calves of granite, marching into battle, victorious before the first blood was spilled.

Hana instructed Lowell in the ritual of the entrance. The great doors opened, releasing a gust of warm, moist air, scented with the odor of hay, burlap, candle wax, and piñon smoke. Although the exterior resembled a miniature San Felipe church, the interior was reminiscent of a rectangular Hopi Kiva, with a dancing area down the middle, serving as a wide aisle, and bancos on either side of the room. At the far end was a raised platform with an altar.

Lowell reached for her hand, holding on tight to be led wherever she would take him. The longer he stood beside her, the warmer the interior seemed, the sweeter the smells, and the more their breathing became a living silence. The air itself was soft and reassuring. His skin felt lighter, his eyes cooler. "Surely this is a place where fear can't survive for long," Hana said softly almost to herself.

On the platform behind the low altar was a throne, painted gold and upholstered in green velvet, made from an old chair Hana had found on one of her many treasure hunts through Albuquerque's alleys. The wings of a golden eagle she'd found as a road kill were stretched out and suspended over the throne. At the top of the backrest, a small, framed sign had been fixed. It read simply "Fear Not." Hana told Lowell the throne was "reserved exclusively for visiting gods." As Lowell's eyes adjusted, he saw that the Kiva was full of fascinating natural objects, icons of Hana's faith in the common sense of the fantastic and the unexpected. Several open sharks' jaws hung from the ceiling. On shelves above the bancos were huge Ethiopian volutes and other shells, along with the skulls of tapirs, pumas, and owls, and many banded river rocks, glass jars of seeds and soil, and a number of stuffed birds. Filling up the far right corner of the Kiva was a virtual field of amethyst crystals, part of a geode that must have been large enough for a small person to stand in it. "This is an amateur's museum of God's imagination," Hana told Lowell. "And a shrine to Her inexhaustible creativity." Lowell was overwhelmed. The Kiva seemed like an Aladdin's cave, cascading with unbelievable treasures.

At the end of the first visit to the Kiva, Hana showed Lowell the most important of the shrine's symbolic objects. In the middle of the brick floor was an uncovered empty square of earth, two feet by two. For Hana, it was a relic of the planet, "the fact upon which this shrine is founded." With great ceremony, Hana and Lowell knelt before it and placed their palm prints in the sandy loam. "This is a sign, Lowell, a mark of intention, displaying to the forces of Christmas that we pledge to do them honor with our play. Our prints will remain here, as tokens of our individuality and common purpose, until midnight Christmas Eve."

Lowell did find a cafe that early Christmas morning in 1964. He read and underlined several pages of Viktor Frankl's *Man's Search for Meaning*, ate a big plate of hotcakes, and returned to Juliet's house before 10 a.m. with the presents he'd brought from Los Angeles. Juliet was sober and dressed in a well-tailored sweater and slacks. She looked drained, but her hair was neat and her make-up in place. They exchanged gifts with a minimum of ceremony but with memories of old affection. When Lowell made references to her disclosures the previous day, she waved them off as "ravings" and would say nothing more. Lowell never again returned to that house while Juliet was alive, although he spoke with her once a week on the phone. Three years later, Juliet was dead, murdered in her bedroom.

Adapted from Lowell Briscoe's "A Nest of Hells."

Intimations of Fatality, 1990

"You're a psycho, you know that? You're a nut. I'm sick of your horrors, sick of your night sweats, sick of your paranoia, sick of your ego. You're a coward, that's all, a psychological coward. I can't stand it anymore! I don't know you. Eleven years! And I don't know who you are! You're all mask, inaccessible, utterly inaccessible. An actor. That's all you do is act, just perform, juggle, dance, spin in the air. You're not an actor, you're a clown. I don't know if you've ever told me an honest word. I'm sick of it all, sick of you, sick of me . . . you bastard! Don't smile at me like that, you bastard!"

And then she hit him, hit Lowell full force in the face. Karen Frank, his "sexual therapist," as she used to say, and his intellectual colleague, slapped him so hard he bit his tongue. This elegant "Manhattan dish," as he called her, "this pampered, high-strung, freelance hotshot," actually slapped him, and then, the cur, she cringed back, fell to the couch, and whimpered "Don't hit me, don't hit me," as if he'd made a practice of it for years. He'd never hit her before, and he couldn't remember hitting her then. In fact, he was almost certain he didn't. But he wanted to. He remembered that. He wanted to grab her by the throat, he told Dr. Tuttle, "squeeze her neck till her veins burst. But I didn't."

He went through her apartment instead, smashing pictures, breaking lamps, upturning tables, hurling books. "There's no question in my mind, I was in a homicidal rage," he wrote in his journal. He had it in him to demolish her. No one had ever hit him before. But he knew the game. "She was trying to turn me into an abuser so she'd have the moral upper hand," he wrote. Karen Frank was good at that sort of jujitsu in the battle of the sexes. So was Lowell.

"You maniac," Karen screamed, "you're destroying everything. You're insane, you know that. Insane! Somebody ought to lock you up!" Karen was running after Lowell, frantically trying to grab him and make him stop demolishing everything in sight. But when she said, "somebody ought to lock you up," Lowell froze in his tracks, turned on her, and gave her a look that made her think he was going to kill her.

"Anyone who tries to lock me up," he said in a loud, hysterically smiling voice, "had better plan to never, ever, have a peaceful night's sleep for the rest of their lives, because I *will* get them. Hear me?! I *will* get them."

Karen took it seriously. She left the room, got her purse, and fled the apartment. Lowell tried to neaten things up before he left. The next day, a delivery man left several boxes full of his papers, books, toiletries, and clothes at his apartment door. Karen had cleaned him out of her life. They never saw each other again, except twice at the agent's office to clear up contracts and royalties.

After Juliet died in 1967, and after Lowell's brief stay in a sanitarium, he settled into his life in Los Angeles, living in Malibu for a while and then around Topanga Canyon. He had more money than he ever imagined, as Juliet left everything to him. He began working in poor neighborhoods and opened a little school for emotionally disturbed children. He became an adjunct professor at Pepperdine, UCLA, and USC, continued to make documentaries, and wrote popular and widely read essays from political hot spots around the world, including a somewhat notorious piece on the 1968 massacre of students in Mexico City that blamed, in part, the U.S. government. He became, in fact, a minor radical guru, something of a celebrity. And he soon wrote and published his Christmas fable, "The Witch and The Star," which brought him international acclaim. But he was still plagued by terrors and desperately lonely when he met the writer, editor, and feminist scholar Karen Frank in 1980. For more than nine years they collaborated on numerous projects that dealt with the ethics of eroticism.

After their big fight, Lowell emotionally caved in on himself, withdrew in self-disgust. As he wrote in his journals of those years, "The realization that I could have killed Karen that day without the slightest remorse genuinely horrifies me. I did not believe I was capable of such a suspension of conscience. What a shock it is for a man in his early fifties to suddenly learn that he is not who he thinks he is, that behind all his habits and ambitions and rationalizations there is more to him, something vaster and more mysterious than anything he could conjure up. For me, that something is not only what I must interpret as a grotesque potential for violence but also a nauseating guilt. The fight with Karen showed that I have within me the emotional coldness of a deeply troubled child. And I can't help, now, but think of my childhood and who I used to be."

To help calm himself, Lowell bought a new house on the beach, went on a diet, stopped drinking and smoking, resumed his college teaching and working with troubled kids. But the catastrophe of Karen plagued him. He started to consciously reconstruct his life to see where the urge to violence came from. "Naturally," he wrote in his journals for Dr. Tuttle, "my thoughts turned to Hana and Juliet and the others. And the more I remembered, the more aware I became of how superficial my relationship with myself had always been. One might say I was suffering a mid-life crisis, but I wasn't prepared to lower myself into the mainstream of pop psychology. Clearly I was at the start of a metamorphosis. And then all shit broke loose."

— ◡ —

From Lowell Briscoe's "A Nest of Hells." A word about the names in this draft of "A Nest of Hells": Dr. Briscoe used the names of real people in the working draft of his book, so as not to confuse himself, a note I uncovered in his journals has affirmed. But he did intend to change all the names, except his own, and I have used the fictional names he suggested for all the characters.

Prelude to the Dreams

About six months after moving into his new beach house, Lowell found himself tangled in a series of traumatic circumstances that softened him up for the spiritual breakthroughs that lay ahead. After the troubles with Karen, these events seemed to widen the cracks in his defenses and let his dream life through. It was a terrible time.

First, his physician, Dean Mendoza, who was his only close male friend, committed suicide by hanging himself in the playroom of his home in the dead of night so his wife and children would find him dangling before their eyes on Sunday morning. He'd left no note and had not given anyone the slightest clue that he was depressed or unhappy with his life or that suicide was on his mind. No one had any idea why such a gentle, seemingly happy man would kill himself in a manner so brutal and angry, in a way that would scar his children for the rest of their lives and, no doubt, seriously undermine his wife's mental well-being. Had Dean discovered he was a Jekyll and Hyde? Lowell wondered. Was Jekyll going to kill the Hyde, only to have the Hyde do Jekyll the favor first?

The death of his friend triggered in Lowell morbid terrors about living a double life, about having been seized by some unknown part of himself. He was dazed and preoccupied with such fears and speculations when he was involved in a traffic accident that came literally within an inch of killing him and a number of others. He was in downtown Beverly Hills shopping, and he jaywalked across Camden Drive. He didn't see that the hunter-green Alfa Romeo was speeding to the left of him, or that a van full of children was making a right turn onto the street. When he saw the van, he stopped in the middle of the street, causing the Alfa to swerve to miss him and collide with the van. "My mind was not paying attention to my life," he told friends later. Luckily the Alfa driver was skillful, and the driver of the van saw him swerving. The crash was not as bad as it could have been, but many parked cars were damaged and several people were injured. Lowell was cited for jaywalking, given a stern and embarrassing lecture in court, and sued by several parties. "The whole process wore me down terribly," Lowell told Dr. Tuttle.

The next traumatic circumstance was what Lowell called "a cancer panic." "I couldn't believe it," he said. "Life, or the gods, or my self-destructive instincts would not let me alone." During the proceedings in traffic court, he became short of breath. He started to cough, and coughed for a week, eventually drawing small amounts of blood. He had no doctor he could trust anymore, so he worried himself to the point of believing he was at death's door. He finally went to a clinic. The physicians there could find nothing wrong, except for a severely irritated throat brought on by nervous coughing. The incident made him realize "how frantically unprepared" for death he was, "how much of my life was unresolved, and how much I could not bear the thought of dying before I'd made sense of what had happened to me," he told Dr. Tuttle.

The final circumstance called for a storm of paranoia. It rose up in him daily like time-lapsed thunder clouds on a TV weather report. It all but depleted his capacity for joy. His next-door neighbor at the beach, a woman of great physical bulk and a flamboyant sort of charm, a person he was growing to like, accused him of building his southern wall two feet over her property line and into her tiny back yard. Lowell knew she was wrong and they argued for weeks. Lowell became incensed. He suspected her of spying on him in his office. When he found her one weekend starting to dismantle the wall—which gave Lowell the privacy he wanted and needed—he threatened to take her to court. But she continued pounding on the cement-block wall with a sledge hammer. If it hadn't been one of those breezy, cloudless, hot but surf-chilled afternoons on the beach, Lowell might not have grown as frantic as he did. But the contrast of her invasion with the free spirit of the day was too much for him. He called the police. Later he even went out and sprayed her with a hose. Whereupon she charged him like a bull; he dodged her, and she ran into the policeman who had just stepped into Lowell's little garden. The cop held on to her and she slugged him. He charged her with assault and battery and resisting arrest and took her to jail. As comical as it sounds, it had been like living in a war zone for Lowell. And it took everything out of him. He even started to feel sorry for her. In jail, she'd gotten into a fight with an inmate, and caused so much trouble they charged her with another count of assault and attempted escape. She'd found herself caught in a web of unintended consequences. But even with her gone, Lowell could still feel her anger pulsing through the garden wall. He didn't want to feel the presence of anyone anywhere near his house. And to have had the power of so much hate directed at him was intolerable. Her negative energies softened him up for the final blow, which came several weeks later when Lowell had two dreams that he considered to be of "cosmic importance." One of the dreams he described as "the most terrifying thing that has ever happened to me. It was so real, so horrible," he wrote, "it seemed as if it were a knot of repressed memories bursting up like corpses from the bottom of a pond." When he awoke from the dreams, he couldn't shake the feeling that he hadn't been dreaming, but remembering. "Was my conscience thumping away like a tell-tale heart? Had Fortunato found a way to tap messages from behind his bricked-in crypt so everyone on the Piazza could hear him while they drank their Amontillado?" The dreams possessed him. He could think of nothing else. "Were they dreams of grace," he wondered, "revelations in horrific code, or images flaked off from the facts of the myth of my life? Is God telling me something? Or am I really some kind of monster? Am I a newspaper headline, heaven help me, a mass murderer? I don't think I've been leading a double life. But the dreams were so real, more like memory than fantasy—in fact, like evidence. My brain began to feel as if it was bleeding, as if my skull had been lined with sandpaper."

Lowell riddled the dreams every way he could. And though he drained them of most of their horror, they appeared suddenly, even in the midst of the most distracting work, like an emotional film, a slick of adrenaline spreading out everywhere.

— ~

From Lowell Briscoe's "A Nest Of Hells."

The Dreams

[Journals of Lowell Briscoe]
August 12, 1992

In the first dream, I'm walking along a deserted neighborhood, in the summer, up a hill, on a sidewalk, next to vacant lots filled with dirt, yellow grass, old foundations, broken and rotting wood. I come to the top of the hill and see to my left a brick wall with Nola, Juliet, Thea Pound, and the Devons standing like victims before it. I'm startled and shocked. In reality, they are all dead, of course, but they are present again, a rogues' gallery, silent and menacing, frozen still like ice statues, gray with pollution. A wind comes up. The wall is enveloped in cold shadows, a frigid shade that smells of flowers, not unlike a florist's refrigerator. I approach the wall and see Juliet sprawled half naked on a rag rug in her bedroom, her old face smashed in by a boot heel, her teeth protruding, her neck purple and wasp-waisted with the belt still cinched around it. I look behind me and there are the Devons, George and Betty, their faces bloated in horror, scratching at the glass of a huge aquarium, drowning. To the side of the tank, in a little heap, is Thea's fat self, a Sunday hat still on her head, and a fox fur around her shoulders. Her black dress, with its floral highlights, is spotted with specks of soggy cereal, orange juice, raisins, and prune skins as if she'd vomited. And behind her in a hospital bed, I see a pair of twisted feet, with curly toenails and thick, cracked, scab-laced skin. They belong to Nola, whose face I see and recognize, despite its cadaverous pallor and gaping mouth. I turn again and walk behind another wall, a white one that looks like a metal garage door. And before me is Hana's garden, the northern part of the Kiva, the grove of olive and myrtle trees and its shrines and redwood table. I walk past the huge, ancient cottonwood and see a patch of ground where, it dawns on me with shaking dread, I seem to remember that all five bodies are buried. I ask myself in the dream, "How do you know this? How can you be so sure?" And then I woke up.

The second dream came to me the same night as the first, after hours of sleepless fretting. It came to me near dawn. In it I see Hana's face, her "mask of horror" in the mental hospital, as if it were a mosaic medallion, a face of Medusa on the floor of a Roman villa. I kneel down on all fours to look at it, and then somehow peel it off to reveal, of all things, my own face as a child. Then I peel that off, too, and see my face as an adult, with a Narcissus smile. I peel that one away and find what must be Hana's face as a little girl. I want to kiss her but I lift up the medallion instead and look down into a tunnel at the sunny end of which I see myself as a boy running away into a happy, forest-walled meadow laughing as if overcome with delight. It's the same sound I hear from myself sometimes when I listen to the "Ode to Joy" while driving in the country.

This entry was found in a brown envelope addressed to Melinda Tuttle.

The First Meeting, Spring 1948

They were an odd lot—George and Betty Devon, Thea Pound, Nola Dasheller, and Juliet Anne Briscoe. Hana Nicholas kept up with them out of loyalty and pity, and the faint promise of learning more from them, about their lives and the way they saw the world. Hana never gave up on people, never abandoned close friends. But by the time Lowell was thirty, in 1967, each one of Hana's old friends, the whole menagerie, was dead. They no longer existed physically in Lowell's life. But they were more than rumors of atrocities and more than memories and dreams. They had become psychic problems. He could never shake them entirely. He didn't want to. "I don't care how dead Nola is. I can still feel her, the dread of her, the chill of her righteousness," he wrote in his journal of those years. Even Karen Frank at her luscious best couldn't completely distract him.

That day in the spring of 1948 when Hana first took Lowell under her wing, Nola was there too, "like an invisible vulture," Lowell wrote. He had been having premonitions about Hana weeks before he met her. He was fascinated by her house, by the acreage it sat on, and by the odd bits of information he'd gathered from listening to conversations between Thea and Juliet. The first time he saw Hana with his own eyes, it startled him so badly he nearly threw up. The thing a frightened child hates above all else is to be startled.

"I don't know why I hadn't seen her before. Juliet might have said it was owing to my selective blindness, the studied self-absorption that caused me to look at the world as if through a soda straw. That's a harsh verdict on an eleven-year-old boy, but Juliet was not all Elizabeth Arden and Prince Matchabelli. There was broken glass in the whipped cream," Lowell told Dr. Tuttle.

Hana came into view on one of those clear blue New Mexico mornings, an exultant morning with a cold sky and a sunny breeze that "makes your whole body feel like a sail," as Hana once remarked to Juliet. Lowell was on the ditch path behind his house, on his hands and knees, focusing on a little pile of pebbles, fascinated by their different shapes and smoothness. He was drowsy with sun and concentration when suddenly out of nowhere his isolation was burst by the cacophonous zing of a bicycle bell and the clatter of a wire basket. Lowell, jolted from his stare, looked up to see a melodious Cheshire grin bearing down on him not ten yards away. "Coming through, sorry, sorry, I didn't see you. . . ." The bike and rider whizzed by. Lowell yelped as the figure on a blue bicycle pounded royally over the bumps and ruts. By the time he'd gotten to his feet, the rider had turned a corner and was gone. "That must be her," he thought. The person on the bike was a big woman, squarely built, sun leathered, her face full of wrinkles and creases. She'd come into his vision with no warning. "She'd just barged right in and out as if all my preoccupations were so much marsh gas and vapor," Lowell wrote. He couldn't focus on anything for the rest of the day. He saw everything in a peripheral blur.

━ ━

From Lowell Briscoe's "A Nest of Hells."

The Grinding of Teeth and the
Clenching of Jaws

The circumstances of the following morning almost caused Lowell to back off from forcing a meeting with Hana. In fact, the whole day was an ordeal. Just after breakfast, at which Juliet had made a pitiful attempt at motherly solicitude, Lowell was seized by a fit of sneezing and coughing, compounded by stomach cramps and tightening in the lungs. If Juliet had not been so dictatorial about giving him a cure of sleeping pills, enema, and a "nice day in bed," Lowell might have allowed his indisposition to overcome him. But he loved to test Juliet's resolve. The tighter she gripped him, the more violently he rebelled. Her attempts that morning to capture him with his own diseases and psychosomatic inertia gave him the impetus to overcome them. The episode developed into one of their ritual aggressions.

Lowell locked himself in the bathroom and wouldn't come out. He was tenacious and his body healed itself with each demonstration of rage. They shrieked and taunted each other. Things were thrown, things were broken, lilac powder was spilled all over the bathroom floor.

"How am I supposed to take care of you, you little son of a bitch, if you won't let me? Come out here this instant! This instant!" Juliet screamed. "This instant, this instant, this instant! If you don't get out here, I'll call the police! I'll have you put in jail! I'll put you in a laundry bag and drop you off at the dump!"

"Shove it, shove it, shove it, shove it, shove it," Lowell screeched back, pounding the bathroom door like a drum. "If you don't shut up, I'll break everything in here. I'll take a razor blade to your hot water bottles. I'll cut my eyes out."

"Go ahead, cut everything off. Bleed to death, go on."

But after twenty minutes of siege, Juliet gave up, contracted an ailment of her own, and locked herself in her bedroom. She let out a final bellow when she heard the front door slam, and Lowell was gone out into the morning, alone, robust, free of everything but fear.

The battle had charged Lowell's emotions to such intensity that his anxieties about meeting Hana were on the edge of being unbearable.

He didn't know how to approach her, and he had no idea what to say. He walked up and down Griegos Road. The longer he delayed the more possessed by dread and panic he became. What would he say to her? Would she run him off? Would she laugh at him? Was she cruel? Lowell paced past her house four times on the opposite side of the road, hoping the Devons would see him and ask him in for milk and cookies. As hard as he tried, he couldn't make himself get any closer. It wasn't courage that made him take the first step across the street. He had to get rid of the pressure of fear. The next thing he knew, he was walking next to the trees along Hana's pine-pole coyote fence, moving closer and closer to the great front door with its crude iron studs, utterly absorbed in being as quiet and invisible as he could.

At the far corner of the driveway, Lowell noticed a small opening in the adobe wall around the house itself, a square hole with wooden bars shaped like lightning. Lowell was just about to summon the courage to take a tentative look inside, when he felt a small hand on his shoulder and heard a soft, insistent little voice admonishing him about being a "peeping tom." He let out a frightened grunt, and fell to his knees as if he'd been punched in the kidney. "Why Lowell, I didn't mean to alarm you." He recognized the voice. It wasn't Hana's; it was Nola Dasheller's. He saw her standing over him, cradling an armful of what looked to him like black roses. She told him that he must not pry and that good little people didn't lurk around and that Hana wasn't home, and that "anyway dear, wouldn't you like to come to my house, have milk and cool down?" Then she put her face close to Lowell's and asked, "What *are* you so afraid of, young Mr. Lowell Briscoe?"

It was at that moment that Nola ceased to be a person for Lowell. She'd caught him with no defenses. She'd accused him of something, he wasn't sure what. She'd grabbed him by the arm and tried to yank him to his feet. She'd violated his person; she'd touched him. Her fingers on his arm didn't feel human, and for a moment her pleasant grandmotherly face took on the appearance of a wasp's. He could see himself reflected in her dome-like eyes, and it looked as if his face were being pulled by the nose from his skull. Nola was half dragging him along when he accidentally stepped on her heel. He tried to apologize, but the words wouldn't come out and she glared at him and hissed foully, "Don't be horrid. Stand up, stand up."

No adult, other than Joel and Juliet, had ever spoken to Lowell in a tone of voice like that. He was enraged. He yanked his arm free and was just about on the brink of exploding, of tackling her to the ground, of God knows what, when he heard the skid of bike wheels on dirt.

When he heard Hana's bicycle, he spun around and saw her smiling the smile of someone who knows no fear. How wrong that assessment would turn out to be. But still on that day, hate, terror, anxiety all vanished from Lowell as dust disappears from a bottle top with the swipe of a finger. Lowell was a little boy again. He moved toward Hana. She took his hand in hers. The two women exchanged some pleasantries and then Hana said to Nola, "No, no dear. He's no bother. I can take care of it. Thank you. I asked him here. He's my guest."

Lowell was trembling and Hana wrapped an arm around him and hugged him to her. Then with her big hand between his shoulder blades, she herded him along through the side gate into her garden. "I did ask you here, after all, didn't I?" she said mysteriously. Lowell nodded, tried to say something but sputtered spittle instead. He followed her around a portal that smelled of animals and feed, and then found himself inside her kitchen. She went straight to the sink as if nothing unusual had taken place. She cut up some liver for her cats. Lowell was still standing at the door, half paralyzed and out of breath. He tried to tell her his name, tried to say something, but the words wouldn't appear. When she asked him if he liked cats, he could only make a grotesque expression with his mouth trying hopelessly to spit out the words, "very much." She seemed mildly impatient, and told him she was pleased to meet him at last and was glad that he'd finally gotten up the courage to come and see her. He stepped toward her, but she stopped him, saying that this was a bad time and that she was in no shape to make new friends. She had work to do that morning, she said, but if he liked he could pay her a real visit the following Saturday. She patted his head, turned him around, and gave him a little nudge out the door. "You've done the right thing. But watch out for rose pruners," she said with a laugh.

"Did you go back on Saturday?" Dr. Tuttle asked.

"Yes, and for many Saturdays and Wednesdays after that."

"What do you think she was doing with you? You don't really think she intuited you needed help, spiritually picked you out as some sort of charity work, do you?" the doctor asked.

"That's as good a reason as any I can think of. I really believe that Hana had a sixth sense, a prophetic vision, some kind of shamanistic power. I know that's wacky, but it seems utterly logical to me. She must have sensed that I was in emotional trouble. Why else would she have sought me out? I don't even really know myself how sick I was. There was a little matter of drugs thrown into the picture, too."

"Drugs?"

"Yeah, but that's for later."

"Why later?"

"Because I don't really remember all that much yet. It's coming back to me as a kind of archaeological puzzle. The dreams triggered everything. But I'm just swamped with bits and pieces, with piles of shards. I do know, though, that Juliet and I were hooked on something strong. And perhaps everyone else was too, everyone who went to that doctor, Dr. Hal Barrows. Hana didn't. In any case. . . ."

"Alright, so charity was her motive, you think? She somehow had a mysterious charge of psychic empathy for you?"

"I don't know, but, yes, maybe. And she didn't need to be a shaman to put two and two together—not about Juliet's and my secret life, I don't think anyone knew about that—but about how crazy we both were together. It must have been obvious to someone with Hana's sensitivity."

"Hana wasn't using you, too, was she ? Like Juliet? Using you to solve her problems?"

"God, no. Not like Juliet, not anything like that."

"No, I didn't mean that way, but everybody does something for a reason. And why would Hana, this brilliant, complicated, erudite woman, take you on as her project? Why would she bother? What was in it for her? She wasn't an Albert Schweitzer, was she?"

"Maybe she was. Maybe it was a matter of dealing with the least of her brethren."

"Maybe she was satisfying deep maternal urges. Maybe she really was close to a breakdown."

"I don't think so," Lowell said sternly.

"No, I mean, really, you should think about that. What was in it for her? I don't want to sound like a skeptic, but I think you should ask yourself if you've turned her into something she never was, idealized her. I'm not trying to be cruel or to burst illusions. I just think you should make sure she's not an illusion."

"She's not."

From Lowell Briscoe's "A Nest of Hells."

Skipping Sunday, Summer 1948

Hana knelt beside him in the tall grasses by the ditch. Lowell had found a large woodhouse's toad in the jungle of weeds on the bank. "Don't frighten him. If we keep still, he might calm down and we could watch him hunt," she told Lowell in a whisper. The toad was motionless and poised to jump. It sat on a matted patch of green surrounded by swaying ditch willows, asters, and Johnson grass. Hana was helping Lowell learn how to be patient, and he was developing a modest talent. The toad blinked. A gnat crossed its field of vision. The toad's tongue slapped out so hard it set him in motion, and he tumbled down the incline of the bank, disappearing into taller, thicker grasses close to the muddy water. Lowell looked at Hana worriedly. She smiled and lightly hugged his shoulder. "He must have been bored with us. He's quite safe, don't worry. He'll probably tell his family about the unfortunate specimens who had such bad manners they were actually going to watch him eat. Toads don't like people to see them chew," Hana said with mock authority.

Lowell saw Hana everywhere on the ditches that freezing Christmas Eve night in 1964 after he left Juliet's house. A clean crust of snow covered the ground. Ice and snow made the tall, dead weeds and willow stalks on either side of the path seem like hedges of clouds. The full moon flooded the sky with a blue white light. Lowell followed the path that he and Hana had taken many times in the summer of 1948. He remembered that "toad Sunday" more vividly than most, but not only because of its toad. Hana also came to call it "skipping Sunday."

Lowell and Hana were out early that morning. The sky was still clear, without a cloud in sight. From the floor of the North Valley, the mountains seemed to rise out of the desert like the landscape of a myth. And looking west across the alfalfa fields and orchard groves to the river, with its tangled cottonwood forest, one got only the merest hint that a big town was anywhere near. They were on the Duranes Lateral, where Albuquerque urban farmers still used updated versions of Pueblo and Hispanic waterways to irrigate their modest holdings.

Hana took Lowell to the ditches, she said, because she wanted to give him an altogether "different view of reality, so you'll know there's more to life than being afraid." She often lectured in a gentle way, "rambling on," as she liked to put it.

"Animals know that fear is the worst fate, far worse than pain and certainly worse than death. Fear is the torture that never stops—until you stop it."

When Lowell protested he wasn't afraid of anything, Hana replied, "not even of being left behind at the side of the road? Not even of being squeezed so tight you're paralyzed? Not even of being naked and found out?"

"Naked?"

"Exposed for who you really are, without disguises, like a snail without its shell; not even that?"

"I don't know. Maybe I am. But you said stop fear. How do you do that?" Lowell asked precociously, dodging her question.

"By pretending you're not afraid of what you're afraid of. Mostly, we're afraid to be afraid, not afraid of what we think we're afraid of."

"Are you ever afraid?" he asked her seriously.

"All the time."

"Why can't you stop fear?"

"Because," she said closing her eyes, "I don't really know who I want to be."

"I don't understand."

"I don't really know where I want to go and so I can be pushed off course by doubt, the bewildered grandfather of fear."

Toad Sunday was midway in their friendship. It became skipping Sunday about an hour after they'd seen the toad. They ambled along the road by the ditch, Hana asking Lowell questions about himself. He was fond of babbling.

"What do you like to do most, Lowell?"

"Play."

"Play what?"

"Playing cowboy or knights, not really cowboy and Indians, but pioneer, gun shooter, a bad guy on his horse, a good guy really, safe on his horse; he never gets off his horse; no one can pry him off; he's safe there, he can always ride away, always, nobody can get him. If he ever gets off his horse, they'll get him. But he never gets off his horse; he never goes into town; if he does, he rides into the store to get his food; he never leaves the saddle. He rides sometimes on the roads I make though the flowers, the places for trucks and tanks and soldiers and secret holes in the ground where I hide under a sheet. . . ."

At various points in the walk, Hana would stop suddenly and freeze, and Lowell would be startled into silence. Hana would point to something in the water or the bushes. Once it was a muskrat swimming like an elegant old man doing the side stroke in his private pool. Another time it was a roadrunner, darting in among the tamarisks, milkweed, willow, and stems of false mallow. In high summer, the ditches were strands of wildness woven around the cultivated fields of the valley and the desert scrub mesas beyond them. Once they were hurrying though a cloud of gnats, waving them away from their faces, when they saw a strange, circular, olive-drab object half buried in the sand beside the road. They stopped, and Hana touched it with her finger. Out popped a little head with a sharp beak. It was a soft-shell turtle that could inflict a nasty bite, they learned after returning to Gloriamaris and looking it up in Hana's library.

Skipping Sunday came to them by surprise when they passed by a small orchard of apple and cherry trees among which were chomping a number of handsome, long-eared goats. They slowed their pace to watch them play and were quite engrossed, when Hana turned to Lowell and grinned, "I think we should skip."

"Skip?"

"Like the goats."

— —

From Lowell Briscoe's "A Nest of Hells."

The Illusion of Flight

[JOURNALS OF LOWELL BRISCOE]

It was preposterous, but there went Hana, skipping down the dusty ditch road, her linebacker's body, in overalls and a work shirt, bobbing up and down like a roadrunner's head. I took after her in a run, and when I caught up to her I naturally started skipping too. Hana had very long legs and was strong as any big man, even in her mid-fifties. In 1948, in fact, she was just a little older than I am now and in better shape. Skipping alters your way of thinking about yourself and the world. We were moving at an incredible clip, gobbling up the ground like flightless birds, flapping their wings in genetic memory of soaring. We skipped in unison, carrying each other along as if we were held together by a force field. After five minutes or so, Hana had picked up the tempo and I couldn't help but keep pace, although I was straining to do so, in fact pushing myself to the limit. As we whipped along at the peak of my endurance, I realized that Hana and I were breathing at the same rate and, astonishingly, I was having to slow down a bit so as not to inch ahead. When we finally stopped, we both felt heavy as sandbags.

"We have defied gravity, we have flown, we are the Wright brothers, how wonderful to be so free, so like goats and birds," she told me beaming, sweat running down the deep wrinkles of her face. "Didn't you feel like the sun was driving your muscles, could you feel the energy of joy, the pure force of the divine hilarity propelling you along? That's what distinguishes us from the herd, the mass mind. Joy can find its way through our defenses and bad habits! Wasn't it holy?"

When Hana was spiritually flying, she gave off so much energy she could even animate someone as deeply cemented in inertia as myself. I have this terrible view of how I used to be as a kid. I know, Melinda, you think that I'm judging him by adult standards. Still he was—or I was—so mature, so devious, so observant that he had a kind of virtuoso quality; he played his life and the lives around him with such precision. But maybe that's all just a wild glorification, an echo of what he had to tell himself to keep from going under, to keep from hanging himself in the garage. That idea came to me many times in the aftermath of the Christmas of 1948.

— —

This journal entry, like many others, was not dated. But it is in the 1992 sequence written for Dr. Tuttle.

Who Can I Believe?

[DIARY OF NOLA DASHELLER]
Thursday morning

I can't describe my consternation. Nothing makes sense with us any-more. I worry about my common sense. I told Hana Tuesday that I felt so lonely sometimes that I'd just as soon go into the mountains and freeze to death, like I've heard old Eskimo people do. I feel use-less. Ancient and useless. And without any roots. Hana is no use to me either. She doesn't understand a thing about this. She is unnaturally happy for her age. It is unnatural. It's not the norm. I'm the norm. Hana's still a child. Or has she "regressed?" Is she becoming more childlike, faintly senile, is she delusional, as Dr. Barrows might say? Am I delusional?

No. I feel terrible. Let's face it, that's how I feel. I feel like I am old, in pain, widowed. That's real. Hana feels happy, young, excited. But she's older than I am. There's nothing wrong with me. This is the way I am supposed to feel. This is why I go to church. This is the neces-sary condition of my faith, as some sage would say. Hana's happiness is exceptional, deviant. . . . No, that's absurd. How can happiness be deviant? Don't be ridiculous . . . but what about senility? Senile dementia? The horrors of menopause? I can't rule anything out. The poor darling. Nothing in my life has prepared me for such responsi-bilities. What if I'm the only one who notices it? What if I'm delu-sional? No. Dr. Barrows, Dr. Hal, told me that I should just "keep an eye on her." Not to do anything. But as a friend. I'm on my own, really. Who can I believe if I can't believe my own senses? I don't think Hal is right. I don't think Hana is an "interesting case." I don't think Hana is a "case" at all. This man is a just a GP after all. He doesn't know the first thing about psychiatry, even if he has been psychoanalyzed and is a follower of Dr. Freud. Hana is no more "hysterical" than I am. She's creative. She's foreign. She's imaginative. She's happy. What's wrong with that? So she does walk around in the summertime naked in her garden. So she does write odd plays for children. So she does vanish for weeks on end, out in the country with "her people," or in her own house, unsociably. So I have found her in what seems to be some sort of neurotic paralysis. So she does befriend strange little boys like Lowell Briscoe and become their "fairy godmother." So she does refuse conventional attire. So she does hate the police and have an irrational loathing of the telephone. So she does live "in a world of her own," an ancient world with Greek philosophers as friends. So what am I to make of all this? Are such things symptoms? Couldn't someone make up such a list about me? No, they couldn't. I'm much too conventional for that. No one would accuse me of being original. Hana is the only person I've ever met who treats me with intellectual respect. And Hal tells me to keep an eye on her. What does he mean by *delusional*, by *delusions of grandeur*? How could anyone accuse Hana of being "grand?" Who can I believe here? According to Hana, she's in the pink of health. If I'd mention the words *mental* health to her, I fear she'd accuse me of trespassing and throw me out of her house. She does admit to dark depressions. But don't we all? I'm puzzled. I'm upset. I feel uneasy keeping an eye on her. I don't think she's any danger to herself. But she does talk more and more about "the door" being always open, something to do with Stoic philosophy's view of suicide. But Hana cannot possibly be suicidal, can she?

I feel that I'm being a snoop.

— —

Written in October 1948.

Medicine and Healing

[JOURNAL OF HANA NICHOLAS]
1 January 1949—Gloriamaris

Thea's New Year's Eve party last night. It's the last one I will ever attend, ever. I despise the chitchat and the forced gaiety.

I encountered Dr. Harold Barrows again. He seems to be seeking me out. Stares at me penetratingly when we talk. There's no sense of flirtation, rather of examination. It feels like he's questioning me, interrogating me, in a very "sweet" way to be sure, but probing me and poking around in my life. He's becoming an unwanted presence. He looks like a clinician, like a pediatrician. Bald, pudgy, dark-rimmed glasses, starched white shirts, Oxford bow ties, benign smiles as if he were hiding a hypodermic needle behind his back. Soft, warm handed, flaccid. I see him coming across a room and I feel like I used to feel as a little girl when I saw a mouse—fascinated, sympathetic, horrified. "Hal," as he told me I should call him, cornered me at Thea's and questioned me about my "medical beliefs." Why he should think I have ideas about healing that are "unconventional," I can't imagine, unless Nola has complained to him, which of course she must have. "Hal" keeps on asking me to visit him "professionally," and I say I have no need to as I am not ill. He just smiles. Anyway, I told him a bit about Pueblo and Navajo healing practices, including herbal remedies (I only know a bit), and speculated guardedly about the mind's role in healing, and talked quite a while about homeopathy and more about herbs that I've been growing and using for years on myself and on neighbors when asked. When I talked about the powers of the mind, he asked if I was a Christian Scientist and if I believe in "mind over matter" and other such maxims. I assured him I know nothing of Mrs. Eddy beyond her reputation, but that I had read a great deal about yogic practices and even engaged in a hatha yoga stretching practice every morning. He seemed riveted. Then he asked me the strangest series of questions—do I have "visions" while I meditate (Nola must have told him I meditated, though she doesn't know what it means), do I bathe regularly, do I see "apparitions" in my garden (I told him my garden is a "farm" and too big for apparitions), do I "commune with spirits" in my "kava"—this man has lived here for such a short time, is such a New York alien, that he doesn't know what a kiva is—and finally he asked me, somewhat bemusedly, if I really did walk around my "house and garden in the nude." At that final question I feigned a sort of humorful indignance to disguise my wariness. I told him that was no business of his, though it might, I said laughingly, do his "pasty city skin" some good to get a little sun. I excused myself and found Thea in the kitchen and spent the rest of the evening helping her. Thea is so sensible and down to earth, and so broad-minded. I asked her what she thought of "Hal" Barrow and she said he was "professionally nosy," and that it was part of his job "to disrobe people." I asked her what she meant and she said to the effect that "he's been questioning me about my life, about Nola, about you, about everyone's land, and the price of land, and about New Mexico in general every time I visit his office." "Are you his patient?" I asked her. She said yes, "he helps me with my feet, my high blood pressure, and gives me injections of what he says are Vitamin B_{12} and calcium. I feel super, just super afterwards."

Why is this man lurking around? Is he a tourist and are we the "natives" he's come to gawk at? Why is he asking so much about me? Oh, I remember one other thing. He thought it was "particularly fascinating" when I told him that I thought certain kinds of things contained healing powers—crystals and other rocks, places in the landscape—and that we could all draw down into ourselves and pass on to others (by the laying on of hands) the healing powers of the universe. "Do you really believe that?" he asked with some astonishment. When I asked him if he thought it was a "loony idea" he said: "Lunacy, Miss Nicholas, has no meaning anymore. But I don't think such practices contribute to science or to the stability of society." Then he immediately began asking questions about how I thought such healing powers were transmitted, and I replied, "by asking for them." He seemed disgruntled and almost angry when I added that science doesn't know everything and dismisses too much to be trusted blindly.

He must think I'm some sort of destabilizing influence. He must, indeed.

PART THREE

Mask of Horror

The Riot of 1992
"I Don't Know What I Know"

"I'm just not sure. I don't know. I keep telling you that, damn it. I'm not sure," Lowell said, almost growling in frustration.

"But surely you saw their faces. You said you did. You said, here in the hospital interview, that, and I quote, 'I'll never forget what they looked like,'" the D.A. countered.

"I was delirious. I was half in a coma; I couldn't remember my own name. It's like they wore latex hoods; I remember their heads but not their faces."

"They were wearing hoods?"

"No, it's a metaphor. They weren't wearing hoods. I mean that's what my memory's like. I can see the form of their faces, but not the faces themselves."

"So you do remember their faces."

"No, I don't. I just told you. It's all murky. No detail. I couldn't tell one if I saw one."

"One what?"

"One of the attackers."

"Of course. Would you like to see someone, Dr. Briscoe?"

"What do you mean?"

"Someone to help you remember. Someone who could help you put the pieces back together."

"You mean a shrink, don't you? You think I know something I can't remember. I think you're right. I don't know what I know. Yeah, I'm already talking to someone."

"Oh, really. Good. What's his name?"

"I think I'll keep that to myself."

"Dr. Briscoe, you've got to cooperate with us. As I've told you over and over, you're our only hope of getting these guys, these ring-leaders. If we can't put them away, all hell could break loose in this town again."

"You mean a rich white backlash at the polls? I know. I know. This is serious. And I *am* cooperating. But I don't want to let you into my head, for God's sake. I don't want the state in my head. She's *my* psychiatrist, not yours. And she's helping. When I find stuff out, you'll be the first to know."

"She?"

"Yeah. And you're not going to get her name, either."

During the year and a half before the trial of Franklin Carter, Frank Thomas, and Marvin Franklyn, the men charged with beating Lowell on the first day of the Rodney King riot, Lowell emerged, as he liked to say, from "a cloud of unknowing," pulling himself free of repressed pathologies like a cicada from its own skin. The beating at Florence and Normandy had been a final trauma that rubbed at the calluses of his unconscious to produce a huge, deep blister that had to be drained. Lowell had suffered a severe concussion. His skull was cracked in two places. He had broken ribs and a broken right cheek bone. His jaw had been dislocated and had a painful hairline fracture. He'd lost eleven teeth and had suffered temporary partial paralysis on the right side of his body. He didn't consider himself brain damaged, though some of his physicians believed he might be "episodically mildly impaired."

"I have all my wits about me," he told Dr. Melinda Tuttle in her rough brick hacienda-style office in a complex on Rodeo Drive. "It's just that from time to time the slides slip, old slides are projected onto the present, or I see a couple of them at once in a maddening confusion. It's like having waking nightmares, or having the brain's filing system spew out images that have nothing to do with what you're thinking about."

"Are you sure they have nothing to do with the present?" Dr. Tuttle asked casually.

"That's a good question."

Lowell had spent several months interviewing psychiatrists. The doctors at the hospital had recommended several, but Lowell knew he needed a special person, someone of subtlety and intelligence and a wide open mind, someone he could trust not to judge him or make stupid stereotypical assumptions about his life. He found Melinda Tuttle, M.D. by accident of synchronicity. As a public victim whose beating, videotaped from a passing helicopter, was played repeatedly on national television for months, Lowell received a seemingly endless stream of solicitations and kindnesses, among them many visits from a faculty colleague named Anabella Orelli, a person for whom Lowell had what he called "clean, real, happy feelings." Ana Orelli brought Lowell a book in the hospital entitled *Dark Memory: The Unconscious Paradigms of Personal Culture*, by Melinda Tuttle. Lowell read the introduction and the author's biography and, hearing that Tuttle was practicing in Beverly Hills, called for an appointment when he was able to walk. What intrigued Lowell the most about Tuttle's thesis were her assertions about the "mysteries of personal culture." "Like shared culture," she wrote, "personal culture, its history of change and its compounding experiences, can become almost autonomic and beyond our control. Most of us, for instance, do not know what we know, in any complete sense. Our minds are a dark sea of experience, a Marianas trench above which we float for much of our lives until trauma pushes us under. And even then, we never come close to sounding the depths to the bottom."

"When I read your book," Lowell told her, "I thought to myself that I've never been able to say what I know about almost anything. And I consider myself someone who knows too much, way too much, about himself. So much, it's embarrassing, melodramatic. . . . so much so that even I have a hard time believing it. Can I know myself and not be sure of what I know, all at the same time? My mind's not a fiction factory, but I'm not clear at all about what's real and what's not, what I've made up or embellished and what actually is and was."

"If it's in your mind, Dr. Briscoe, it's real," Dr. Tuttle replied.

Thanksgiving, 1948

The gathering was at Thea Pound's dark old Edwardian house near downtown that year. It was rather like a candy feast at the Mad Hatter's. The table was piled with puddings and pies, relishes and chocolates, nuts and sweet wines, along with a twenty-pound turkey and a crispy ham smothered in pineapple and brown sugar. The guests sat at an enormous round oak table in Thea's dining room. It was Juliet's and Lowell's second Thanksgiving with Hana and her friends. Thea put out her party best. Linen napkins, folded to resemble camellias, sprouted from silver goblets. Each guest had a delicate pewter basket full of mints. The chairs were oak and squeaked throughout the meal. Lowell was dressed in the brown wool suit his mother had bought him for Joel's funeral. He loved the thing, felt handsome in it, and refused to give it up even though he'd outgrown it several times. Juliet understood its sentimental value and had not begrudged the alterations. Juliet herself was done up in her Hollywood best: a broad-brimmed cavalier hat and a swank gray suit with immense shoulder pads that were slightly out of vogue. George and Bette Devon looked tweedy and smelled jointly of bay rum. George was in a suit of brown herringbone, wearing his gold watch chain, a bow tie, a dark blue Oxford cloth button-down shirt, and hiking boots. His big moustache, wildly tufted eyebrows, and sprigs of hair made it seem as if he were sitting in a high wind. Betty was in herringbone too, wearing sensible shoes, and looking vaguely like an Eleanor Roosevelt impersonator.

And then there was Thea. She had swaddled herself in bright green satins, topped with a lavender turban. She was decked with string upon string of shell beads and turquoise. If she'd been taller one could have called her stately as well as gaudy. But she really seemed like a squat shrub covered with unlit Christmas lights. Thea's impishness and gusto, though, overcame her dumpiness. She carved the turkey like a drum major, wearing elbow-length white leather gloves, and waving the knife and fork to inaudible carols. Nola, for some reason, had festooned the left breast of her frock with so many lodge pins and fobs that she looked like the Queen Mother inspecting the officers of the

Empire's private social club. Her burgundy pill-box hat, though, brought dignity to the proceedings, and gave her the aspect of a four-teenth-century Florentine merchant. Hana was wearing an orange silk Chinese coolie suit, with little black shoes and no socks. Around her neck was a heavy silver chain and a beautifully worn old turquoise and silver Navajo cross. She wore no makeup, of course, and her smiling, beautifully lined face and Joan of Arc haircut made her the handsomest person in the room in Lowell's eyes.

To an outsider, the party might have seemed like a gathering of the Flat Earth Society. But when Hana gave the blessing, she asked the Lord "to preserve this company of players from the illusions of pros-perity, make thy abundance known to the suffering children of the world, and warm every heart with the merciful power of thy self-knowledge." The assembled amen-ed and were lifting their forks to their faces when Nola, quite out of character, shot to her feet and blurted something about protecting us from "false metaphors" and "the contamination of unconsecrated thoughts." She seemed aston-ished by what she had done and Lowell even detected a blush. But when she sat down, the assembled amen-ed again, and she fell to feast-ing with the rest. It seemed for a moment as if Nola were contesting with Hana for control of the "congregation," as ludicrous as that might seem. And during the bubbling of conversation and general mirth that evening Lowell overheard some telling banter. Nola was saying to Hana "orthodoxy is humility, it is submitting yourself to the wisdom of your betters, it maintains the hierarchy, which in itself is an instru-ment of humility."

"You're sounding particularly Greek tonight, my dear," Hana replied. "The gods don't punish hubris anymore, only hypocrisy. Zeus has joined an opera company somewhere, and Athena and Aphrodite are both selling cosmetics in Beverly Hills."

"I hate it when you're clever," Nola smiled back. "You know exactly what I mean. Pride is the first vice. It takes a proud person to like the sound of her own voice and words more than the words of the . . ."

"Don't say the Bible, Nola dear. It's a wonderful book, but it's just a book. And I know it better than you do; you've said so yourself. Why are you so prickly tonight?"

"I know you know it better than I do, oh don't I know it. I'm not prickly," Nola said indignantly. "If you know it so well, then why don't you stick to it?"

"I'm not going to tell you it's a tar baby, Nola. But *it's* the thing that sticks to everybody; that's a tacky pun I know."

"Will you stop it!" Nola hissed. "Is there nothing you won't twist and tangle? You used to stick to the Book; you used to read psalms for the Thanksgiving prayer. Do you remember when you led us in singing that wonderful 'Come Ye Thankful People Come'? It was so sweet, so real, so in the spirit."

"Well, my spirit's been off with Huck Finn for a while, you know that . . . out adventuring. What's the difference? You know, you're beginning to sound like an officer for the Biblical thought squad. You must be having me on."

"This is no joking matter. Five hundred years ago, you'd . . ."

"I'd what?!" Hana said with a frightening scowl.

"Just look at the way you dress. It's no joking matter. It's really shameless," Nola sputtered.

"Have you been drinking too much?"

"How dare you!"

"Have you?!"

"A very little bit."

"Would you like some more sweet potato?" Hana gestured, trying to slow their growing anger.

"I really think you must get hold of yourself," Nola said in a low, emphatic voice. "You're becoming someone else, someone I'm not sure I know, or really like very much anymore. You think I'm silly. But just look at yourself. You're not the same. You've changed."

"Nola dear, if you don't like me, stop associating with me."

"You know what I mean."

"No I don't, but I'd wait till coffee and dessert before you had another drink."

"Don't lecture me about drink, Hana Nicholas! Really, this is insufferable," she fumed, lifting a wine glass to her lips.

"Nola, Nola, let's stop this," Hana sighed. "Please, let's just stop this. There's so much to be grateful for today. So many years of friendship and trust. Why do we get into these ridiculous tiffs over nothing? We're just chewing on old bones."

"It's not nothing to me, Hana. I do worry about you, out of friendship. I worry. What kind of friend would I be if I didn't tell you? It not theological, it's psychological—that's where the differences lie," Nola said with feigned sobriety. "You have changed. Can't you see?"

"I think I have. And I know you have. I'm happier than I've ever been. You don't begrudge me that, do you? *Do you?* You don't begrudge me my delight, my spiritual pleasure, do you? If you do, you're the one who's changed, and you're no friend of mine, Nola dear. But I don't think you have. I've trusted you with everything, you know that."

"Of course, but that's only money."

"It's much more than that, Nola. Your prudence protects me, I've told you that a million times."

"Let's don't be sentimental," Nola retorted with a teacherly smile. She picked up a celery stalk, waved it gently over her plate, as if she were contemplating an inspired reply, then turned to Hana and kissed her on the cheek and said with obvious pleasure, "Perhaps we both *have* changed, Hana dear. I am seeing life so much more clearly now. And you still need a change of glasses."

Hana patted Nola's hand like that of a naughty child who has not exactly apologized but who has stepped back from confrontation and relieved the tension. Nola patted Hana's shoulder in return, not to be outdone in the battle of gestures. Then both turned and looked for other conversation.

— ~

From Lowell Briscoe's "A Nest of Hells."

An Unworthy Disciple

"Hana is the key, don't you think?" said Melinda Tuttle. "She's not just a tragedy. She's a real person who has become a myth—or so it seems to me—a part of the myth of your life. You must take her seriously—I know you do, but more realistically than allegorically, if you understand. Through her, you can see how it must have been like to know Orpheus, or St. Teresa, or Buddha as living people, before they were reinvented by their followers. Lives are lived and they leave behind stories. They can't help it. The past is made up of their leavings. The stories are not the same as what actually happened. They might seem the same, but they are merely descriptions, loaded with meaning of their own. Their precise reality, their accuracy as reproductions doesn't matter. They are stories laden with meaning. The meaning is what matters. The meaning makes the myth. And with Hana you came close to seeing what actually happened, you breathed the same air as the source of a myth, really, isn't that what happened?"

"I hadn't thought about it *quite* like that before. But I think you're right. Useful information could turn up in the discrepancy between the description of Hana and my actual memory of her—presuming, of course, that I could make such a distinction," Lowell replied.

"And your assailants, too, Dr. Briscoe. The whole terrible incident has become part of your personal myth, has been folded into the overall fabric of how you describe your life to yourself."

Melinda Tuttle was forty-four, a decade younger than her new patient. An elegant dresser with expensive tastes, she was aristocratic in bearing but comfortable and unpretentious with her patients. People remarked how much like Doris Day she looked, but her sweet demeanor was edged with an air of authority. Educated at Harvard and Stanford, married for the last fifteen years to a plastic surgeon, Dr. Tuttle seemed unshakably solid, the kind of person who was self-confident enough to enter with sympathy into the difficult lives of difficult people. Whenever she spoke in therapy, she leaned forward in her chair reassuringly, increasing her vulnerability to her patients while conveying to them the healing power of her own autonomous strength.

Dr. Tuttle struggled with her tendency to fit patients into the templates of her clinical experience and education. When she looked at Lowell Briscoe, she saw a handsome, white-haired older man with terrible deep bruises and sutured cuts on his face, a man who had come within a minute of being murdered. She realized, as well, that the wounded face was a mask, an unintentional mask that partially disguised an oddly fascinating man, refined and yet feral, a patient she was keenly interested in as a subject and slightly afraid of as a person.

"I think, Dr. Briscoe, that your difficulty in identifying your assailants is mythological—not that you're being untruthful, but that it pertains to the mythological descriptions."

" . . . my repressions and sublimations. . . ." Lowell interjected.

"I don't like to use those terms, but they will do for the moment. Let me continue and say that I think your lack of memory here is tied to your confusion about other issues in your past."

Lowell Briscoe might be simply a charming, neurotic charlatan with an elaborate fantasy life, Dr. Tuttle thought to herself after one of their sessions. But he was probably for real. She imagined that the grosser details of his life—his education, his professional positions, his books and political activism and charity work—had been verified by the D.A.'s office. But the jury was still out on his description of his childhood, as far as she was concerned. "Dr. Briscoe is a man of sly cunning, considerable intelligence and breeding, a person who has obviously spent much of his life reading and manipulating language. He's both verbally and emotionally facile with a storyteller's skill at narrative," she wrote in his file. "He's both evasive and candid, often at the same time. I do not, any longer, entertain the possibility that his confusion about himself is a theatrical hoax. He does appear to be genuinely riddled with subconscious defenses and projections, and he may well not be able to identify his assailants in the long run. I don't think he is a multiple, but he is deeply alienated from traumatic events and emotions in his past. He'll have to let off a lot of psychic steam before any progress is made. Do I doubt the incest with his older half-sister? Is it a wish fulfillment? Do I doubt the marital quality of their quarrels and dependencies? I can only intuit so far that he is giving an accurate picture seen through the eyes and emotions of a boy."

Once Lowell told Dr. Tuttle that he sometimes "felt trapped in my description of myself. It's possible I was not a mad child who Hana rescued, that I was not emotionally deformed, fated to be unintelligible, a boy Cassandra speaking out about myself. But the facts are the facts. They happened. So what is self-acceptance all about? What roles do perception and perspective play in one's own beholding of one's self? I feel like my description of myself. That's what I know the facts to be."

"I think I understand," Melinda Tuttle replied. "My mother once told me that I should never smile at strange men, anywhere, even in the grocery store. What she told me is a fact. And what I did with it, how that message was interpreted by me and embellished and pruned and espaliered by me, that's my description. And that's what's hard to get a clear bearing on. And my history of interpreting her admonition, and interpreting my own interpretations *ad nauseam* is a fact as well," she said with somewhat startling candor.

When Lowell told Dr. Tuttle about the Christmas of 1964 when Juliet had made her bleary confession, Tuttle said something that showed Lowell she might be trusted. "That sounds like the holocaust," she said matter-of-factly. "You're the lone survivor, aren't you, the last left. I'd have contemplated trying to hunt them all down, too, I don't think it's an unnatural response."

— ~

From notes left by Lowell Briscoe for "A Nest Of Hells."

Juliet, Hana, and Other Friends
Summer 1947

Juliet's behavior toward Lowell didn't much change when she and Hana became close friends, but her general mood and demeanor did. She was still unbalanced and madly possessive; her exuberance, though, had returned. Lowell remembered the first time he'd heard Hana's name in the summer of 1947. He'd asked Juliet who lived in the big adobe up the road and Juliet replied, "the dearest person I have ever known, Lowell. Her name is Hana Nicholas, that's Hana as in Ana. She's saved my life." Juliet had a particular radiance about her that afternoon. Sometimes Juliet could look like a perfect ingénue, adorably pretty, like Juliet in Wonderland, girlish and romantically prim. Juliet craved her anonymity in Albuquerque. And though she liked to pretend she was famous, she kept mostly to herself, a seductive, vaguely pitiable, but uncomfortably foreign figure from Hollywood in the eyes of some of her Anglo acquaintances and the university faculty who'd heard of her film scripts, books, and exotic reputation. But as protective of her privacy as she was, she still craved intelligent conversation. When she learned that Hana owned and had read nearly all her books, and had found them "stimulating," it made Juliet feel she had a "new lease on life," as she liked to say. "It was sweet, sweet fate," she said, when she bumped into Hana and Thea at the old Alvarado Hotel on her first visit to Albuquerque in 1945. Her friendship with Hana took time to mature, but it was "instant recognition" when they met, Juliet said. Hana didn't even ask her name but "intuitively knew" who she was, Juliet told Lowell with inflated certainty.

Juliet carried on endlessly that afternoon with Lowell, saying "Hana *feels* things, sees right into the heart of everything. She *knows*. She understands. Do you have any idea what that means to me?" Juliet even confessed that in Hana she had discovered her "master, the mentor of my spiritual fruition."

When Hana made Juliet feel good about herself and her talent, she also gave her evidence of how far she had fallen, how deeply mired in sloth and self-pity and addiction she really was. Hana's moral vigor made Juliet more ashamed than ever about undermining her talents with gin and pills, though she still said things like "the fruits of Dionysus are the essential lubricant, they tone up my instrument, my imagination." As an adult Lowell often wondered why she didn't die of that hazardous mix of alcohol and sleeping pills, but he also knew that she'd tried a number of times to stop doping herself and get back to work, under the influence of Hana's example. But every time she fell off the wagon, she hit the ground harder than before and could barely get to her feet. She couldn't live up to Hana's influence. It tortured her. And she tortured Lowell. That was the beginning of those crazy oscillations, from days of exuberant optimism to weeks of starvation and alcoholic binges. The more unpredictable she was the more angry and rebellious Lowell became.

One night Juliet had a friend over to the house for dinner, a man many years her senior, a former film writer whom Juliet thought was safely old and gay. The evening turned into a catastrophe when this "sweet old guy" made a grossly lewd and unwanted pass at Juliet after supper. She was half drunk and became enraged. Lowell watched as she took a big glass ashtray and threw it at him, grazing but gashing his scalp. The man was furious. He lunged at Juliet across the dining room table, grabbed her by her hair, lost his balance, and fell on the glassware, breaking it and cutting his chest and hands. The blood mixed with his sweat and made him look like he was hemorrhaging. He chased her around the house, bleeding on the rugs and floor, roaring and yelling obscenities, crashing into furniture, and throwing whatever he could find. Juliet was screaming hysterically and running as fast as she could. It seemed almost funny to Lowell at first, but then Juliet ran past him, grabbed him by the arm, and pushed him in front of her attacker. The man fell over Lowell, crashing down on top of him, bleeding all over Lowell's face. The man disentangled himself when he saw Juliet standing by the door and gave chase again. He finally slipped on his own blood in the kitchen and fell to the floor with a stunning thud. Juliet had the look of a wild thing. She was really quite magnificent, Lowell remembered, her nostrils flaring with satisfaction and her chest heaving as she stood over the man and delivered a well-aimed kick to the ribs. Lowell jumped out from under the breakfast nook table and was going to pounce on him and finish him off, as he imagined Ming the Merciless might do, but Juliet kept him back. The man was unconscious. Lowell began to scream and cry with relief; Juliet poured herself a drink and slid down on the bloody floor and soon passed out herself. Lowell thought about calling the police, but then locked himself in his bedroom. He listened at the door for what seemed like hours for the man to wake up, terrified he'd come to get him. At some point, though, Lowell fell asleep at his post. The man was gone the next morning. The front door was wide open, but nothing had been taken. Juliet didn't get out of bed until late afternoon. By then Lowell had cleaned up much of the mess and had put some soup on the stove. From that night on, Lowell made a fetish of checking and rechecking the locks on all the doors and making sure the windows were secured.

From Lowell Briscoe's "A Nest of Hells."

The Infamous Rehearsal

A week after Thanksgiving, another oddly important event occurred. Hana and Lowell were in the Kiva, rehearsing the Christmas play as they did every day after school and on the weekends before the great day. The whole idea of performing before an audience appalled Lowell, and Hana worked diligently to help him free himself from his fear. They spent rehearsal time building sets and costumes, choreographing the action, going over the lines again and again, methodically breaking down Lowell's barriers of self-doubt and timidity.

Hana wrote, directed, and performed her Christmas play as a gift to her friends. She saw it as a contemporary offering in preparation for the more traditional New Mexican celebration of Los Pastores. And she guarded its subject and philosophic content with good-natured but absolute secrecy. Rehearsals were always closed. And Lowell grew to feel utterly safe in the Kiva, with its big front doors bolted against intrusion. The day they were interrupted says much about the mood that Christmas.

They were working intently on the final scene in which the first faint strains of the "Ode to Joy" filtered again into the play. The music came from the Victrola behind the sky-blue star-covered backdrop when Lowell was torn from his concentration by a noise at the door, not a knock, but a "mushy thumping," Lowell recalled later. It startled him terribly and he scurried to the far end of the banco near the altar and slouched there sullen and dangerous. Hana turned off the Victrola, removed the costumes and other paraphernalia that would betray the content of the play, and strode to forcefully open the door.

It was Juliet, Nola, and Thea, all of them breathing heavily and in a state of delighted agitation, bearing good news. With them inside the Kiva, its sacred spaces were transformed for Lowell into merely another room, a dank somewhat embarrassing place where silliness and childish rituals were indulged in.

Nola spoke. "Hana, we're sorry to barge in like this. I know how you hate it. But we just had to tell you. We know you wouldn't mind. George's book is going to be published at last, and Betty's decided to make a celebration supper tonight. We thought you'd like to know right away, so you can adjust your plans."

The women had been at the Devons' all afternoon, listening to George read from his manuscript about bird imagery in Pueblo religion. Hana had long been fascinated by George's research and felt well-disposed toward him, both as a person and as a scholar. Their friendship was warm, lighthearted, and very safe. But no bookish good fortune could justify this interruption.

Juliet noticed Lowell hunched over in the corner and called out to him just as Hana said in a sharp tone, "For heaven's sake, darlings, is that what you disrupted us for? You almost spoiled the Christmas surprise. Couldn't you have left a note at the gate? I would have seen it in plenty of time. Well, it matters not. Tell Betty I'd be delight to come to dinner. The usual time? Good."

Juliet was about to make a worried move in Lowell's direction, when Hana wrapped her arm around Juliet's shoulder and backed all three of them out the door, saying, "You know the rule at Christmas. No peeking, dears." Hana walked with them through the garden to the back gate. When she returned, she was annoyed and Lowell was in a fury, pacing up and down, babbling in expletives about their stupidity for interrupting and how awful their intrusion had made him feel. Hana calmed him down, told him she understood, but said strongly that he "must forgive them and see through them," and never speak such words, or use such a tone of voice, in the Kiva again.

"You were rude to them, Lowell. You lost control. You were no longer a player. They took you out of yourself. You were the victim of a chance event, vulnerable to whatever came along. That's no way to live. Rudeness is a sign of weakness. I had to apologize to them for your behavior. And I do *not* like to make excuses for anyone," she told him with painful emphasis.

The repercussions of that interruption were severe. The mood at the party was almost ugly, and the questions were all but insulting. Hana was interrogated, or so she hinted the following day when Lowell told her of Juliet's reaction. Hana told Lowell that Nola, Thea, and Juliet had used George's publishing success as a "convenient ruse" to pry into their rehearsals, "just like naughty little girls." When Juliet interrogated Lowell, she whined angrily at one point, "What is going on in there!? Why were you so sullen? What are you hiding, you little satyr?"

"It's supposed to be a secret," Lowell said. "The play's a secret. You know that. And stop spitting in my ear."

They screamed at each other for a while, but it was a minor skirmish and eventually the cold war froze over, as it always did, into another stalemate.

"I just think you're working too hard at this. It's getting to you. You're not strong enough." Juliet was using her motherly tone. "If you get too tired, you'll have to give it up and rest, you'll just have to. I can't have you being exhausted."

Nola came over to Lowell's and Juliet's house the following day and told Juliet that she thought Hana was "overworking the little fellow," and that it was, after all, "only a neighborhood Christmas pageant" and that there was "no need to get so intense about it."

"Hana is becoming so extreme, don't you think, Juliet? And what is wrong with Lowell, cowering like that in the corner. You'd think they had something to hide."

"Well, they do," Juliet answered reasonably. "They're keeping the play a secret, a Christmas secret. There's nothing extreme in that. It's fun. It's a surprise. I've hidden your present in the closet. Haven't you hidden mine?"

"Juliet, don't be such a little girl. It doesn't become you. And why would you think I'd even want to know what my present is? How do you know I've bought you one?"

"You haven't?"

"Of course I have. But I haven't hidden it. And why would Hana be silly enough to think that we would be interested in the play at all? You'd think they were doing some kind of magic rites in there, or God knows what."

"Nola, you're such a kidder," Juliet chuckled.

— ~

From Lowell Briscoe's "A Nest of Hells."

The Terrible Possibilities

"These dreams! They always leave me limp and confused," Lowell told Dr. Tuttle. "I woke up this morning with the image of Hana's face in the mental hospital, frozen in a hideous grimace, her 'mask of horror' I called it."

"What do you mean 'mask of horror'?"

"When I went to see her there when I was a kid, I found her sitting motionless with a horrible, howling look on her face. It was a Medusa face. It could turn you to stone."

"Was she being mistreated, do you think?"

"No, she just looked like she was wearing a mask, a mask, maybe, of her true feelings. I don't know. I do know she was a totally nonviolent person. Totally.

"Maybe that look was her way of getting revenge," Dr. Tuttle surmised.

"Let's stop talking about it."

"Is something blocking you?" asked the doctor.

"Jesus," Lowell said with vast irritation. "This is my life. I can talk as little or as much about it as I like."

"Of course. I'm sorry."

"You want to know something else?" Lowell asked with pointed nonchalance. "I think I might have killed those people."

"Ummmmm."

"That's what really worries me."

"Why do you think that?"

"That's what I'm afraid of."

"Why do you think that?"

"It seems impossible that I could have killed them all. Betty, George, Thea, Nola, and Juliet."

"All of them? It certainly does."

"It seems impossible, impossible that I could have done it, impossible that I could have hated them enough to do it, impossible that I couldn't remember it if I did, impossible, impossible . . . but I'm going nuts with the fear that I might have. They all died violently . . .

unnatural deaths. Not one of them went out peacefully. I think that kid hated them, just hated them."

"What kid?"

"Me, back then."

"You're not two people, you know."

"I'm not him," Lowell said with hushed emphasis. "I'm not him anymore. Hana freed me from him. She was *my* mentor, not his. Alcibiades had Socrates. I had Hana. Students never live up to their teachers. Alcibiades betrayed Athens so many times, the Athenian populace came to love him for his daring and bravado. Socrates was the most pious and steadfast patriot Athens ever had, and they killed him for it. Hana would have done anything to avoid hurting another creature, human, beast, or bug. She was even jokingly kind to stones, talking to them when she moved them around her garden so they wouldn't feel displaced or lonely. There wasn't a drop of violence in her. Like Socrates, she wouldn't save herself."

"But she gave them something to think about, as he did."

"What?"

"The mask."

"Maybe so. But . . . I don't know, it's not her style."

Dr. Tuttle tilted her head. "There could have been a message, a whole lecture, a complete philosophy in that grimace."

"Hana wasn't violent," Lowell mused, "but here I am, knowing full well I could have broken the bones in Karen's face with a single blow after she hit me. And knowing, thank God, that I didn't. But I wonder if *he* could have."

"He?"

"The kid."

"You mean you."

"Me, the kid, or some part of me. I didn't do it, but the impulse was there, an impulse Hana never even remotely experienced in herself, I'm sure. The question that keeps coming back and back is, Was I an Alcibiades to Hana's nonviolence? Could I have repressed it all? Did I methodically pick them off? Did the student turn into the polar opposite of the teacher? It seems to me to be a common pattern."

"Don't you think you're idealizing her? She was human. We're all deeply flawed. Aren't we?"

"Some of us more than others," Lowell said in a low voice.

"Are you telling me I ought to watch out for you?" Dr. Tuttle asked.

"No, I'm not trying to do that. I'm sorry. I'm really sorry. You must think I'm nuts. I'll shut up. I shouldn't be yakking like this. You'll think I'm crazy for sure."

"Is that what you think?"

"Well, not really," Lowell said, squinting and turning his head. "But the worry's in my brain. It's a philosophical worry, and a dread of being bad. I don't want to be a bad man. Hana was the source of the great asymmetry of my childhood, of my whole life really. She was more than just an opposite. She was a transcendence."

"What do you mean exactly?"

"I mean, the world seesaws between dualities, polarities, contradictions. Opposites run the stuff of life. But I believe that underneath there is an asymmetry in favor of . . . the good, for lack of a better word. Hana was that asymmetry for me. But I'm superstitious, too. Terribly superstitious. What if she was one half of a duality, and I was the other half, the evil half? But she wouldn't have picked me for her Judas, surely."

"Betrayal hurts less when it matters less," Dr. Tuttle said pointedly.

"But I mattered to her. I know I did. But I worry that I'll die like she did, that the end of my life will be a mirror image of my childhood, that I'll end up in a rest home that treats everyone like children, that it's the policy of the place to make life so miserable and contradictory that old people want to die just to get free. The personnel there are instructed to love the old folks, indulge them, manipulate and exploit them, chain them down, reject them, lie to them, give them treats and kindness, and make them totally dependent. Intermittent reinforcement it's called. These rites of dying are so claustrophobic that the old people are ready to pounce on any opportunity to run away from home. Their freedom's waiting for them; it's an ashcan where they'll be dumped like the old fetuses they are."

"Now that's a great punishment for a bad little boy," Dr. Tuttle said with clinical irony.

"You sound like a shrink," Lowell said raising his voice.

"I am."

"Is that all you're going to say?"

"No. Lowell, all children, young and old, need love. That 'kid' who you were . . ."

"Needs me, right?"

"Exactly. He doesn't need to be blamed or banished from your life. He needs you to love him. Just that and all that it means."

"But I'm not Hana. I'm not big hearted. I'm afraid of him. I'm afraid of myself. I'm terrified, just terrified all the time. Just paralyzed with fear, frozen, motionless."

Summer 1992.

A Cartoon of the Devil

Nola Jones Dasheller. What a role she assumed in Lowell's unconscious. His memory saw her as living in a castle surrounded by a moat of pink petals and a forest of rose trees. Her hybrids had won first prize at the New Mexico State Fair for years. She was always trying to develop a thornless St. Francis, but it escaped her.

Lowell's imagination saw Nola as a retired elementary school teacher who had turned to real estate and investments to keep herself busy. A pragmatic, helpful soul, she was permanently right about absolutely everything. Nola, for him, had the qualities of a maternal nun, a salesman of moral good works who owed her spiritual allegiance to a strict, charismatic fundamentalist vision. Her great fear, as Lowell heard Hana once express it, was "spiritual pollution" and negativism. Hana apparently never feared such things, or so Lowell thought. She just dismissed them as unworthy. And this, he surmised, Nola could not understand and perhaps secretly admired and therefore resented.

The God of this Nola of Lowell's was a fanatic about conformity. A compulsive hand washer Himself, the divinity demanded of His followers a worshipful hygiene. On the surface, Nola seemed a kindly and dapper grandmother-widow who knitted sweaters, baked pies, and knew what was the best for children, animated by what she called "pizzazz." Nothing could keep her down for long; she'd smile it right out of existence.

Lowell saw clearly that Nola would not tolerate contradiction. Her world was without mystery. Once she saw the truth, she would have it, or know the reason why. Everyone's problem with Nola was that she saw the truth for others as well as for herself. It was a standing joke among her friends: if you had a problem, you kept it to yourself when Nola was around. She would solve it on the spot and rain cheery scorn upon you if you didn't follow her solution to the letter, right or wrong.

There was no question that Nola meant well. If nothing else, her starched aprons with their Raggedy Annes and Andys would tell you that she was prim and kindly. But Nola was subject, like everyone, to doubts and momentary terrors, which were made all the more dangerous by that "inward smile" she bragged about and by her growing anxiety that she would somehow become tainted by nonconformity and unredeemable just at the moment of her death. She lived in a constant state of vigilance.

Lowell found it almost impossible to be fair about Nola. "I remember her, and my feelings about her, with the clarity of a hunter," he told Dr. Tuttle. "As a child, I hated her like a mongoose hates a cobra. She was the enemy. I could smell evil every time she'd enter the room. My loathing for her was instinctual. I couldn't have reversed it if I'd wanted to."

But Lowell learned he was wrong about Nola in a number of ways. She was not a retired schoolteacher. She was a retired economics professor, well published, academically cosmopolitan, though archly conservative. She was not a fanatic, though she did have a strong opinion of her own intelligence that was undercut and made ever more intractable by her intimations of inferiority when in the presence of Hana's overflowing mental élan. Nola, Lowell came to understand, must have been on an odyssey herself, which was not of the same intensity or vivacity as Hana's, but nonetheless risky and requiring an adventuresome spirit and bold curiosity. Otherwise why would she have formed such a close attachment to someone so utterly unlike her? Lowell did not understand, however, why Nola began to rigidify, why her thoughts froze up and fixated on the religious myths of her childhood, or why Hana remained loyal to her even when Nola clearly was no longer useful to her own explorations, when she had, in fact, become something of a yoke and an ordeal.

"What was Nola's relationship with Hana? What was at the heart of it, do you think?" asked Dr. Tuttle. "Were they merely friends, or was there something romantic, or secret, or unrequited going on? Did Nola have some kind of hold over Hana, or was Nola threatened by her? Were you, Lowell, some sort of pawn in their relationship?" she asked pointedly.

"I've been asking myself similar questions for years. I have no clue, except my intuitions and suspicions," Lowell replied.

"And they are?"

"I'll bring you a draft copy of a novel I'm working on about these people. That will give you some clue to my thinking, though I have to admit that writing the novel has left me more confused and riled up than ever."

From Lowell Briscoe's "A Nest of Hells."

Supper at the Alvarado, Fall 1948

Thea Pound had nothing of Nola's suspicious nature. Thea was too fey for subterfuge and insinuation. She was Juliet's and Hana's mutual friend. They had met at Thea's house and had discovered an instant rapport. Thea was a friend of Lowell's as well, if friendship is the word for the bond between an eleven-year-old and someone past sixty. Maybe she was more an admirer of Lowell's. Thea liked children; she made a fetish of them. Her house was everyone's favorite stop on Halloween. Her candy basket was a cornucopia. She also managed the annual Easter egg hunt for her friends and their grandchildren, serving as the Master Bunny, dispensing little hints like Toscanini urging on his orchestra. She'd send Lowell birthday presents, Christmas presents, Valentine candy, St. Patrick's Day cards—she never missed a holiday, and she remembered all the children of her acquaintance. On Thanksgiving and other feast days, she rounded up her friends to deliver a caravan of groceries and toys to various orphanages and charities around town. She and Hana were especially close, and saw their friendship as being rooted in a shared history of "struggling to do some good," as Thea put it.

Lowell loved to remember Thea. She had a round little face covered with down, dry lips, slick gray hair, and fingers that looked painfully like turnips. She tended to wear black dresses, and always wore a choker of real pearls, even while gardening. Lowell used to imagine her having very long toes, as her shoes, either saddle oxfords or patent leather pumps, were huge.

"Thea was gorgeous," Lowell wrote in his journal. "The more I think about her the more I miss her. She seemed to understand me, even though I can't remember a real conversation between us until after Hana's tragedy. Perhaps it was that she never treated me like a child, but always made me feel proud and grateful to be one. Childhood in her eyes must have been a state of grace. And she saw herself as one of the helpers of the guardian angel that dispenses sugar plums and keeps tabs on the justices of delights."

Those towering turbans she wore, those fabulously ratty fur coats! Lowell thought no one ever had a sweeter smile. And on the scale of musical laughter, one would have to put Thea right up there with certain meadowlarks. Her laugh erupted out of her, filled the room, then stopped so abruptly that it seemed to leave the air full of expectant silence.

Thea had mothered five sons, buried three husbands, and lived alone in a handsome, but vaguely ominous, two-story Edwardian manor near downtown about five miles away from Los Griegos and Hana, Nola, Juliet, and the Devons. Thea's house was completely hidden from the road by a constricting ring of Arizona Cyprus. Inside, her house always smelled of fresh baked cookies and dog food. Thea's bearing was both formal and madcap. She was one of those older women who always had her purse with her. Lowell thought she might have slept with it, and brushed her teeth with it hanging from her arm.

When Juliet, Thea, and Lowell went out to supper at the Alvarado Hotel, which could be as often as three times a week, Thea would give Lowell a crisp one-dollar bill, pulled from under a dark green glove, folded into a tight little square, and placed in his palm like a wafer on the end of a supplicant's tongue. Their suppers in the hotel's grand dining room were always formal, and Lowell never relished them, though the building itself had a strong effect on him. It was next to the railroad station and designed to look something like a vast and rambling California mission. It was everywhere appointed with Indian ornaments and motifs and dark Spanish colonial furniture and tile. It had a sumptuous and rustic Southwestern savoir-faire that might remind one of a desert ocean liner, manned by crisp-suited porters and kindly waitresses in white aprons, black dresses, and starched little napkin-like hats. And even though Lowell had nothing to compare it to, he knew the Alvarado was a regal place and that there was some honor in being its habitué.

Still, the dinners were hard on him. "I'd have to put on my best face and spend the evening looking in mirrors, making sure it was still in place," he wrote. "It was exhausting having to be pleasant to Thea and still have to carry on the usual flirtations with Juliet. I should explain the word *flirtation*. I think I never felt I belonged to Juliet, or that I had a solid place in her life. I was struck by the profound meaning of the title of *orphan*. And Juliet's moods were so transitory that I never really knew where I stood. It is only in retrospect that I know she'd made a commitment to me. So I was constantly checking my status, and seeing what kind of mood she was in, and that amounted to an insecure and flirtatious kind of communication of smiles and side glances. It sounds grotesque, but Juliet seemed to thrive on the attention and on my unease."

What did the worldly Juliet Briscoe have in common with the motherly and pixilated Thea Pound? Hana was their common interest, but they also liked the oddity of each other in their lives. They were such misfits that they constantly amazed each other and were delighted by the differences in their backgrounds and outlooks.

Thea had known Hana since 1925 when they'd both moved to Albuquerque. They had met the Devons and the Dashellers at the same time. And although Juliet hadn't met Hana until more than twenty years later, she and Thea were swimming in the same sea of ignorance about their mutual friend. The conversation one evening over dinner dealt almost exclusively with Hana's elusive personality and past.

"Hana is a Godsend, Thea, really one of the most important people I have ever met, important to my soul. But I don't know a thing about her, really," said Juliet with a stare.

"Well, we've been close for over twenty years, and I don't know all that much myself, you know," Thea smiled, sipping pink champagne. "Hana has always cherished her solitude. Being an enigma does tend to keep one separate. All I know, and I'm not even sure about this, you see, is that Hana came to New Mexico and Albuquerque from abroad after what you might say was a disastrous relationship. She bought her acreage near Guadalupe Trail and like a Robinson Crusoe started to build an independent, solid, secret life behind those great wooden fences and adobe walls, the life of a castaway that was punctuated by charity of every sort. That's how I met her, you see, and Nola and Betty Devon too. Hana hates gossip, always has. Gossip about others and gossip about herself. You couldn't say she was 'one of the girls,' see, if you know what I mean. She's always been odd, but not aloof, off to herself, but not standoffish."

"Yes, yes, I know what you mean," said Juliet emphatically. "That's the way she strikes me too—utterly present, but somehow apart."

"Exactly. If it weren't for her positiveness, her positive thinking, her optimism, her Christian glow, as someone said, if it weren't for all that, you see, you might think there was something wrong with her. She's so solitary, so imaginative, so inward, if you see what I mean, so otherworldly."

"I do know. She's an artist. Needs lots of license."

"Yes. If there were visions to be seen anymore, she'd see them."

"You know, I think she would. . . . So you know nothing about where she was born, about the defunct romance, about her accent?"

"Nothing really."

"What about all the animals. How many are there? Why does she have so many of them?" Juliet asked.

"Hana has always called them her children. Maybe they are substitute children. I don't know. She has always been fiercely involved in what they call anti-vivisection, do you see. It's not a cause of mine or Nola's. But Hana and George are adamant about it. We'd work with orphans and Indian education—Hana would join us, of course—and they'd work to stop companies and the government from using living animals, even guinea pigs, as guinea pigs."

"How many animals does she have?"

Thea, delicately dissecting a shrimp, answered. "Hundreds, I'd say, if you count the birds and the fish, those huge and spotted carp of hers. All the dogs and cats are neutered, of course. The turtles, the rabbits, the goats, the horses, the chickens. I think she likes animals better than people, or as much as she likes children. The animals are everywhere, but you get the feeling they are discrete, that they move in the shadows so as not to draw too much attention to themselves or to Hana. But out there in the country, what does it matter, you see? Besides, many of them are wounded. I saw a limping fox there once, a limping roadrunner or two, several three-legged cats over the years, I think. There were even snakes, nothing poisonous, mind you, that's what she says, but fearful, fearful things.

"Are they wounded too?" Juliet asked with a smile.

"Who can tell?"

"I wonder where she's from," Juliet mused again.

"I always thought she came from a winter country, had black forests in her blood, and had a private tutor. Maybe she's royalty, the last child of the queen of somewhere. It's all those books of hers, too, do you see, those vast walls of books. And she insists she's self-taught. I'm sure she's read every one of them, every one. And those longshoreman's hands of hers: she can still play Mozart like a prodigy."

— ~

Adapted from Lowell Briscoe's "A Nest of Hells."

The Bird Walk

George Devon once used the word *prodigy* about Hana. At Juliet's pleading, he had taken Lowell on a therapeutic bird walk down by the Rio Grande, through the bosque with its miles of giant cottonwoods. Lowell had gotten into a fight at school and had lost all control. A boy humiliated him, calling him names because he'd dropped the ball in a baseball game at recess and Lowell went berserk. Teachers had to pull Lowell off him. Lowell had broken his antagonist's nose. There was a loud and nasty encounter between Juliet and the boy's parents. They threatened to sue her if she didn't keep Lowell "on a leash." Lowell reflected years later, "I must have been a horror. Raging one moment, blubbering the next. Anyway, Juliet sicced me on poor George. It was almost impossible not to like him."

George Devon was a well-to-do engineer. He'd spent most of his salad days doing important things with uncanny inventions. When Lowell knew him, he was in his mid-fifties, a semi-retired, cheerfully reticent malcontent who enjoyed good company but more often than not preferred his own to others. He'd traveled all over the world, working on projects that ranged from road building in South America to the construction of gas pipe lines in Siberia. He was a worshiper of the twentieth century. He adored the growth of knowledge and the speed and power it produced. George's fascination with the present and how it turned into the future had caused him to decide early on in favor of longevity. He neither smoked nor drank, nor did he eat meats or animal fats of any kind. He told Lowell that he "specialized in grains, like the birds."

Lowell felt a natural affinity to George Devon. He was a success-ful odd man out. They remained acquainted all through Lowell's high school years, even after Hana's tragedy. George was thin and bald and sported a heavy white moustache. He often wore a blue bow tie with red polka dots. Wherever he went, he carried a knapsack full of worn bird books that were bound together with thick rubber bands and a beautifully weathered, canvas-covered notebook in which he would record new birds, new cars, new thoughts, and even new inventions or improvements of some public utility that he'd seen on his daily walks. George was the closest thing Lowell had to a father when he was a teenager. Lowell admired George's tidiness, the precision of his life, and his forthright autonomy. George was who he was. He had no secret agendas, no hidden shames, no neuroses Lowell could detect. He was happy, solidly happy with who he was. And it was a great comfort to be around him for that reason. Lowell didn't have to perform for him. He really didn't even have to talk if he didn't have something to say.

George and Lowell rarely spoke of Hana, but when they did George's tone was reverential.

"She has a prodigious mind, Lowell. You would do well to listen to everything she tells you. She must have been a child prodigy, rather like yourself. She's interested in everything. The conversations we've had! She knows more about the real life of birds than I do—well, as least as much. She's interested in ancient cities, in water works, in folk technologies, in how things work. She never fails to amaze me. And she's the warmest of souls."

George was not a confidential sort of person. But Lowell's interest in what he was saying about Hana caused him to blurt out his true feelings, almost to the point of saying too much. He caught himself in time, however, and picked up his pace. As he strode out of the woods, he scattered a congregation of ravens that swooped away behind him like a wake, flying so low Lowell could almost touch their feet. When Lowell finally caught up with him on the levee, George hid his embarrassment by telling him that if he and Lowell and Hana were together, every raven in the area would gather to greet them.

"I've never seen anything like the way they come to her," he said. "I've watched her actually pick a wild raven up in her arms. They won't land on her shoulders, she insists, because they know they're too big and could hurt her. She understands them, knows what they think, if they think," he said with a chuckle. "She's like that with most animals. It's almost as if she could speak to them."

Late that afternoon big Betty Devon, a handsomely robust, grandmotherly New Englander who referred to women as "gals" and wore slacks and men's shirts, stuffed Lowell full of ice cream and apricot jam from her orchard. Betty had been educated at Mount Holyoke and still studied political science and frontier history. She was a kind person with a mean streak. Fiercely independent, with a loathing of "girl talk" and domesticity yet with a fondness for comfort and "the hearth," she'd been known to throw tantrums if men tried to help do the heavier, menial tasks around the Devon spread on Griegos. Early in their relationship, she threw a pail of water at George, pail and water both, when he offered to carry it for her. He never tried again. Betty would have liked to live far out of town, behind the mountains somewhere, raising horses and a few head of cattle. But she was oddly unassertive for a person of such striking appearance and original behavior. Their small orchard and vegetable farm, with its modest stables and small vineyard in rural Los Griegos, was a compromise she probably wouldn't have had to make if George had known from the start it was a compromise. There was an edge to their relationship, but it rarely sliced though the surface of their routines. After ice cream and jam that day, George showed Lowell more of his stamp collection and his current jigsaw puzzle. And Betty asked Lowell "back over any time. George needs young friends, kids he can lecture to." George smiled uncomfortably at the remark and Lowell was quickly out the door.

Spring 1948.

Brotherhood, Choice, and Pleasure

I'm in such a fury. How can a person with so much happiness, and so much to be happy for, be so angry, have such an angry heart? I don't think of myself as an angry person. And yet I know I am constantly making angry judgments against people. I flew into a rage the other afternoon at Thea's when I heard some of her friends talking about Japanese Americans and how it was "prudent and moderate" to have had them locked up for the duration. One "patriot" said, "and we should have thrown away the key." I actually attacked him, verbally, calling him a bigot to his face. He was startled. I was ashamed. It was such a prim little coffee klatsch. And Thea had put us all together for a good cause: to create a little assistance group for people flooded out in the North Valley around our various neighborhoods. It was to be just a food and clothing bank, and perhaps a tiny cash reserve for people stranded until the water subsided. The idea didn't go anywhere, largely because of my anger and the disruption it caused. I have no business getting involved in politics anyway. My days of being of service aren't numbered, but my days of working with others might be if I can't control myself. But why should I need to control myself? Am I wrong about the evil of locking away Japanese Americans during the war? Absolutely not. We should be putting together a fund for them to help them refinance the businesses, homes, and possessions they lost or had confiscated. Valley flood victims need help too, but. . . . I just got in the way. I couldn't let such grotesque prejudice pass without response. But by attacking him, I ruined all hope for discourse. Nobody likes to be assaulted and accused of being a fool, not even a blockhead.

A Failure of Imagination

[JOURNALS OF LOWELL BRISCOE]
Tuesday

Reading old news magazines and papers about the riot. And lo and behold the goddamn president of the United States said in public "I can hardly imagine—I try, but I can hardly imagine the fear and the anger that people must feel to terrorize one another and burn each other's property." A failure of imagination is at the heart of all the miseries of the world.

He can't imagine the fear and anger, so he won't do anything about it. And Hana's demon neighbors and their fucking doctor couldn't imagine what a healthy person would be doing thinking thoughts like she thought, so *they* did something about it. Los Angeles will boil for years. You won't be able to tell what's going on. And then one day it will just explode again. And the bastards in power won't be able to imagine why. They'll just go on making money, getting elected, fucking their secretaries, and snorting candy with a Jim Beam kicker. And other folks will go on living decent lives trying to keep their children from starving while others kill each other and snort a whole damn department store full of goodies. Someone like me, like Rodney King, and some pathetic householders will get the shit kicked out of them, or lose everything they have, but where it counts—in the think tanks and in the virtual reality of Washington and City Hall—no one will remember.

I'm so angry about so much. I've got to try harder to separate the past from the present. I don't know how to do it. I have Hana on my mind all the time since the beating. She's been with me every day. I see her smile. I feel her hand on my shoulder. I smell her kitchen and her barns. Oh, my god, I miss her so much, so much. I can't bear it. I need her; I need someone. There's nothing I can do. Nothing I can do to save her. Nothing I can do to change anything. I just wish I hadn't loved her; I wish I hadn't fallen in love with her. How could an eleven-year-old boy fall in love—in a pure sense—with someone forty years older? For God's sake, it happens all the time, all the time. It's called a crush. Shrinks call it transference. It happens to kids, to troubled people, to therapists all the time. I'm not some pervert, some monster here. I loved her. Boys fall in love with their mothers. This isn't incest. It's the highest admiration.

Hana at some point became the source of all the good feelings I had about myself. I was grateful. I loved her. She mothered me. Maybe even she couldn't imagine exactly what it was that she meant to me, what it felt like to be so utterly overjoyed and swept away with the mere sight of her, the merest smell of her house, the merest glance she gave me, the merest word she uttered. And I couldn't have imagined then either what my declaration might have done to her, what odd effect it might have had. But I can imagine this: that somehow my love for her made her vulnerable, changed the atmosphere of her life, set her up to be attacked. I was probably too much for her, too demanding, too needy, too ever-present for her, perhaps I was just the last straw, that one thing too much that drove her over the edge.

But I don't think she went over the edge, do I? No, I don't. I don't think she was crazy. I don't, do I? Is insanity the ultimate easy answer? Yes. It's the answer of least resistance. It's the kind of thing that stupid arguments lead to—stupid conclusions. "Well, if you think we should take care of the poor, then you must think we should level out all incomes, that everyone should make the same wage." That's as stupid as saying, "Well, she does seem odd. I don't know what to make of her. She's withdrawn. She seems not to like our company anymore. Is there something wrong? She has always been prone to depression. Has she gone over the edge? She might be going over the edge." Talk about stupid conclusions! Talk about "going slack." No, I do not think she went crazy. I do not. Do I? Am I coming to believe it too? Has their stupidity gotten to me, too? Am I so bereft of imagination that I couldn't think of any other answers, anything else but a canned answer of the Mass Mind? What's happening to me??????!!!!! Maybe all the hells on earth are failures of imagination.

＿＿

Late summer 1992.

Playing Athena

"I play the Athena figure every now and then, pushing him along on his Odyssey, that's all," Hana told Nola defensively one afternoon after her friend had mildly, but pointedly, questioned the amount of time Hana was spending with Lowell. "And besides, my dear, this really isn't what should concern you. He's the little friend of my girlself. Utterly sweet and harmless," Hana said with mild irritation as her friend peered over the top of her reading glasses looking up from a pile of bills. Nola was working on Hana's taxes at a card table in Hana's "thinking room." "Well I wasn't prying," Nola said snappishly. "It just seems to me that he's such a strange child, so unnatural, so unhealthy. And really, Hana darling, everything about you concerns me, you know that, how could it be otherwise?"

"If Lowell is strange, does that mean that I'm strange too, 'strange by association?' . . . Well, it doesn't matter. Lowell's a boy that needs a little help, that's all. Juliet is pleased with his progress. He's something of an orphan, and orphans and I communicate. I wouldn't worry about him any more than you'd worry about the water bill," Hana said with increasing casualness. "You're just used to your nephew, Nola, and the obedience you demand from your graduate students. Lowell's just fine, really. Let's don't bother ourselves about this anymore," Hana said softly, but with definite closure, returning to her correspondence.

"You're never a bother to me, dear," Nola said half audibly under her breath.

— —

Early fall 1948.

PART FOUR

Sticking to the Shadows

The Riot of 1992
Nightmare Man

During a daytime television interview, Lowell was heard to say to a young reporter, "Yes, I think you're definitely right, Mary Margaret. I *have* become a symbol of their deepest dreads. I am sort of a nightmare man. What white folks have always feared might happen to them some day actually happened to me. And they saw it with their own eyes over and over again. I've even watched my own beating, maybe twenty times. It's never off the air. It's like a brilliant piece of propaganda. Do you want to terrify the populace? Just show the Briscoe and King tapes ten times a day for a week. Black people and white people will never be the same. Those images have become part of the common experience of the city, of the nation. For most of the white and Asian people in this city, my beating was like helplessly watching a man being burned alive with a blow torch. There are no words to express the horror they experienced as part of their daily image fare. For most of the Black people in this city, the images of King's beating were visual confirmation of their deepest intuitions and experience of oppression. The Klan was just wearing badges, that's all. King was their nightmare man."

"You had such a dazed look, Dr. Briscoe," Mary Margaret McLeod of the Channel Eight News Watch Team said sympathetically. "Did you know what was happening to you after the initial blows were landed, or were you pretty much in shock?"

"Well, it's strange. I can remember everything about the beating, and I can recall nothing. I emotionally, viscerally, remember every blow and kick, every act of outrage. But if I consciously try to recall a particular moment, or a face, I come up blank. After the initial blows, as you put it, my adrenaline was racing so hard I was on the verge of blacking out. I don't think the blows hurt terribly much after the first five or six. Adrenaline works like an emotional steroid. In strong enough jolts, it overrides all normal nervous responses. Everything was happening in slow motion. But it was slow motion of something terribly fast, so it was over almost before it began in my mind, and in my recollection, do you see?"

"Yes, Dr. Briscoe, of course, of course. But you must still dream about it, don't you. Do you ever want revenge?"

"Oh, absolutely. I ask myself over and over if I'm ever going to get satisfaction. Will the rape victim ever know the pleasure of society's just retribution against her assailant? I imagine stalking those young men. I know that sounds sick and weird. But I do; I imagine stalking them in their neighborhoods and bit by bit destroying everything they love. I'm not proud of such thoughts, by any means. But I do have them. You have no idea how angry something like a beating can make you. I want to kill those guys. Something deep inside me wants to kill them. But the trouble is, you see, that I can't personally remember their faces. I can't see who they are. So all my anger is fruitless and stupid, as all anger is anyway. I must sound like I'm losing my mind! Do you have any idea what it's like to watch yourself on television being beaten nearly to death? Sometimes I cringe with every blow; sometimes I just go on eating my ice cream as if I were watching a news clip on the savage war in somewhere unpronounceable. I've learned how sensitive and callous I can be."

"Oh, Dr. Briscoe, I can understand how you feel, I really can. Most women could. Anyone who's been threatened, or physically coerced, or raped, or beaten could."

"I'm sure they could. Have you had such an experience, Mary Margaret?" Lowell asked in a serious low voice.

"Aaaaa, well, uh, I ya, I ya have ... but a ... ahhhh. ... Dr. Briscoe, there's a, there's a caller on Line 1. Hello, you're on the air."

"Yes, Dr. Briscoe?" a soft maternal voice asked.

"Yes, I'm here."

"We all want you to know we all admire you out here. You're a hero. We want you to know that. Your courage, your dignity, your manliness in the face of adversity. ... You're just an inspiration to us."

"You're too kind."

"No, it's true. Our question for you, though, is this. Don't you think that any kind of mob violence should be subject to capital punishment laws? Wouldn't that put a stop to these kids looting and dragging people from their cars?"

"What's your name, ma'am?"

"Lilian, Dr. Briscoe."

"I'm sorry, Lilian, I don't think any kind of mob hysteria should be a capital offense. As angry as I can get at mob violence, executing people for looting or assault and battery would be a gross injustice and a terrible precedent. What if conditions got so terrible in America that you and I needed to riot to work people up? I'd hate to get shot or hanged for that."

"But surely your attackers deserve the death penalty, Dr. Briscoe."

"I don't think the state should kill anyone. But I'd like to be given amnesty so I could kill them," Lowell said with a smiling irony in his voice.

"I'd like to help you string them up," she said in her softest voice. "I'd like to string them all up, every one of them, all of them. There's not enough rope in the city. . . ."

"Thank you ma'am," Mary Margaret said breaking into the conversation. "We have another caller on Line 3."

"Dr. Briscoe, will you carry around a gun for the rest of your life now? I have two guns with me at all times. And I swear that any animal who tries to do to me what they did to you, I swear I'll blow their balls off."

"Thank you," Mary Margaret said abruptly. "Here's another caller, Dr. Briscoe."

"Yes, I just want to say that I think the perpetrators of mob violence should be treated like the animals they are. They should be put to sleep, that's what you'd do with a dog or a horse that's turned killer. That's what you ought to do to anyone who's turned into a rabid killer. Put them to sleep . . . which is the nice way of putting it."

Mary Margaret looked relieved. "I'm sorry Dr. Briscoe. We have to go to a commercial break. Thank you so much for being with us this morning."

Unreasonable Searches and Seizures

[JOURNAL OF HANA NICHOLAS]
3 March 1949

Privacy is not only a divine right, it is a Constitutional right. Privacy is not secrecy. I can't get that through anyone's head. I'm almost desperate with anxiety and frustration over the constant pressure to be more "available," more "sociable," more "communicative," more "transparent." Nola harps at me for "suddenly" becoming "secretive" and "evasive." Even Thea has been wondering out loud "what's become of you?" I don't think I'm being evasive. I'm just in a period where I need privacy. And I have a perfect right to it. Don't I? All this prying and meddling. It's exactly like an unreasonable search, and god knows what they want to seize. Maybe it's me . . . absurd, absurd, absurd. Their surveillance now has become so objectionable to me, though, that I'm starting to seize up when I see them. I find I have nothing to say to them and don't want to be around them, and the more I shut up, the more concerned they get, the more meddlesome they become, the more intransigent my responses. It's come to the point where I think I should take a long trip, and I would if it weren't for Lowell, who is going through a particularly rough time of it right now. I can't quite make sense of what's happening to him. He seems so much angrier than I've ever seen him and so much more reluctant to return home from Gloriamaris. I wonder if he's psychic, if he's having premonitions. . . . Rubbish!

I have got to find some humor to survive this. If I could only become my "jolly old self again" as George told me the other day. That's what's troubling me. Nothing is funny anymore. My sense of humor is gone. I can't laugh at Nola because I am afraid of her; AFRAID. I am, I'm growing more and more frightened of her all the time. I find nothing amusing when I'm around her. I can't even laugh at her when I'm alone. I think about our arguments obsessively. And Gloriamaris doesn't feel very safe to me either. Could Lowell survive if I vacated Gloriamaris for a month? Just took off and drove around the country? He was so happy and relieved when I returned from my meditation retreat. Why is that boy so important to me? He's so hard, so defiant, so marvelously gentle, perceptive, kind. I just feel more and more compelled to look out for him, more and more. It's not that he's like a son to me; I have no desire for children. But he is like a windfall. I have changed so much since I have had to explain everything in such detail to him. I feel I'm more myself than ever. That must be the greatest reward of teaching. Knowing what you know twice as well after having "taught" it to others.

Where would I go on this vacation? Would it be fair? Would Lowell go into slump? Would Nola send out an all points bulletin?

Thea Pound's Funeral

It was October 1958. A crisp, bright wind ruffled the dresses and suit coats of the mourners. The priest was eloquent in his praise of the charity and generosity of Thea Pound. "She was an angel of mercy," he said. "She would often joke and call herself the orphans' flighty fairy godmother. But she was anything but flighty. Steadfast, ever ready to help, even at the most inconvenient times, she probably did more for St. Thomas's over the years than even her devoted friend Hana Nicholas, who has gifted this parish with such munificence of spirit and worldly goods. When our beloved Thea was with children, she was a cherub of happiness herself. The children knew she loved each one of them individually, knew that for them there was, in her, true unconditional love."

When Lowell heard those words, he felt a flush of sentiment foreign to the hardened image he had of himself. Even at twenty-one Lowell felt secretly jaded, as if he had already lived a hundred years, as if his just post-adolescent self was the thinnest of facades, a veneer of innocence over the entrance to a huge cave of unknown darkness. His memories of Thea were still largely emotional—feast day memories associated with cookies and turbans and high humor and memories of the smells of roast beef and sherry and how it felt to be singled out of a crowd of adults to become the object of her attentiveness.

After Juliet phoned him at Yale about Thea's death, Lowell had expected an intimate funeral with just Thea's close friends, an image he dreaded as he flew into Albuquerque. But the crowd that morning was perhaps a hundred people, many of whom Lowell had never seen before. He liked knowing that Thea had been so important to so many others. But, of course, the rest of the old group of Hana's friends was present too—Juliet, Nola, and the Devons, each one wearing an expression of the gravest sorrow and aggrieved befuddlement. Lowell was in a state of shock himself. He'd been summoned home by Juliet two days before, just three weeks into his junior year. Thea had died suddenly and tragically, an inexplicable death, almost as horrible as suicide. Juliet had told him on the phone that Thea had choked to death in her kitchen on the weekend.

"How did it happen?" Lowell asked Juliet.

"Well, Nola told me she'd inhaled some cookie dough while she was making chocolate chip cookies for the St. Thomas retarded Girl Scout troop. She just choked to death, that's all. All alone in her kitchen. Struggling all alone, gasping, with no one to help. God, what a horror! How useless, rotten; it makes no sense. Just like that. Just like that. Here one second and then suffocated by cookie dough, for Christ's sake, the next. It's impossible!"

When the priest was finished with his sermon, and Thea's many friends had given their eulogies, the crowd drifted apart and broke into little groups. Lowell joined Juliet, Nola, and Betty and George Devon in uneasy banter near some flowered headstones. The adults, as Nola would call them, showered on Lowell what he thought were bogus and defensive expressions of affection. The small talk was directed at him, with many questions about Yale and his studies. While the others were merely exaggerated in their welcome, Nola was pointed and nosy about school and Lowell's general health and well-being. No one felt particularly comfortable. They'd all suffered so much together, and no one forgot that when Lowell was a child, he hounded them mercilessly about Hana's disappearance and caused terrible anxiety and guilt. Lowell knew from long and intimate experience that Nola disliked him and suspected him and that she had spread rumors about him and had tried in countless subtle ways to discredit him and to cast doubt upon his soundness of mind. The instant Lowell saw her at the funeral he was aware of a stale, metallic taste in his mouth and a jolt of adrenaline. He despised her; she despised him. Their masks of conviviality were convincing to all but each other.

"I'll only be here for one more day, otherwise I'd love to visit with everyone. But I thought this time I'd go up to the state hospital again, up to Las Vegas, and see Hana. I haven't seen her since I left for Yale. I'd hate for her to die or something without trying to see her as much as time permits, though I know she must still be strong as a horse. She was always so tough," Lowell told the little circle of friends.

"Oh, Lowell, don't you know? Weren't you told?" asked Betty Devon with great distress in her voice.

"Told what?"

"Hana died last February," Nola said matter-of-factly without a touch of sentiment or sympathy in her voice.

"What!" Lowell shouted in amazement and consternation, running his hand through his hair. "She's dead!? God, Juliet how could you not tell me? How could you?" he said with piercing accusation. "Is she buried here? Where is she?"

As Juliet stumbled and almost gasped, Nola said dryly, "She's in her beloved Rio Grande, Lowell. She was cremated, and I put her ashes in the river as per her request."

"How did she die?" Lowell asked with sudden calm.

"We think she had a heart attack," George Devon replied.

"She had to wait a long time to die, didn't she?" Lowell said with deep contempt. "How long was she in that mad house, eight, ten years? God, it's monstrous! Unbelievable."

Lowell was about to turn away and walk off by himself when Nola asked accusingly, "How did you know she was in the State Hospital? How did you get in to see her?"

Lowell took two steps and was standing not six inches away from Nola's face when he answered softly with all the menace he had in him, "Even you aren't a perfect jailer, Nola. You could do everything else, everything else, everything," Lowell was shouting now, "everything else, but you couldn't bury her alive, just torture her, just torture her for years on end, years and years and years," he shrieked, stalking off up a grassy hill into another region of the cemetery.

"It seemed like forever," Nola said under her breath as he walked away. No one followed him.

He could not believe Hana was dead any more than he could believe three years before that her house and Kiva had been torn down and the land subdivided. He remembered that event as one of the many turning points of those years, and the stimulus for why he broke so thoroughly with Juliet and Albuquerque and chose distant Yale over the other schools that had accepted him.

"Lowell, Lowell, Lowell, I'm so sorry about yesterday," Juliet said trying to break the ice. "I didn't know either until after she was dead and cremated. Nola told no one until after it was over. She told us her grief was too personal and profound to share it. George was especially devastated and Thea sobbed for hours in my living room. I don't know why I didn't tell you. I knew you'd find out, of course. But I just couldn't bring myself to hurt you with such wicked news. And now, of course, I've hurt you even more. I'm so sorry. I'm such a coward. Lowell, please say something. Scream at me or something."

Lowell didn't say a word. When they arrived at the airport, he got out of the car, took his bag from the back seat, and slammed the door, never looking back or acknowledging Juliet and her explanation in any way.

"That was really the final cruelty," Lowell told Dr. Tuttle. "They treated me like a cipher, like a shadow from the past that no longer mattered. It took months and months for me to speak to Juliet again. And my silence made her so frantic and desperately sad that I felt guilty in the end. What's worse, though, is that I came to see that no matter how much I loved Thea, I held a coldness for her, too. She'd helped put Hana away. And she didn't think to tell me either. I found it incomprehensible how someone as close to Hana as Thea was, and someone with the kind of sensitivity that Thea had, could permit such a thing to happen, even though I understood her reasoning. It was so awful to realize that I despised her too. When I flew out of Albuquerque after her funeral, I felt something different than the recognition of long-denied rage; I felt a shameful sense of justice having been done. I was glad Thea had died awkwardly, terrifyingly alone, even though side by side with such hideous feelings were the sweet memories of what Thea had meant to me as a child. So, you see, there are emotional grounds for me to question myself about her death. Very good emotional grounds."

"But Lowell," Dr. Tuttle said seriously, "if she had died on the weekend, and you were in New Haven, how could you have done it? Isn't it logistically impossible? Aren't you just beating yourself up for nothing?"

"I'm so glad to have some place to dump all this and someone to help me organize my thoughts. . . . See," Lowell said with pinched urgency, "I *could* have flown out and killed her and then flown back before Juliet's call. It could have been done."

"Could you have paid for two flights like that?"

"Yes, I had plenty of money."

"But that was 1958, the planes were terribly slow then."

"I know, but it's still possible. And I remember nothing about the events prior to her funeral. I'm just a blank."

"I don't mean to be harsh, but I think you're stretching this whole thing out of proportion in order to make some sense out of the senseless. And besides, how do you kill someone with cookie dough? What do you do, make them laugh while they're sampling it? Pound them on the back, go boo?" Dr. Tuttle said with a sly grin.

"Of course, you're right. It sounds terribly improbable. Maybe I am just titillating myself with the possibility. . . . But would it have been possible for me, or someone she knew, to be in the kitchen with her while she was baking cookies and when her back was turned hit her over the head with a frying pan so it would look like she hit her head on the floor? Yes, I think it would. She'd no doubt gulp the cookie dough with the blow. Or maybe someone was going to kill her, but Thea choked on the cookie dough before they actually could do it. Maybe they scared her, frightened her into choking. Maybe they were in the room when she was struggling for breath and didn't help her or call for help. That would be murder by omission."

"Why would anyone want to kill her?" Dr. Tuttle mused.

"Because she might have started to talk after Hana had died, because she might have begun to put two and two together, because she might have become accusatory in her grief. Or because someone just got fed up with the memory of what she'd been a party to and polished her off."

"Why couldn't Nola have done it?" Dr. Tuttle asked innocently.

The idea had obviously never crossed Lowell's mind. He was flabbergasted. "My god, I don't know. Maybe she did. Maybe she was covering her ass. Maybe there really was something underhanded going on, and Thea's conscience couldn't stand it anymore. Maybe Nola did kill her, maybe she killed them all," Lowell said with a vehemence that bordered on gladness.

"Or maybe it was all just a series of hideous coincidences," Dr. Tuttle said rather blandly.

The thought that it might have been Nola and not him who'd been the secret serial killer filled Lowell with a temporary but profoundly relieving calm. Was there anyone else his battered conscience could blame? What about Dr. Hal? Was he in cahoots with Nola? Lowell felt like a six-year-old released from the principal's office, thrilled at the possibility of being free.

From Lowell Briscoe's "A Nest of Hells"

Flooding and Trusting

[JOURNALS OF HANA NICHOLAS]
3 January 1949

There is nothing I can do. It's like that terrible flood in the North Valley in the late 1930s. The river rose up, the rains wouldn't stop, the whole valley was saturated. The streets themselves were like the Mississippi. Some places had three feet of standing water. There was nothing you could do. You just had to wait and trust in time. It feels like that now. And I'm not sure I know what's happening. I feel exhausted, mentally soggy, bobbing up and down on waves of mud. I feel threatened. I sense disaster. I'm not totally in control of how my life is seen. I don't like this doctor friend of Nola's, this Harold Barrows, this Dr. Hal, with his serious solicitude and menacing curiosity. If I didn't know better, I'd think he was somehow "casing the joint," the joint being me and my property. That's ridiculous, I hope. I would like to take everything back from Nola, especially my finances. That was a big mistake. A very big mistake. And it started out innocently enough. I asked Boris for advice with my investments. And slowly, inexorably I allowed them to advise me on taxes and bookkeeping and other basic chores of money management. When Boris died, I told Nola I'd learned all they could teach me and wanted to go it alone with my books. It hurt her deeply, I think. She accused me of no longer trusting her. She practically begged me to let her be my "financial secretary," those were her words, so we could stay "close." When I told her that we would always be close, she implied that actions speak louder than words, and I relented. Now I'm stuck. What a terrible error.

Nola has changed. She is becoming a dangerous version of herself, a horrible caricature really. Hysteric and authoritarian; immobile and oblivious. If she weren't such a little girl, such a pouter and foot stomper, I'd be worried about her. As it is, you can hear her coming ten miles away, rather like old Tumble Tummy, his feline urges racing as he stalks a sparrow and then takes a running leap at it from fifty feet out. The birds just blithely lift off the ground when they see him coming.

Trust is everything here. Trusting the cosmos. That's the funda-
mental saving grace, the only worthwhile personal virtue: the belief in
the neutral good will of the All. It's not that life knows best. It's not
that kind of absurd optimism. Everything is going to work out all right
in the end for many of us. But that's not the point. We are not the
center of the universe. Trusting the totality is what matters. Trusting
the miracle of the possible. When the universe was created, it was created from stuff in the Field of the Possible, not the void, not the ether.
The Possible is the matrix of the universe and the imagination of the
divine. And the divine is not evil.

There is nothing I can do except keep an eye out for Nola skulk-
ing through the bushes. I don't know what's going on, but I sense
danger. And like any prey, I have to stay far away from where preda-
tors congregate, especially one weasel. Dr. Hal has to be avoided like
the plague.

The Destruction of the Kiva

It was the late spring of 1956. Hana had been in the state mental hospital in Las Vegas for the better part of six years. And Lowell had decided to leave Albuquerque for Yale. He had come home from school early one afternoon to tell Juliet of his decision when he saw bulldozers battering down Hana's Gloriamaris. He was stunned. He knew if the house was being leveled, the Kiva would be too. He'd walked past Hana's place every day since that terrible summer of 1949. He loved to imagine himself inside Gloriamaris with Hana. And now this last tangible connection to her was being demolished.

Lowell couldn't stand the sight, so he made his way to a darkly shaded, dense part of the bosque beyond the main ditch near the river. Sitting cross-legged on a pile of leaves, Lowell felt orphaned again. He was muddled and numb. There was that old drip of loneliness distracting him, maddening him, that itchy noise and anticipation of sinking and loss. The destruction of Hana's house made it real to him what he'd struggled to avoid since the winter of the Christmas play. Hana was gone for good. Something had happened to her that shouldn't happen to anyone. And now the visible remains of her life were being erased. The image of bulldozers and the brutal simplicity of their blades set his imagination to producing images of bodies being cut in half by dozer blades, and his own arm being crushed under the treads.

When it was dark that evening, Lowell slipped through the deep, green fields and went down the back paths to Hana's property. He wanted to see exactly what had happened. It was a sight that disgusted him. Many of the great trees had been pushed over by the bulldozers. The sacred groves of oak and laurel, myrtle and olives, decorated with ceramic statues she had made like huge jigsaw puzzles in effigies of Zeus, Apollo, Aphrodite, and Athena, were smashed to the ground. The great central cottonwood that had shaded so many wonderful years of Hana's merriment and gentle sociability lay on its side like a mutilated animal, the last of its species. Most of her gardens had been crushed by the big machines moving across them with their treads for hours. The acreage looked like photos Lowell had seen of World War I battle sites, barren, charred, and damp with black stumps of trees poking up randomly from dead soil in the moonlight. The rambling old earthen house itself, the Greek Revival–trimmed Gloriamaris, had been reduced to a bombed-out pile of timber, vigas, white plaster, and broken adobe bricks. No light would ever shine out through its windows across the winter night again. No one would ever be able to sit in the Thinking Room in those overstuffed leather chairs by the fire, drink hot apple cider, and go on "eye adventures," as Hana said, around the room, stopping on Pueblo pots, Navajo rugs, bultos and retablos, rocks and shells, and some of the endless titles of her wall-to-wall, floor-to-ceiling bookshelves. The sweet comfort of being in that badger's den of a house, secluded from the harshness of weather and neurosis in the outside world, had been ripped from his life.

Juliet didn't seem to mind that the house was gone. She didn't mention it; Lowell had to bring it up, and when he did, she gave a mild gesture of futility and returned to the television. And yet, Lowell thought, she had long, wonderful times with Hana in that big room herself. What seemed to him to be her callousness about Gloriamaris gave him one more reason to detach from her.

Juliet did in fact, however, mourn the passing of Hana's place. It signaled for her the final sealing off of one of the most tumultuous, yet safe and candid times, of her life. With the demolition of Gloriamaris, Juliet felt, as well, an evaporation of her energy and ambition. She still worked at her manuscripts, but only to keep up appearances so she wouldn't judge herself too harshly and could keep pretending she had a reason to live.

Lowell walked through the rubble sobbing and shaking his head in bewildered rage. If Nola were Hana's "guardian," as Juliet had told him, he thought she must also be behind this travesty. For that, and so much more, Nola should be punished, bulldozed and turned under the ground, Lowell said to himself as he approached the Kiva. The building was still standing untouched, waiting for its execution, he was sure, first thing in the morning. He walked carefully to the great front doors, but knowing they squeaked and not wanting to make a sound, terrified Nola would find him, he skirted around to what Hana had referred to as the "secret" side entrance, the "theatrical device," and opened what looked like a good-sized wood box, ducked his head, and entered the Kiva behind the altar. His cigarette lighter seemed like a torch, the light was so fierce. He could see through the thick shadows, to his relief and immediate delight, that nothing had been removed.

But that meant that when the bulldozer battered the Kiva down it would be with everything inside it. None of its treasures would be saved. The luminous shells, the crèche that Hana had made from pine cones, the hawk, goose, and raven wings she'd collected and preserved, the raw crystals and crystal spheres would all be crushed and ground up like the bones of corpses.

This was the ultimate treachery. Even as a cynical and rebellious teenager, Lowell believed the Kiva to be a holy place. Its low ceiling, thick walls, and complete silence made him feel safer and more alive inside it than in any place he'd ever been, including the dark seclusion of the bosque and the river. The smell of candle wax, incense, and years of cedar and piñon smoke on the walls and vigas was intoxicating. When the Kiva came down, Lowell knew he would lose an emotional space never to be duplicated but always yearned for. In fact, for the rest of his life, Lowell would work to create studies in his various homes that reminded him of the Kiva.

He knew he could do nothing to stop its destruction. He was completely helpless. There was no use trying to carry away all the treasures either. Juliet wouldn't know what to do with them. Nor could he tell Hana about the eradication of her house and shrines when he went to see her. It would be a vast cruelty for her to know. So Lowell paced the Kiva in the darkening shadows, looking for a small object to take away for himself, and something also for Juliet, a remembrance he could keep with him wherever he went. He came to the small square of soil in the middle of the room where he and Hana had placed their palm prints before rehearsing the play. He thought about taking some soil from it, but he didn't have anything to carry it in. He thought of taking two eagle feathers, but rejected the idea, knowing the feathers would eventually decay. He'd long coveted the crystal and amethyst spheres, but they seemed too important and somehow too powerful for him to take; better they be buried with the Kiva itself. Lowell settled on the row of circular pebbles he could barely see, round stones that Hana had collected from the river and placed on the altar over the years. She told him they were "perfect circles, each with perfect imperfections, just like us."

With the lighter burning his fingers, Lowell searched for the almost perfectly circular gray stone with the little bump on the edge and the dark circle of smooth basalt with what looked like bands of clouds across the albedo of the new moon. He found them both, put them in his pocket, took one last look around the Kiva's calm, snapped the lighter shut, then ducked out the secret entrance and ran home.

Late that night, he put the dark circle at the bottom of Juliet's jewel box, visible but not glaringly obvious. She'd have to be sober to recognize it. Five weeks later, he drove his Ford northeast to Las Vegas to see Hana and eventually to New Haven and Yale.

— ᵔ —

From Lowell Briscoe's "A Nest of Hells." It remains uncertain in my mind what actual legal conditions existed regarding the property of a living person committed to a mental institution in New Mexico in the 1950s. Dr. Briscoe's vagary on this point reinforces the fictional nature of his account.

The Only Visit, July 1956

"Visiting Hana at the state hospital was one of those sobering, maturing, indelible experiences that inform everything serious that you think about for the rest of your life," Lowell told Dr. Tuttle.

Lowell was on the verge of turning eighteen. He was shy but self-confident. Little deterred him. But he didn't know if he'd be able to see Hana at all. He hadn't gotten permission from Nola, in fact he hadn't even said goodbye to her, or to anyone but Juliet and Thea. It was two years before Thea's death. Despite his suspicions and resentments, Lowell looked to Thea for comfort and the security that comes from being treated like someone important. Thea was always glad to see him, once she'd forgiven him in the early 1950s for accusing her of conspiring with Nola to harm Hana. She always made a great fuss with cookies, milk, cloth napkins, and his favorite chair. He always told Thea what was on his mind at the moment. And he couldn't resist telling her that he planned to visit Hana on the way to New Haven.

"Lowell, dearest one, dearest one, don't be shocked when you see her. Don't cry out! Don't run away!" Thea said to him theatrically.

"You mean you've really seen her?"

"Yes, my sweet, yes I did. I did sneak up there behind Nola's back once, fully expecting to lie my way into a meeting with dear Hana. But the hospital staff was so happy to see anyone who wanted to visit her, they let me right in, right away. Oh, it was a terror to be there, Lowell. Hana looked like a dead Egyptian queen just unrolled from her mummy wrappings. Such a look I've never gotten from anyone."

When Lowell reached the state hospital the next week, the red brick buildings on the outskirts of Las Vegas reminded him of the film about Frankenstein's monster he'd seen the weekend before. The manicured gloominess of the place made him anxious. Though the lawns were mown, the hedges trimmed and leaves raked from the flower beds, the place seemed seedy and down at the heel. Lowell approached the main building with exaggerated foreboding. But once inside, he found the staff to be, as Thea had said, welcoming and eager for him to visit their patient.

An orderly named Anselmo led Lowell down long, white corridors to the far wing of the hospital. Lowell couldn't keep from shuddering now and then, half with anticipation of seeing Hana and half with a cold dread of being even temporarily confined to such a place.

The orderly was somewhat distant but not unpleasant. He explained that Hana never spoke and appeared never to listen to anyone, but that she was not immobile and was really quite able to care for her own basic needs. She was never rude, the young man said, but simply went about her business as if she were all alone. He asked Lowell if he knew about her face. Lowell said he'd heard about it from a friend. "Well, it's pretty bad. Don't be surprised. I'm used to it. I just look at her eyes. But, boy, she must be angry!" They rounded a corner in the corridor, and the orderly pointed out a figure with her back turned to them sitting in a big red chair in a small, walled patio attached to the building. The woman's face was raised to the sun. Lowell almost turned and ran. The intervening years backed up and flooded his awareness with anguish. But there was Hana, sunning herself in the morning; she was alive. It had all been real, Lowell thought to himself. The orderly turned to leave, but Lowell stopped him and asked nervously if there was any chance of a recovery. The orderly shrugged his shoulders. "Well, I think she's given up on us," he said. "She's gone wherever you go when you're sick and tired of other people. I don't think she's ever going to come back." Lowell thanked the man and then turned and walked ever so slowly to Hana's chair.

The Mask of Horror

[JOURNALS OF LOWELL BRISCOE]

A pleasant breeze was blowing through some evergreen shrubs. The sun was hot, its light glaring from the walls of the patio enclosure. I stood behind Hana's chair for several minutes, dead still, not knowing what to do or say. Finally, I exhaled worriedly and moved around the chair, squatting on my haunches before her. I greeted her somehow, my eyes turned toward the ground, but when she made no reply, I looked up at her face. Her head was tilted to get the sun, but her expression was one of furious agony. Her mouth was wide open in a mute scream. Her expression looked as if it were frozen in permanent horror, as if watching the approach of the hooded flayer bringing his knife to the first layer of her flesh. My revulsion was overwhelming. I felt the dome of my brain shudder and parts of it break off and crash to the floor of myself. The rest of Hana, however, was a picture of perfect peace. Her legs were crossed serenely, her big rough hands cupped in her lap, the breeze ruffling her short gray hair. She was wearing slacks and a work shirt open at the neck. Her breath came in steady, regular waves, as if she were meditating.

I bowed my head and whispered, "Hana, Hana, it's me, Lowell." She made no sign of recognition. I moved from my crouch and sat cross-legged on the ground before her, holding my head, and began to tell her all I had tried to do for her after the Christmas play all those years ago. I had no idea beforehand that I would try to justify myself to Hana; it just came out, punctuated frequently with ardent apologies for my failure. The more I talked the more my composure deserted me; my ideas came blurting out in a jumble of disconnected thoughts and ramblings. I wasn't sure she was hearing anything I said. But she did hear. When I would look at her face from time to time, I could see beneath the mask of her rage and horror that her eyes moved in recognition. My confessions exhausted me; I couldn't stand the accusation implied in her expression. I finally shook my head and told her I couldn't stand it any longer and that I'd have to leave. "Could you, though, give me just one small sign that you've heard me and know who I am?" I asked her. And I know I saw her hand raise ever so slightly. I know it. I was overcome with happiness. I asked her if she wanted me to get her out of there. I promised I wouldn't fail her "this time."

"I can rescue you," I told her emphatically. I thought I saw her hand flutter delicately for an instant as if to signal no. "I don't understand. You don't want to leave? You don't think I can get you out? Are you worried about where you'll stay? You can stay with Juliet. It's Nola, isn't it? It must be Nola. You're scared she'll get you again. That Dr. Hal will put you away. Is that it? I won't let her do that to you. I won't. I'll kill her, and him, first. Just tell me what you want to me to do. Just tell me and I'll do it. I'll do anything."

Hana remained motionless, and I knew immediately that she'd never say a word or make any other gesture. She was no longer present; she'd chosen to leave and she wouldn't return for anyone, not even me. I told her I loved her, that I loved her so much more than I could ever tell her. And I promised to come back. Then I put my arms around her and kissed her on her cheek. She felt soft and warm, and smelled of baby powder, but she was as unresponsive as the body of a dead animal on the road.

I left Hana's room like someone sneaking away from the scene of a crime; I was jumpy and relieved to be gone. I found the orderly and quizzed him about Hana's overall health and learned that she was apparently not in any physical pain. When I asked if I could see her dossier and other records, the orderly dismissed me out of hand as a mere visitor with "no legal connection to the patient."

The whole encounter with Hana had taken a little over forty-five minutes. It was the last time I would see her, and our meeting has become the supreme symbolic moment of my life. I'll never forget that face she wore. I remember it with the deepest sadness and admiration. It's like an icon. It reminds me of how I feel whenever I see a crucifix. Something cultural happens to me. I am not a Christian in the formal sense. But when I see Christ on the cross, tears well up, even if it's an ugly crucifix with no aesthetic power. My memories of her mask are like that. When its image comes into my mind, I am overcome with grief. What a price she paid for her eccentricity! What a horrible price for honestly living her life as she really was. Her candor was utterly noble and utterly fatal. Even in the wilds of a northern New Mexico mental hospital, even as a so-called catatonic, Hana was true to her feelings. That face was her protest. It wasn't effective; it did nothing to change her condition, but still she reacted. She didn't chicken out; she didn't choose against her integrity. But maybe she didn't want to defend herself and return to a world so dangerous and so catastrophically disappointing. Maybe she just wanted to punish them. Maybe the trauma turned her into someone who gains satisfaction from tormenting others. That scream on her face would have been heard in the eyes and minds of anyone who had to deal with her. And if Nola and Dr. Hal ever visited her, it would have greeted them too. Perhaps it was designed for them in the first place, and no one else, and it just got stuck as her only persona. Maybe Hana wanted to give Nola nightmares, to become her nightmare. Maybe that was her final pleasure, to think of Nola squirming in her dreams. . . . No, that's not Hana. I think that face was just a shriek of pain, of the knowledge of unendurable suffering that she'd have to endure for the rest of her life.

I can't think about it anymore. But I can't stop myself.

Who Would Have Thought?

[DIARIES OF NOLA DASHELLER]
August 4, 1949

I visited Hana yesterday. No change. A complete blank. A menacing blank. Who would have thought? Such obstinacy. Such resistance. Such obvious hatred in her face. It breaks my heart. But Hal assures me it will pass, "in time." It was going to happen anyway, he says. He's just glad it happened in the hospital. But I can't imagine why she's still so vacant. I would have thought she'd be railing, furious, damning everyone. That would be so much healthier. I thought she'd be home by now. But I don't think she'll be home for a long, long time, no matter what Hal says.

I can't care for the animals forever. I dread it, but I might have to sell them, or have them destroyed. My life's being dictated by them. I can't do anything. As guardian, I have a right to do what's best. When she's healthy, she can get more stock and some pets. She'll never, I'm sure, accumulate a zoo like this again.

I'm frightened even to write this down. But did what Hal and I cooked up for her own good cause her to get worse, much, much worse? And why would that be? Were we not only tiresome but also malicious meddlers that unsettled her? Does she hate me so much, now, that she can't stand the sight of me anymore? I miss her so. There's no way to describe the pain. I have no one, now, really no one. I feel the void hurrying to my doorstep. Which is to say, I worry for myself, I really do.

Thea, the Devons, even Juliet Briscoe are very solicitous. But they can't make up for Hana. And every time I set out to work on her papers, or deal with her finances, I get to thinking of what we once had together, and I just can't bear it.

Hal was right, of course. He's a medical man, and he should know. She was on the verge of a breakdown. She was. That's beyond my control. Give me the strength to feel that in my heart! I had no control over her mental health. No control.

I feel no guilt, of course. Why should I? Hal's right about that too. When someone you love needs help, you must not let them down. Hana will thank me in the end, I know it—if there is an end, that is. Hal's disappointed about the land. I've told him repeatedly that it will never get settled until Hana's settled, one way or the other. Beside, as I told him over and over, Hana will never sell. And I won't either. Why can't he get that into his head? Easterners just don't understand about land. It means everything here. He's really like a child about it. Petulant. Ignorant.

Hal wants me to dine with him tomorrow night at the Alvarado. Too many memories there. And he's getting under my skin in a bad way. He's too insistent. Too charming. Too full of secrets and protestations of affection. And way too fleshy. I'm starting to think Hana was right about Hal in some ways. And I'm not under as much stress as he thinks I am. I don't trust him anymore. How odd! How fiendish.

Poor George and Betty

In the early spring of 1960, George and Betty Devon's bodies were found floating up against a wooden check dam in a community ditch near their acre-and-a-half farm on Griegos Road. They were fully clothed, and it first appeared they had somehow fallen into the ditch and drowned. The ditch boss told the sheriff's officers what they already knew. The Devons hadn't opened the floodgate to their property before they fell in the water. That's why the ditch was so high and flooding the neighbors' gardens. Local boys on their way to school found the bodies early in the morning. Their corpses were a frightening sight, face down in the water, coated with leaves, mud, and brown silty foam. It was a beautifully clear and carefree morning. The boys screamed with shock and excitement when they first saw them. They recognized George's overalls and old tweed coat. They knew him and liked him. And Betty Devon was always a favorite of the local kids, especially at holidays when she baked mountains of special cookies and offered them to everyone she met.

When the deputies arrived, they fished out the bodies and checked for evidence of foul play. George had a deep bruise and cut on his left cheek, as if someone had kicked him or hit him with a two-by-four, as one officer suggested. "Or he might have just smacked his face on the sharp edge of the check dam," the deputy went on. There were no visible marks of violence on Betty. Later, one of the deputies found what looked like scratch marks and disturbed soil on the side of the ditch where the Devons might have fallen in. Did it look like the traces of a scuffle, or was it where George and Betty had scrambled helplessly to get out of the water? The deputies couldn't decide. "How old were these folks?" one of them asked Nola at the scene. "I've known them for more than thirty years. They were dear, dear friends. They were both seventy-three and not in the best of health, though they continued to plant every spring." Nola told the officers that she had heard the boys' commotion when they found the bodies and had made the first call to the sheriff's department. She watched with evident emotion as the Devons were pulled from the water and examined. "They were so frail. They should have hired help to do the heavy work," said

Nola sobbing into a handkerchief. "They look in pretty good shape to me," the deputy answered absentmindedly. "Poor George and Betty, poor George and Betty," Nola moaned.

The findings of the autopsy were inconclusive, but they officially ruled out wrongdoing. Splinters were found in George's cheek that matched the old, waterlogged pine planks in the check dam. And water was deep in both their lungs, which showed they had been alive when they entered the water. The ditch was deep, and the sides extremely slippery with no grasses in the early spring to hold on to. It's probable, the coroner theorized, that the seventy-three-year-old Devons simply could not climb up the ditch banks and exhausted themselves in the effort. Despite the scuffle marks, the coroner wanted to rule out foul play altogether. But he couldn't be "absolutely positive and definite," he wrote, because he didn't understand "why the deceased didn't cry out for help. If they had, it is likely that someone would have heard them."

Lowell's imagination wouldn't let go of the Devons' drowning. He obsessively examined and reexamined the possibilities, goaded by the horror of possible guilt. Finally he fixed on the following narrative: It was late twilight when George and Betty were at the ditch to divert water for their early spring pea patch and leafy green garden. They had been kneeling by the check dam near their land, trying to pull up the flood gate onto their field. Betty fell in first. Just as he saw her hit the water, George caught a peripheral glimpse of someone behind him, right before he too felt a hand at his back shoving him over and down the bank into the ditch. Had the deputies been able to figure it out, they might have suspected the killer was someone George and Betty knew. Whoever it was jumped into the ditch with them, at first glance appearing to try to rescue them. The person quickly pushed George's head under the water and then forcefully shoved his face into the wooden check dam several times, dazing him enough so that he took in a huge gulp of water and began to choke and flail helplessly. The killer then turned to Betty, who was still so flustered she could hardly breathe, and with a heave pushed her head under the water and kept it there until her body stopped moving. The Devons were both so stunned to find themselves in the ditch, and were attacked with such efficient ferocity that they barely uttered an audible cry. It took less than forty-five seconds for George to be dazed and drowning and for Betty's head to be held under the water. In two or three minutes they were both dead. The attacker had a hard time scrambling out of the ditch with nothing to hold on to, but eventually did, leaving what looked like scratch and scuffle marks on the ditch bank. It was completely dark and moonless as the killer trotted down the ditch road in the direction of the other farms and houses on Griegos.

Lowell filled this fantasy with vivid scenes. It seemed so logical and perfect to him he was astonished no one else thought of it. The killer, if there was one, got off scot free. No one was ever charged, or even suspected, in the Devons' deaths. Lowell remained uncertain for years whether he'd been in Albuquerque the weekend they died. He had no memory of where exactly he might have been. He had only his obsessions, what he knew of the coroner's report, and his scenario of their drowning to go on. And the image of the aquarium with George and Betty scratching frantically on the glass in his transformational dream was reassuringly remote from the actual site of their deaths. Still, the look of their horrified, bloated faces pressed against the glass, the sound of their pounding and muffled scratching was with him too many nights to ignore. He was certain, though, that he had not attended their funeral. He was sure he would have remembered Nola and Juliet's cosmetic displays of emotion and stoic resolve. Nonetheless, the old itch of imaginary guilt wouldn't leave him. He didn't have the wisdom and life experience until much later to think that his conscience might be feeling what dentists call referred pain—pain in one part of his life mysteriously appearing in another, perhaps unrelated, part. After the Los Angeles riot of 1992 he had come to reason that his moral anxiety about himself as a young man might have nothing to do with the deaths of Hana's friends, but with something even more mysterious and hidden in life. It was not until after Dr. Tuttle's suggestion that Nola, or even Dr. Barrows had just as much motive as he might have had for the "killings," especially if there had been a conspiracy involved, that Lowell could momentarily console his conscience with what he sardonically called "the refreshing possibility."

— ◄ ►—

I have adapted this from very sketchy notes I found in the back pages of Lowell Briscoe's novel "A Nest of Hells."

Invisible Dust

[JOURNALS OF HANA NICHOLAS]
27 October 1948

"We are mere feathers of compassion, leaves with hearts in the cold inferno of the Nothing-In-Between the annihilating stars. All we have are our feelings, our feelings that are less than the invisible dust on stones, feelings and desires and kindness that are as invisible as solar storms in the night." I wrote that this morning on my walk. Very cold. Cottonwood leaves rattling like brown insect skins. Why am I so depressed? Am I falling into an endless rabbit hole? I can't shake these feelings of leaden inconsequence. I didn't know I could feel such desolation. I didn't know that writing could double my misery or that words could make me feel so terrible. Still, what a cure for solipsism! Ever the optimist, Hana! Why not?

Nola's Last Stand

While Lowell was never certain about the Devons and Thea, he was quite sure that two years later, in the summer of 1962, he was in New Mexico. That summer, five years after Hana's death, Nola was in the hospital, on the verge of dying herself. Lowell was in Santa Fe doing research on the Pueblo Revolt of 1680 for a magazine article and possible dissertation project.

"No, I won't do it. I'll be damned if I'll pay a 'mercy call' on her," Lowell said to Juliet, practically yelling over the phone.

"She's in terrible shape, and a kindly gesture wouldn't hurt you one bit. I know you hate her; I know you have odd ideas about her and Hana and her and me. I know all that. But for God's sake, she's dying. A little visit wouldn't hurt. I just can't visit her alone. And she called me and begged me to see her. Maybe she wants to tells us something. But I just can't go alone."

"Why not? Are you afraid of her? I always knew it. Of course you are."

"Yes, I am. I'm terrified of her. I need your help."

"Is she blackmailing you or something? Does she know something about you? Why are you so afraid of her?" Lowell asked with bitter innocence in his voice.

"Do not, I repeat, do not psychoanalyze me. Do not—just don't do it! Just help me, please. Come with me, Lowell. Please. Please."

"This is unbelievable. I won't go. Can't I ever get away from this woman? Does she always have to bedevil me? I'm busy up here; go see her yourself. All she'd want to do with me is attack me, make me say something or do something I'll be sorry for. That would be her last revenge. Go see her yourself," Lowell said almost shouting into the phone.

"Baby, I can't. I can't. Hal says I must come."

"Hal?"

"Dr. Barrows, you remember. He's her doctor. He's insisted that I come see her. And I must go. I just can't ignore her. Too much has gone on. God, I've known her for nearly twenty years. She's my friend.

She's family. I'd feel guilty all the rest of my life if I denied her. She's got no one left. Everyone else is dead."

"Hal's not."

"But that's not the same. It went sour."

"What went sour?"

"You know."

"No."

"Everyone else is dead, honey. It would be cruel, monstrous, to deny her," Juliet said with moral certainty. "What if someone did that to you?"

"What's wrong with her? Isn't she a little young to be dying?"

"Lowell, please," Juliet said with exhaustion. "It's cancer or something."

"OK. OK. OK. I'll come down, I'll come down in a couple of weeks."

"No, it has to be tomorrow, Lowell. She'll be dead before the weekend."

"How do you know that."

"That's what her doctor thinks."

"Hal?"

"Yes, Hal," Juliet said with impatience.

"I just can't tomorrow."

"Tomorrow! I mean it. Please, you just have to. Please."

The first thing Lowell saw as he entered the hospital room was a pair of bloated, painfully twisted feet with curly toenails and thin, cracked scab-laced skin. Nola was flat on her back, with tubes in her nose, snoring loudly.

"Boy, she is old," Lowell said whispering to Juliet.

"Not that old," she replied.

The room stank sweetly of talcum, sweat, and pee. Nola looked to Lowell like a shrunken head. Her whole body had shriveled up. It was as if she were filled with hot sand. The demon had become a gnome. God had made the devil into a bad-smelling old baby with a wasting disease. If Lowell had not been so repulsed, he would have been almost glad to see her like that. What a satisfying contrast she made to the old image he had of her—her formidable physical presence, her dark hair, erect posture and straight shoulders, her dainty but muscular hands and forearms. She was almost six feet tall and seemed to Lowell as a child like a bean-stalk giant, a tyrannosaurus busybody. To actually see her bare feet sticking out from the hospital bed was as unlikely and upsetting as seeing the toes of the Pope or Stalin. "It's come to this," Lowell thought. "There she is, a tragic little old lady, stripped of all her menacing powers. Juliet's right. It's too pathetic. We should be here. I'm glad we are."

"Juliet, do you think Hal's doing a little mercy killing here? She looks yellow."

"You idiot. I'd slap you right now, if we weren't in a hospital."

"Well. . . . Look at her."

"Lowell, this is too much."

"OK."

Just as Lowell moved to pat Juliet comfortingly on the shoulder, Nola let out a loud gasp and raised herself on one elbow.

"Who's here?" she shouted. "Be careful. I'm not dead yet."

Her voice sent a barb of adrenalin through both of them. It had not shrunken up. It was as forced and sharp as it had ever been. Lowell had always hated it. It was the whine of the Cyclops, the bitching of a giant squid.

Juliet gripped Lowell's arm. "How are you, Nola dear?"

"Who's here? Don't touch me. Don't stuff me in a bag. I'm still quick."

"Nola dear, it's Juliet and Lowell, Juliet and Lowell Briscoe."

"I know who you are. Don't come too close, you'll compromise my tubes. . . . *Who* are you?"

"It's Juliet and Lowell, Juliet and Lowell."

"Juliet and Lowell, Juliet and Lowell," Nola replied tauntingly. "Juliet and Lowell, so what?"

"Honey, don't you know us? It's just us, Juliet and Lowell. Don't worry."

"Ouch, this crucifix is biting my chest!" Nola shouted. "Take it off me, take it off," she begged, tears rolling down her cheeks.

Juliet bent over the bed to see if there really was a crucifix around Nola's neck, and as she did Nola grabbed her head with both arms and hands and pulled Juliet down on top of her.

"Nola, please, please," Juliet pleaded in a muffled, desperate voice. "Nola, let me go, now you just let me go, let me go."

Juliet couldn't get loose. Nola held on to her like a person in a panic who can't swim might hold on to a beach ball in a wading pool.

"I'll never let you go, never, never, never," Nola said gritting her teeth. "You're a fence post, you're a light pole in a high wind, you're a snow plow. I'll just hang on; they'll have to break my fingers to get me off."

Lowell made a move toward the pair and grabbed Nola's wrists, hoping to pry open her hands.

"Oh, no you don't, you little rat," Nola roared. "You won't nibble away on me."

"Please Lowell, make her let go, she's really hurting me," Juliet said in a squeaky, terrified voice.

Nola had the strength of rigor mortis in her grip and her arms were still unnaturally strong, but Lowell wouldn't let go either. He tugged at her arms like a referee trying to pull apart squirming wrestlers. Juliet couldn't keep on her feet any more and Lowell, too, lost his balance, pulling Juliet and Nola almost off the bed. Nola set her jaw and still hung on to Juliet. Nola's head was almost touching the floor when she finally loosened her grip, sending Juliet and Lowell crashing against the wall.

"There, now you've done it. You've compromised my tubes, they're leaking all over the room," Nola snorted, trying to reinsert the prongs of the oxygen tubes into her nose. "Help me up and back into bed, you idiots," Nola boomed like the Queen of Hearts. "You idiots, I can't get back into bed!"

Juliet and Lowell scrambled to their feet. While Juliet hurriedly adjusted her dress, Lowell pushed and yanked Nola back onto the bed and then tried to help her rearrange her hospital gown, which had become twisted enough to expose much of the left side of her body.

"Get your disgusting, vile little hands off me, you pervert," Nola hissed at Lowell. "You won't touch me, you won't find my privates," Nola said, emphasizing "my."

Lowell reared back in amazement and rage. "What on earth do you mean? Your privates? What are you talking about? You are incredible!" he yelled, throwing her left arm against her body. "Why would I ever want to touch you?"

"You've touched everyone else, haven't you," Nola sneered.

Lowell was beside himself, engorged with anger. The adrenaline of the struggle had almost unhinged him. "You keep your Goddamn mouth shut, Nola! Who the hell do you think you are? Do you think that just because you've gone senile," Lowell said with acid snideness, "that you can insult anyone you want?"

Nola tilted her head back into her pillow, squinted at him intently, looking like a bad caricature of Long John Silver, and said with a level voice, "You're the one who poisoned me, I'd recognize you anywhere. You're the one."

Like a rattler, Nola's hand flashed out and grabbed Lowell's wrist, "I've caught him, I've caught him. Help! Help!" she yelled at the top of her lungs, "Help! I've caught him."

Lowell was desperately trying to pry Nola's fingers loose, when two nurses came into the room and tried to calm Nola down. But no matter what they did she wouldn't release her grip. And Lowell's hand was beginning to go numb.

"Mrs. Dasheller, is this any way for a professor to behave?" one of the nurses asked in mock indignation. "Please, Professor Dasheller, let the gentleman go. You can hang on to me if you like. Here, take my wrist."

Nola ignored her, looked Lowell in the eye, and said with razor precision, "I know you. I know who you are. I know what you've done, I know, I know and I've got you. See! I've finally got him. I wish I could get him between my fingernails and pinch his head off like the dirty little tick he is."

Lowell gave the nurses the kind of look one gives a doctor when one's child is screaming in fear of an injection.

"Dr. Dasheller!" said the nurse hoarsely, "if you don't let the young man go we will have to sedate you. These rages are not good for your heart. The doctor won't permit it."

Just then Dr. Barrows appeared at the door. "Good gracious, what's all the commotion? Nola what are you doing? My heavens, it's you, Lowell, and Juliet. Um . . . Nola let go of him like a good girl, let go. Let go."

"Oh, it's you. You're the one who poisoned me," Nola said in an almost inaudible whisper of recognition. With that she sighed in resignation to authority; her anger suddenly deflated, her grip loosened once again. Lowell yanked his arm free, and she collapsed back into her pillows.

Lowell started to thank Dr. Barrows, but he'd left the room.

"There, Mrs. Dasheller. Would you like some tea?" the nurse asked.

"Yes, dear."

Juliet and Lowell waited in the hallway while the nurses rearranged Nola's bed cloths and hospital gown. "No, I hate the bed pan," they heard Nola say.

"God, what a scene! What was all that about? What did she say to Dr. Hal? 'You poisoned me'? What the hell's wrong with her?" Lowell growled rhetorically as Juliet tried to compose herself by putting on fresh lipstick.

"She begged me to come to see her," Juliet said distractedly.

"I thought she had cancer. She seems like she's insane to me, demented, maybe drugged and senile," Lowell said pointedly.

"I thought she might have something she wanted to get off her chest."

"Yeah, like the stiletto she's hiding there waiting to plunge in your back."

The nurses left the room together. Seconds later, Nola called out in a sweet, pathetically weak little voice, "Lowell, I'm sorry dear. I'm sorry. I'm so groggy. Come here and give Nola a hug."

Lowell looked at Juliet, she gave him a quizzical look but shrugged her shoulders and nodded yes. Lowell entered the room alone. "Close the door behind you, dear, would you please," Nola said with teacherly gentility. He glanced at Juliet, raised his eyebrows in mock alarm, but did as he was told.

"OK, Nola, what do you want?"

"Just a hug, dear, just a hug. I'm sorry for becoming so emotional."

"You're not going to hang on again, are you? You won't get me in a stranglehold?" Lowell asked as seriously as he might ask a child not to squirt him with a water pistol.

"I said I was sorry . . . it was just Dr. Hal."

"What? Oh, OK," Lowell said, leaning down to hug her. "It's OK, everything's OK." But Nola didn't want a hug. She grabbed Lowell like a bear would, pulled him to her with great force, and whispered in his ear like a torturer taunting her victim, "I saw you dancing in Hana's living room; I saw your disgusting gestures! I saw how you manipulated her, preyed on her weaknesses, you filthy little satyr! I saw it all, how you tempted her, how you provoked her. I saw it all, all of it, all of it."

Lowell almost fainted from the rush of hysterical anger that filled him. He saw spots in the corner of his eyes. His mouth dried up. He began to pant. Half in panic and half in a vindictive fury, struggling to wriggle free, he whispered back hoarsely, "I saw you too, Nola. I saw you and Hana naked in the sweat lodge together. I saw what you were doing to her. I watched you night after night in bed through the window, too. I never knew people could do such things to each other."

Nola gasped, almost squealed in pain. "Lies, lies, lies," she shrieked, flinging him from her. "Oh, monstrous lies, monstrous. You devil, you swine. Lies, lies, lies, lies."

Nola covered her face with her hands, shivered, began to tremble, then shake violently. She almost turned blue; she grabbed her throat, coughed with a deep rumble, and stared at Lowell in astonished sadness, as if he had just put a barbeque fork in her belly. She tried to speak, but her first garbled words were accompanied by grimacing convulsions that Lowell thought must have signaled a heart attack or a massive stroke. Whatever the cause, she was dead.

When the nurses and Dr. Barrows rushed into the room, Lowell watched the doctor's face with every ounce of attention he had. It was expressionless. He checked her vital signs, closed her eyes, pulled the sheet over her face, and calmly wrote on her chart.

For weeks after her death, Lowell felt pangs of hilarity mixed with guilty remorse. He had never seen Nola and Hana in bed. He had come upon them one day as they were entering the sweat lodge, but he'd seen nothing else. He had no evidence that Hana was the love of Nola's life, until the moment Nola had died presumably in horror of the thought of having been discovered. It wouldn't have mattered to Lowell if they'd been lovers or not. But he knew that by accident he'd hit Nola in her most vulnerable spot.

"Maybe I found her fondest wish, her deepest secret desire, the agony of her unrequitedness with Hana. Maybe I snagged her in her darkest shame, or most precious secret pleasure," he told Dr. Tuttle years later. Lowell would never know, of course, what actually killed Nola, beyond the doctor's descriptions. Maybe Dr. Hal had poisoned her. Maybe she had a stroke. Perhaps her cancer had weakened her so much that all the trauma and activity of that afternoon sent her over the top. But he knew one thing. The relationship between her death and his words, his passionate but vicious retaliation, was one on one. He had spoken and she had died.

➤ ➤

From Lowell Briscoe's "A Nest of Hells."

Juliet Was My Charybdis

[JOURNAL OF LOWELL BRISCOE]

The confusion in my mind about the deaths of Nola, the Devons, and Thea Pound was nothing compared to the superstitious befuddlement I've always felt about Juliet's murder, especially in 1967 when she died and during the trial of her alleged killer. I really began to worry that I was cursed, or that I was the curse myself. My studies had led me occasionally to art history texts and depictions of demons and nightmare forms. I fixated on such images and in my worst moments began to see evil as a cosmic force that was trying to find its way into the deepest part of my psyche.

When Juliet died, I was twenty-nine, well-tailored, sleek with intellectual pride, and full of dread. The boyishness that many men of that age still retain was missing from my enthusiasms as well as from my politics. I was armored and armed for the kill. You could say I'd become an extremist, a radical even. And I supposed I had. It was fashionable to be angry. And I had to do nothing at all to be in the height of fashion. Optimism and idealistic good will were polished features of my persona, too, which others found attractive and, I was told, even inspiring. But such charms and lures did not occupy my private thoughts. I wanted to believe the world was neutral, neither doomed nor blessed, but the experience of my life made me shy away from true hopefulness. Maybe the most generous thing to say about myself in those days is that there was a hiddenness to me and an unaffected heaviness that kept me apart. People liked me, though, but I refused to submit to their praises of my difficult life, or what they thought they knew of it. And from time to time I even thought I was well turned out with my new Ph.D., my good teaching assignments, my prosperous grants and trips to Europe and Mexico, and the remarkable success of my public television show that treated Los Angeles as if it were a modern Pompeii. My friends did notice that I had an amazing capacity for alcohol. I drank all day, bourbon and "branch," without really showing it. And I was not shy about admitting to taking amphetamines, which I only mentioned, however, when name dropping my many projects to convey how hard I was working.

I learned of Juliet's death when my old high school friend Reg Sandoval called me from Albuquerque one night during a dinner party at my house. It was one of those oceanic summer nights in Los Angeles that left people feeling as if nothing bad would ever happen again. I was entertaining academic acquaintances in my garden overlooking the Pacific. The scene looked like an advertisement for tonic water in *The New Yorker* with lean, well-dressed young people apparently engaged in intimate, but carefree, conversation. When I heard that Juliet had been strangled and stabbed to death, I exploded, ripped the phone from the wall and threw it through the kitchen window. My guests looked like people who'd just seen a truck drive through the window of a diner they'd left not minutes before. The guests fled without much show of sympathy, though a young woman I was idly courting, a precocious student who thought she liked professors, did linger to make sure I was "OK."

I was numbed by Juliet's murder. I wrote in my journal then that "It feels like my head is encased in ice. I can't believe this. This is madness, some cosmic insanity. It makes no sense. Where was I when she died? Where was I? I still can't believe the preposterousness of it. Why should she be killed? That's not the way the story of a life like hers should go."

My numbness eventually turned into an odd nonchalance as I drove east across the Mojave desert. I'd stop at small cafés, have coffee and a smoke, indulge myself on greasy foods and desserts. At one geranium-jungled café in St. Christopher, California, after a plate of bacon and eggs, I drifted into a reverie, remembering every detail of one of those legendary weekends with Juliet when I was ten or so. I remember them so clearly, but I don't know how they started. Juliet and I were aware, though, almost from the start, that we found each other adorable. We were infatuated. We had a kind of childlike zest for each other and a delight in each other that was, on one level, completely natural and animal like. We loved to curl up in each other's fur and heat. We loved to nest, to hunker down with our pleasures and keep the world at bay. On those weekends, we agreed to pamper each other from Friday night to Sunday night, to take the phone off the hook, lock the front door, and indulge each other completely. I remember our shopping sprees in preparation for what Juliet referred to in any season as our long winter's nap. The ice creams and candies, meats, wines, and eggs and thick maple-cured bacon, and fashion magazines and comic books by the pound.

Juliet had been my Charybdis, a soft, warm whirlpool I couldn't resist until the very last second before I drowned. With her, I could pretend I was still a very little boy, and Juliet could imagine she was still in complete control of her life. We were safe together. There was no danger. It was like masturbation—rebellious, indulgent, illicit. It was also like Russian roulette. The longer we hibernated, the greater the chance that claustrophobia would finally overcome intoxication.

In the café my memories didn't shy away from Juliet's body and her amazing gift for losing herself entirely in the pleasure of the moment. I remembered us both drawing the curtains all over the house, locking doors, checking windows, and then dancing long, slow dances in the kitchen. I was jarred from my reveries by a waitress pouring coffee and still felt weak and fuzzy headed an hour and a half later as I paid the bill. When I pushed open the café door to leave, a rush of adrenaline hit me like a shot of speed, as the image of Juliet's soft, white back merged with the thought of her dead body on the gray carpet in her bedroom. I wanted to run out into the desert and never stop. What I couldn't bear was the insane, though utterly "normal," contradiction of emotions. I felt guiltily relieved that Juliet was dead and could no longer plague me, though of course she does to this day. I felt an animal joy in "justice being served" and a bitter self-recrimination for the pleasure it gave me. When I thought of her being strangled, I felt the deepest sadness and pity bordering on hysterical empathy, a somatic response that resembled choking, which doctors told me was an esophageal spasm. And I felt a gray but electric loneliness, the kind a child might feel, lost from her parents in a bazaar.

When I left the café, I sat in my baking car, trying to calm myself down with sweat and heat. I went back to the café, half-dehydrated I think, took more coffee and water, and then continued east to Albuquerque, windows rolled down, with cowboy music blasting all the way. When I rode through the Duke City's modest downtown again, I felt protected and childishly safe—until, that is, I went to the newspaper office and its morgue to find accounts of Juliet's death and of the arrest of the man accused of killing her. I remember reading about her murder propped casually against the morgue librarian's oak front counter. One story said that a neighbor found her body some two weeks after she'd been killed. When I came to a passage that read that "the electric cord around her neck had been pulled so tight it almost severed her head from her body, police records show," I almost fainted. Albuquerque's clear light became as blinding and frigid as twilight sun glancing off snow. I thought I might be going mad. When I recovered my composure somewhat I searched through the papers for accounts of the arrest of her alleged killer. The stories were repetitive and vague, and his trial was still weeks away. The man's name was Mark Spindle, a prematurely gray-haired, fortyish white man who vigorously protested his innocence, claiming that another graying, middle-aged white man, and "hopeless bum like myself," boasted in a bar of "murdering the hag" after Juliet refused to give him some work when he came to the back door on a cold Friday afternoon. The newspaper accounts said witnesses identified Spindle as a man they'd seen "lurking around the neighborhood for weeks." I felt guilty but satisfied, I guess I could say, when I read how certain the police were about their suspect. But I knew I needed more evidence. I had no choice but to wait for the trial and go through the ordeal of witnessing it from start to finish. I spent the next weeks in New Mexico trying to keep myself together, periodically driving back and forth to Los Angeles to attend to business, always grateful for the desert and its anonymous motels and cafés.

What happened to Hana, what happened to Juliet, what happened to me and to everyone else in this story all has something to do with who controls reality, with who has the right to be believed, with whose version of reality is the one with the political clout, the perception of choice, the one people can understand, not necessarily the true version, not necessarily the right one either, but the one that fits the normal organization of things. Hana clearly didn't fit. I don't either. That's why it's so hard to explain myself to the prosecutors, so difficult to tell you, Dr. Tuttle, what's really going on. Maybe that's why Hana didn't defend herself at the sanity hearing. She knew her version wasn't wanted, that there was an enemy version already in place and that to oppose it meant you were insane, or unbalanced, or a fool. A classic double bind.

I've always been caught in double binds, suspended between impossibilities. Do I really know what happened to me in the riot? Is my version official enough? Is my doubt official, my reticence, my uncertainty, my confusion? No! I am not official enough. Cold, hard facts; objective truth; no interpretations; just the data, the identities, the matter-of-facts, that's all that's wanted. I am not an instrument, a stimulus/response mechanism. I remember what I can.

Here's an interesting "fact" I've never pursued. When I was in Albuquerque in 1967, I checked at the Bernalillo County Clerk's office to see who owned the subdivision that used to be Hana's land. A corporation owned it, called Far Frontier, Inc. Far Frontier is a term I heard Dr. Hal use more than once when he was fresh from the army and upstate New York and I was a kid. Is he the monster of the piece? I almost don't want to know about it. I don't want to know, period. But why?

— —

Late October 1992.

The Irrational and the Insane

[JOURNALS OF HANA NICHOLAS]
9 March 1948

I was thinking the other morning driving to Santo Domingo that Western culture equates the irrational with the insane. New Mexico completely disproves that assumption. Pueblo mysticism, its beliefs about harmony, about the human spirit being inseparable from the world around it, one and the same, in fact, without distinction, so that a bad mood or an angry thought or a discourteous attitude toward the day can spoil the weather—we would think such a concept was irrational and for all practical purposes insane, more insane even than the idea of an omnipotent male god who washes his hands of evil and knows all things and causes all things and lets his children flounder in his mystery like suffocating trout flapping on the sand. But no one would ever dare to consider the idea of such a god irrational or insane. No one would think that the atom bomb was anything other than an act of supreme clarity, genius, and sanity; hardly anyone would call "the bomb" inherently lunatic, created at enormous cost for one purpose alone and none other: mass annihilation. That is perfectly, gorgeously, patriotically sane according to the world of the supremely rational homicidal maniacs who invented it and used it. But the Pueblos, they are looked upon as primitive, paleolithic, even "savage" by some, on a lower peg of cultural evolution. Yet this week, when the drums began, even I, as an outsider, could feel the peace, the holy harmlessness come over all of us. The "real" world of the midpoint of the twentieth century seemed even more mad, more hysterical, more full of misery and mayhem than before. Even Nola thinks the Pueblos live a more peaceful life than we do, but she attributes it to irresponsibility, to escapism, to a childlike perspective on the world, which she denigrates and really, at base, abhors.

But who's happier? The Pueblos, without a shadow of a doubt. Even as conquered people, even in their seeming poverty, the Pueblo people have a secret joy that nothing of our world or the world of the friars could take from the them. And they kept it a secret, too, so we wouldn't pollute it. Inside them is a mystery, a belonging, a faith in the day, in the weather, in the world, a marveling, a profound respect for everything around them, the simplicity of care; little goes unnoticed, little goes by without some acknowledgment, without what I would call gratitude. There's nothing really mysterious about it; it doesn't require social science to comprehend; we're all humans under the skin, under the songs, under language and culture; we're all the same; their pain is the same as ours, their joy is the same; it's just that they have a different set of things to emphasize—they are more intent on the pleasures that endure than we are, on cultivating the feeling of religious exhilaration, on nurturing the safety of family, on being happy and doing the things one needs to do to keep happy: be quiet, be frugal, be calm, go as slow as you can, uncluttered with ambition and free of the solitary ego, the separate self, that being who thinks everyone is looking at her and judging her. The Pueblos, of course, are not immune to self-consciousness, or to any other of the emotional ills that befall people of the West. We are the same, all human. It just seems as if the way they've organized the world, and their place within it, is healthier than ours, even though their life-expectancy is lower than ours. At least they're more fulfilled while they're alive; they don't need the promise of some palace in the sky to keep the joyousness about their days, shrugging off suffering, looking at the beautiful rather than the bad, laughing as much as humanly possible at everything there is to laugh at.

Oh, tut, tut, you're romanticizing again, Hana, aren't you.

George and Betty wouldn't approve. Nola scoffs even as I write, even without reading a word of what I've written.

PART FIVE

The Disappeared

The Riot of 1992
My Attackers

Lowell felt frighteningly vulnerable in the hospital. Off and on in the early hours of the morning he suffered paranoid fantasies about his attackers tracking him down and finishing the job, icing the only witness. But it wouldn't take him long to remember that his beating had been televised. And that if military spy satellites could read license plates from two hundred miles up, surely the technological wizards at the FBI could identify his attackers from the videotape. Surely they must know that too. He was both relieved and befuddled when four young men associated with a criminal gang were arrested on suspicion of attempting to murder him, as well as on charges of arson, conspiring to incite a riot, and other crimes. He found it odd, though, that their arrest seemed to him like just another news story. It didn't seem to have anything to do with him, beyond allaying subsurface fears. He knew rationally that he had been beaten with uncontrollable brutality and that his attackers had enjoyed doing it. He certainly felt the pain of his wounds. But he had no emotional recollection of anything about the incident. And the painkillers he needed made the present seem like a child's shadow show.

After the four young men were arrested, the press named them the Normandy Four. Lowell was quoted in the *L.A. Times* as saying "as far as I'm concerned, they are innocent until proven guilty. But if the jury convicts them, I hope the court throws the book at them." He told television reporters that he hadn't seen their pictures yet. "So I don't know if I can identify them. But I know I don't identify *with* them, that's for sure." To other reporters' questions he answered harshly, "Of course I believe in due process, but how could a punishment fit the crime in this case? Would I have to be given by the courts the right to beat the hell out of them?" he asked with a mocking grin. "I would like the law to afford me some satisfaction. If it won't, why have it at all?"

When the parents of one of the young men demanded that the charges be dropped, claiming mistaken identity caused by racial bias, Lowell told reporters, "It's a logical argument. Just like all white people looked the same that day at Florence and Normandy, so do, I'm sure, all black people look the same, so to speak, to white cops, judges, and prosecutors. It's perfectly possible that those young men are the wrong people, that the system made a mistake, though it's not highly likely."

In a long session with Dr. Tuttle, Lowell's anger got the better of him. "Christ, I'm the victim here! I'm the one who had to have his skull stapled back together. Jesus H., drop the charges? Shit, I'd like to charge everyone! The city, the chief, the parents of the kids, the voters who wouldn't support decent schools. Everyone. I told Chuck Lewis yesterday . . . my attorney. . . ."

"I didn't know you had an attorney, Dr. Briscoe," Melinda Tuttle said with slight surprise.

"Well of course I do. What do you think I am? A mental minnow? I told Lewis to sue the city of Los Angeles for not providing me, as a citizen, with adequate police protection. It's the mass mind, Melinda, you know that. The cops, the politicians, the goddamn thugs. They all have the same kind of mind. That's why I could sue the parents of the accused for violating my civil rights by raising monsters like that. That's why I could sue the higher-ups who ordered the officers to retreat from the intersection. That's why I could sue the goddamn politicians who wrote our crummy laws, and why I could sue every member of the jury who acquitted the cops who beat Rodney King. It's all the mass mind. They are all the same. The same!" Lowell's voice had a hysterical edge to it. "Our culture is rotting in their brains. They'd all crucify a saint. They'd all do it. I'm no saint—no, no, no! But hand them one, and stand back, the blood will be spurting all over the place in seconds! In seconds."

"Are you all right? Would you like some water?" Dr. Tuttle asked.

"No, no, no, no, no, no. I'm fine. Sorry. I'm fine, really I am. I just can't stand this idiocy. I'm not going crazy am I?"

"Of course not. You're angry. And you have a right to be. Better you blow off some steam in here than in the D.A.'s office."

"You don't report what I say in here to the D.A. do you? Am I your client, or is he? That's an impertinent question, but. . . ."

"You know better than that, Lowell. You are my client. There's no ambiguity about it. I say nothing to the D.A. I don't even know him. You're the one who is dealing with him, not me. Just relax a bit now," she told him.

"I'm sorry. I know I'm your client. I didn't mean to imply anything unethical on your part. I really didn't. It's just that this is so important. There's so much at stake. And I know so much about betrayal, so much. I don't need to know any more. And yet I know I will. Somewhere along the line, someone's going to get me, use me, sell me out, exploit me, somehow; I know it. I'll be the one who ends up being scapegoated or blamed or hunted or something. I just know it."

"Tell me about betrayal, Dr. Briscoe."

"Lowell, OK."

"Lowell. Tell me."

The Anger of the Gentle and Kind

The sky to the far southeast was almost black with rain and hiding the mountains as Hana and Lowell walked hurriedly back up the Griegos drain to Gloriamaris in the high summer of 1948. Weeds and willows had completely taken over the ditch bank. In some places, they walked through the tunnel of overgrowth for many yards before the sky could be clearly seen again. Lowell and Hana had walked as far as the big bosque east of the river to look for birds and tree lizards and scout for beaver and coyote spoor.

"Do you live alone because you're 'broken hearted' or a 'lesbian'?" Lowell asked.

"What? What did you say?"

There was a tone suddenly in Hana's voice that Lowell had never heard before and would never hear again. It was terrifying in its ferocity.

"Where did you hear such absurd things, Lowell? Where did those questions come from?"

Lowell was startled and frightened. He stammered and gulped. His heart raced so fast he seemed blinded by the rhythm. He felt that frenzied numbness come over him when he was terrified and defensive all at once. It was the feeling one must have, he thought, just before they cut off your head.

"Tell me, Lowell," Hana insisted, staring at him with a look that could turn anyone to stone.

"It was Juliet, Juliet and Nola, Juliet, Nola, and I don't know, Hana, maybe Thea, I don't know, I don't know." Lowell was holding his breath, his voice was squeaky and edging on hysteria. "I didn't think it was wrong, I didn't know it was wrong."

Hana stood back, took a deep breath herself, wiped her hand across her forehead, and smiled with resignation.

"Lowell, I'm sorry. I didn't mean to frighten you. It's going to be fine. Really. . . . No, I'm not broken hearted. And no, I am not a lesbian. Do you know what that word means?"

"No," he said, but he did.

"Good," she sighed. "Lowell, let me be very direct. Don't be frightened. But hear me clearly."

"OK, I will." Lowell's heart was still pounding, but Hana's smile had taken the edge off his nausea.

"I live alone because I am a free person, because I like to live alone, and because I cannot think of anyone in my life who I would like to live with. It's that simple. Questions like the ones you asked me are just gossip. Meaningless, dangerous, tawdry gossip, prying, malicious gossip, manipulating rumor—that's all. I have a horror, Lowell, of being spied on, of being meddled with, an absolute horror of being misunderstood and misinterpreted. It's the one thing I will not abide, the one thing for which I have no tolerance," Hana said with agitation. "Do you understand, Lowell? I am afraid of what other people say. I don't like to be afraid, but I am. I live in terror of no longer being in charge of my own definition of myself, not able to shake someone else's inaccurate assessment of me and my life. Am I making sense?"

Lowell nodded yes. She was making sense to him, even if he didn't understand all the words exactly.

"I don't want to be treated like someone I'm not. Do you understand?"

"Yes, yes, I do, I really do. I'm not what Juliet says I am either."

"What does Juliet call you?"

"Words I shouldn't say."

"You can tell me."

"No, I can't."

Hana took Lowell's hand, kissed him on the forehead, hugged him to her for a moment, and then led him back to Gloriamaris.

"We never have to speak of such things again, Lowell. I'll never ask you again. And you . . ."

"I promise I'll never ask you either."

"Good! What a beautiful day! Maybe we'll make it home before that rain cloud catches us."

From Lowell Briscoe's "A Nest of Hells."

The Goose Step of Suspicion, Fall 1943

Hana had bought her wide-banded silver bracelet from a Navajo at the Alvarado Hotel in 1926. By 1943, its symbols were worn down to a rounded smoothness.

"Do you really think you should be wearing that bracelet now, Hana?" Nola asked over coffee after supper.

"It could easily be misinterpreted," Nola's Boris chimed in. "I've worried about you wearing it since 1933, when Hitler took power."

"I know you have, Boris, but as I keep on telling you both," she said, pointing to the symbol on the bracelet, "this is not a Nazi swastika. It's backwards. I've shown you so many times. It's an Indian symbol of wholeness and a Hindu symbol as well. People in New Mexico recognize such things. Really, it's all right."

"I know it's your favorite, and that you never take it off. But wearing that thing now has the same effect on me as someone carving their initials on the crucifix. I know it's not sophisticated of me, but that's how I feel. And I'm sorry I have to say it," said Nola staring into her coffee cup. It was her first disagreement with her marvelous friend, Hana Nicholas, who knew so much about New Mexico and how the world really worked. But the problem seemed self-evident to Nola. "We're fighting a war," she pointed out.

"Well, I'll think twice about wearing it again," Hana responded with a stoniness that Nola had never heard before. Nola worried the rest of the evening that she might have stepped over some invisible line and that her fascinating intellectual friendship with Hana might have been damaged. But when Hana bade Boris and Nola good night that evening, Nola could sense not even the barest hint of hostility in her voice and demeanor. Nola told Boris that she thought Hana would show "good sense about this." And when Nola went to bed that night, she drifted off to sleep thinking about having gained stature with Hana and how deeply and quietly good that felt to her.

The next day Hana lunched with George Devon at the Alvarado. They met there every week, sometimes twice a week when ideas were flowing, and could talk for hours about wildlife, the workings of nature, mythology, philosophy, and the struggle to live a free and useful life.

Hana felt at peace with George. She could try out ideas in his presence without fear of judgment, or dampening of enthusiasm. George did not compete with her. She would take risks and let him take risks in response. And George's reading fascinated her. He was an intellectual omnivore, she liked to say. He wanted to understand how things worked as much as she wanted to know why they existed in the first place. George was a spiritual person in his own way—"a mild and genial ecstatic, excitable, enthusiastic about the miracles of the commonplace," Hana wrote about him once in her journal.

George and Hana knew their friendship was inconvenient and even marginally dangerous. "The world clucks so," Hana chuckled that day at the Alvarado after a waitress had told them what a "sweet couple" they were.

Betty Devon didn't begrudge Hana and George their "little talks" but she could never quite convince herself there wasn't something "more" going on, although she was sure she would be able to tell if there was. It wasn't sex that Betty worried about from time to time; she knew George well on that score. It was more personal than that. Betty worried that she couldn't keep up with George's curiosity and that Hana could.

George and Betty stuck to each other like suction cups. Betty liked it that way and she could sense even the slightest, most transitory pressure to detach, even for a moment. George was true to his feelings, whatever they might be, or however confused they might seem to him. He loved Betty deeply and he loved Hana in a way that he couldn't quite explain to himself. She felt to him like the proverbial long-lost friend from centuries ago. The first time he met her in 1925, George felt a strange kind of comfort come over him. He was absolutely unself-conscious in her presence, right from the start.

Hana's feelings for George were just as intensely pleasant. "He finds everything that's on my mind interesting, he actually does; and I'm always eager to see where his mind is going. What a blessing! What a treasure! A man who listens," Hana wrote in her journals a year or so after they met and began their dialogue. "The great gift of George Devon in my life is that I have a male friend I can deal with who wants nothing 'institutional' from me, no 'romance,' no 'possession.'"

At lunch that day in 1943, Hana allowed herself to be agitated. "This poor old bracelet of mine. I can't understand their worry, really, George, nor yours. But you all mean well. So I'm not wearing my old friend today, and I feel a little naked. I bought it when I first got here almost twenty years ago. I researched all the symbols. And the reversed swastika is truly sublime, full of motion, strength, tolerance, and acceptance.

"Last night. . . . When we're in a crowd, it's always impossible to communicate with each other at the level we reach alone together. People get oddly jealous if friends are too friendly. I'm always so inhibited in those situations. It sounded last night as if you thought Nola and Betty were right. Do you think that? Please tell me if you do, and tell me why."

"Oh, Hana, I don't know. I don't mind it personally. But I can see it a bit from Nola's and Betty's point of view. The black swastika on those brutal red flags and arm bands. I've even dreamed about them. It means something horrible."

"It does now, indeed, of course it does. It's just a word that's been reinterpreted or has had a new association attached to it." Her big grin widened and she said, "It's like Hollywood, isn't it? When it means the wood from holly brambles, or woods of holly, it had a far lovelier meaning than it has today."

"I think that's it exactly," George answered. "Nothing remains the same, particularly in the world of symbols—unless, of course, their meaning is fixed in public discourse and made rigid by some kind of power."

"I'm not clear . . ."

"Well, the meaning of the swastika has been made rigid by Nazi power and by Allied power. Nola would not have as much trouble with it if the allies hadn't amplified on the common sense awareness that it's a Nazi symbol. They turned it into a symbol of hell on earth. That's a pretty powerful thing to buck."

"I agree. It's about coerced conformity. That's why we could get a kind of Babbitt Nazism in America if we're not very careful. All that totalitarians have to do in conformist America is to keep on making conformity fun and profitable. Then the middle class will be led to the slaughterhouse with smiles on their faces and Bing Crosby in their brains. The slaughterhouse won't be for them, of course. They'll be zombie spectators. The middle class won't wake up until it has torn the nation apart with its greed, pounding the poor, the strange, and the smart on the head with a righteous hammer—a reign of terror by the convinced and disappointed. And when they finally do wake up, the gore will be so sickening, it will lead them to their only relief—sweet, sweet denial, cathedrals of denial, whole universities of denial, a cosmology of denial."

The conversation that afternoon carried on, with the indulgences of the waitresses, for another hour, until almost 2:30. It moved deeper into politics and then emerged suddenly into an open field of talk about birds and animal behavior, and "man, the naughty monkey," as Hana liked to say.

It was a phrase that caught George by the funny bone and caused him to take what he called "a preposterous digression" into the *Divine Comedy*, populating its lower depths with "naughty monkeys of the modern era, baboons like Father Coughlin, Huey Long, Himmler, Hitler, Stalin, all those yackers swinging in the trees, crapping on the sidewalk of life. What I want to know is, How did cannibal-brained beasts of prey like us come to dominate the whole planet? I don't think our conquest was foreordained. Maybe we're just wretchedly effective busybody parasites who feed off everything and everyone else on the planet. What do you think?"

"I think we've come to dominate the world," Hana smiled, "because the world is pure consciousness, and we are the masters of consciousness on this planet, even the stupidest of us."

From Lowell Briscoe's "A Nest of Hells."

Intimations of Heresy

"What fascinates you so much about them?" Juliet asked Hana with more than polite interest.

"You mean the pueblos?"

"Yes, what attracts you."

"It's hard to describe simply," Hana said distractedly but with a serious tone in her voice. "I suppose it's that they are genuine, distant, and seemingly unafraid. They are who they are with no apologies. They've survived us Europeans and our rapacious ways for centuries. They are pragmatists in the best sense of the word. They've done everything they've had to do to preserve their right to be who they are as they see fit. They interest me, Juliet, because of their strength, because I want to be as strong as they are. As a gringa, a nice white lady, who treats them with respect, they take me for what I am too, or for what I choose to show them. They withhold from my view about nine-tenths of their lives, and I withhold from them an equal amount of mine. We get along so well because we're absolutely alike—almost totally camouflaged. It's just that *what* we camouflage is different," Hana said with her characteristic smooth ironic smile. "Well, not so different. We both hide who we really are so no one can take it away from us," Hana said softly as an aside.

"You always have such good reasons, Hana," Juliet said with a student's enthusiasm, hiding a slight sense of bafflement with an ingratiating smile. "I'm so grateful you want to take Lowell out there with you next week."

"You don't mind, then?"

"No, why should I?"

"I thought you might be leaning toward Nola's camp on this."

"I lean toward you, Hana, always toward you," Juliet said with impassioned understatement.

"I hope you lean toward yourself, too, a bit, dear," Hana joked. "I think Lowell will come away from the experience quite deepened. It's hard not to be changed by something that's both strange and fun."

"I didn't think fun would enter into it," Juliet said with some surprise.

"Everything important in life is fun, in the sense of being an adventure. What's the use of taking risks and growing if it isn't fun?"

"I hope he won't be bored."

"It's hard to bore someone with a brain like Lowell's. He's far and away the most curious child I've met. I like his enthusiasm. He must be a delight for you."

"He *is* incredibly smart, I'll give him that, almost a prodigy, almost an idiot savant," Juliet said with amused malice.

"It sounds as if you like him about as much as Nola does," Hana said feigning a wince.

"Nola's a crank about Lowell," Juliet backpedaled. "I adore him. He's just difficult, not bad or more flawed than the rest of us. Just a handful for someone my age and with my disposition. But he's my lot. And I asked for it. He is a delight, of course. I wouldn't know what to do without him now. He can be an angel, an absolute angel."

"Angelic, indeed, but prematurely dusty in places, if you know what I mean. Maybe a little trip will clean some of his windows," Hana said studying her lunch, then gracefully changed the subject.

A week later, in early August, 1948, when Lowell was eleven, he and Hana took their first "far adventure" alone together to Santo Domingo Pueblo, halfway between Albuquerque and Santa Fe. The most traditional and secretive of the Rio Grande pueblos in New Mexico, Santo Domingo had made a small but special place in its life for Hana. The pueblo's people first saw her in 1925 when she attended a Christmas Eve mass in their whitewashed adobe mission church and stayed through the night to witness the dances on the snow-packed and icy plaza the following day. She had attended virtually every public ceremonial each year since and considered the pueblo her "spiritual parish." It was a sign of her "otherness," she said, that her religious community was made up of people whose language she didn't speak and whose indigenous religion she knew about only from direct observation and the speculations of anthropologists. She and Thea went to Santo Domingo together from time to time. But Hana liked it best when she could slip out of Gloriamaris alone early in the morning and head to the pueblo before anyone knew she was gone. She felt utterly safe there and completely cut off from the ordinary troubles of life.

The Santo Domingo people who knew her considered Hana to be one of the few white people they didn't have to keep an eye on. Some of them were even glad to see her when she came to ceremonials, in the same way they'd be pleasantly disposed to the appearance of a congenial distant cousin. Hana knew the right way to behave. She was scrupulously deferential, friendly, and full of humor when humor was called for, especially when confronting the ribald horseplay of the koshare and quirana, the sacred clowns that stir things up and keep the ceremonials from becoming more important than the spiritual purposes they serve. So her friends at the pueblo were always happy to have her watch the dances from their porches and bancos, share their food on feast days, and take shelter in their homes in bad weather. Hana trusted their generosity and thought they were kind to her because she seemed to them like an anomaly among whites, like an exception that proved the rule.

Hana felt herself at home from the first moment she walked into the wide dirt street that served as the pueblo's ceremonial plaza and felt the drumbeats and the footfalls of the dancers like another heart in her body. After witnessing her first dance in 1925, Hana understood how Santo Domingo had survived the European conquest for four hundred years. "It has its own communal sense of the Tao. The Pueblo and its kin never broke," she told a distracted Lowell. "They kept what was important to them *to themselves*. Secrecy was their best weapon and their sharpest tool. And they never let down their guard. When you see the pueblo, you'll understand. It has only seven streets, as far as I can tell, all parallel and each one very long, like streams in canyons of square earth hills. But as simple as the layout is, it's a maze, a puzzle to keep people outside out and people inside in."

"What does Tao mean?" Lowell asked, staring out the windshield at the gravel hills and bright river of green leaves that hid the Rio Grande.

"Good question. I think it means, to me anyway, The Way Things Are, the way things are beyond opinion, beyond our knowledge, the ebb and flow. Do you get what I'm saying?"

"No," said Lowell with a hint of petulance.

"Ummmm. The Tao is the way to survive. You bend and give and hold your ground, or you break and die. Any clearer?"

"Not really."

"See those mountains over there?" Hana asked, changing the subject. "They are the Jemez. We'll go there one day. Way at the top is a place called Los Alamos where they invented the atom bomb. Did you know that?"

"No."

"It's not more than fifty miles from Santo Domingo and even closer to other pueblos. The bastion of the nuclear age, our dead fall from grace, cheek by jowl with the people of Eden," Hana said almost to herself.

"What? I couldn't hear?"

"Oh, I'm just musing, Lowell. You know, I've been told that, at least at Santo Domingo, people feel that anyone who witnesses ceremonials with sincere appreciation adds to the potency of the ritual. So we'll be just fine."

"You mean if you and I like it, it makes them do it better?" Lowell asked with a serious look on his face.

"Well, yes, yes, sort of."

Adapted loosely from Lowell Briscoe's "A Nest of Hells."

Infatuation

[JOURNALS OF LOWELL BRISCOE]
October 2, 1992

Like most kids, I never thought I was going to die, and I never thought anyone I loved would die either. I had more than an inkling that life was dangerously fragile, but I still really didn't know what death meant. And I certainly never thought about the possibility of Juliet dying—although I did think about killing her, but that wasn't the same. And it never once occurred to me that Hana was mortal.

Physically, Hana was one of those people who actually are what they appear to be—solid, strong, "childly," as she'd say, wide open. She had a chameleon face. She looked like a Hispanic around Hispanics, an Indian around Indians, a kid around kids. She was Athena with a girlish grin one moment and had the smile of the Madonna the next. She was not fat, nor was she a giant. I imagine her height must have been something around six feet and, though she didn't have the body of a man by any means, she had the strength and roughness of a carpenter or a brick layer. Yet she was delicate, too, delicate in the way that certain big cats can be when they're at rest, limpid, disturbable, easy but easily moved.

I remember her smell most of all. It could be herbal and sharp when she'd been doing physical labor; usually, she smelled like greens, fluid and fresh. On summer evenings, she had the odor of brambles, a dry, flowery, pungent smell that wasn't sweet, but rather slightly thorny. I loved to hug her and be close to her. I loved to sniff her skin through the button holes in her work shirts. I loved to feel her big flat hands on my back and shoulders, patting me, almost burping me. She was as companionable to me as Walt Whitman was to New York. She stuck by me. She slung her arm over my shoulder. She liked me. She enjoyed who I was. And I never for a moment thought she was going to die.

The older Hana got, the younger and more innocent she became. It threatened her friends to see her so happy, so willing to live out her contradictions no matter how odd they seemed. That must have been why I was so drawn to Hana. She wasn't a normal adult. I couldn't smell the stench of compromise and disillusion in her.

I remember her telling me once that children were like quiet ponds, reflecting the beauty around them, but that the slightest breeze, the smallest stone, could cause that reflection to become distorted, and a big stone, or a falling limb, could make the pond chaotically opaque, for a while.

A Good Strange Story

"What a good strange story our lives have become," Hana said to Nola one afternoon in 1946 while they were weeding the tomato patch in Hana's garden at Gloriamaris.

They were inseparable in those days, working on each other's land, cleaning their common ditch, riding together through the bosque, working long hours for their charities, and above all "discussing," as they used to say, "everything we can get our teeth into."

"How could two people with such particular tastes and outlooks be as close as we are?" Nola would often ask.

"It really is a good strange story," Hana smiled.

"Yes, you're so right. I mean who would have ever believed in Chicago that I would have a dear and irreplaceable friend like you when I grew up? But this isn't a 'story' you know. I object to that. This is very real. We aren't fabulists inventing our lives."

"Oh, but we are, Nola. Look what you've done since Boris died. Look what you've created from yourself, the life that you're living, the good work that you do. You've done that yourself. You've constructed a new story for yourself. And it really is quite fabulous."

"Thank you, dear one. But I still think a story implies that something is untrue, told for effect."

"A story is a construct. It's one of the things we say about the world," Hana answered.

"But there has to be something more than our constructs. They are just approximations of what's real," Nola said with precision.

"But constructs *are* real, in and of themselves, are they not? Just as real as another's thoughts. And who's to say which 'approximation' is closer to the 'what's real'? Who knows what's real?"

"Only God knows, I'm sure," Nola said with mock contempt.

"And She isn't telling, is She?"

"I wish you'd stop saying that. She."

"He's just another construct. So, for that matter, is She."

"I don't believe that, Hana," Nola said with stern and resigned seriousness. "God is the masculine and rational principle of the universe. Mary is the feminine and suffering principle of the universe. Mary is not God."

"We've trudged this trail before, haven't we? To repeat, how can any one 'approximation' of the divine, one 'construct,' be right and all the others—and all their billions of believers over time—be wrong?"

"It's called evolution, Hana, spiritual progress, as I've said over and over. Christ is the end result, the fruition of eons of trials and error. Isn't that abundantly clear?"

"'By their fruits shall ye know them,' Nola. An idea—a construct—is no good unless its consequences are good. Murderous, cold-blooded closed-mindedness is not good." Hana returned to rooting out grass from her tomato patch.

"Power has its prerogatives. Evolution makes that clear," Nola said almost under her breath.

"Now there's a fascinating topic," Hana laughed with what might have seemed like a mocking glee.

"What?"

"The misplaced application of the idea of evolution. It seems to work with animals and plants; the life force changes from the more simple to the more complex. But it cannot be said to work with, say, art or, in my view, religion, or spirituality. Minoan dolphins are just as 'great' as a Rembrandt or a Van Gogh, different but just as great. The spirit is a pure flame in all of us. How can it get better? Our ideas about it are merely different, that's all. It's just that some ideas are more dangerous than others."

"The spirit seeks us, Hana, it wants us for its home. But we close the door and will not let it in. Without it, we are merely history, a series of empty, dark events, barren of God, the spirit, and the holy ghost, barren and desolate. We must open the door. Christ is the only key."

"The *only* key?"

"The only means evolved enough to work," Nola said with satisfaction.

"Oh, dear."

— —

Adapted loosely from notes left by Lowell Briscoe.

The Sweat

Nola agreed to do a sweat with Hana in the summer of 1946 more out of curiosity than comradery, though she was always happy to do whatever she could to strengthen the bond of their friendship, even things that frightened her and were distasteful, though never what she considered "debased."

"I'm very pleased that you'd want to join me. I admire your spirit of adventure. I didn't really expect you to say yes," Hana told her.

"I'm nothing if not open-minded," Nola smiled.

Nola didn't care much for the idea of Hana making a ritual out of it, but it made good sense to her that sweating could be a kind of purgation. She reasoned that experiencing its medicinal properties would distract her sufficiently from Hana's annoying practices, whatever they might prove to be.

Nola was "in a state," she told Hana, and felt she was not thinking clearly in those days. She was lonely and bewildered by her emotional neediness and attraction to Hana. Boris's death had left her "completely at sea." Hana had become a kind of anchor for her, a relief from her isolation, a friend she could say anything to, "almost." Hana has caused warm feelings in my heart, Nola thought, feelings that she described as admiration, but which she worried might be something "more."

Still, that she had feelings at all after two and a half decades of life with "hollow Boris," was amazing to her. And she was always ready to deny her worries about neediness and looked upon her new feelings for Hana as "something of a blessing, a windfall of grace, if you will."

Hana had built her sweat lodge from willow poles covered with blankets, tarps, and deer skins in a grove of young cottonwoods and Russian olives at the far southwest corner of her property, close to the ditch. It was secluded from view, though it didn't need to be as she had no neighbors on any side of her land for an acre or more. One could undress in a pine bough shelter outside and enter the sweat lodge with a feeling of security that no one would accidentally pass by and "catch us like Actaeon caught Diana without her robes. We wouldn't want to have our cats tear them limb for limb, would we," Hana laughed, pausing to unbutton her shirt.

"Why are you taking off your shirt?" Nola asked worriedly.

"To take a sweat."

"Oh," said Nola with a rise in her voice.

Nola had not counted on having to undress before entering the little hut. She didn't like to see herself naked in a mirror. She treated her physical self as a disagreeable afterthought. Her "physique," as she called it, had never given her much trouble or much pain or pleasure. She wasn't used to it, but as she aged "little things" started to go wrong—the first glimpses of menopause, hot flashes, mild arthritis in her thumbs and toes, problems with her teeth, and what irritated her most of all, "irregularity." These innocuous but startling changes were proof enough to her that the body and its world were corruptible and untrustworthy. And that the physical was the "lowly servant of higher purposes."

As the two women undressed, Nola was astonished to see that the rest of Hana's big, strong body was nearly as darkly tanned as her face and arms.

"Do you go nude often, Hana?" Nola asked with a faint whiff of judgment in her voice.

"As often as I can when no one's around," Hana replied. "I feel so at peace that way, so much like my animals."

"You *do?*" Nola said in amazement.

"I'd like to ride Thunderhead naked if I could get away with it. I'm surprised myself that I feel absolutely no shame or uneasiness. Of course, I don't go anywhere I can be seen," she said facing Nola without embarrassment.

Nola clutched her skirt to her chest. She still had her underwear on.

"Indians don't go around nude, do they, Hana?"

"Of course not. Me liking to be naked has nothing to do with Indians. I like being a critter, a critter with a mind."

"And a soul?"

"And a soul, of course. But my soul doesn't separate me from the world of flesh and blood. It doesn't make me less an animal, less able to love my beasts or to be loved by them," Hana said standing naked before Nola with as much ease as if they were talking on the phone.

"You see yourself on an even keel with animals?" Nola asked, trying to keep her eyes looking straight at Hana's. "Now, *that's* Indian, isn't it? Don't they believe that animals have spirits?"

"I suppose, but that's not why I believe that."

"You mean you haven't been 'converted' but actually have come to this yourself?" Nola asked half jokingly.

"What's this animus you have against Indians?" Hana asked, turning her back and stooping down through the lodge door. Nola caught herself looking happily at the muscles in Hana's back and legs, and then abruptly averted her eyes.

"Oh, my goodness, Hana," Nola said in a painful whisper as she felt the moist heat of the lodge on her face and shoulders and legs. "This is unbearably hot, unbearably."

"Move over to the far edge, over there, get as far away from the rocks as you can. You'll get used to it very soon. Here's a moist towel. Hold it over your nose."

Nola did as she was told but had a hard time breathing and talking at first. She coughed and buried her head in the towel.

"Breathe calmly, Nola," Hana instructed. "Breathe calmly and pay attention to sensations other than the heat. Think cool thoughts to soothe your brain."

Soon Nola smelled the sage and mint that Hana had brought in, and felt the smooth cedar planks under her thighs. The room was very dark, lit only by thin rays of sun shining through the cracks in the walls.

"Feel better?"

"Sort of," Nola said meekly.

"You're a lot gamer that I thought," Hana said with evident admiration.

"Well, thank you, but I don't think so. This is very hard. And you're a lot stranger than I thought. Do you have any more secrets like this in your life?" Nola asked.

"Secrets? No, I just prefer to live a private life. A life of my own. If I'm strange then so be it."

"I didn't mean strange in a negative way, but do you have other things you do like this?"

"Other strange secrets? I'm not a witch, Nola."

"Oh, I'm sorry. . . ."

"No, you have a right to your opinions. We are very different kinds of people. And that's fine."

"I don't think we're so different, really, under it all. And I don't think you're anything like a witch."

"Are you getting more comfortable now with the heat? Sorry, go on," Hana said.

"Yes, yes, I'm fine."

"I'm going out to get more rocks, then."

Nola crossed her legs and put her face once again into her towel.

"It's getting too hot for me, Hana, way too hot. I can barely stand it," Nola whispered after Hana had poured water gently over the new hot stones.

"Here, moisten your lips, drink some water, and try to put your mind somewhere else, think about something else. Let's think more about how different we are, and how odd it is that we should like each other so much."

"I don't know if I can think.

"Do you want to go?"

"Nooooo. I'm sorry. Don't mean to be a complainer. I'm just not used to this. . . . We are different, but I can't put my finger on it."

"Perhaps we just stand on either side of the Great Wall of Europe or, with us, the Great Curb."

"What are you talking about?" Nola said with slight irritation in her voice.

"I mean, perhaps we just stand right next to the line on either side of what creates the duality of the West. We are so close but so far apart in so many ways."

"What duality are you talking about?"

"Try pagan/Christian, classic/romantic, liberal/conservative, orthodox/heterodox, artist/scientist, logos/mythos, nomos/physis, body/mind, patriarchy/matriarchy, I could go on and on."

"What are you talking about, Hana? Do you mean that we take sides on such matters, and that we, you and I, fall into these different camps? I don't think so! Not for a moment!" Nola said with astonished emphasis.

"Oh, I don't think so either, really. But I do think that we're like different cuisines, spiced distinctly, delicious but easily told apart."

"Now, that's not true, Hana. We're much more similar than that. We've always been marinating in the same sauce, haven't we?"

"Maybe so," Hana said with a smiling sigh. "But our differences can't be counted for by declaring we're fish and fowl. I like thinking about us both being fish, but spiced and cooked differently. That makes us seem much closer than being different critters in the same marinade."

"Well, now that's indicative," Nola said thoughtfully. "I like the same marinade, you like the different spices. How does that fit in with the Great Wall of Europe?"

"You're quite wonderful, Nola. Do you know that?"

"So are you."

"Well, anyway. The heat's a little softer now, why don't we try to meditate, or do a little silent prayer with each other. What do you say?"

"I don't see why not," Nola said gladly.

— —

Adapted from a number of clues taken from letters and Lowell Briscoe's "A Nest of Hells."

How Do I Manage Unmanageable People?

[Diary of Nola Dasheller]
June 2, 1948

If she just wouldn't walk around in the nude out there in her garden. She says nobody can see her. But I can see her, at least in my mind. Am I nobody? She says her land is the "hat of Hermes," which she apparently thinks makes her invisible. God! She's impossible. Hana's becoming as unmanageable and worrisome as sister-in-law Ida. How that old monster hated me! And I returned the compliment. She was utterly unmanageable. Boris told me that when they were kids, their parents had to commit her and she was given cold water shock treatments. Intolerable. Eccentric all the way around. I like no-fuss people. No fuss. I can't stand all this trouble. I can't stand trouble, period. Hana reminds me of myself so much. She's becoming like a little girl. A petulant little girl. She's causing so much trouble. If she could just not stand out, control herself a bit, put a lid on it, as my mother used to say, just be more manageable, then no one would have to do anything. But they told me years ago that if I didn't keep a lid on it, if I didn't settle down, I'd have to go to the hospital. And that settled me down right away. Right away. Pronto, as they say. I wanted my own way. I wanted everything my way. I wanted to be left alone. And what terrible trouble that caused me. I've never forgotten mother's look when I told her I'd do whatever I damn well pleased. She looked at me as if I'd gone mad. Such shock, such disgust, such despair in her eyes. And I didn't care how sad I'd made her. It didn't really matter to me how mother felt. I was concerned just with myself. Then daddy made it very clear to me that I either "shape up or ship out." I know all about being unmanageable. About being too smart for your own good. About being high and mighty, above it all. That's a kind of insanity itself. People are required to be predictable, otherwise the world falls apart.

These are all dangerous, dangerous ideas. And yet if you don't conform to them, the danger is worse. Hana is on the verge of becoming someone that nobody can understand. Oh, I know how painful that can be. Once you start down that road, your loneliness compounds. It gets thicker and thicker. There's no escape. I remember so well Donald Buchanan. Donald, who told me at the junior prom that I was becoming "weird." No fun to be with, too headstrong for my own good. Little did he know all the headstrong women in my family. All the wild women no one could ride, who bit their fists their whole lives to keep from crying out, to keep from going after their idiot husbands with an axe. Manageable. Everyone wants everyone to be manageable, no fuss, no problem, predictable. If you're not, you get into trouble. Nobody wants to get into trouble. If you do, you're really nuts. Daddy was right. So right.

The Orthodox Body

[JOURNALS OF HANA NICHOLAS]
April Fool's Day, 1948

My nudity has now become an issue. Even George had the temerity to question me about my "sunbathing." What I do in the privacy of my own house and grounds is being looked upon as moral turpitude. I can't stand this! I just can't stand it. What has gotten into these people? My inner garden is completely secluded. No one can see me but God and the Muses. My sweat lodge is completely hidden from view. And no one can see into my house. Nola actually asked me if Lowell and I "nature bathe" together and if I'd taken him into the sweat lodge as I did her. These people have some aversion to the human body. I am so brown anyway that people would think I was wearing fur. Is this Dr. Barrows at work again? Do I ask them questions about how they live their lives? I find myself spending a great deal more time alone than I'm used to and much more time with my farmer acquaintances. I'm beginning to despise my academic friends. They've simply got to stop this asinine prying into my affairs. They do not understand the differences between the erotic and the sexual. They can't fathom the connections among the physical, the mortally spiritual, the joy of being an animal in the wild and the joy of being a civilized, fully developed, individual human being. In Nola's conversations lately, I'm hearing much more sexual gossip and rumoring—about everyone, even Lowell and Juliet, even Lowell and me, even the Devons, even Thea, for heaven's sake. What is Nola up to? Is Hal Barrows a secret Freudian? Nola's sounding like an inquisitor, like a witch finder general, rooting around in people's private lives. When I asked her about *her* "sex life," as she calls it, she was outraged. When I asked her what she thought about her body, she lost her composure and replied with blustery testiness that she respected hers more than I respected mine. I asked for those responses, of course, having questioned her in aggressive self-defense. Still, I am stunned by what's happened to her.

I've been going animal in my various gardens and houses for as long as I can remember. The first time my mother caught me nude in the apple orchard, I must have been ten, she was so kind and so generous. She worried about me hurting myself, but she never accused me of immorality or even impropriety. She just worked out an agreement with me that I could become an animal—that's what I called going without clothes—just as long as I knew where I was and that no one could or would see me. I've always been scrupulous about that. But in victorious America, a nude old woman walking around in her garden is a sign of subversion. What would Artemis think? Would she set the dogs on them?

Responsibilities and Faith

June 9, 1948

I am my brother's keeper. Whenever I shirk my responsibility to help others, I lose my self-respect. I lose my way toward the Father. I stop hearing his voice rise out of the Book. I become deaf to him. Hana is always arguing with me that the voice Socrates heard told him only *not* to do certain things. It was the voice of restraint, she said. But God gives us a full rule book. Everything we need to know is there. I feel a childlike certainty about that, an innocent sureness I love beyond speaking. Everything we need to know about being good and therefore happy is in the Book. Perhaps not literally. But by implication. How could it be otherwise? If life was as complicated as Hana makes it out to be, no one would be able to live it! They'd just become like sleepy puppies and curl up and forget they are alive.

I am terribly torn, terribly. I know that I am my brother's keeper. That is the rule. To love my neighbor as myself. Nothing could be clearer. That's not the advice of restraint, but an admonition to action. But how do I do that without trampling on another person's freedom? Their freedom to make choices, their God-given free will? How do I know when it is right to take charge? It's so simple when people are hungry or in need of warmth. You feed them and give them clothes. But what do you do when someone is in jeopardy of committing heresy? And is it their own free choice to do so? Do I even believe in heresy? I must. If I believe the Book is right, then I must believe all else is wrong. And yet that doesn't make sense to me. Hana has a point. How can everyone else be wrong? How can the whole rest of the world be in a state of helpless heresy?

I am certain about this: To be my brothers' keeper, I am obliged to care for them when they are sick and needy. But am I obliged to do that if *they* don't think they are ill and in need of help? When do I trust my judgment *over* theirs? One does that all the time with children and pets and mad people, and people too immobilized by disease to make a clear decision. When do I intervene? I must try to think this through more clearly. I wish mother was alive. I have no priest or pastor. I'm a modern intellectual. I can't really talk to Hana about it, either. She denies the need for intervention except in situations that to her are without question—someone is sick, wounded, starving, or about to be persecuted. The rest of the time, one must work to make the conditions of life so good that sickness and misery are less and less likely to occur. A nice theory. But childish. The world is beyond our control. We must let it go. And work for the souls who inhabit its brutal illusions. I can't talk to Hana. Thea does not ever wish to speak of religion. Juliet is an atheist. George and Betty are preoccupied. Hal is a scientist, but at least he understands about caretaking, about when illness is real and not. Or at least he thinks he does. He is such an obliging man. Every pain I have he wants to cure forever.

The Vulnerable Hibernations

Hana's interest in Lowell's life made him feel so important, so useful, confident, and strong that his hours at Gloriamaris had become the only time during the week that he felt truly alive. He hadn't missed a single weekly meeting with Hana for more than half a year. So when an acute case of hay fever kept him from school, it filled him with feelings of worry that Hana would think he'd forgotten her. As soon as the stupor of congestion had lifted he went to Gloriamaris to explain what had happened, completely forgetting Hana's admonition about no unscheduled visits.

There was something pale and frozen about Gloriamaris that afternoon, as if it had been lined with wax paper, hermetically sealed, with all life suspended. Lowell knocked on the thick front door for more than three minutes with no response and began to imagine horrible scenarios. But when the door finally opened, it wasn't an angry Hana who greeted him, it was Nola. She was the last person Lowell would have imagined at Gloriamaris. He didn't know what to make of it; she was a total non sequitur. His shock was converted rapidly to intense anxiety and he all but demanded that Nola tell him where Hana was, what was wrong, and why she was there.

In a voice that was at once demeaning and consoling, Nola explained that Hana had been "severely stricken" and was "very ill and ghastly."

"But you mustn't worry, Lowell. I've been here day and night since the beginning of the week."

Lowell was terrified that Hana might be dying, or murdered, or worse—as his panicky imagination might have it—and insisted he be allowed to see her. When Nola refused, Lowell raised his voice. They argued for several minutes until they were interrupted by a desperate little voice from far away, saying "Let him in, let him in, for heaven sakes, I can see him. Let him in." In triumph, Lowell brushed Nola aside and ran down the corridor in the direction of Hana's voice. Electric lights were on all over the house, bare bulbs glaring in every corner, the dark mysteries of Gloriamaris stripped naked by the cruel presumption of the light. The walls and paintings were dusty and cobwebs looped from the ceilings. There was a strange smell of herbs and disinfectant.

Lowell had never gone all the way down the corridor before and had no idea where Hana's bedroom was, but she kept calling out to him softly and he followed her voice, with Nola right behind him, to a small room at the back of the house, dominated by a large window whose curtains were pulled tight. For someone who had only seen Hana in the peak of health, the vision that greeted Lowell was imponderable. Hana was propped up like a dummy on some pillows in a small four-poster bed opposite the big window. Her face was frozen in a gray and flaccid scowl, drained of all vitality, a dead face in an open coffin without benefit of the mortician's rouge and stuffing. She looked as dispirited as a prisoner until Lowell walked into the room. The instant she saw him her face began to thaw and in a matter of moments it was smiling, brown, alive, and strong again.

It's hard to describe what happened next. Nola and Hana threw themselves into a strenuous argument that began when Hana asked Lowell to open the curtains so she could see her garden and fields. Nola was indignant and expressed her "disappointment" in Hana's "childish ingratitude" and disregard for her "prescription of secluded, shaded rest. You know how you need peace and quiet, dear." Finally, Hana refused to put up with any more of it, threw off her covers, stood up in her enormous linen nightshirt, and in the nicest possible way told Nola to leave, reassuring her that she'd be "just fine now." Then, completely unwittingly, Hana sealed Lowell's fate by asking him to show Nola to the door. He did as he was told. Nola was blue with anger and stalked down the corridor faster than Lowell could walk. But when she reached the door, she turned and smiled saying, "You'd better go home soon. If anything happens, come and get me, darling; don't worry, I'll drop everything and come right back. Hana just isn't herself right now. Pay no attention to her, Lowell," she said striding across the front patio to the big gate. "Take her with a grain of salt. She doesn't mean to be cruel, she really doesn't."

When Lowell returned to Hana's bedroom, he found her seated on the edge of a big chair, wrapped in an Afghan, looking a bit like Lord Byron after a long swim—exhilarated, but relieved. She could see that Lowell was agitated, confused, and frightened, and that he needed some answers and reassurance right away.

"We've both been sick, haven't we, you and I?" she said. "And look what it's done. We've missed our meeting and made an enemy in the process . . . well, not exactly an enemy. I've been sick by opinion and

I bet you've been sick by convenience, tricking Juliet, no doubt, to keep you out of school."

Lowell, frowned and said, "No, I couldn't breathe very well. I was wheezing, ya' know. I'd never miss a meeting."

"Oh, I know, Lowell. I know. I'm just being sour." Hana explained to Lowell that for three days, Nola had been accomplishing a "feat of psychological capture." She had a hard time explaining what she meant, but said that in essence she had gone on "a retreat, a journey of transcendence," in which her metabolism was slowed to almost a stop, and all her attention was directed on inward things. "I do this quite a lot, for short periods of time. I'm sure you don't know what I'm talking about, but let's just call it an intense kind of prayer that I have to do and want to do all alone." In such a state, she likened her mind to two rooms, connected by a tiny corridor. She lived most of her life in the front room, she told him, but on retreats she went into the back room, "the outback" of her mind, as she put it. It was there that "God germinates and comes to visit his garden."

All her energy was diverted from the physical world, she said, and she became totally vulnerable to intrusion. Usually she took every precaution to protect herself and her privacy. But this time she was "so mightily consumed by the inward journey" that she was "literally carried away, transported from consciousness," before she had a chance to secure herself from the world.

Nola, it seems, had stopped by three days ago for an uninvited cup of tea and had found Hana's door unlocked, and Hana in a seemingly unconscious state, upright in a big chair in the thinking room. Nola had judged Hana deathly sick, and, Hana told Lowell, "began nursing me back to health, out of the goodness of her heart. But I was helpless to stop her intrusion. It was like a nightmare," she said. "I knew what was happening. She was in my house, rearranging things, looking at everything, prying into nooks and crannies. Not only was I distracted from my concentration, I was also inert and unable to affect anything."

When Hana reached the back room of her mind, she told him, her "spirit swelled, nourished on the sustenance of higher things," and she couldn't "return to the front room because the passageway is too small." A lengthy time of "secularization" was needed for her to "shrink back to normal size and normal occupation."

Hana praised Lowell lavishly, saying that he had rescued her. "I heard your voice and it melted the barrier of timidity that the soft spirit without its worldly shell must build. I'd been clawing at the corridor, like a mole in a cave-in, and when I heard you so close to me, it gave me the hope and energy to burst right through. You've been my savior, and I shall not forget it."

From Lowell Briscoe's "A Nest of Hells."

In The Lair of the Devil

[JOURNALS OF HANA NICHOLAS]
23 June 1948

I wonder how I would have held up in a Nazi concentration camp. Could I have endured it with dignity? With sanity? With my faith intact? I ran into B. Bettelheim's *The Individual and Mass Behavior in Extreme Situations* in Zimmerman Library yesterday. It described, in part, how he kept sane by observing the horrors around him with something of a detached, or clinical, perspective. An admirable project, but not one for me, I think. Dignity, sanity, faith. The Nazis startled us so terribly because we had no idea that lurking right under the grass in our backyards, right under the sidewalks in our town, right in the closet behind the lecterns in our little churches, right there, so close, so invisible, was the lair of the devil. Open one window, allow one fury or frustration to go unchecked and the entire world is transformed instantly from coddling coziness and sweet books of virtues over high teas into the devil's excrement, the mire of Hell, without so much as a click of the fingers.

All of us know that hell is all around us. When will it find its way here? Sanity. Dignity. Faith. How do you stand that, the suspense, the incredulousness at undeserved tranquility, with the knowledge that some trigger, some tripwire exists somewhere that would switch the mirrors of reality? How do you cope? When all your life you have lived as if slippers and warm robes and hot porridge were the natural rights of the body, the body's due?

Faith. Sanity. Dignity. I think I would lose my faith immediately in a concentration camp . . . and spend what little time I had left scratching my eyes out trying to find it again. I think I'd go insane. And what is dignity on the gallows, anyway? Not complaining? Being poised? Showing no fear? Being a mere object for them to destroy. I'd much rather give them something to think about. I'd rather speechify about freedom so much they'd have to gag me. I'd rather try to kill a guard than be hoisted up by my neck like a gurgling pig.

Why am I thinking about this? For very good reasons. You can't avoid it; the truth is everywhere you look. Last week, Nick Archuleta's nephew Ruben was shot by the police across town on the edge of Martineztown. Nick told me they had stopped Ruben on the street for looking "suspicious." They could do that to any of us at any time. Could they? Or am I just getting "hysterical?"

Why didn't more Jews leave Germany? Couldn't they see what was happening? Or were they just so sweetly moral themselves they couldn't believe the devil was so close by? Could the sheriff shoot me? Of course he could, if I were Spanish or Indian and male in the wrong place at the wrong time. Would they shoot me, though? A white old gal, odd, but grandmotherly? Something tells me they probably wouldn't, but something else tells me that they probably wouldn't have to. They could just slip me quietly into a box and send me on to my maker the slow way.

This is preposterous. Stop it, Hana!

Preposterous but not completely untrue. We just don't want to think the devil is there behind the two-way mirror watching and waiting.

The Mask of Odysseus

[JOURNALS OF LOWELL BRISCOE]
July 6, 1993

What caused me to bring such intensity to Hana's Christmas play was, as might seem obvious, my adoration of the author and my intuition that she was right about the wearing of masks. You wear the right one long enough, you eventually become what it means and represents. Not that I have become Odysseus, of course. But I am certainly wily and I *have* survived. So, something must have made it through my bunker skull.

I also realized in those days, I think, that the play was more than "just a play" as far as Hana was concerned, it was more than even creative fun, more perhaps than a gesture of faith and charity. For her, and then for me, the play had magical properties. She intended it to be, I think, a rite of initiation, a transformative event. Something inexplicable happened to me while I worked with her to create my character and give life to the situation she'd created in the play. In pretending to be something I was not, I became who I am. That was the essence of the Christmas miracle in the winter of 1948. We were all in danger that year. I sensed it; I didn't need Hana to tell me. Something was about to fall apart, some straw was about to drop and crack the camel's back. The sense of urgency was almost unbearable at times during rehearsals. Hana was never tyrannical but her fervor was sometimes too great a charge of energy for me to cope with. It burned me out. I'd find myself so exhausted that I'd fall asleep waiting for her to close up the Kiva.

Who can say what the source of the play's magical power really was? It makes sense to me, though, that when you have to resort to magic, things have gotten pretty bad. Magic is the technology of the helpless. And if my sense of things is accurate, Hana's despair and apprehension were far greater than she ever displayed. She must have had some sort of presentiment. This has to be what happens in extreme situations, even if their extremity is completely internal. Hana might have been on the verge of achieving a highly sophisticated form of sanity that appears as a kind of simplicity, an unshakable innocence. But the quest for sanity is a burning ladder, a holy ordeal to undergo and eventually to overcome in the sheer joy of living without fear. Most of us live out our lives shriveled up on the bottom rungs with madness lapping at our heels. Hana was at the top, beckoning us to climb as fast as we could to join her. By performing the Christmas play, I think she believed that some of its clarity would rub off on the world. And there is no doubt that it did change me. But I can't remember more than a few of the opening lines. She passed her message on to me like a shaman to her student. I knew it by heart. She whispered great secrets into my ear, and I have forgotten the magic words, the formulas, she used.

This entry was written during the preliminary work before the trial of the Normandy Four in 1993.

"I Told Her Phooey."

[JOURNALS OF HANA NICHOLAS]
18 March 1949

I don't know what to make of this. Nola told me the other day that she thought there was something "wrong, seriously wrong" about Juliet's relationship with Lowell, and that if she could "do something about it" she'd "see to it" that Lowell be placed in a foster home. She admitted, of course, that it was no business of hers, but she said she couldn't stand to watch "that libertine destroy the moral fiber of a little boy." When I asked her to be specific, she said to me that I must be sensing something wrong too. She likes to do that, get someone into a conspiratorial huddle and see what develops. When I told her that I'd sensed nothing wrong and then asked her what she knew and how she knew it, she replied that it was their hostility to each other "one minute" and their "embarrassing affection the next" that had her worried. She said it was a sign of "a sick relationship." I told her "phooey." She looked hurt. Everything that isn't peaches and cream isn't "sick," I said. Look at us, we're always off and on. Is that any reason to want to ship us off to a foster home? I asked her. And she mumbled something about it being "just wishful thinking."

I don't really understand what's happened to Nola. She's beginning to fixate on the normal. Anything that doesn't match her template of what's right and proper is somehow "sick." Life is becoming a box of chocolates for Nola: if some are missing, or if someone nibbled the edge of one of her nuggets, it's a sign of corruption and "morbidity." She told me the other day that society itself had become "infected" with wrong thinking, with promiscuity, with collectivism, and even "communism," and that if we're not careful soon we'll all be feverish with the same "sickness and rebellion" and "subversion." What any of this has to do with Juliet and Lowell, I'm not sure. They do have an unconventional "family." Juliet is very high strung. She does imbibe. She's not a maternal soul. Lowell could be called a misfit, but then so could I. So could Nola.

I wonder if this has anything to do with Dr. Hal. I wonder if he puts ideas in Nola's mind about the Briscoes. He seems so eager to find something wrong with people. He's so concerned with their tiniest aches and pains. I find him odious beyond belief. "Dr. Hal" probably thinks Juliet is corrupting Lowell with drink. It's entirely possible, of course. But I know Lowell too well. There's nothing wrong with him that some sympathy, some attention, some sanity won't cure. Juliet is not a bad person. She is often on the edge of breaking down, though. I know that's true. Her troubles are so terrible and her fears so huge.

I don't know when Nola met Dr. Harold Barrows. I think they might be going out together. He is a very strange, prying little fellow, as I've observed many times before. He's too snoopy, almost a Peeping Tom, too curious, too much like a moral policeman. He's like a burglar casing the joint, he's always casing people, looking for what he can get. He reminds me of news photos of Heinrich Himmler, without the moustache. That's being unfair, except every time I see him I want to laugh at the thought of him in leather short pants and a Tyrolean hat. Dr. Hal is so fastidious, annoyingly tidy. You get the feeling he keeps records like a Nazi. He's the kind of physician who lectures patients on general principles without really understanding what their lives are actually like. I must remember too that he's very rich and very interested in land.

I just don't like him. I think he's sinister. Nola likes to bake cakes and cookies. She's taken to quoting him fairly often, ominous platitudes about cleanliness, right thinking, and capitalism. It's really quite preposterous. It really is. A year or so ago, Dr. Hal did not exist. Now he's offering to help Thea with her poor toes and esophageal spasms, and George and Betty with their sore backs, and he even offered to "look into" my various little moles and age spots to see if "we could clean up your complexion." My God! My complexion! He blames my wrinkled face not on character but on too much sun. . . .

PART SIX

The Turning

The Riot of 1992
"You're Certifiable"

"Look, I don't care how important this is, I can't tell you what I can't remember. I can't just take your word for it that these kids are guilty and fake it, just to make it easier for you, or just to get them put away."

"We're asking you to do no such thing, Dr. Briscoe, you know that," District Attorney Cates said, indignant at Lowell's air of ethical superiority.

"Then why are you badgering me? Why are you complaining that I'm not cooperating? Why are you implying all the time that I'm holding out on you?"

"Dr. Briscoe, that's all in your mind. We're just trying to help you remember, help you organize your thoughts. I'm sorry if you feel pressured." Cates was beginning to sound antagonistic.

"Yeah, I bet you are."

"Come on, Dr. Briscoe."

"Don't use that tone of voice with me. You've been cross-examining me. You're treating me like a hostile witness. Right from the start, you've suspected me, you've antagonized me, you've treated me like a rape victim, as if I were somehow responsible for what happened to me."

"That's grossly unfair, Dr. Briscoe. You're sounding a bit paranoid, don't you think.?

"God damn it, man, don't go psychoanalyzing me. Who do you think you are?! I'm trying to be as helpful as I possibly can. I'm just not functioning as well as I might. How do you think you'd react to being beaten half to death by a mob?"

"Bullshit!" Cates exploded. "That's not the point. You've just dragged your feet at every opportunity. You've got to recover sometime! You've never given us a straight answer. Where's your common sense? You're unstable, you're undependable. And I don't think it has anything to do with the beating. Trying to build a case from your testimony is like trying to build a house out of sand. I don't think you want those fuckers to go to jail at all, for some weird, sick reason that I'll never understand."

"Sick? Weird? Sick?! Weird?! SICK!? WEIRD!?" Lowell shouted louder and louder.

"That's what I said! You're Goddamn certifiable. I can't tell what kind of Goddamn crap you're going to say next. You're nutso, Doctor, just nutso. You're just not normal. I don't care how fucking famous you are, how 'beloved' you are by the fucking 'children of the world.' I think you're a creep. I'm just trying to get you justice here." Cates was yelling hysterically.

Lowell could feel an urgent, gurgling release rumbling through him, an emotional constipation just about to break loose and flood the room. He jumped up and, as loud as he could, screamed in Cates's face, "Certifiable!? Certifiable!? I'll cut your fucking heart out, you miserable fucking pinhead! You're the fucking nut case! You're crazy as a Goddamn Nazi, you sadistic bastard, you're not going to put me away!" Lowell glowered at him, practically baring his teeth, and was on the verge of lunging across the table when he felt an amazing calm overwhelm him, the sweet comfort of comprehension. It coated the inside of his head and body with a warm soft light. Why should he care what Cates thought of him? Why should anything matter now? Cates's outburst made him know he was in control of the situation, not Cates or anyone else. These were mere functionaries. They were not angels of retribution in a tragedy he'd dreaded all his life. Knowing that made him feel as if he were walking in a cool meadow at twilight. No one could do anything to him. They needed him. He was indispensable. He had done nothing wrong. No one was out to get him. And he didn't care what the courts could or could not do to avenge him. His rage was personal, his urge to vengeance was personal. And as far as that red-headed bow-tied D.A. Cates was concerned, he was a non-entity, a servant who had asked him impertinently to raise his feet while he swept the floor.

"Briscoe! Don't you touch me, you crazy fucker! Don't you lay a hand on me! I'll charge you with assault and battery, you crazy bastard! Get outta here, get outta here!" Cates screamed in terror.

"What *are* you talking about?" Lowell asked quietly as his expression changed to one of detached serenity. "Are you all right? You're not getting sick, are you?"

"What? You sorry bastard, what are you doing?" Cates asked with an expression of horrified suspicion.

"I don't have any idea what you mean, Mr. Cates. Maybe you should sit down and cool off. Would you like a glass of water?"

Cates stood up, looked at Lowell as if he were a conjurer, and walked out of his own office petulantly, as if he were being sent to the cloak room by his second grade teacher. He reappeared ten minutes later with his hair combed and slightly damp. He looked refreshed and had, like Lowell, become ruthlessly smooth and settled.

"Now, Doctor Briscoe, could we return to those first moments when the mob approached you. If you close your eyes, does any face, anything recognizable at all, come to mind?"

From then on, the tension between the two men was not unlike the strain and jumpiness you might feel moving a cocked mouse trap into place under a sofa.

At Dr. Tuttle's that afternoon, Lowell said D.A. Cates was a "sociopath with no feelings for others. Calling me 'certifiable' pushed all my buttons, naturally. I practically jumped right out of my skin. He was terrified. I could see the fear harden under his skin like cold wax. I snarled at him like a baboon. I've hardly ever felt such hate, such terror."

"What did that remind you of?" Dr. Tuttle asked.

"It's obvious, isn't it? Hana, of course. But it was all unconscious at the time. It's like there's an invisible force field of past associations just below the surface of awareness that gets activated by the present, and that turns the present instantaneously into a living version of the past that has long ago ceased to exist all together."

"And the calm that came over you? What was that about, do you think?"

"I really have no idea, no rational idea, other than I'm a cunning devil, in full control of myself. It was the calm of an assassin. I really wanted to get even with him. I still do, to some extent, but without the fury. If I were myself thirty years ago, I might have thought it was Hana coming back, Athena-like, to temper my rage and keep my sword in its scabbard. The sensation of raging fury one second and complete calm the next really felt Homeric."

"I'm afraid I'm not up on my Homer."

"Well actually, it's pretty universally Greek. From Homer to Socrates, inner voices, goddesses, or daemons are forever counseling restraint, patience, planning."

"Good advice."

"Yes, indeed, but I worry about even needing such advice in the first place. I worry about being so angry, so prone to terrible rage. It frightens me. I frighten myself. Do you know what I mean?"

"Of course. But you've always remained in control of yourself, haven't you? That's one of your life-long patterns, if I've heard you correctly," Dr. Tuttle said reassuringly.

"Yes, I think I've never unleashed my anger completely. But I've often worried, as I've told you, that I might have a kind of rage-induced amnesia that allows me to be a Jekyll and Hyde without knowing it. When I say that in here in this room with you, it just sounds so fanciful, but I *have* woken up in sweats from terrible dreams in which I am tearing people apart, literally rending them."

"Can we talk about that some for a while?"

"Let's not."

What Must It Be Like?

[JOURNALS OF LOWELL BRISCOE]
Summer 1992

What must it be like to be someone wrongly accused of a crime, suffering the torment of hate and the threat of death at the hands of those who despise you without cause? What must it be like to be so utterly alone? So completely helpless? So absolutely without any outside comprehension of who you might really be? What must it have been like to be Leo Frank, innocent of any crime except being a Jew, standing with a noose around his neck, a handkerchief over his eyes, with all those righteous redneck bastards jeering at him just before they slowly pulled him off the Georgia ground to strangle him for a half an hour of their pleasure and satisfaction? What must it have been like to be the Scottsboro Boys facing trial after trial and whole lifetimes in prison for crimes they knew they never did? Or those men and women herded like cattle from the Warsaw Ghetto on the way to the gas chambers. What must it have been like to be Hana pulled from Gloriamaris in what she thought was an act of "diabolical murder?" And what about the so-called Normandy Four? What if I'm so messed up in my head that I *really* can't tell if they're the ones, I mean *really* can't? Do I have reasonable doubts? What if I'm insane? Can they be reasonable?

In The Foyer of Christmas, December 1948

It was snowing at last on the day of the performance, a sweet, heavy snow. The clouds seemed carved by a jeweler from polished blocks of concrete, the wind thick and warm. It was just the way it should be. The weather intensified the refuge of the Kiva.

Hana and Lowell had spent the morning together going over last-minute changes in staging, costuming themselves, cuing their lines, putting on make-up, and strutting around the Kiva taking deep breaths and puffing loudly to tone up their diaphragms "whence all actors live," as Hana said.

An hour before the audience was to arrive, Hana took Lowell's hand and they both knelt before the crèche. In her most melodious voice, smooth and sweet as hot apple cider, Hana prayed aloud, "Please help us to give our gift as gently and with as much free strength as you deserve. Please give Lowell his courage and me my focus. It is an honor to be alive. It is an honor to be who we are. Thank you."

When Hana and Lowell had finished with the candles, the Kiva glowed, Hana remarked, "as if illumined by a hat rack of halos." Lowell couldn't help laughing as they swept the floor, put fresh pine boughs over the portals, and dusted the shells and crystals and masks and bones in all the nichos in the walls.

Half an hour before the play was to begin, when the audience was about to arrive, Lowell was whisked off to his hiding place in Hana's bedroom, there to wait until exactly 4:45 when he would leave the main house, walk through the orchard that led to the Kiva, and present himself at the door, waiting for his cue.

The audience consisted of Juliet, Nola, Thea, George and Betty, a Mrs. Willcraft who was an expert on Shakespearian flora, and a Professor Williams who specialized in nineteenth-century German romantic poetry and was one of the few consistent recipients of Hana's writings. Several other older ladies, all Hana's friends from some time past, were also present, as were the Gallegos, whom Hana consulted from time to time on matters of Church history and the lives of the saints. Filling out the crowd were Mr. and Mrs. Archuleta and their five daughters, the Candelarias and their brood, the Contreras family, older members of the Chivera clan, and the stork-like, frail, but regal Grandmother Lucero, who was ninety-two and had come to all of Hana's Christmas plays since the first one in 1928. Grandmother Lucero appeared to take a contemplative delight in the fantasy and impossibility of Hana's moral and imaginary stories, as well as a doting pleasure in the courage of the various children who had starred in Hana's productions over the years. Theresa and Bruno Duran, proprietors of the Griegos Grocery down the way, came with their aging and enthusiastic friends the Anayas, who, as was their wont, greeted Hana's thanks for their presence with "We wouldn't dream of missing this, any more than we'd miss Los Pastores." Miss Cumberland was in the audience that day as well, a woman whom Juliet had described as a "missionary type lady" who was an officer in various charitable organizations and as such the only "official guest," Hana said. Miss Cumberland would be entrusted with the task of equitably distributing the proceeds from the play to the needy of the neighborhood.

The sound of the guests as they walked through the orchard to the Kiva was uncomfortably foreign to the insular calm of the gardens of Gloriamaris. Shy laughter, whispered gossip, the rustle of dresses, the clop of dress shoes and boots—it sounded disconcertingly like a funeral to Lowell, as if he were the corpse around which everyone was walking. Lowell could sense the uneasiness in Nola's voice in the distance that day, her round little voice, churchly and diffident, asking where Lowell was "hiding." The mere sound of his name coming from her lips set all Lowell's nerves on edge. The composure he'd so longed to achieve almost vanished with one motion of her jaws. But Hana had said he was not to think of the audience. He was not to think of pleasing them or of what their reaction might be to his performance. Hana had stressed that point over and over again in each of their rehearsals. "Give to them, but do not live for them. You must never forget yourself," she would tell him. "Play for yourself. What they think matters not, until you have given them something to think about. Allow nothing to make yourself slip your mind."

The chattering in the light snowy garden went on in the distance; the last footsteps Lowell heard, or thought he heard, were Hana's on the flagstone path. Lowell listened at the window for the final sound—

the great Kiva doors closing—and when it came, he knew the whole world was inside the warmth of their refuge with the fragrance of wax and pine and straw, dazzled by the lights sparkling from crystals and candles, protected from even the smooth, gray calm of winter twilight in the Valley.

The clock showed 4:44. Lowell placed the Odysseus mask over his face. It would take him a minute to walk from the bedroom, down the great corridor and into the kitchen. He arrived at the back door, took a deep breath, saw the clock on the stove move to 4:45, and stepped out into the gentle snowfall. Once he did, he was no longer himself. He was Odysseus the Kachina. He had become, for the moment, the best that Hana had thought he could be.

━ ━

From Lowell Briscoe's "A Nest of Hells."

"Great Star Mother, Athena, Weaver of Light"

Lowell stood outside the Kiva door. His great Odysseus the Kachina mask gave him a sense of power and anonymity. A gourd rattle in his left hand, turtle shells with pebbles tied behind his knees, feathers on his arms, and a leather kilt with a fox tail around his waist, Lowell had become a fusion of Athens and Hopi. As he collected himself and took deep breaths, he could see a tiny crack of light through one of the panels in the door. It was like a jolt of Benzedrine. He held himself perfectly still. Everything was hushed inside. Then almost automatically, he knocked four times, repeating the sacred incantation: Beauty, Work, Gratitude, Truth. The sound of his voice broke the stillness and the heavy door opened. He stood outlined in the snowy sky, a breeze picking up behind him, making the feathers dance on his arms. All heads turned when he entered the shimmering, candle-lit great room as the strong door closed mysteriously behind him. Strains of Beethoven's Ninth followed him as Odysseus the Kachina danced methodically to center stage, and then wheeled around to face the world of faces before him. As he spoke his first words, a blast of wind rattled through the frost-brittle cottonwoods outside.

I am Odysseus, Kachina supreme,
Ithaka's always right where I dream.
Nothing evades me, nothing can hide.
I find my way home, eyes open or blind.

As he spoke, the stage lighting changed abruptly to make it seem as if Odysseus had been locked away in a terrible, dark cave.

All life is a test
to see who's the best.
No cave can become
the home of the brave.
The grave swallows up
all who are dead;

habit and fear
make a grave of the head.

As the minutes unfolded the play to the audience, an amazing amalgam of local history, science, and Homer emerged. Odysseus the Kachina is suffering a "great captivity," locked away in a "horrible cave" by the "terrible, one-eyed, closed-minded Monsters of Atomic Mountain" at the ends of the earth on "Los Alamos Isle." The Odyssey of Hana was one of redemption rather than return. And in 1948, it must have seemed patriotically sacrilegious to some members of the audience when the heroic scientists were turned into remorseless monsters.

For Lowell, the sense of political impropriety was the last thing on his mind. For a little less than three quarters of an hour, he was the absolute ruler of the Kiva, the master of the evening. For those brief minutes, he lived without fear, without anger, without suspicion, and without fraud. In the mask of Odysseus, his majesty was compassion, and his rule was generosity. He gave to each member of the audience a glance, a gesture, some personal moment, donating to each a victory of theatricality, like a small sacrifice laid before their feet. What gorgeous moments! Lowell remembered them years later as one would recall the sweet savorings of a former life. In the darkness of his most desperate fantasies, he felt time after time that his real calling, his ideal vocation, was to be Odysseus, the cunning being who followed the Christmas Star home to Ithaka, who transformed the myopic Atomic Cyclopes into Kachinas of hope and hospitality. The comparison between that dream and Lowell's life helped to give him a self-deprecating charm, a sense of humor about himself that verged on sneering self-mockery but was redeemed always by the gentle forbearance he inevitably, at the last minute, directed toward others even in the heat of combat. Recalling Odysseus the Kachina as a former life gave Lowell if not a sense of superiority, then a kind of awkward dignity that even he didn't quite understand, though his friends and students, even some of his lovers, found it to be disarming and endearing.

About two thirds through the performance, during a battle between Odysseus the Kachina and the last of the Atomic Cyclopes, the voice of the Great Star Mother boomed out from behind the backdrop.

Jesus, the redeemer, had a hard job:
To lead us from sin, the course of the mob.

But God was His master, She led him to work,
an urge inconsistent from which he ne'er shirked.

Lowell's back was to the audience when the last lines were uttered, but when he heard footsteps he turned to see Nola striding contemptuously down the aisle, opening the great door, and slamming it shut with a gruesome clatter. As Odysseus, Lowell was ready to chase after her and bring the barbarian back to the fold. But the music rose up loud and deep to signal the next scene. Lowell's response was, by then, nearly instinctive and he wiped her departure from his mind. The rest of the crowd was shuffling and badly distracted, but the spell had not been broken. Lowell and Hana recaptured the mood deftly, carrying on the Odyssey across the Terrible Atomic Mountains to Ithaka, the reconstituted home of the infant Jesus. Lowell and Hana stood beside a tiny manger. The music began again; Hana flicked the flashlight on under the straw of the manger and a beam of light shot up across the ceiling, as if the star was in the Christ Child's heart instead of the sky. With that, the music ended and the Christmas play of 1948 had come to a close.

Hana removed her helmet and blew out the candles, the audience clapped politely, if somewhat slowly, and without great enthusiasm. Lowell experienced an instant, plunging depression. There should have been kettle drums; God himself should have descended and placed a laurel wreath around his head. The muttering applause was crushing. That the play was actually over made it even worse. It was over! Lowell was shaking with grief. He had never given a moment's thought to the fact that the play would actually end. But there he was suddenly metamorphosed back into his daily, painful little self. Juliet, right when Lowell needed it the most, broke the somber shuffling of hands, exclaiming "Oh, how beautiful, how beautiful! It is Christmas. Thank you, thank you blithe spirits!"

Hana had deliberately stepped out of character with the first applause and wrapped around herself the protective role of supreme hostess. She thanked her friends in the name of the "world's poor and hungry children" and announced that festivities would continue in the big house.

From Lowell Briscoe's "A Nest of Hells."

Après the Play

It was quite dark when Lowell and the audience stepped out of the Kiva into the feathering snow. Hana rushed ahead to ready the food and Lowell was left to pamper and guide the assembly to the big house. George Devon patted Lowell on the shoulder and told him he'd done a "really fine job." Juliet snuggled Lowell under her trench coat, smashing his cheek into a gold and emerald Christmas tree pinned to her bodice. "And you remembering all those lines, Lowell! How did you do it?" she said kissing the top of his head. Despite other kind words directed his way as they walked along, his depression was deepening. The secret play was no longer a secret. Everyone had seen it. And Lowell was just a little boy again. How he hated being who he was! He knew his performance deserved more than pats on the shoulder, but he could not lower himself to ask for more.

The group arrived at the kitchen door and were ushered in from the cold by Hana with Nola by her side. There was not a hint of any bad feelings between them. If anything, Nola looked a little sheepish. Inside the house there was the same glow that had been a spiritual radiance in the Kiva, but here it was a domestic warmth as sentimental as it was comforting. The Thinking Room was decorated with pine sprigs, red bows, and holly wreaths. The room smelled like a winter forest and a bakery shop. Tables were laden with cookies and breads and cakes and candies and fruits and bowls of nuts. Thea had baked and constructed one of her famous gingerbread houses, covered with gum drops, white icing, and jelly beans, with a Santa climbing into the chimney. In the corner was Hana's triumph, her "Children's tree." Lowell was drawn to it with such power that it all but absorbed his depression. He examined it inch by inch, ornament by ornament—the strings of rose hips and asparagus berries, the ropes of silver and gold tinsel, the glass balls, the angels, the glittering birds with real feathers, the pixies and elves, the little houses and tiny stockings, candy canes, and crowning the tree was a beneficent, smiling, rosy-cheeked angel, the most beautiful he had ever seen, made by Hana's own hands, with a child's innocent smile, deep glad eyes, golden wings, a halo, and a resplendently beaded blue gown.

Lowell's reveries by the tree were interrupted when Hana told the gathering that it was time to distribute the presents, saying, "for all of you who have given so generously as Magi to the children's Christmas fund, some token from my heart in your honor."

Hana picked presents to fulfill the needs, likes, and enthusiasms of each of her friends. She reasoned that it never hurt anyone to be, even for a moment, childlike in curiosity and anticipation. The more adults could empathize with children through their own excitement, the more children would be treated as real people rather than as "little machines forced to do their parent's bidding and live the dreams they could never fulfill," Hana was fond of saying.

The most surprising of Hana's gifts was the one she gave to Nola. Despite Hana's extreme displeasure in the pretensions of those who see fit to embellish the craftsmanship of nature, she had found for Nola a superbly ornamented Emperor's Helmet shell from the West Indian Ocean upon which appeared the full nativity scene carved in the intricate Neapolitan style. It was a masterpiece of its kind and one would have expected Nola to be more than superficially pleased, especially since she must have known how offensive the gift was to the giver. But Nola could only react with strained surprise and mock gratitude. Her theatrical and obvious discomfort reminded everyone in the room that she had stormed out of the performance and loudly slammed the door. When Hana gave the nativity shell to Nola, the spotlight for a moment was turned on her, and she could sense that everyone was perturbed and curious about what had set her off.

"Oh, Hana, dearest, what a splendid acknowledgment of Jesus and the Holy Family," Nola exclaimed with forced delight when she'd examined the present. "It's so like you, isn't it, to be munificent, legendary in your munificence, at Christmas. And what a gift you gave us with the . . . how should I call it? . . . the kachina play. I really feel embarrassed about it all and I apologize if I shattered the mood when I left. Let's just write it off to religious conviction. I don't want to say any more to spoil this festive occasion . . . but I was dismayed, I must admit, by the pagan and political qualities of the characters—the philosophical eccentricities, shall I say? But that's not a matter for a warm and jolly Christmas season, and I hope you'll forgive me and try to go on as if it never happened . . . although I'm sure a more fitting and innocent theme could well have been found. . . ."

Nola carried on this way, trying to avoid speaking her mind, but no one would change the subject, and as none of the people in the room would signify any recognition of what Nola was saying, her thoughts tripped over themselves in ever quickening succession, filling the silences of her friends' polite but unsatisfied curiosities. By the time anyone wanted to interrupt, Nola had built up quite a temper. It was unintentional on her part, and she would have given anything not to have done what she did, but as if by a chain reaction her voice grew louder, and even Thea's plaintive little "now, Nola, now," couldn't slow her down. Hana watched with a compassionate silence as Nola reached a crescendo, "We were tainted by politics, by propaganda," she mumbled loudly. "It will take me weeks and weeks to clean up my thinking, weeks and weeks."

The Thinking Room was deathly still. One could hear only Nola's heavy breathing. Nola sat down next to Juliet on the big couch, looked at everyone, and burst into tears, apologizing, beseeching Hana to forgive "this spectacle. I'm mortified. Why have I done this? Will you all ever forgive me?" She got up abruptly, took her present, gathered up her coat and purse, and without another word or expression ran down the corridor and out the front door.

Everyone stared at Hana and then walked over to her and hugged her and said how sorry they were that such a thing should have happened. But Hana dismissed it with a wave of her hand and, after pouring everyone another round of eggnog, gallantly toasted Nola's outburst with a "vivre la difference."

Hana might have fooled everyone else, but she didn't fool Lowell with her offhand chivalry. For the rest of the evening, Lowell could see at the edges of Hana's eyes that she was close to tears. When Christmas Eve was finally over, and Lowell and Juliet were leaving, Hana gave her "little Odysseus" a powerful and emphatic hug, whispering in his ear, "You were magnificent. I will never forget our night on the stage together."

<hr>

From Lowell Briscoe's "A Nest of Hells."

Detoxification

[JOURNALS OF LOWELL BRISCOE]

Hana must have been enraged and in a state of shock after Nola's self-righteous explosion following the play. I didn't see her for three or four weeks. When I went to Gloriamaris for my weekly visit, I was greeted by a curt little note on the door, asking all to forgive her but that she was "unavoidably indisposed." I felt abandoned. And Juliet began harping at me about spending too much time with Hana anyway, saying that I should "wean" myself from her.

Then in the Friday mail, a little note addressed to me in Hana's hand appeared. Juliet tried to hide it from me, but I saw it in the stacks of bills and letters and snatched it up. I still have it. It read:

> *Weary is the world*
> *without two sides at least;*
> *but weary is the man who knows*
> *both sides play for keeps.*
> *Now I'm at home again, and fresh and clean. Please come and see me*
> *   Saturday morning,*
> *usual time, if you can.*
> *Love, Hana*

When Hana opened the front door the next morning she was thinner and paler than I'd ever seen her, physically haggard and depleted, but almost aglow with an inner vigor and optimism. We spent almost the whole morning in the Thinking Room—now stripped of Christmas and altered back to its original dark and wizardish state, as if nothing of the holidays had ever happened there. We spoke of the play, what effects it had on me, and what had happened to Hana that would have kept us apart for almost a month. I can't remember what I told her about wearing the mask of Odysseus the Kachina, but I suspect it really did have an impact on me. Perhaps that is why I became so wily, so forceful and devious after Hana's disappearance.

When I asked her where she had been, her answer amounted, in so many words, to a declaration of war. Without ever directly mentioning Nola, Hana told me that she "too" needed weeks and weeks to "cleanse" herself after the turbulence of Christmas Eve, and that she had gone away into the "back room" of her mind to sort things out and nourish herself with the "vitality and potency offered to those who keep current their friendship with the universe," or words to that effect.

She had apparently fasted for a week, took what she called "dream travel" to the "shores of conviction" in the second week, and the last five or six days in "spinal meditation, wordlessly in touch with the intelligence surging across the emptiness between my atoms." Those aren't her words exactly, but that's the way she used to talk and the words I'll use to describe this event if I ever have time to finish the novel.

The intensity of her gaze, the crisp deliberateness of her words, focused my attention. This was a new Hana, a Hana whose substance was not at all disguised or metered out in doses she expected I could take. She was thinking full blast in my presence, as if I were her peer.

She said something like this:

"Some might say that I am obsessed with freedom. That liberty is my neurosis. But I am only now just learning what it means to be free. One must be unfree first." The lessons she had learned, she told me, while secluded with the "crude uncoded message of my spine" concerned her own "free feelings of hate." She had never allowed herself to acknowledge an enemy before, "not a person," she explained, but concepts, attitudes, views that might animate a person into actions contrary to the purpose and pleasure of the "Mighty All." She admitted that she'd finally allowed herself to acknowledge danger, to recognize "the forces of the lie" that live in the real world, to "demythologize" them, identify their "ministers and agents." She had never been afraid, never "philosophically wrathful" before, she said, considering such feelings to be a slight on the "omnipotence of beauty."

She told me, in effect, if I may mimic her, that "it was the Mass Mind, the workers of conformity, the treachery of Order at the cost of variety—these are the hoplites of the Lie." She had known this all before, she affirmed, but "on a different plane," one on which "redeeming fact" did not exist. The individual, she told me, is in danger of being crushed by a world that cannot accommodate surprise. She was adamant that the individual is the final and everlasting hope, and that there were centuries of struggle ahead before the human universe would come to accept the irreplaceable value of each human life.

In those three weeks, Hana had undergone a drastic "conversion to effort," as I think she would have put it. Before Little Christmas—and from what I can tell that was the decisive moment—Hana's faith was a given; there was no difference between faith and deed, no space between them. Now a space had become apparent. In a mundane sense, she said she'd become aware of her purpose (although, I am sorry to say, I'm not fully clear on what that might be). In any case, I realized that my relationship with Hana had been transformed. In retrospect, I can see that I became for her what a mute might be for a monarch: a silent ear. I was her only confidant, a partial one to be sure, during those final months. Through it all, I was mute with incomprehension and kept her secret safe.

What was her secret, I wonder. It might have been that she'd discovered the two spoilers of human life: appearance and evil. She'd seen a separation between her sense of being and who she appeared to be. And had understood that separation to be very dangerous, a space through which evil could slip and do terrible, cruel damage.

In the final analysis, I remain completely ignorant of Hana's state of mind, or her mental health, or the extent of her spiritual evolution during the early months of 1949. I'm just as puzzled today as I was as a kid.

"The Light Has Gone Out of Our Lives"

2 Feb

Juliet Dear,

I'm not in the habit, as you know, of dictating topics for our weekly talks and mental repasts. But I desperately want to discuss with you the assassination of Mahatma Gandhi. I say "desperately" because this catastrophe may be one of the turning points of my life. I have followed the Mahatma's achievements and philosophy since I first learned of him twenty years ago or so. I have read everything I could about him and have accumulated quite a file of clippings and transcriptions from books and articles. He *was* one of the great lights of the world. I need to understand why gentleness and kindness are greeted with suspicion, violence, and hatred. I understand why, I think, when it comes to human psychology—the Mahatma's assassin was a fanatic Hindu who loathed the Mahatma's open-mindedness and open-heartedness toward Muslims. That somehow makes sense to me. Small minds and small hearts are terrified by spirits that see through their smallness and try to join them with the bigness of everything else. They fear losing their identity, rather than embracing the opportunity to identify with a larger sphere. What I cannot, cannot understand is why, cosmically, such horrors must occur. What principle of the cosmos does Gandhi's assassination reflect? What principle of life does cruelty manifest? Is there some supernatural/natural law that says tenderness must be sacrificed? Why were Christ, Gandhi, and Socrates killed and Buddha and Mohammed spared?

I'm heartbroken, Juliet, by Gandhi's murder, really desolate. But the only way to survive such senselessness is to take it on and find some sense to it, if we can. Can we put this on the "menu" for next week's talk?

Love to you, dear friend and fellow adventurer,

(signed) H.

Letter from Hana Nicholas to Juliet Briscoe, 2 February 1948.

An Encounter with the Beast

Lowell left Gloriamaris one late February afternoon in a particularly buoyant mood, having spent time examining more of Hana's shells and listening to her read long passages from the *Song of Myself*, which he was surprised he understood. Lowell was walking down Griegos, heading home in the dusk, when a blond boy with big feet, freckles, and a nasty sneer stepped out from behind a bush and practically knocked him down. The boy confronted Lowell, telling him that he knew who he was and had seen him at "the ugly old witch's house" and that he must be some sort of "pansy ass" for spending so much time over there. Lowell had no idea why the boy was picking a fight with him, but, though ridden with terrors, when pressed passed a certain point, Lowell was at a loss to contain himself and prone to furious rages. The boy goaded him, hounded him, stepped on his heels, hit him hard on the shoulder as Lowell tried to walk away. But when he said more monstrous things about Hana, Lowell lost control and kicked him as hard as he could in the shin. The boy doubled over in pain, fell to the ground, held his leg and howled. Lowell pounced on him, hit him in the face with his fist, put his knees on the boy's biceps and hit him again.

"If you ever say another thing about that woman," Lowell yelled, unable to utter Hana's name in such company, "I'll gouge your eyes out." With that, the boy wiggled free one arm and threw a punch, which missed, and Lowell hit him directly in the nose; the boy shrieked in pain. Lowell lifted himself off the sobbing body, as one might dismount a dead horse, and casually walked away.

In a sense, that encounter was the beginning of the end. Lowell relished the violence of his victory, but was plagued by guilts and trepidations. He had really hurt that boy. He was intermittently terrorized by fantasies of being caught by the police, put into an orphanage for terrible kids or worse, ostracized by Hana. But his fantasies were mild when compared to the truth. That would-be bully turned out to be none other than Nola's beloved grandchild, who'd moved to town when his father was hired by the U.S. Air Force as a weapons consultant.

When Nola learned it was Lowell who had demolished her grandson, she reacted with an insane fury. There was mention of bringing charges against him, but the idea was dropped when Juliet explained that her brother had "been under a doctor's care for quite some time" and that she would do her best to restrain him in the future and would even take Lowell to a psychiatrist if Nola thought it fitting. But Juliet never made the appointment. Nola tried to get Juliet to promise her that Lowell would be kept from seeing Hana, too, but Juliet would not agree.

Going to Gloriamaris now became for Lowell like trying to get behind enemy lines. Lowell had to sneak down the back ditch as far away from Nola's property has he could. And Hana didn't let Lowell off the hook either.

"I know you did it for me, Lowell, and I'm sure Karl started it, but you must never do anything like that again. You've jeopardized me and our friendship. You must learn self-control."

Hana then proceeded to lecture Lowell with a harshness that astonished him. "You have two lives, Lowell, one is brilliant and kind, the other base and mean. You know I adore you, and you know that I will always take the bad with the good when it comes to you, but this time your mean side has almost undone me. You cannot imagine the encounter I had with Nola over this whole sorry business. The Lowell of Gloriamaris must defeat the angry Lowell as soundly as he defeated Karl Dasheller. The violent Lowell must be expunged; he is what stands in your way. Take him in hand, or he will destroy both you and me."

Lowell was mortified at first and beyond consolation that he should deserve such a dressing down from Hana.

"I'm saying this to you, Lowell, because you have a cruel streak, a fear that turns to violence, a cowardice that destroys. I tell you this because of all that you are to me and all that I have come to love."

"You're right about me, Hana," Lowell brooded. "Please don't hate me."

"Lowell, I could never hate you. It's the mark of friendship to overlook the faults of someone you care for. I don't like you sometimes, but I will always love you."

Lowell felt a surge of exhilaration. Hana knew exactly who he was; he could hide nothing from her. She knew the truth and was his friend in spite of it. His love for her at that moment was religious in intensity. It was an ardor that would never fade.

From Lowell Briscoe's "A Nest of Hells."

Who Do You Believe?

Sunday, May 5, 1949

A beautiful morning today. I feel so happy, so light. My worries have been brushed away by the bird song and the morning breezes. What grace to be relieved of burdens, to feel that old hurts are silly! The world is as it should be. Nothing could be clearer on a day like this.

I was so worried last night when I talked with Hal about Hana. He seems more convinced than ever that she is in need of some sort of psychiatric consultation, "for her own good," and "to take the burden off you," he told me. This morning, Hal seems preposterously nosy. Hana has always been a difficult person. We've never seen eye to eye. And she was always been standoffish more or less, off and on. What is in her best interests? What is in mine? To be treated with loving care; it's the same for everyone on earth. If you see a child about to touch a hot plate, you stop it. But Hana is not a child.

The question of "Who do you believe?" has come up repeatedly in my mind over these last months. This morning I feel steadfast in believing my own experience. Hana is acting more oddly than usual, but is it dangerously odd? I think not, not yet.

Hal asked me again about Hana's land, how many acres she had, when she bought it, how much it cost, its current value, etc. You'd think he coveted her holdings—if he weren't so smiley and oval faced. Honestly, he looks like a bushy-browed, graying ten-year-old sometimes.

What Hal said about Lowell Briscoe, however, still has me troubled. Hal thinks the Briscoe brat is verging on being dangerously psychotic. I'm still so vexed about his brutal treatment of poor, dear Karl. I come close to hating that child. Does Hana have a bad influence on him, and is her anger coming out through him, or is he just a perverse little demon that even she can't control? Can I legitimately intrude on Juliet's business? Does she need some help in taking care of him? Is he a danger to himself and to us? Is it my duty to intervene and straighten things out? Again, no. Unless my interests are directly challenged, I should just enjoy my mornings and let these people go their own ways. I gave Lowell a piece of my mind already. He won't attack Karl again. He fears me. I'm glad.

The Tutorial

The day after Hana had scolded Lowell for his cruelty to Nola's grandson Karl, she spent the afternoon tutoring him in the delicacies of human nature. She knew that Nola was taunting Lowell and that he hated her as intensely as she hated him, and that if Lowell was to be relieved of that hate, he would have to see into Nola and see himself from her point of view—and in a sense take her side.

In her usual way, Hana was working hard to see Nola in a different context; she had placed her in an abstract terrain and had commenced to deal with her not as a person but as a concept instead, a generality with albeit very specific qualities. She had transposed Nola onto an intellectual map, as a general might transpose a strategic position, the better to deal with it, having made it, for a while, stationary and predictable.

Hana spoke to Lowell in conspiratorial tones. She made him feel in league with her, as if he were being initiated into her most secret and valuable knowledge. But the Imp of the Perverse was lurking in that discussion too. Because Hana had managed to see Nola as existing on a "different plane," because she had codified her opinion of the woman and made her static, Hana had committed the general's greatest mistake. She had ceased to see the situation with Nola in terms of possibilities to be prepared for and had instead cast it all in the reality of probability, thereby leaving herself ultimately defenseless to the inevitable improbabilities of reality. Hana, of course, had no recognition, either, that she was involved in a war, or that she was required to be a general.

"Nola is not an evil person, Lowell. She is blighted, blighted with the terror of death. She has been flayed alive and relieved of her beauty by guilt long ago." Hana said that Nola saw "the world as being polluted by deviance, as being an Ideal continually tainted and insulted by everyone other than herself."

Nola had, Hana said with a whisper, "more likely than not set Karl upon you, herself, unknowingly of course, egging him on by her attitudes and disregard for you, by her feeling that she was on a crusade against this child of ill, which is yourself, dear Lowell."

Nola was a "perfectly sane, splendidly sweet grandmother," Hana told Lowell. She had "fulfilled her duty to her times," raised a family, tended her husband, found refuge in her God, performed her profession as a scholar and lecturer with admirable accomplishment, and sought to glorify her drudgery with a pristine and backbreaking set of standards. Nola was also, Hana warned, an empire builder, a conqueror who, to achieve the status of a rose pruner, had overcome all odds, including her husband's infidelities and her own reprehensible, and therefore deeply repressed, appetites. She was a master survivor, Hana said, and got what she wanted, when she wanted it and how.

Lowell sat there listening as if Hana were describing the remains of a creature so prodigious that it died of its own immensity. Fascinated, he nodded agreement with every word.

Then Hana said something Lowell found puzzling. "Nola is not to be feared as a person, Lowell. She can do us, or the world, no harm. She is but one short hair in an ocean of stubble, the stubble that grates eternally on joy. It is the stubble as a whole that must be feared."

"Nola alone," she told Lowell, "can do nothing but rant and be unpleasant and be a discomforting dread in the heart of a little boy. She is the Mass Mind, dear, but incapable of evil unless in a mob. So fear her not. We are safe. She is trapped like a fly in a bell jar feeding on leftovers, while the great feast is being prepared outside. She has the curiosity of a ground snail, but do not forget, Lowell, the courage of a centipede. She does not live in the world we inhabit. She sees only the surface of things. But she can crawl on us and cut us with her pincers if we don't keep out of her way. We, on the other hand," she added, "can see through, through into the teeming glories of variety."

Hana's face smiled with mock, sheepish pride, "She is safe in her jar, for she cannot see the feast. She is gobbling up the debris so fast she's panting and has misted the glass. She is safe, and we are safe *as long*," Hana stressed these words most sternly, "as long as she never sees again the slightest glimmer of what lies beyond her reach and understanding. *We must become invisible, Lowell.*" Hana was at once informing Lowell and pleading with him. She made him swear on their friendship that he would work diligently to become "unapparent."

Eager to please her, Lowell withdrew from his pocket the perfect circle stone Hana had given him and pledged on its "fearful symmetry" to do as she had asked. His use and mastery of such a phrase appeared to please Hana and he liked nothing more than to be the cause of some joy or relief for her. To say or do something that would cause her great, broad face to smile had become one of his principal occupations.

The longer Lowell knew Hana, the more beautiful her face became to him, the younger it seemed and the more predictable. He would wait for certain wrinkles to appear around her eyes, for a certain pressing together of her lips, the way her nose would rise ever so slightly when she was thinking about something he'd said. Her face became Lowell's medium; he toiled to bring out the desired effects. And he became a master of his craft; never a meeting passed when Hana's face and voice didn't at some point bathe him in admiration, didn't respond to him with smiles and affection, with her intimate civility.

By the end of their meeting that afternoon, Lowell understood what Hana was driving at, and it was he who suggested that they find a better way for him to come and go at Gloriamaris, some way that would not bring him directly into Nola's field of vision. They agreed upon a section of movable fence at the far south end of Hana's property, completely cut off from Nola's sight. They disguised the secret passage with honey-suckle vines growing all around, so other children and thieves wouldn't find it. When Lowell asked Hana if she would tell Juliet about the passageway, Hana replied, "Of course not. She's too old to know."

From Lowell Briscoe's "A Nest of Hells."

Rumor Flies

[JOURNALS OF HANA NICHOLAS]
17 April 1949

"Fama volat"—Virgil's phrase is so marvelously terse—"rumor flies." How that phrase governs my life these days! And then there's always Horace—*"sapere aude,"* dare to be wise—and the phrase that motivated Michelangelo—*"saper vedere,"* learn how to see. With rumor all around me, inciting friends to rash impertinence regarding my life, I really must, now more than ever, dare to be worldly wise enough to understand what I am seeing, and to learn how to see more. I really do feel I am under siege. I've been turned into an object of interest and suspicion and fear. This feels exactly as if I were an eccentric old woman in a small town, or someone who was too innovative and personally successful in a pueblo. The viciousness of the gossip is turning me into a witch or a dark power somehow. I'm becoming a Freudian demon, a "hysteric." That's what Dr. Hal thinks. His ignorance terrifies me. He knows nothing about human beings. He reduces everyone to a medical false front of a person. His background is East Coast provincial patrician, which comes with the inflated superiority of science. It leaves me gasping in amazement at its emptiness, bombast, and lethal naiveté. Ah—that's how to see him! He's a provincial missionary who has gone to the Plains tribes and presumes to know more about holiness than they do. Arrogant, stupid, invincibly self-righteous. How could I have fallen prey to such an idiot? At cocktails the other evening at Nola's, one of the few times this spring I've ventured out, Dr. Hal and I found ourselves admiring Nola's magnificent chief's blanket that we bought together at Chinle many years ago. I was explaining to him about the Navajo and their relationship to the Pueblos, when he said something like, "You've really escaped from the twentieth century, haven't you?" I was flummoxed by his comment and, as I dislike him inherently, I shot back, with anger in my voice, that it seemed to me he was escaping from the realities of New Mexico and the Southwest by constantly denigrating indigenous peoples as historical throwbacks, living now in the wrong place and at the wrong

time. I said this with a certain wry gentility, forming my words and thoughts almost sweetly. He replied that people who "sequester" themselves in "the provinces by choice" are "fooling themselves," for "real life" will not "just retreat in the face of their fantasies." "Life," he said, "is progressive; New Mexico is a museum, dead and preserved." I should have kept still, smiled, and turned the subject to something else. But instead I told him that the most provincial people I've ever met were city slickers who escape from pressures they cannot bear, colonize a rural area, and then have the temerity to criticize its culture and history as somehow lesser and more provincial than theirs. He looked at me fiercely and asked with accusative intensity if I were talking about him. I told him he could take it any way he liked. The next thing I knew he put his drink on the table, stared me straight in the eye and in a high, barely controlled voice, replied that I was becoming hysterical and paranoid about outsiders, that I was immaturely resistant to change, and that my "ostrich syndrome" would only cause me to become increasingly withdrawn and "neurotic, hiding in the past." I laughed at him and said that his amateur psychoanalysis was "charming if sweetly pathetic, like a ten-year-old who's angry at his mother for not letting him have the last word in a petty squabble." By now, Dr. Hal had gotten me very angry, and I was, I must admit, a little shaky with adrenaline, but very calm in appearance. Dr. Hall looked at me dismissively, and then abruptly took on a professional air, distanced himself, and looked at me as if I were a specimen. "Do you always become so verbally violent when you're challenged?" he asked me as if he were wearing a doctor's smock and a stethoscope. I replied by asking him if he always became aggressively professional every time he was challenged. He smiled at me and said softly to himself as he was turning away, "definitely beyond the bounds of acceptable behavior."

And that's exactly it, isn't it? I am, my whole way of life is, being questioned by Dr. Hal, and his protégée, Nola; they are squinting at me and there is a narrowing, a constricting of acceptable behavior in their eyes. Is this all preposterous? Am I having a nightmare? I really don't understand.

I have got to learn to see. I've just got to. I feel eerie, terrified. As if I had just stepped into a very, very slow pit of quicksand.

I think today I'll take a long drive, go Santo Domingo, where I'm welcomed with respect, and try to forget for a while his asininity.

"Unacceptable Behavior"

[DIARIES OF NOLA DASHELLER]
April 19, 1949

Hal told me the most astonishing thing. At cocktails the other night, Hana attacked him viciously, he said—no, he used the word "hysterically"—and no matter how hard he tried to disengage, the more vehement and outrageous she became. He told me that she might have had an "episode," a "psychotic episode." My God, is that possible? Hana seemed quite normal to me all evening. I noticed she and Hal were having a discussion. I thought they might finally have become friendly. But no. This is frightening. Now, I'm in the middle. Hal is furious, I know, but remains polite and courtly. And I'm sure Hana will tell me all about it in charming, philosophical detail. And I'll be left again trying to make sense of the senseless. Hal was so upset that he said at one point Hana should voluntarily submit to analysis by a colleague of his, or if not, that a court order might be required, "if she gets out of hand." He then said something about "unacceptable behavior," smiled, and changed the subject. Hana has a right to her opinions, surely. She's unconventional, even eccentric, and New Mexico makes her seem more abnormal than perhaps she really is. This is all getting out of hand. Hal has a terrible temper. I can see that now. And Hana provokes him any chance she gets. I wonder why she dislikes him so much. I am made wretched by all this bickering. Poor Hana, I'd better have a long talk with her about Hal. I wonder if she thinks Hal and I are. . . . I'll certainly be able to disabuse her of that. Jealous perhaps? Hana?

The Infamous Letter

29 April 1949

Dear Ones,

We've had some strong differences over the last year and I thought I'd write you all to tell you something about who I am these days, sharing with you my already ancient resolutions for this year that nears the halfway point in this century. I know some of you have expressed "concern" over the way I have been "acting," over the way I have been living my life, perhaps more reclusively than before in the history of our long friendships. Your concern has, from time to time, taken on what I consider an inappropriate diagnostic tone, as if my "behavior" was a "symptom" rather than a mere reality. Let me state the obvious, dear friends. My "behavior" is my own business. There is nothing more to be said. I am not an object of conjecture; I am not a set of aches and pains; I do not "exhibit" the clues of a malady. There is nothing more to be said. Nor am I in the throes of that dreaded subject, the Change; I am not undergoing hormonal depression; I have not been rendered maniacal by the supposed "change" in my "womanhood," to quote another dear friend of a dear friend of mine. There is nothing more to be said. I am not offering myself, out of my own concern, for diagnosis. As that is so, all speculation about me and my "behavior" is intrusive gossip. I do not want you, or your friends, or your physicians, to be "concerned" about me, as I am not, I repeat, not concerned about myself—in any other way than my normal concern for my development as a free person, in charge of herself and her life. There is nothing more to be said. I am not on "the brink" of a "collapse," or of anything as sinister and flamboyant as a "crushing depression." I am gestating new ideas, new hopes, new possibilities, which I will share with you in my own good time. There is nothing more to be said. Please, please do not confuse your loving concern for me with my reality; please do not replace me, the person you have known so well, with your suspicious worries about me. Please do not replace me with your worries about yourself, disguised as worries about me. Worry about yourselves, if you need to. I will, as always, take good care of myself. There is really nothing more to be said.

As you know, I am perfectly capable of caring for myself and for you, if necessary. We all are deputized by the Goodness of the Universe to look out for ourselves in the absence of a credible personal God figure, to care for ourselves and for all others. Bring me your worries, if you need to, but do not bring me your worries about me.

I ask you to promise me four things:

1. You will not meddle in my affairs and substitute your gossip about me for my own knowledge of who I am. In other words, you will believe me.

2. You will stop talking about me among yourselves and with acquaintances, especially those in the medical profession.

3. You will listen to me when I have something new to tell you from this period of gestation. And that you will not interrupt me by imposing your opinions upon me until I am through. And if you don't agree with me, you will let me be and not employ SS tactics and police state methods against me. Really, dears, all this meddling and sniping is vicious.

Do stop it!

4. You will look to your own problems, your own fears, your own concerns about yourselves, your own "oddnesses" and "preoccupations," and "seeming obsessions," to use words and phrases used recently about me. Please, concern yourselves with yourselves. "Know thyself," has always been the first commandment.

I love you all very much, as you know. Please, please do not cast a net of worry around me. I do not want to have to break the knots and escape for good. I cherish you all too much for that.

Your long loving and devoted friend,

(signed) Hana

Preventive Measures

May 1, 1949

I showed Hal Hana's infamous letter today. He read it with what he called "bemusement." "I'm always somewhat taken aback when I meet face to face a person who actually suffers from delusions of grandeur," he told me. He went on saying how unusual and "pathetic" it was to see someone of Hana's "bearing" and "profound moral character" begin to slip into what I think he termed "mental recklessness." Hana surely does have delusions. Hal's right. "Police state," "SS tactics"— is that kind of accusation sane? How can she turn the most genuine sentiments of concern into the most tawdry of accusations? She's not in her right mind.

But why don't I question my own motives? Why do I assume it is her? Am I a meddling so-and-so? I've asked these questions over and over for months now. Am I going slightly wonky in the head myself? But isn't it our duty, our absolute duty, to yell a sharp warning to someone who's about to step into an open manhole? Isn't it our duty to take preventive measures? What if you saw your best friend walking down the railroad tracks with a train a quarter of a mile away? Wouldn't you do everything in your power to get her off the tracks, even if you had to use violence as a last resort? But what if the train is a mirage? What if she just wants to be left alone? What if Hana thought I was in trouble and thought she should take preventive measures? What would she do? And what if I didn't want her help? What if I thought she was meddling in my affairs and it was none of her business? Would I be furious at the intrusion? Yes, I would. But what if I were insane? And didn't know it? Who would be right then? How do we know these things? What is right? What is the right thing to do? I am so confused. But I cannot abandon my responsibility. What if Hal is right? What if he prescribes her a period of rest and observation? He could do it. But would she agree? Of course not. Absolutely not. She would never agree to such a thing. She would see it as a gross impertinence. She would resist it with all her might. But is that the sane thing to do? Would that be in her own best interests? Don't you just have to, sometimes, do what's best even if others condemn you for being wrong? Isn't that what being moral implies—a sense of obligation to the right, no matter what you feel or how much it pains you, or the people you love.

I'm coming to a dreadful moral decision. I'm not there yet. But I am approaching it. There may come a day when I must do what is right for Hana, no matter how much it pains me to cause her TEMPORARY suffering. It might just have to be the burden I must bear.

Still, the basic question is, Is my judgment to be trusted? Not alone. I must confer with Hal and the others. We must concur. . . .

The Incident of the Police

[Diaries of Nola Dasheller]
May 15, 1949

I was stunned. Hana was completely immobilized. It was just a traffic stop. She'd apparently made a rolling stop at a stop sign. But the police officer just scared the wits out of her. It was as if she were an escapee who'd been suddenly caught. I had to handle the officer all by myself. I'm sure if I hadn't, Hana would have been in a lot of trouble. He might have thought she was drunk or having a hysterical fit—what did Hal call it, a psychotic seizure?

Hana came by yesterday trying to explain herself and actually told me that she did sometimes feel "a little at odds" with reality, that she experienced "projections from the past," she said, referring to Dr. Jung. I must ask Hal about his ideas. Hana asked me if I didn't from time to time slip into the past and lose touch a bit. I think she was seeking reassurance that she wasn't going crazy. I humored her and told her of course, we all feel that way sometimes. But I never have, and I am sure most of us haven't disconnected from reality even once in their lives, except perhaps as children who believe nightmares are real, or that ghosts are living under the bed. I really do not like what I am seeing here. In all these years, Hana has never behaved in this way in my presence. The last year or so she seems very different. Is it Lowell Briscoe? Is she going through menopause at last? Is she having a breakdown? Is Hal right about her needing a rest and some "clinical help?" I think he must be. He must be. Menopause is a terrible thing. It unsettles so many. To be suddenly barren. And it's worse for Hana; she's never had children. Her hormonal system must be drying up in horrible ways. And if you're odd to begin with, or even a little different, it just exaggerates the problem. A good rest always helps. . . .

Lives Like Compost

Lowell had learned of Hana's encounter with the police from Juliet. She told him that Hana had almost had a "nervous breakdown." He wasn't sure what that meant, exactly, but when Lowell asked Hana if she was all right the following day, Hana replied, "Oh, you mean about the police? Of course. I'm just fine. There was nothing to it. It's happened before. It's just that I never had a gossip in the car with me. Nola told Juliet, am I right? Of course I am. Perhaps I should explain."

Lowell felt relieved. But then Hana launched off into a monologue that left him if not exactly shaken then uncomfortably perplexed.

"I am more afraid than even you are, Lowell. I am more alone than you and more vulnerable and weak."

"No you're not, Hana. How could you be? Besides, you said there was nothing to worry about."

"Nothing now, Lowell. But the future is growing from the pit of the present. The now is a slimy mire and our lives are like so much compost. I have spent all my life trying to learn to be a willing helper, but I cannot, it seems, learn to like being a rotting leaf eaten by other leaves around me. I don't like being compost. I'm terrified of it."

"What do you mean? What does that have to do with the police?"

"I'll try to make it clear. All of us go into the compost that feeds the future. Each of us is duty bound to develop in herself sufficient nutrients—developing our minds, our imaginations, our souls, our ability to love—so our slaughter will bring the compost worthy ingredients. But, oh, Lowell, how I abhor the slaughter and the slaughterer. For most of us, the slaughterer is our own bodies and disease, for some it is politics, for others it is convention and the law, and for the very few the slaughterer is the fever of divinity, the passion, the calling to feed the garden of God, to supply him with humble grain, at his request."

Hana's voice was as calm and steady as if she were telling Lowell how to change a bicycle tire. "That is what planets are, Lowell. Gardens, spiritual fields from which God and the future nourish themselves. The slaughterer will not be my body, Lowell, I don't think, nor my calling, as I really have none. I will be slaughtered by my time, and that is why I sometimes get so afraid. I see the slaughterer coming in his nice blue uniform. And I ask myself, Is this the moment my special life has come to? Has God fattened me up already? Could it be he would surprise me so? I know there is a purpose for us all, Lowell, and I know the purpose is to nourish change. But I love the present so much. The present needs me as much as the future does. I could live on forever, Lowell, and never be emptied of the joy I feel for my life and the life around me."

Hana smiled. Lowell waited for some sign that she wanted to do something else. But she continued. "I am not afraid of dying, only of being unspent, of going full, of being taken before I am through, of being raped by time. Fear is my great weakness too, Lowell. Dread is the ugliness that mars me. Once it was so big in my life, it almost consumed me. But then I came to New Mexico. I have whittled it down all these years, shrunk it until now it's only a pinprick, and some day I will drive fear from my life altogether."

Lowell spent most of that evening huddled in the back of his closet at Juliet's house, trying to piece together in some coherent way Hana's confession of fear. It astonished him. It made him love her and want to protect her all the more. He felt a kinship with her of such aching intensity that it frightened him almost to tears. He knew nothing of what it meant. Nothing except that the only word that seemed right was "love." "I love Hana," he told himself. "I want to join her and protect her."

— —

From Lowell Briscoe's "A Nest of Hells."

Calm as the Whole Ocean in a Storm

[JOURNALS OF HANA NICHOLAS]
30 May 1949

My prayer is that I can find a way to be as calm inside as the whole ocean is calm in the middle of a violent storm. It's not the ocean itself that's stormy, just the day; the ocean will always be the ocean; the desert will always be the desert, no matter how much sand is swirling in the air. I want to be like the mountains, unmoved despite the ice and snow and wind, circular as the earth always is, whether parts of it are eroding or uplifting. I always scoffed at those old sages who wanted to be "imperturbable," "self-sufficient," "effortless." I will only survive this if I can float above the flood, if I can become buoyant enough to breathe, if I can remain calm enough to become the water rather than the storm. I pray for this. I pray for it. I'm losing my strength for anything else. I'm becoming depressed!

I can't imagine that, but I am.

This is absurd. Their definitions of me border on the lunatic. I am "unresponsive," "defensive," with "minor delusions of grandeur," "maladjusted," or so says Dr. Hal, who also claims I exhibit "unacceptable behavior." This is about conformity. I am enervated by this, completely de-energized. I feel them looking at me. I can't get them out of my mind. I can't seem to keep my guard up anymore.

Why is this happening? Do they want my land, my money? Is that what it's about? Petty material greed? It cannot be! It cannot be. That is simply impossible. I am not the victim of some monstrously small-minded extortion scheme, am I? Am I being driven insane so my friends can have my land? That's preposterous, isn't it? This isn't *Gas Light*. Why should Dr. Harold Barrows question me about my life and my real estate every time he sees me? And why does he only see me with Nola? And why does he want me to become his patient? I need no doctoring. Is this a heinous scheme? God help me. I've got to find some calmness inside me, some focus beyond these hideous thoughts, beyond these hideous people.

PART SEVEN

The Hat of Hermes

The Riot of 1992
The Mob Can't Think

"It's only now, after all these years, that I'm coming to understand, inside myself, what Hana might have meant by what she called 'the mass mind,'" Lowell told Dr. Tuttle a few days before the trial of his alleged assailants began.

"I see this automatic, fear-driven, dangerous, and unreflective way of thinking all around me now, even in my own thought processes once in a while. The mass mind infects common sense with idiot conformity. Mass mind contagion takes the form of reflex consensus, no matter how mad the propositions or the goals might be. It's like IQ tests. What is intelligence and how do you measure it? Is intelligence a real thing, or just an idea, just a passing notion of no substance that has become a quantum in the mass mind's view of human worth? I think intelligence is an invention of statisticians. If you don't have something to measure you can't measure it. The mass mind view of IQ is that it actually is something, that it doesn't change and that it is separate from what a human being does. Everyone agrees that's so, no matter how preposterous, or how utterly unprovable such a notion might be. But the tendency of the mass mind is undeterrable. It never questions itself or its beliefs. I can see the mass mind at work in D.A. Cates, in the cops, in the thugs of the mob that nearly killed me, and in the psychiatric industry too, yourself excluded, of course," Lowell said with shallow sincerity and in need of reassurance.

"Of course," Dr. Tuttle nodded with a smile.

"The mob had a mind of its own; it followed a course of action as a single creature. Everyone did what they saw everyone else doing; it was like the sudden movements of a school of fish, everyone reacted in the same way, without reflection. Violence became the norm. Studying the norm of any group or any profession, one discovers the mass mind scheming to exclude and drive out whatever disagrees with it, whatever it cannot incorporate into its irrational consensus. For normal people like us—excuse me, I don't mean to laugh—the twistings and torturings of the mass mind are enough to drive us mad. Take the D.A.'s insistence that I must think and remember as he thinks and remembers. He wants my mind to work the way he expects his to work. Well, it doesn't work that way, does it? The worst stress there is in daily life comes from the pressure to behave in expected ways and the terrible punishments exacted when one strays from what people can understand without having to think about it. Once they are required to reflect, the crazy mass mind takes over and projects onto all exceptions and eccentricities one of its vast array of devious suspicions. I know that is exactly what happened to Hana. The mass mind is ignorant of options. So, it turns what it doesn't know into the object of its worst fear, the secret fear, the unbearable and untenable fear that its rigid view of how things are is somehow wrong. It can't stand that, so its form of denial is to destroy what it doesn't understand by transforming it into something it does. . . . God, I'm just rambling on and on."

"No, I think this is very sensible and completely in keeping with what you have told me about what happened to Hana," Dr. Tuttle said with a particular warmth in her voice. "Hana understood the dark history of fear very well, didn't she?"

"That's well put, Dr. Tuttle."

Two days before the Briscoe Trial, as it came to be called, Los Angeles found itself worrying about another riot. Pre-trial newspaper stories had magnified the brutality of Lowell's beating by describing him as "the author of one of the most beloved children's stories of our time." The papers also recorded, with the relish of sports writers proclaiming "the fight of the century," that the defendants and their parents were "incredulous over the charges" they faced. The defendants, the Normandy Four, vigorously and consistently denied their guilt. But the evidence seemed overwhelmingly against them. "Only Dr. Briscoe knows who his attackers really are. His eyewitness testimony is the key to the prosecution's case," the *Times* editorialized. In the black ghettoes of Los Angeles, the question was simple enough: Would the Normandy Four be scapegoated for the whole four-day riot, and for the beating that someone else gave to the "beloved [white] author," or would justice prevail? It all seemed to hinge on the conscience, memory, health, and character of Lowell Patrick Briscoe.

"I think the case is being handled with dignity and authority," Lowell told a television reporter. "I am sure justice will prevail and that the human and civil rights of the defendants will be scrupulously protected. I hope they are. As a long-time 'card-carrying' member of the ACLU, I believe with all my heart that these young men must be given a fair trial. And let the facts speak for themselves. There are no devils here. Just the poisoned soil of injustice from which anger always grows."

In the quiet office of Dr. Melinda Tuttle, Lowell was not as magnanimous.

"I'm terrified of my anger. It frightens me to talk about it, to admit it, to show it, to keep it under wraps. I feel like such a hypocrite. I am a hypocrite. My persona in the media is smooth, calm, detached. I am the saintly children's book author, an esoteric Mr. Rogers, an ACLU good guy. And part of me is like that. But I'm beginning to see that I am a crazy tangle of contradictions . . . that there are other parts of me that are totally unreasonable, enraged in fact, a maniac who'd just as soon kill the defendants as look at them, guilty or not. And I don't honestly know if they were the ones who beat me. And I don't trust the videotapes; they're seductive but too blurry. And maybe they've been doctored. . . ."

"Why would they be doctored? By whom?" Dr. Tuttle asked.

"I don't know; maybe the cops. Maybe the cops had a grudge against them and framed them. Maybe they're drug dealers. I don't know. But that's not the point. . . . It's me that I'm worried about. I know I'm not going to kill those young men. I know that. But I'd like to. And a part of me is busily working up imaginary justifications for doing just that. I know I won't. But, God, I want revenge *for something*. I can't stand this feeling of fury, these ranting monologues, the combustible fake dialogues going on in my head. I can't stand the frustration of seeing everything I love destroyed without being able to strike back."

"Who are you having those dialogues with? And what's been destroyed?"

"I'm having imaginary confrontations with everyone, with Juliet, with Nola, with Cates, with you, with the Devons, Thea, everyone, everyone. I even dreamed last night that I was in the courtroom with Hana. I was ten and hiding behind her as she swore to tell the whole truth. When she sat down, I was left standing behind her with a shotgun pointed at the judge. I pulled the trigger. I woke up with the sound of the explosion. . . .

"My God, what's happening to me? I can't stand it. I feel just possessed. I don't know what to do. I'm conscious of all this stuff. It's not like I'm a split personality or anything like that. But no matter how aware I am, I can't shut off the feelings once they start; they're there until they've run themselves out. I know they're all about the past, but they're right now, too. What if I just blow up on the witness stand? What if I just lose control? What if my persona just cracks apart, if the force fields shatter and I go in there with my shields down? I've been afraid of that happening for so long, and afraid that it already happened once, that I can't shake it, I can't get free of it. It just comes back and clogs me up terribly. I look at those young men, and I think to myself, 'I don't know if they did it or not, but I'd like to make mincemeat out of them.' It's a very, very old feeling. Very old. I think I wanted to kill my father once."

Lowell almost mechanically recited the details of the past, once again for Dr. Tuttle. His rage at Hana's circle of friends, his anger at Joel, his contempt for Juliet, his worship of Hana, his loathing of Nola.

"I used to worry that I'd somehow killed them all, that I'd betrayed Hana, hired someone to butcher Juliet and Thea, and killed the Devons and Nola myself. I know that I was the cause of Nola's last heart attack. I told her that I'd seen her and Hana having . . . well, why not? . . . having sex. I hadn't, of course, but it bollixed Nola so much that she had a stroke or a seizure or something. I felt such rage, such guilt at being so angry, so impotent, so useless. I did love Hana, in a way I have never loved anyone before or since. And I did declare my feelings to her, in the form of a dance. . . . I've never told anyone this before. . . . I really can't go on. . . . I was caught, I think, by Nola, who was spying while I did my dance for Hana. I felt so horrible, so guilty, so outraged."

"Why?"

"Because Nola turned something honest and guileless into something dirty. I wanted to show Hana my love and allegiance. I knew she was terribly stressed. So I did a Kachina dance for her. It was totally innocent on my part. It wasn't sexual. It was intimate, a dance of affection, a dance to declare myself her ally. A child's fantasy, but true hearted."

"What happened then?"

"Then Nola raised a stink with Juliet, which Juliet ignored to her eternal credit. Then I didn't see Hana for a month. And when I did, she was different, conspiratorial, very shy and withdrawn, as I thought about it over the years. She was still herself, not crazy, but deeply suspicious and deeply afraid of something. I think it was Nola. I think Nola accused her of corrupting me, or something like that. That's what I think happened. I don't know for sure about anything. I do know, though, that Nola thought I'd seduced Hana somehow, infected her mind, that I was a malignant influence. I don't think though that she suspected at all about Juliet and me."

"What about Juliet and you?"

"I haven't told you that, have I?"

The Ultimate Disclosure, May 1949

Lowell sat in his closet for hours at a time that weekend after Hana had talked with him about the incident with the police. He was preparing himself to make the ultimate disclosure. He wanted to join her tribe, fight at her side. He would either secure for himself a permanent place in the myth of Gloriamaris as a partisan in Hana's company, or he would be kindly and indulgently rejected. This, he knew, would be the final risk and commitment. He thought and thought about how to give Hana a gift that she would accept and understand completely as a token of his truest feelings. Of course, the gift would have to be a dance, a kachina dance. But what kind? Would he play Odysseus again? Would he extend Hana's play? No. That would be impossible for his skills and he might betray his misunderstanding of Hana's whole idea, which he thought he knew but maybe didn't. He would play himself instead, make a mask of his own face. He knew Hana would understand the joke; wearing such a mask would mean to her the complete unmasking of himself. He was thrilled with the idea. He would disguise himself as himself. He knew Hana would understand immediately.

Once he'd settled on a plan, his whole being became animated by the thought of the dance, by the danger of showing himself, of even letting Hana know that there was a real self to be shown. And this passionate danger was made all the more thrilling and noble by the shadow of repression that Nola cast over everything Lowell did. Nola's image plagued him. He thought he saw her everywhere, could feel her presence hiding behind trees and around corners. Nola was the dust on his life. He hated her so much and was so frightened of her, he sometimes could barely walk around his own bedroom for fear of Nola hearing his footsteps a quarter of a mile away.

Lowell worked hard to put Nola out of his mind while concentrating on making the mask and choreographing the dance. His performance would have to do the job of words. It would have to explain his intentions and his motives thoroughly. Once it was over, Hana would have to know unequivocally where Lowell stood. But how should the dance be performed? The harder Lowell thought, the less he liked his strategies. It finally came to him that he would have to improvise, do a kind of "on the spot mime," the kind that Hana had taught him in preparation for the Christmas play. He'd have to trust himself and let go, as Hana had instructed. He was confident that such a performance would not only please her, but convince her.

Lowell stayed home from school early in the week, feigning a bad cold, and managed to avoid Juliet's suspicious curiosity. He spent every moment he could in his closet with a flashlight, making his costume and drawing over and over the mask of his own face. "I'll become a bird for her," he thought. "I'll dance for her the way birds dance for each other in the spring."

Little sleep, deep concentration, and growing stage fright all served to rub his nerves to a fine, hot sheen. He'd never thought of anything as exciting in his life. He had never felt such anticipation, such joy. He was about to create himself for her in his own image and likeness. This was to be the first true gift he'd ever given in his life, and he convinced himself that nothing would go wrong.

Adapted from Lowell Briscoe's "A Nest of Hells."

A Most Remarkable Gift

[JOURNALS OF HANA NICHOLAS]
31 May 1949

Lowell gave me a most remarkable gift this afternoon. He definitely senses the "troubles." He declared his loyalty and allegiance to me by performing a kachina dance of his own invention. It was quite marvelous. His mask was a drawing of his own face! What subtlety. Does he really understand the nature of a healthy persona—that you disguise yourself in who you really are? He must. I have been so right about him. He danced with absolute frenzy and almost collapsed when he was through. I told him I was honored, and I am. I think he loves me in a way that is profound and that might be hurtful to him, if anything happens to me before he's strong enough to survive a broken heart. I must be more careful. My responsibility is sobering with Lowell. He feels I am his guardian, the mother of his better self, but there is also something of a "romance" involved, all very Platonic for him, I'm sure, but still extremely compelling, as he approaches adolescence. I have mothered him. And my advice to him has been sound: dream up who you want to be, and pretend to be him, wear that mask, let it become you. It's perfectly in keeping with practices ancient and contemporary all over the world, from religious ritual to parental and military role playing. But has he become someone that I've dreamed up for him to be; is this the Lowell that Lowell wanted? He is stronger, there's no doubt about that. He is wiser. He is less vulnerable to his own neuroses and borderline manias. But am I anyone who should be someone else's mentor? I do a very good job with myself. But someone else? Lowell is not a little boy anymore.

My intuition was strong with Lowell. He sensed it; I sensed it. We needed each other. I needed to confirm in myself, by teaching, what I knew was true about how people should be treated. Lowell brought out the best in me. Good students make good teachers. When he appeared in my living room in full costume—with his "life mask," his kilt, his feathered leggings, his own little drum and began dancing and singing "I am with you, I am with you," in a deep, chanting voice, which grew increasingly hoarse and frantic as he lost wind from his efforts—when I first saw him I felt such a rush of pride and gratitude. For all his innocence and tenderness, and all his cruel savvy about the world, Lowell understands me better than anyone else could, on a visceral level. I wish he were thirty years older and a friend, rather than a troubled "son."

Demonic Peeping Tom

[JOURNALS OF LOWELL BRISCOE]
Summer 1992

I remember my horror that evening so clearly. It was late twilight when I left Gloriamaris. I was exhausted but flushed with a feeling of acceptance and success. I thought Hana really understood the message of my gift, crude and full of bravado though it might have been. I wish I had been as imaginative as the Lowell in "A Nest of Hells." But I was just a scraggly kid. But I did make a costume of some kind. I did want to tell her I loved her, without any doubt, stripped, so to speak, of pretense and convention, though I'm sure that in the late spring of 1949 I didn't know what such words might have meant. I do remember that Hana wanted to walk me home that evening along the ditch, but at the last second changed her mind. I don't know why. I blew her a kiss when I waved goodbye and almost skipped home. I'd forgotten completely about Nola and my troubles and was humming a tune, I think, when I almost swallowed my tongue in fright. There was Nola, standing at the front door, arms folded, a terrible pinched scowl on her face. She was just leaving, and Juliet looked stricken. Nola stalked by without even looking at me.

I can't describe the power of the adrenaline that was rushing through me. I instantly suspected that she had somehow found out about my dancing for Hana and my declaration of love. My nerves screamed, "She knows, she knows!"

I tried to remain composed and seem natural if not nonchalant. I asked Juliet if she and Nola had a good talk, trying to scope out the situation, but Juliet was sad and stern and fiercely adult. She would tell me nothing of their encounter, saying only that it would be best "for all of us," if I'd stop seeing Hana for a while until "things blew over." I begged her to tell me what she meant, but she wouldn't. And when I pressed her, she adamantly refused and wouldn't budge. And then she went into her bedroom, locked the door, and sulked.

In the space of less than a half an hour, I moved from euphoria to becoming possessed by the worry that Nola had seen me, that she'd seen "everything," that she knew I loved Hana. And what made my worries feel like dead certainties was Juliet's "suggestion" that I stop seeing Hana. What a calamity! What trauma! Of course, now I think it's possible that Nola was setting up her psychiatric assassination that afternoon. And perhaps she was. But I still dread the suspicion that Nola had found me out and that somehow set her off to take after Hana.

I wanted so badly to rush back to warn Hana that Nola was on the warpath, but I didn't dare, and really couldn't have anyway, so dizzy with fear and anger I'd become. I lay in bed that night paralyzed with apprehension and hate. I remember those hours vividly. It felt like I was in an iron lung turned into a pressure cooker. I was burning up, drenched in sweat, seized by a claustrophobic panic that tightened around my throat until I could hardly breathe or swallow. There was no escape, no place to go, no way to get my questions answered. I couldn't see Hana. I was completely helpless. Who I used to be before Hana mothered me now moved to repossess me. The demon of fear could smell my despair. I became prey to the worst of myself.

I have no direct personal knowledge of what took place following that long, mad night. By all accounts, I didn't wake up the next morning, having fallen into what was described as a "traumatic coma," a kind of temporary catatonia, that left me bedridden and mentally exhausted for the better part of three months, or so I was told. I've often suspected, though, that I was drugged, or, more politely, sedated. I was taken to a clinic, apparently, and had moments of lucidity. I can recall such things as the leather straps that kept me from falling out of bed, the wristwatch of the girlish therapist who tried, unaccountably, to get me to make paintings, and the countless occasions nurses came to give me pills, stick me with needles, and change my bedpans. The rest of the experience is a complete blank.

When I was released, everyone at home was solicitous and cozy. I stayed in bed for another month, I think, generally unaware of anything but the warmth of the blankets. It seems to me now that I must have been heavily sedated. The only sense I can make of what happened to me is that either I was stricken by a massive psychological shock, or I was literally drugged and kept out of the way. Perhaps my collapse was a welcome convenience and merely exaggerated by prescriptions "until it blew over," or equally possible, I could have had just an old-fashioned nervous breakdown. It seems preposterous that I'd be kept drugged up for months on end, unless, of course, people really were conspiring to get Hana's land, and were very carefully driving her insane. But that can't be, can it?

When I finally came to my senses, I realized, slowly at first and then with greater clarity and intensity, that there was an enormous void between the day of the ultimate exhilaration with Hana and the present, a huge dark hole splitting me apart from my life, leaving me literally stranded in a foreign dimension of time. When I awoke from my "illness," I found myself in a totally different world. I was a Rip van Winkle.

Some Bad News for You

Lowell's recovery and convalescence was a frozen blur to him. He slowly thawed after being sedated and kept in bed for months. In late summer, when the sun in Albuquerque is searing even near twilight, the day of his liberation came at last. Juliet reassured him that only a final visit to the clinic was needed before he could return to school and "be your old, wrangling, raunchy self again."

Juliet seemed to Lowell very strong and beautiful that day. She was wearing one of her summer suits, with wide shoulder pads and an elegant print pattern on the rayon skirt. Her long brown hair glistened in the breeze as they drove through the North Valley in her black Chevy. Dr. Harold Barrow's office in the Sunshine Building downtown was a nest of clichés—a replica of an Elizabethan globe, the Florentine leather pencil holder, sweat-inducing vinyl-cushioned captain's chairs, framed reproductions of seascapes and dewy glades awash with prancing children. The doctor, himself, had the look of a bemused friar, a halo of hair crowning his pate, a saccharine smile stitched on his face. He stared at his green ink-blotter pad, searching for the best words to explain to Lowell what had happened.

"Lowell's high strung and temperamental, aren't you, Lowell?" Dr. Barrows said with high hopes for a congenial response. But Lowell sat motionless, beside Juliet, sourly staring out the window behind the doctor's desk.

"He experienced a terrible trauma of some sort, as you know. We remain, uhhhhh, uncertain of the cause," Dr. Barrows said, obviously ill at ease. "He's had an emotional experience he was just not capable of enduring. He simply evacuated reality for a while."

"I understand, Hal," Juliet said with some annoyance, urging him on.

"Yes. The cure is now complete, Lowell. But if you have any questions, or a relapse for any reason, please know we will be more than happy to take care of you for as long as you need." Dr. Barrows sounded positively corrosive in his superficiality.

"Hal, please," Juliet whined.

"Yes, yes. . . . Lowell . . . Lowell . . . uh, you need to brace yourself.

We . . . I, uh, have some very bad news for you. Do you think you can handle bad news right now? Do you?"

"What!?" Lowell responded with frightened impatience.

"Lowell, if this is too much for you to handle. . . ."

"What? What?"

Juliet put both hands around Lowell's right upper arm, as if to soothe and restrain him.

"Lowell, it's about your friend Miss Nicholas."

"Hana? What's wrong? What is it?"

"Lowell, Miss Nicholas . . . Miss Nicholas . . . is dead. . . . She died two months ago, quite suddenly, of a massive stroke. I'm so very sorry. Believe me, she felt absolutely nothing, no pain at all. It was so sudden, so very sudden. . . . Lowell, are you all right, young man?"

Lowell didn't say a word. He tilted his head toward his right shoulder, moved his attention away from Dr. Barrows, smiled quickly at Juliet and looked out the window to the Sandia Mountains and the slash of Tijeras Canyon. He took a deep breath, then closed his eyes, as if he were waiting calmly for the executioner to pull the switch. Lowell felt cold and empty, but not surprised. He spoke very softly, his eyes still closed, and Juliet released her grip.

"When did it happen, exactly?" he asked Dr. Barrows.

He shuffled through some papers unsuccessfully. "As I said, two months ago."

"You don't know the exact date?"

"I do but I can't find it," the doctor said flatly.

"How are her animals? Who is looking after them," Lowell asked methodically and as adultly as possible.

"Honey, nobody is. The estate sold them, or had them put to sleep. You can imagine how hard it would have been to care for them all," Juliet said.

"No, I can't imagine," Lowell responded impassively. "Are they really all gone?"

"Yes they are. I'm so sorry."

"All of them? How is that possible? Didn't anyone take the pets?"

"I really don't know," Juliet said with slight impatience.

"Can we go home, now, Juliet, please?" Lowell said wearily.

"Lowell, tell me how you feel before you go," said Dr. Barrows with some renewed authority in his voice.

"I'm OK, I'm fine. I just want to go home, now, please."

Then Dr. Barrows looked at Juliet. They both said nothing, waiting for Lowell's next reaction.

Lowell's mind was racing. His seeming composure came from an intuition of extreme danger. He had to protect himself. He knew if he didn't behave, Juliet and "Dr. Hal" would have him sedated again. And this sense of personal jeopardy was sharpened by the total certainty he felt that Juliet and Dr. Barrows were lying to him, that Hana was not dead at all, far from it. Perhaps it was the doctor's tone of voice, perhaps it was the almost imperceptible theatricality of Juliet's silent comforting. Whatever it was, Lowell knew the room was stale with fraud.

Hana could not possibly be dead, he thought. She had not finished herself. She would never submit to death until she was through. She could not be dead. They are trying to keep me from her. And if she was dead, it was not an illness that killed her.

"Is she really dead?" Lowell squinted, now on the verge of tears, at once manufactured and real.

"Yes darling, she is. I'm so, so, so sorry. We all miss her so much. And I know you will miss her most of all," Juliet said with sincerity laced with restrained exaggeration.

With that Lowell let out a howl and began crying loudly and rhythmically, doubling over in the chair, sometimes seeming almost unable to catch his breath. Juliet and Dr. Hal looked at each other with relieved expressions. And Juliet took Lowell into her arms and rocked him as he cried.

Adapted from notes left by Lowell Briscoe for his "A Nest of Hells."

Stepping through a Stormy Mirror

Once at home, Lowell's demeanor and temperament changed. Juliet could tell immediately, and she wasn't happy.

"Honey, I've missed you so much. Come on. I know you hurt terribly. Let me take care of you. Come here, come here for a while. Let's cuddle and talk," said Juliet in a nurse-like, madonna voice.

But instead of moving as always to her, Lowell backed away, surprised at his revulsion and at the spacious distance he felt between himself and who he used to be. It was as if he had stepped through a stormy mirror, been blown to smithereens, reassembled, and deposited exactly where he started—only now where he started was no longer there.

"I feel real bad, Juliet. My head hurts. My tummy's upset. My eyes are burning. I feel like you look when you're hung over."

"Lowell!"

"No, I'm sorry, I mean I just feel crummy. I'll cuddle tomorrow, I really will. I'm going to bed now. Is that OK?"

Juliet looked at him as if she were examining a wasp that had perched too close to her face. Her head tilted back and slightly turned, her nose was almost wrinkled.

"Of course, dear," she said pointedly. "Are you all right? You're not feeling bad as before, are you? No dizziness? No raging headaches?"

"No, I'm really fine, except that I've been sick for months. I don't remember a thing. I just learned my best friend is dead. How do you think I feel?"

"Aren't I your bestest friend, Lowellie? Aren't I still?"

"Of course, Juliet. Of course. Don't worry. I'm just tired."

"You rest now, dear," she said more softly. "You've had a terrible shock. I'll look in on you in a while. I'm going to have a little drinkie. Sleep tight."

Lowell was flummoxed by how different he felt to himself. He just wasn't the same. He felt heavier and stronger, despite his physical weakness. He felt, in fact, cold and stern.

"I've been drugged, haven't I?" he thought to himself as he moved down the hall to his room. "How long have I been 'sick'? How long has Hana been 'dead'?" A wash of emotion made him tremble.

"Nothing's the same, nothing's the same. The whole world's changed. The last thing I remember is Nola at my front door."

Lowell was battered with surprises. His brain seemed to be squinting into a glaring light, his mind swarming with events and circumstances he had to give some order to. In his closet that night, behind the wall of clothes, he gave in to burning pangs of anger, homesickness, and grief. He had been away from himself for what seemed like a lifetime. And now suddenly, just like that, he was back again. Aware, alert, alive, with all his old fears intact and all the new strengths he'd learned from Hana feeling dangerously sharper than before. Lowell felt utterly and devastatingly alone.

"I have nobody now. I have no Hana, no Hana at all," he sobbed. It was not all a terrible dream, he knew. It was real, Hana was real and Lowell loved her. And now she was missing, but, he was absolutely sure, not dead.

"Something's wrong. They've done something to her, just like Dr. Barrows and Juliet did something to me. But who did it and why?" he wondered. "Why did they lie to me? Was I to blame? Are they keeping it from me so I won't feel bad? Did Nola see me?" Lowell gasped for air. Hana was not dead. Something was terribly wrong. He would go to Gloriamaris and see for himself.

"Am I to blame?" The question rang through his head, endlessly, all night long and for years thereafter.

The next morning, from down the road at a distance, Gloriamaris seemed the same. The house was there, the cottonwoods and Russian olives were strong as ever, honeysuckle and trumpet vine swarmed up the trellises and telephone poles. Everything was the same at the secret side passage into Hana's garden—the same muddy puddles, the same flagstone chips, the same rope and stick to latch the movable part of the fence. Lowell began to feel slightly giddy, half expecting Hana to pop out from behind an apricot tree at any moment. He stood perfectly still, watching and listening. Except for the rustling of the leaves and the gentle hush of silence in his ear, there was not a sound of life in the whole, gigantic garden. It was as if something had drained the spirit from the place, sliced out its will. It had become inanimate. Everything in the landscape was there, but it was all a reproduction, a diorama. The animals were nowhere to be seen, but that was always the case. What was missing was the smell of fur and food and vitamins and oils, and the subtle sense of movement here and there. Lowell hardly dared stir himself. It was as if some force had abolished motion. He crept as silently as he could through the forests, groves, and gardens, whispering Hana's name, and the names of the animals. Then he came upon empty food troughs and the unattended shrines. He checked the back doors and windows of the house, but they were locked and the curtains drawn. He went to the Kiva, but it was sealed with an enormous chain and a heavy padlock. He didn't have the heart try the secret passage.

Surely the goldfish and carp must be in their pond, he thought. But the water was dark and smelled faintly like tar, with not a fish in sight. Death and pestilence. The gardens of Gloriamaris had been plagued, blighted by some hideous malady, and Lowell was standing in the middle of it; it might catch him, too, if he didn't get out.

Could it be true? Hana might really be dead. She, herself, might have been seized by this dreadful curse, seized by some ghostly enemy that swept through her lands, harvesting non-human souls.

"I better leave. I'd better get outta here fast," he mumbled as he hurried to the hidden gate, turned, held his breath, looked for what might be the last time on the deep green landscape of Gloriamaris, then stepped back into the other world and right into the arms of Nola Dasheller.

Her fingernails dug into his arms. She spun him around, stared him in the eye and smiled. "I knew you would return, that you couldn't keep away from the scene of the crime. I've been waiting for you, waiting for the final pleasure of driving you off for good," she said sweetly in a soft voice. "I am the guardian of this place now. It is mine to care for as I please. And it pleases me very much to inform you that you are never to set foot in here again. Do you understand?" Nola grinned. "Do you understand?"

Lowell stepped firmly on the arch of her right foot. She grunted loudly and released her grip. Lowell scooted around her to a safe distance. And smiled back at her, almost shouting, "You killed her, didn't you? You killed her or had her killed! I know all about you," Lowell said, lowing like a bull on the "you."

Nola stood straight and tall, collected herself, and said with magisterial bearing, "You know nothing but your crime. Nothing. Absolutely nothing. You are insane. And you drive others insane. God help you if I catch you here again. God help you."

"God help you, Nola," Lowell howled and laughed as he ran down the ditch into the morning. "God help you, too."

By the time he'd stopped running, he was tightrope walking over a culvert across the mother ditch and running into the bosque by the river, shouting and screaming at the top of his lungs, "God help her! God help her! God help her!" As he walked, his rage and fear were slowly replaced by an aching, intolerable sorrow, the most fertile ground of all for guilt. What "crime" was she talking about? The question remained there, lodged between his fury and his despair. Such questions were the first motive that drove him to the extremes everyone would come to regret.

From Lowell Briscoe's "A Nest of Hells."

No Longer a Boy

[JOURNALS OF LOWELL BRISCOE]
Summer 1992

Even I have a hard time distinguishing between my fiction of 1949 and the so-called reality. It's almost impossible to clear it up. But my nonfictional memory of those days is about one thing only: coming to terms with the facts—the fact that Hana was gone, the fact that I really didn't believe she was dead, the fact that I was alone again, the fact that I had been sick, or drugged, or had a mental breakdown for the better part of three or four months, the fact that Nola hated me, the fact that Dr. Barrows and Juliet were very friendly.

During that summer, I resolved to try to look something like a regular boy, working with desperate concentration to block out the sorrow that threatened to drown me. I had always been alienated from everyone by my secrets, by what I did not wish to reveal, and by those realities I thought I could never explain well enough for anyone to understand. That summer, the alienation deepened. Juliet was still playing nurse and was particularly sweet. I have to say here that it is a mark of my mental uncertainty these days that I want to disclaim very clearly any relationship between the fictional Juliet and the real one, but I cannot actually do that. My fantasies and recollections, my novelist's imagination and my historical perspective as a player in my own story "interpenetrate" from time to time. Images shuffle together. And since the beating, I've not been able to arrange the decks with complete accuracy or objectivity. Be that as it may, Juliet did pamper me with movies and model airplanes and whatever else she could think of that summer. And although I feigned gratitude, nothing could really distract me. I had, in fact, left my childhood. I had become something quite strange in my own eyes, something rather fabulous, I thought, and more enviable than the cartoon heroes I so enjoyed. I knew I had more secrets than anyone. I knew I was a spy. I was so much more than I seemed. I could not regress. Childhood could not hold me; its delights could not absorb my feelings; there was simply no distraction that could turn me. Every time I thought I had escaped into some trivial delight, the questions, the rage and the sorrow would pierce my reveries, insisting on their presence.

Hana was gone!

I had only one person to turn to: Nurse Juliet. Surely, I thought, she would have some answers. We shared so much. Yet, she had never spoken a word of what had really happened, never an intimation, never the slightest clue that something was wrong. She stuck to the story of Hana's sudden illness, but I didn't believe her. If I, a boy, knew better, I reasoned, so must she.

Early Questioning

Lowell came to see Juliet as the source of everything he needed to know. Whatever had happened to Hana, Juliet was as close to her as anyone and would surely have an inside track on the truth. At first he prodded very gently, enquiring about the funeral, wondering if it was at Gloriamaris where he was sure she would have wanted it, asking who was present, what animals came to pay their last respects. Juliet answered with fancy lies, and Lowell knew it, and Juliet knew Lowell knew it. But she wouldn't give an inch. Everything was tragic, but, Lowell thought to himself, sort of rosy too. Juliet had not a word to say about Nola, or Dr. Barrows. But he could see worry in her eyes.

One morning at breakfast, in a most meticulous and masterful way, right when Juliet was most relaxed, smoking her second cigarette with her second cup of coffee, Lowell told her that he had run into Nola after he'd taken a look at Gloriamaris for himself, finding everything lifeless and detecting no sight of a grave or burial ceremony for Hana. When he added that Nola had scolded him terribly for even being at Gloriamaris, Juliet inhaled a drop of coffee and sputtered and coughed. She averted her eyes, tried to speak of something else, and demanded that Lowell take all his pills "right this minute." It was the first time he knew for sure he was on to something.

He pressed his point by rolling up his sleeves and showing her the scabs on his arms left by Nola's fingernails. "She did that to me, Juliet. What are you going to do about it? Aren't you going to call her and read her the riot act? She did that to me!" Lowell said melodramatically. Juliet got up and strode forcefully to her bedroom with Lowell hounding right after her.

"You lied to me, Juliet. Didn't you? You and that doctor lied at the clinic, you lied at home. You lied. My sister, the dirty liar. You are a dirty liar, Juliet!" With that she spun around and slapped Lowell hard across the face. Lowell just stood there, hardly blinking, and continued to harangue her as if nothing had happened.

"She screamed at me, Juliet. She threatened me. She said if I ever went to Hana's house again, 'God help me.' And then she said that she was 'the guardian now,' and could do anything she pleased with

Gloriamaris. What did she mean?" Lowell yelled, starting to cry. "What did she mean? Please tell me, please, please!"

Juliet opened the bedroom door, took Lowell into her arms and tried to hush his sobbing. "You must forget. You must forget. You can never go to Gloriamaris again. You must never go there. I don't know what happened . . . hush, hush . . . but Hana was my dearest friend, too, Lowell," she said with deep insistence, "and I hurt too, very, very, much. Leave it be, leave it be, please, I beg you."

Lowell tried once more to worm free some morsel of truth, but Juliet clung to her story as tightly as she clung to him, smothering his questions and dampening his will.

Realizations come in layers. It was not until many days after that first confrontation with Juliet that Lowell realized how hopeless he had become. He was being purposefully kept from the truth, held at arm's length, while he flailed away at thin air. There was no way a boy his age could get to it. His mad frustration was worsened by his growing sense that his life and his happiness had been taken away from him, stolen. The more he felt his loss, the more he came to resent it. The more he experienced his pain, the more it transformed itself into a longing for vengeance. He felt himself to be the sole surviving member of a despised race, horribly wronged. He bore within him scars of mutilation and excruciating injustice. If he was to avenge this crime, he would have to think of himself as something other than a mere child. He would have to follow Hana's advice and pretend to be someone so strong and so smart that he could cause the unknown to be known and the unreal to perish amid reality. If Hana was not dead, he would have to find her. If she was dead, someone would have to pay.

Lowell now concentrated on what Hana had taught him about pretending to be "more than who you are." Through make-believe, Hana said, you could overcome your fears and gradually become who you really wanted to be. Lowell knew he needed to become a kind of Odysseus, someone who wouldn't give in, even to the Gods. If Lowell were to become Odysseus, he would have to drive out all sloppiness, beat back the little boy that kept seeping into his life, dismantle all childish appetites and consecrate himself to the task.

Lowell put himself through weeks of what he thought Hana would prescribe for him, all kinds of exercises, most of them designed to toughen him up, to endure discomfort, and to find where his limits really were. He would do endless calisthenics, squeeze his fingers with pliers to see how long he could take the pain, hold his hand under the hottest tap water. He would close his eyes and imagine the most horrible tortures, what it would be like to drown in a submarine, how it would feel to burn up in a car. And whenever he would tire of his training, he had only to remind himself that he was barred from the joys and refuge of Gloriamaris forever and ever.

From Lowell Briscoe's "A Nest of Hells."

"For Us, Hana Is Dead"

Despite all his wiles and cunning, Lowell probably would never have learned the fundamentals from Juliet if it had not been for a chance encounter with Nola in the grocery store.

Juliet and Lowell had planned a weekend of utter self-indulgence, locking all the doors, taking the phone off the hook, indulging their weakness for sweets of every kind. They were shopping rapaciously, their cart brimming with pies and cookies, nuts and candy bars, when they ran right into Nola coming down the condiment aisle. Lowell hadn't seen her since their confrontation at the hidden gate to the garden of Gloriamaris. Nola was wearing a simple blue frock, her hair was done up in a bun, and she was sporting ridiculously modish dark glasses. She looked almost girlish.

When Lowell saw her, he turned livid and Juliet began to tremble. She averted her eyes when Nola passed them with an expression of total disregard. Lowell wanted nothing so much as to trip her, but he, too, averted his eyes when the crucial moment came. After Nola left the aisle, Juliet clutched him fiercely, moaning pitifully, "We must get out of here right now. Quickly, quickly. We'll lock the doors and pretend it never happened." She put some money in his hand to pay for the groceries and said she'd meet him in the car.

Alone in the market, Lowell wheeled the cart around trying to kill time until Nola paid her bill and left. Then something marvelous came over him, a wonderfully fresh sensation, a realization that he was not afraid of Nola at all. He'd expected to be, but instead he was giddy with a sense of carefree invincibility that shocked and delighted him. And it came to him quickly that if he wasn't afraid of her, then he could make her miserable. Any discomfort he could bring her, he would do so with happy abandon. So he shoved the cart to front of the store as fast as he could, found Nola waiting in line and pulled in right behind her, bumping her buttocks with his cart. Nola wheeled around, saw it was Lowell, and raised her hand to slap him in the face, but caught herself just in time.

Lowell said, "Hi honey bunch. How's tricks?"

Nola made no reply.

Lowell said in a loud voice, "Hey, aren't you going to talk to me? Why not? How come? What's wrong, don't you like me anymore? After all we've meant to each other."

Heads turned in other lines around them. When the cashier got an odd look on her face at Nola's seemingly ungenerous behavior, Nola turned around and patted Lowell on the cheek. Lowell wanted to spit in her face, but he restrained himself and continued, instead, to pat her on the bottom the entire time she was writing her check.

Lowell paid his bill and pushed the cart into the parking lot, eager for another confrontation. There was Nola at their car, almost pounding on the rolled-up window with her open hand, Juliet inside, scrunched down in her seat.

Nola was almost yelling, "If I ever see that little deviant again, I'll tell him what you did, then I'll call Dr. Barrows, then I'll call the police about your so-called family. I can hurt you, you know, hurt you terribly! Don't forget it! Don't you ever forget it!"

She saw Lowell running at her with his cart. He wanted to crash it into her hip, but she escaped into her Studebaker and slammed the door before Lowell could reach her. He contented himself with dinging and chipping the paint on her door. She looked at him with all the wild fury she could muster, but Lowell detected, to his great pleasure and relief, what seemed to be a trace of fear in her eyes. He gave her a big grin, made an obscene gesture, then skipped with his cart back to their Chevy.

Juliet was paralyzed. They rode home in the steaming car, windows rolled up tight, Juliet scowling and shaking her head and not saying a word. This was the break Lowell needed. Now he knew that not only was Juliet in terror of Nola because of "our secret" (whether Nola really knew anything or not was unimportant), but because Juliet had apparently done something that under no circumstances did she want him to know about. Lowell had her where he wanted her.

When they got home, Juliet immediately locked herself in her room. Lowell was content to let her get away with it for a while. He wanted the chill of the encounter with Nola to sink in. He wanted Juliet to fully realize how aggressive and uncontrollable he was where Nola was concerned. He sensed as well, from Nola's reaction, that there was nothing to fear from Dr. Barrows at the moment. If he had been drugged before, the will to do such a thing again appeared to have dissipated. By that evening Juliet was still in her room and Lowell was beginning to lose his patience. He paced up and down the hall, damning her to himself, wanting to shriek at her, but remaining silent. He was so close. He had the precise weapon he needed and he wanted nothing to ruin his chances. If Juliet really set her mind on it, she would clam up forever, no matter what the consequences. He couldn't risk her indignation. He had to find the right lever.

Finally, he knocked on her door, sobbing, "Juliet, I'm scared out here all alone! She's going to get me! I'm really scared!"

He gave his best performance, whimpering a bit, shuffling shyly. Slowly the bedroom door opened, Juliet was there, her arms wide open, "Oh, my darling, I know, I know."

It was 8:00 p.m. when she let him in. By 2 a.m., he had everything she could tell him, for the moment. He conducted a masterful interrogation. He allowed her to soothe him for nearly an hour before he told her, sobbing again, how terrified of Nola he really was, that she plagued his dreams, that he was sure she was out to get him, that he knew she had done something terrible to Hana, and that he thought she suspected him of knowing about it and wanted to shut him up "for good."

"I went after her in the store because I wanted to scare her. But the trouble is, Juliet, I don't know what I'm supposed to know. I don't know why she's after me."

Lowell paused while Juliet blew her nose, then, almost whispering, said "I know you're afraid of Nola, too. I've never seen you like that, so scared, so tiny. Why does she frighten us so much?"

Then, with a master stroke, Lowell continued, "Is it because we are afraid that what happened to Hana could happen to us?"

And then he said more softly still, "And what did she mean about telling me what 'you did'? What did you do? What did she mean? Was she trying to get me mad at you or something?"

Juliet made a move to soothe him, but he pulled away. "I want to know, Juliet, I want to know right now. If you won't tell me, I'm going over to Nola's right now, tonight, and break a window or cut down all her roses or do something so terrible to her that she'll never bother us again. I can't stand it," Lowell screamed. "I will not have her treat you like that again. I hate her, I hate her, and I'm going to stop her."

Juliet turned very cold and totally focused. She said methodically and with menace, "If you do that Lowell, you will be killing us. Do you understand? Killing *us*, *us*, do you understand? You have to stay away."

"Then tell me what you did," Lowell said loudly. "Tell me now. Did you help her? Is that what she meant? Is she . . . blackmailing you or something? What did you do that she knows about that terrifies you so much? What is it? Tell me now, or I'm going over there right this minute! I'm not kidding. I swear I will. There's nothing you can do to stop me! And you know it!"

Lowell ran from her bedroom, got dressed, and was almost out the front door when Juliet grabbed him and gasped that she would tell him "everything" if he promised "to be done with it," and never tell a soul, and, especially, never bother Nola again. He promised her he would back off once he knew.

"The reason I haven't told you, Lowellie, is that I'm afraid for your mental health, honey. Do you know? I'm afraid you'll have another breakdown. The truth is brutal. I didn't know, I don't know, if you can take it. Can you take the truth?" she said seriously searching Lowell's eyes and demeanor.

Lowell laughed. "What could be worse than anything else in this rotten world?" he said dismissively. "What could be worse than having her dead?"

Juliet smiled wanly, took him by the hand and walked back to her bedroom. "You're so young, Lowellie, I don't know how you're going to understand all of this. I don't know if I do. And I'm real frightened, honey, that you'll hate me. I did nothing really bad. I did help Nola, I think," she said wrinkling her lips, "but in a very, very small way. And I didn't know it at the time."

"Help her do what?"

"Be patient, I'll tell you everything."

When Lowell heard that Hana had not been stricken dead by a sudden and terrible disease, he whooped and jumped around the room quite out of control. Juliet finally calmed him down and told him with blunt certainty that he "didn't quite understand."

"What happened to Hana, Lowell, is a fate worse than death." With those words, Juliet told Lowell a deft, sanitized, children's book version of what happened. Near the end she said, "In the final analysis, Lowellie, what dementia means is that she lost her mind. She went insane. Do you know what that means? And nobody really knows why."

"But she's not dead, right?"

"But she might as well be. Nola says she recognizes no one."

"Where is she?"

"That's not important now. We can't see her. She's as good as dead, I think, and there is no way to get her back," Juliet said in an ever darker and more deeply depressed tone of voice.

Lowell was transfixed, fascinated and horrified. Juliet told him that she herself had seen the men from the pound come to Gloriamaris several months after Hana was "taken away, mad as a hatter." The "dog catchers" spent hours and took as many as ten trips to collect and remove all of Hana's creatures. "It seemed to me they didn't make a sound when they were taken from the forest. And they knew where they were going, I'm sure."

"Where was that?"

"Do I have tell you what you already know?"

"You mean, they killed them?"

"Yes."

"What did Nola mean about what you did?" Lowell asked now in a calm and settled voice.

"Lowellie, we all knew Hana went mad: Thea, George and Betty, me. We all knew it. We didn't do anything. Nola told me to stop seeing Hana for a while. And I did. That's all. The next thing I knew she was gone."

Juliet turned her head away from Lowell and reached for his hand. "I saw Hana, you know, before her hearing, what they call a 'sanity hearing,' and she looked mad to me. The sanest person I've ever known, just standing there disheveled, utterly dumb."

"She didn't say anything?"

"Nothing. She was stoic, steadfast, but I could see the spirit had been drained out of her. She was trying to keep poised, but her energy was draining away so fast, she seemed limp, almost flabby, unaware of what was really going on. I think it had taken her by complete surprise."

"Why did you lie to me? Why did you and Dr. Barrows tell me she was dead?" Lowell asked shaking his head.

"Wasn't that easier to take than what you know now?"

"Not really. What did you do to help Nola? Please, please tell me. I won't hate you. I just want to understand."

"Well, if you want to know the whole truth," Juliet said melodramatically, "Nola went a little nuts herself. She saw your dance, Lowell. She was a peeping tom, a peeping Nola," Juliet laughed to herself. "She told me you were naked. But I know you made a costume. I don't know why. But I do know you well enough to know that even though you're wicked, Hana brought out the best in you, not the worst. You'd never dance that way for her," Juliet said, kissing Lowell on the cheek. "But Nola just raved on. She was so enraged by your dance that she threatened to charge me with child neglect and complicity in ghastly moral crimes with Hana if I allowed you to ever see Hana again. I was terrorized. Nola had all the evidence against Hana that she needed, she said, and she went about with Dr. Barrows methodically convincing Thea, George, and Betty, and trying to convince me, that Hana had gone utterly mad and had become a child molester, 'polluting the minds of innocent children.'"

"That's crazy! Just crazy!" Lowell bellowed.

"I know, but we were all frightened of her. I was beside myself," Juliet said, her tongue loosening more and more. "She was blackmailing me. And she demanded help. It seemed like nothing at the time. I didn't know what was happening. I told her, when she asked me, that Hana had no living kin that I was aware of. That's all I did. I swear it. But somehow everything seemed to revolve around that one fact. Nola even asked me to check with Hana and make sure, which I did, very deviously and indirectly, of course. When I asked Nola why she just didn't find out herself, she told me she wanted to double check. Apparently Dr. Barrows told Nola that it was Hana's one vulnerability, under the law—she had no family to care for her. Nola has been made Hana's guardian. She has her power of attorney too, Lowell. But I laughed at her when she told me Hana was insane. But now I think she must be right."

Juliet stopped. Lowell was looking at his feet.

"Lowell do you understand anything I've told you. Do you understand now why I didn't want you to know? . . . Lowell, we have no friends anymore. Do you understand what I'm saying? We have no friends. But everything now is back to normal, so to speak. Nobody's doing nasty things anymore. The wind's out of their sails. I don't see anyone. I don't trust anyone. I don't bother anyone. It's utterly hopeless. Short of leaving here, there's nothing else to be done. And I can't leave. There's no place else to go. Hana is gone. Gone. And I'm not equipped to handle any of it anymore. There is nothing that can be done, except to forget the bad and remember the good. Do you understand?"

"Maybe if we talked to Dr. Barrows. . . ."

"Lowell, stay away from that man. I mean it! Don't go near him. He's poison. Absolutely lethal. If you don't want to end up like Hana, stay away from him! I'm not kidding: he's dangerous to me! Dangerous to you! He has no scruples. Do you understand? It's all science or something to him. He's like a Nazi, cold blooded, small-minded, confident enough to do anything. Are you listening?"

"Yes, ma'am."

"That's why you must stay away from Nola. Nola and Hal are friends, or were. I'm not sure anymore. But let sleeping dogs lie, Lowell. Wake that one, and he'll have us all screaming bloody murder."

Lowell nodded. Then he asked, "Was I really sick? Or did somebody give me things to keep me out of the way? What happened to me? Was it Dr. Hal? Was I . . . doped, or poisoned?"

"Honey, honey, honey, do you think I'd let that kind of thing happen to you?"

Lowell looked at Juliet and smiled his most angelic smile.

— —

From Lowell Briscoe's "A Nest of Hells."

The Next Interrogation

What did Juliet mean, Lowell wondered, when she said that Hana's fate was "worse than death?" That's what stuck in Lowell's mind, not all of her hysterical admonitions and pseudo explanations. Lowell's imagination took hold of him; it was easier to deal with fantasy than to accept even a thin semblance of the truth. Was Hana being tortured somewhere? Was she in chains? What did going insane mean? Sometimes at night Lowell would be frantic with worry. His mind would fixate on a particular torture and then all the horrors he'd read in Juliet's library and heard in school about the Inquisition, about Nazi and Japanese sadists, filled his mind with addicting images. Only when morning came would they disperse. Then he'd wander through his days in a chilled, intoxicated stupor, affected only by the awareness of a shadowing malevolence everywhere he turned.

How could he help Hana?

Instead of going to school, Lowell took off for the bosque with paper and pencil, hid in a grove of cottonwoods across from the marshy oxbow, with all its trees and willows and birds, and let the river calm him. He recorded in his journals all the information Juliet had given him. He put it into an outline. He made a map of it, but he could still find no reasonable sum of truth. He made lists of all the facts he didn't know. He fretted about Dr. Barrows and couldn't bear thinking about confronting him. His fear of the doctor felt cowardly, but it was insurmountable. When he waded into the river to cool himself off, he thought about the quicksand Hana had warned him about and then imagined her being sucked under in a kind of social quicksand, a slurping trap made up of people. The river always washed away his fears. Its smoothness, its untroubled grace always reminded him of Hana, of the way she walked, the way her beautiful hands moved through the air when she talked. The river, he thought, felt like her smile—slow, peaceful, an ever present possibility. And there was nothing her smile could not cure.

One river morning about ten days after Juliet's confession, Lowell decided that he had stored up enough energy to break out of the inertia of his terrible fretting and despair. Everything he had to do became clear to him. He would have to confront them all if he was to find out the whole truth and check Juliet's story, all of them—Thea, George, Betty, and Nola. Could he possibly get to Dr. Barrows? Maybe he could, though the thought of it almost made him vomit with panic.

He decided to go after George first. He was the safest. But how could he force George to disclose his shame? What tactics could he use? What if George really was in league with Nola? Would he tell her that Lowell was snooping around? Would she sic Dr. Barrows on him? How would George react? Would he strike out, get violent? Lowell felt pangs of terror that Nola might try to silence him, drug him, run over him with her car, or drown him in the back ditch.

He prayed in his closet that night, asking God and Hana and the Kachinas to help him try his hardest and to forgive him if he failed.

The next morning he dressed to look as young and helpless as he could—in sneakers, baggy jeans, and his favorite old plaid shirt. He slicked back his hair in the kind of pompadour that Juliet liked so much and set out to the Devons' house down Los Griegos and up Guadalupe Trail to a cluster of old cottonwoods by the irrigation ditch that ran past their rambling adobe compound. Lowell almost turned and ran when he saw George standing by the ditch, binoculars up to his eyes, looking for some mysterious feathered presence in the trees. But George heard Lowell scuffle twigs behind him, turned, and gave him one of his tremendous Cheshire smiles.

"How are you, old boy?" George seemed genuinely pleased and excited to see him. "I'm so glad you're better. I really missed you! What's going on? Catch me up."

George was jauntily attired in hiking boots, a fatigue jacket of some sort, a blue-and-white-striped seersucker shirt, and a blue bow tie with red polka dots. His pipe was billowing clouds into the early autumn wind.

"So how are you doing?" George asked again.

"Oh, not so good, I guess. I can't believe . . . Hana's gone," Lowell said looking at his sneakers. "I miss her so much."

"Oh, boy, I do too," George Devon said with a sorrowful grunt. "I do too. I sure hope she's getting better."

"Getting better?" Lowell frowned. "What do you mean?"

"Well, she's very, very ill, you know. You do know that, don't you? I'm not surprising you, am I? . . . Are you all right?"

"Oh, yeah, I'm fine. Go on."

"Well, you know she's been in the hospital for a very long time. Very, very sick," George sighed, shaking his head. "You didn't know?"

"Yeah, I knew, but I don't understand what's wrong with her. Juliet can't tell me much. I really miss Hana. It really hurts."

"I know, I know," George said putting his arm around Lowell's shoulder. "Well, the poor dear," he began, "she. . . ." He stopped mid-sentence, puffed his pipe, looked up at the tree, and said almost under his breath, "I'm not so sure I should be the one to tell you this, after all you've been through. She'll get better. You and I must just trust that."

George pointed to a particularly cocky robin hopping along his coyote fence, trying to distract Lowell and change the subject. "Boy, look at that little guy strutting! I really like it when robins stake out territory; they're not afraid of anyone, even big bruisers like us. They just won't back down. Look at him giving us the evil eye!"

"I'm not going to back down, either," Lowell thought, smiling to himself.

"Why is everyone so afraid to talk about Hana, George? I don't understand. Juliet even lied to me at first. She and Dr. Barrows told me Hana was dead. Then Juliet said she wasn't. Hana's my best friend. I know her better than anyone. She trusted me. And now she's suddenly gone. And nobody will tell me what happened!" Lowell said with his voice rising dramatically. "What really happened? Has she been murdered or something like that?" Lowell asked with mischievous sarcasm. "Did somebody do something bad to her? I can't sleep at night, I worry so much," Lowell said, his voice trailing off theatrically.

"Oh, Lowell, I know how it is. I can't sleep either many nights. Betty too. It's tough. Real tough."

George Devon took a few steps up the ditch, picked a cottonwood leaf off a trailing branch, twirled it around by the stem, then approached Lowell and stared off into his fields. He hesitated and stumbled at first, but once he began to tell Lowell the story, he couldn't stop.

Hana had been acting "very strangely" and she had done some "very strange things," he said, and had some "very strange ideas." He mentioned some "dangerous thinking," some "odd-bally politics," some "lapses in her ability to perceive reality."

"Well, so everyone got worried about her and thought she might need some help. She was getting on, you know," George said gently. "She must be in her late fifties . . . but so am I . . . she'd lived here a long time and all alone, and was having an awful hard time keeping things going.

Rough job for a woman running a spread like hers," said George shaking his head. "I suppose what with the change of life and all, that kind of stress would addle anyone's head after a while, and the war took it out of everybody, especially sensitive people like Hana. It's not that Hana went crazy. It's that she started to become someone else; she changed in very odd, odd ways. She began to be noticeable to the wrong people."

"What's wrong with changing," Lowell asked. "And what do you mean 'wrong people'? Who was watching her?"

"That has to do with politics, Lowell. And probably no one was actually watching, but she was drawing attention to herself with strange ideas, dangerous ideas. Enough said. I don't even like to talk about it. I'm sounding like Nola and Thea."

"I don't understand any of this. She never seemed like she was having a hard time at Gloriamaris when I was around. And I was there all the time," Lowell responded with a frown.

"Well, I think she always put on a good face for you. Nola was the first to notice it, after the play you two were in. Poor Nola's not so well herself at times, but she was right. Hana was acting 'queer,' as Nola said. And even that guy Dr. Barrows, Hal, thought so, according to Nola. Hana wasn't eating properly, Nola told us, even when she brought over Hana's favorite breads. She seemed terribly depressed— know what that means?"

"Yep."

". . . depressed and tired and listless. She just seemed like she'd run out of gas a lot of the time, got slovenly, let herself go, wouldn't keep to her regular habits. And she was getting suspicious of everyone."

"What's wrong with all that? Doesn't everybody get sad once in a while?"

"Sure, but this was pretty severe, and it went on for a long time. A real long time. In fact, it seemed to be getting worse; that's what Nola thought, and Betty, too. We all got worried. Then she'd just shut down, lock her doors, wouldn't see anyone for weeks and weeks, it seemed. . . . We think she had what you'd call a nervous breakdown after you got sick. Maybe it was in the air. Betty came down with the flu just then, and Juliet had something or other for a long time after you were in the hospital," George said lightly.

"I was in the hospital, too?" Lowell said squinting in disbelief.

"My gosh, young man, you didn't know *that*?!"

"No."

"Yes, yes. You were out like a light for weeks and weeks, maybe months. You had to have round-the-clock care, somebody said."

"Golly, I don't remember any of that," Lowell said with mock surprise. "Is that why Nola's been so mean to me?"

"Why, because you were sick? Nooooo. She's been mean to you? I can't believe that, Lowell. Why would she be mean to you?"

"I don't know. I think she hates me. I went to Hana's the other day, and Nola kicked me out and said if I ever returned I'd be real sorry."

"Well, it's a hard job running a ship like that. And she's responsible now until Hana gets better."

Lowell was surprised at George's peaceful demeanor. He wasn't ashamed, or scared, nor in the least bit nervous. He didn't seem to be making anything up. "He must think that Hana just got sick," Lowell thought to himself. He'd expected powerful things to happen, things that George would say that would let Lowell trap him, pin him down, and twist all the truth out of him. But George was calm. Lowell didn't know what to do at first; then he got brave.

"But what *really* happened, George? You're leaving stuff out, aren't you? What happened to all Hana's animals, and why can't I go to Gloriamaris anymore? Something's wrong. I don't like it. It's like everybody's hiding something," Lowell said backing up a yard or more from George to get a better look.

"Well, I'm sure nobody is hiding anything. Hana's up in a sanitarium east of here toward the Sandias, recuperating. They thought she'd get better but she's getting worse and worse, apparently. If she doesn't get better soon, Nola told me, her estate won't be able to keep her in a private facility and she'll have to go to the state mental hospital."

"Have you seen her?"

"No, visits weren't advised."

"What do you mean?"

"The doctors thought friends would only upset her and push her further into darkness.

"Darkness?"

"That's Nola's word. . . . As for the animals, well, you know, how can you properly care for all those creatures? It was a full-time job for Hana herself. Twenty cats, eleven dogs, my gosh! And all the others. We decided the best thing we could do was to find good homes for them."

"But that doesn't make any sense, if you really thought Hana was going to get better and come home," Lowell said convincingly, but with an argumentative whine. "Why didn't you just feed them? I know why, don't I? You didn't really expect Hana to return at all, did you?" he said accusingly and on the verge of tears. "And besides, all the animals are dead. Juliet told me that."

George Devon tapped his pipe on his shoe, put it in his shirt pocket, took Lowell by the hand, and walked up the path beside his front lawn. He stopped midway at a wooden bench he'd made years ago, sat Lowell down and said slowly and with genuine anguish, "They *were* all killed, Lowell. Somehow, something terrible happened, some horrible misunderstanding, some unforgivable breakdown in communication. It was so awful. I can't even explain it to myself how such a . . . such a dreadful, dreadful thing could have happened. I went down there myself and tried to make them explain. They promised to call me and tell me who the new owners would be in each and every case, so I could report to Hana that they all had good homes. But they had them all put to sleep the next day, for gosh sakes, the next day. They told me it was some clerical mistake. They would say nothing more. I take all the blame for this myself. I shouldn't have let Nola handle the animals as well as all the other things she had to do. She was so upset herself and so troubled by Hana's illness and the business with the courts that she let things get out of control. I should have taken charge, Lowell. I should have taken charge. I'm no good at taking orders. I wonder now if *anything* we did was right. One of the main reasons Hana's not better, I believe, is that she learned about the death of her animals. I don't know how she found out, but she must have. She just seemed to cave in completely after that, Nola said. I'll feel bad about it, Lowell, until the day I die. I'd known those critters almost as long as Hana had. I loved them. I guess you could say I loved Hana too.

"It's unforgivable what happened. But it happened. Remember that, son, things like that do happen *if* you leave it up to others. That's certainly a lesson I'll never forget."

"I loved Hana, too. I didn't know you did," Lowell said with a shy smile.

"Well, I mean, I loved her like a dear, dear friend, Lowell. She and I were allies when it came to protecting animals and birds. We talked once or twice a week for more than twenty years. I miss her terribly."

Lowell could see wetness in George Devon's eyes. His despondency, the crack in his voice, his sad expression as he tried to help

Lowell understand, made Lowell instinctively pat him on the shoulder to reassure him that he didn't think George was to blame.

But when Lowell asked him to explain what he meant by "court business," George became uncomfortable, though he didn't hesitate to talk about it.

"It's very confusing, Lowell, very confusing. I don't really understand why we had to do it. But Hana was all alone, all alone in the world and had no one really to look after her. She didn't like to admit that she was sick and in need of care, but we all knew she was, and we were afraid for her, afraid that she might get really ill and hurt herself if we didn't do something for her and do it quickly. Hana would not have gone to the hospital unless the court had told her she had to."

"What kind of illness did she have? I never knew she was sick. She was never sick when I knew her. She got tired, maybe, but she was never sick. Do you mean sick in the head, is that what you're trying to say?" Lowell asked.

"That's one way to put it."

"What's another way?"

"Well, she just couldn't take care of herself."

"What do you mean? She always took care of everyone. Me, too. And Juliet with their lunches and talks, and even Nola, and I bet you, too."

"Yes, Lowell, she did. But she started to wind down. She got confused. She got angry. She didn't want any help. She couldn't manage."

Lowell looked baffled. "What business was it of yours?" he asked pointedly.

"Well, son, if you think your best friend is in trouble, is about to hurt herself, to hurt someone else, you have to help her. We are our brother's keeper, you know."

"I don't get it. Hana didn't want to hurt anyone. She was the kindest person in the world. And how could anyone that good be a danger to herself? In what way. I don't understand."

"You do know what depressed means?"

"Well, yes, I guess."

"Hana had severe bouts of depression."

"But is that any reason to take her to court, put her in a sanitarium, kill all her animals, and God knows what else?"

"Lowell, Lowell, of course not. Of course not. No one thought it would turn out this way. No one."

"If she was sick, couldn't someone have come to stay with her?"

"Lowell, I swear to you, I was appalled when I heard that the sheriff's officers came and took her into custody."

"Oh my God, really? Why would anyone do that?"

"Well, it seems she didn't want to go. Nola and that Dr. Barrows thought it best, thought they had to get her out of the house before she did real damage to herself. I don't know, Lowell, I don't know," George responded with a hint of irritation in his voice.

Lowell took the cue immediately. He slid down the bench, moving away from the older man, stood up, stuck his hands in his pockets, and stared off at the volcanic cones to the west. "I'm sorry, George, I don't mean to make you mad. It just seems stupid and strange to me. And I don't understand . . . anyone, or anything. I'm sorry. I'll shut up."

"No, Lowell. You've asked good questions. I wish I had better answers. I'm sorry. I'm really sorry. I don't know what else to say. I've got lots of work to do this morning, Lowell, maybe in a couple of weeks we could walk down to the bosque and look for birds and see if we can track that coyote family we found last summer. That would be fun, wouldn't it?"

"Sure. I'll drop by in a couple of weeks. Maybe I could talk to Betty then."

"You mean about Hana? No, no. I don't think so, Lowell."

"Why not?"

"Let's just say that Betty is too close to it now, and very upset. And let's say no more," George said with resolute finality.

"OK," Lowell answered as he turned away and almost ran down the long path to Guadalupe Trail.

Lowell felt thoroughly muddled. George Devon had been honest with him, he thought, but now he had two very different interpretations of what had taken place. And some horrific visions, especially of Hana being carted off by the sheriff. George's tale did not fit with the picture of events that Juliet had given him, though they did have one thing in common; they both pointed in the direction of Nola and Dr. Barrows. Lowell did feel some relief, however, in that he no longer had to hate George Devon. He was not a fiend, any more than Juliet was. And Betty? He'd never cared much for her anyway. And he crossed her off his list.

—-—

From Lowell Briscoe's "A Nest of Hells."

PART EIGHT

The Starry Mire

The Riot of 1992
Going Slack

Franklin Carter, Oliver Smith, Frank Thomas, and Marvin Franklyn—
the Normandy Four—had spent the last eleven months in jail in Los
Angeles, held without bond for the beating of Lowell Patrick Briscoe,
the "beloved children's author." Only Frank Thomas had heard of
Lowell's Christmas fable. The others hadn't had much experience with
Christmas in their lives. Franklin Carter's father, a fry cook, had left
Los Angeles for San Diego where a good-paying job in a Marriott
kitchen promised better things for his family. He left when Franklin
was eight and didn't return. Franklin's mother raised him and three
other children, working two jobs. Oliver Smith's father was a preacher,
a person of rigid standards, a widower, who died when Oliver was sixteen, leaving him without a family. Frank Thomas's parents were teachers—a mathematician and a historian—at Fremont High School. They
were strong, upstanding, hardworking people who Frank thought
never quite understood him or his needs. Christmas was plentiful in
Frank's house, but it meant little to him or to his friends who were
busily teaching him to grow up in a hurry. Marvin Franklyn was an ath-
lete who'd lettered in four sports. He was a muscular, big young man
with a tiny mother, two tiny sisters, and a father who had been killed
in 'Nam. Marvin worked in an auto repair shop. His friends wondered
if he sold crack to pay for his beautiful Buick.

None of the Normandy Four belonged to a gang, as far as anyone
knew. They were not members of the territorial armies that ruled the
neighborhoods in South Central Los Angeles. They verged on being
middle class, and they had known each other all their lives. They were
angry at their parents, angry at school, angry about Rodney King,
whose beating seemed to symbolize the hopelessness and danger of
their lives, and angry as hell that they'd been caught up in a riot and
charged with beating some crazy white man who they'd heard spout-
ing off on talk radio and interview shows on TV. Did they beat Lowell
Briscoe almost to death? All they cared about at the moment was getting free of their orange prison jumpsuits, the terrible prison food, and
their dangerous notoriety in jail, where half the inmates admired them

and half wanted to kill them. They were frightened all the time, bored all the time, angry all the time.

Lowell wrote in his journal three days before the trial began: "All day with the prosecutors again. Cates more civil. Everyone trying to treat me with kid gloves. About time. This is my first trial. I am not on trial, but I feel like I am. I feel as baffled as Hana must have felt. . . . Well, of course not. I'm not fighting for my life. But then, she didn't actually fight either. Still, I feel as if I am fighting for myself, if not my life. I really don't know who I am anymore. I know that I've created myself. I know that what I have created is real. Yet I feel inauthentic, or at least disgusted with what I consider to be the 'most real' part of me—my anger. I feel so much anger at so many people, so many, many people. I find it unbearable, this inner madhouse. I can't identify with it. It's the hidden misery I live with all the time. I feel inside, sometimes, like the people who talk to themselves on the streets, chattering, shrieking, getting even, telling people off, saying to themselves what they could never say to others. I can't turn the monologue off sometimes. Yet, it's the only thing I can do something about. I can't change my history. I can't change the world. I can't change what happens to other people. But I think I can change what goes on inside me. I want to be at peace. And the only way I can do that is to be able to forgive, forgive everyone everything, to get rid of my anger, forgive Nola and Juliet, forgive the bastards who beat me up, forgive the jury who freed the cops who beat up Rodney King and caused the Goddamn riot, forgive Goddamn D.A. Cates, forgive everyone. Forgive myself. But it's one thing to say that, and quite another to sincerely feel it. And I don't know about my motives. Is it permissible to forgive people so *you* feel better, or is it something you give to them? And is it possible to forgive in the first place? Isn't it extremely arrogant? 'I forgive you.' Big deal. But I can't think of anything else to do. And it seems hopeless. I've programmed myself to hate these bastards. I'm addicted to hating them. The patterns are so pervasive in my neuropeptide system that anger just spontaneously appears. How can I sincerely forgive these people if I keep having hateful thoughts and feelings of rage about them? Is it enough to intend to forgive them? Will that help quiet me down?

"I've got the feeling that the so-called Normandy Four are feeling the same things I am. How could they not, trapped as they are in their lives, the riots of the 1960s as powerful a trauma for their families as the Great Depression, all of them inheritors of the worst possible kind of persecution and oppression that cannot be, and must not be, forgotten or forgiven.

"It's so ridiculously odd: At the same time I'm struggling for sincerity, praying for kindness and compassion in my heart, I feel overcome by an exquisite, childish urge, by an intense, almost erotic compulsion to take charge of the trial, to 'give in' to the prosecution, to do what they tell me to do, to hoodwink everyone and agree that the 'defendants' are indeed guilty and point them out. The feeling I get when that thought comes to mind is one of delicious retribution. The case against them is very, very strong, even if I don't remember their faces. And my desire to let go, to stop fighting, to get some satisfaction and have everyone love me—so childlike, so sweetly familiar—is irresistible. How can hatred and this insane need to be loved exist side by side?"

Later that afternoon, at a pre-trial briefing, District Attorney Lewis Cates looked at Lowell with a soft, grateful smile. "Now are you sure about this, Dr. Briscoe? I want you to be able to live with this."

"I am. I don't know what could have confused me so much before. I think I was just pissed off at the world. And I felt you were pushing me, forcing me to agree with what I couldn't confirm in my own conscience. I don't know what happened over the last few days, but as I looked at the video, I've emotionally, if not perceptually, become convinced that they are the ones. I trust my emotions more than I trust my senses. I think feeling is a way of perceiving."

"This sudden change, Dr. Briscoe. We haven't just worn you down and made you willing to go along just to get us off your back? We know how much torment you've suffered, but that would not be right."

"No, this is real. I'm not playing around. I'm ashamed of myself for being so stubborn. I haven't paid attention to you. I've tried to focus on my own sense of what really happened. I've been so afraid that I'd forget, or that I've really been somehow brain damaged, and that this stuff would just slip out of my head. The images are so fuzzy and they come in and out of view. I was pissed at you, too, because I didn't think you really understood what happened to me and were expecting too much of me. But I've realized that I've just been working off of fear. It's made me pig-headed. It seems to me now that your evidence is overwhelming."

"We think it is too, Dr. Briscoe. And I apologize if I was overly hard on you. I was probably out of line. I want these suckers real bad.

What they did could have happened to any one of us. It was a racist mob. And they are racists! That crap cuts both ways. And I'm going to show them that it does," Cates said with finality.

Lowell nodded and smiled benignly.

"Dr. Briscoe, let's go back over your testimony, just for a moment if we could."

"As I said, I know emotionally and intuitively that they're the ones, though I'm still not absolutely sure I could tell them apart in a line-up. I have no moral qualms, though. I know what I know. They are the ones."

"I hate to say this, but making such a distinction between emotion and . . ."

"Perception. . . ."

"Yes, perception. That won't quite hold up in court. The defense will tear you apart."

"Well, being emotionally certain is more convincing to me, personally, than being perceptually certain, so I'll just say I'm certain. Is that OK?"

"I think so."

"Good. But how could I respond when the defense asks me if I can identify the actual people on the video footage?"

"I was just about to get to that. Let's run the tape and I'll show you."

Three days into the trial of the Normandy Four, Lowell wrote in his journal: "I testify tomorrow. Everyone's so cocky. The kids, their defense team, the D.A., and his people. The media is all over me every time I come to the courthouse, leave the courthouse, every lunch break, practically every time I take a leak. I feel anything but cocky. The whole town is waiting for me to point the finger at those kids, not only as my attackers, but by implication, as the plotters of the whole riot. The D.A. wants me to help him make them the riot scapegoats. My team, the prosecution, is so arrogant, so vehement, that I feel embarrassed. I feel like the key witness in a witch hunt. I brought this on myself. I manipulated them, and now I feel manipulated. I look at those young men, the backs of their heads, and I feel compromised, morally compromised, cowed, and bullied into submission. By everyone. There are riot police outside the building. The national guard has been put on alert. People are buying handguns and all because of me. And, of course, the parents of the 'accused' demanding 'equal justice' for their kids. 'You let the cops off, even with a video tape, you can let our kids off too.' The oddest thing now is that I actually believe the prosecution's evidence. Those *are* my attackers, those are the people I used to want run over with a steamroller and watch their brains and guts spurt out. The damn D.A. has convinced me. And now I feel totally vulnerable and used. I don't know how to defend my interests. I don't know how to look after myself. There seems to be only one thing to do, revert to form, be consistent with my past, and *lie*. Would Hana laugh! If I'm going to save L.A. from another riot and an enormous social crisis, I've got to forgive those kids, even if it's only a gesture. I've got to forgive them and rid myself of the horror of wanting to kill them."

The next day Lowell took the stand in a courtroom that looked like a stage set. The D.A., himself, examined him, moving through all the events that led up to his beating and asked Lowell to describe in as much detail as he could the suffering he'd undergone. Lowell largely repeated the testimony of medical experts who had been on the stand the day before. And he told the court what he'd been telling Los Angeles television viewers and radio listeners for more than a year. He was dressed for court like a professor. And really, from a distance, seemed no different than he always had, except for his nose, which seemed uneasily crooked. If you looked at him long enough, though, you could see that one eye appeared not to work very well, that he wore two dental plates that discomforted him, and that his right cheek, forehead, and lips had formidable scars.

When the D.A. asked him what it was like to be pulled from his car by a mob, Lowell replied, "It was like staring down the throat of a big shark that was about to chew off your head. A primal terror comes over you, a horror that's in our genes, somehow, and that compels us to do everything we can to escape. And, of course, that's what makes it all so unbearable. There's no escaping sharks and there's no escaping mobs. You just have to be eaten alive or beaten to death, or half to death in my case," he said with a wry smile.

Lowell began to feel nauseated. The courtroom smelled to him like sauerkraut and dusty blinds, with cat pee along the floorboards. The room was hot and packed with reporters and police. He had shuddered several times during his testimony and had pressed his palm to his brow briefly as if he had a headache. Now, he could sense that his moment was approaching. He knew D.A. Cates was moving inexorably and with exquisite finality to the fatal questions of identity. Lowell had given much of his testimony looking at Cates and then staring at the defendants, who never met his gaze.

Lowell knew that he was about to seize the whole proceedings. He felt an uneasily thrill in his guts—what a slave must feel when the chains are being cut from his neck, no longer a victim, no longer under anyone's protection but his own. He straightened himself in his chair. He felt good about himself, he enjoyed the tension of finally doing what he thought was right.

"Dr. Briscoe, you've stated you have a clear recollection of who your attackers were, that you've seen them and recognize their features," Cates said almost nonchalantly looking at his yellow pad. "Do you see them anywhere in this courtroom?"

"No, I do not."

The courtroom was silent as ice. The defendants looked up and stared at Lowell with amazed intensity. And D.A. Cates rolled his eyes, stared fiercely at Lowell, and said with massive indignation, "I beg your pardon. What did you say?"

"I said I don't recognize my attackers anywhere in this room," Lowell said softly.

"What on earth do you mean," Cates bellowed. "You have led us to believe all along, Dr. Briscoe, that you had identified the defendants as your attackers. Are you changing your mind, now? I don't understand. What's happened? Are you afraid of reprisals?" Cates's voice was sounding hysterical. "Are you falling into some kind of post traumatic stress syndrome?"

"Excuse me?"

"Are you suffering from post traumatic stress syndrome?!" Cates shouted. "Have you lost your senses? Are you losing your mind?!"

"Objection, your honor," the defense attorney stammered, "the prosecution is attacking its own. . . ."

"Sustained," the judge said impatiently.

"May I respond, your honor?" Lowell asked in his best professorial tone.

"Go ahead, Dr. Briscoe, you're not on trial here."

"Thank you, your honor. Mr. Cates, I cannot in good conscience, and upon months of ceaseless reflection, point the finger at these young men, despite the seemingly airtight nature of your case against them. As I look at them now, what I thought I knew was true dissolves into doubt. I have always had doubts that I could identify them. You know that. You've tried endlessly to talk me out of them. . . ."

"That's a very serious charge, Dr. Briscoe, bordering on libel. I'd be careful if I were you," Cates shot back.

"Libel doesn't apply to public officials, Mr. Cates," Lowell said softly with a smile.

"What are you trying to do to me, you little. . . ."

"Objection."

"Sustained. Mr. Cates, I'll thank you not to threaten and insult your own witness."

"You *have* tried to talk me out of my doubts," Lowell continued. "And while I know you did so, in your own mind, to help me to remember, I also know that you become extremely agitated when you think someone is endangering public safety, which is an admirable quality. My doubts, I think, have caused you to consider me a danger. But I have doubts. I was beaten senseless. And as much as I admire your zeal for the public's welfare, I have felt twice victimized by this whole situation—first for being in the wrong place at the wrong time with the wrong color skin, a condition many people, and countless black people, have suffered horribly in our nation's history, and second by you because I am a person who is unwilling to deny his conscience. You've badgered me, accused me of being everything but insane. . . . No, no. I'm being unfair. You were trying to do your job. I'm sure you did it ethically as far as your conscience is concerned. But we've never been anything but hostile to each other. Isn't that so? And you could never quite get it through your head that it really did matter to me. . . ."

"Your honor, please, do I have to listen to this?" Cates bellowed from his seat.

"Mr. Cates, there'll be no more outbursts from you, is that understood?"

"Yes, sir."

"Dr. Briscoe, please continue, but keep it short."

"As I was saying, you could never quite get it into your head that it really does matter to me that the right people get convicted of this crime, not token or symbolic defendants, but the actual, as they say, 'perpetrators.' There's too much negative stereotyping going on in this country. I don't want to be a part of the interchangeability of people who have lost their personal identities in the negative images imposed on them as members of a financially lower, untouchable caste by the existing power elite."

"Power elite?!" D.A. Cates blurted with indignation. "I am an employee of the people of the County of Los Angeles, I am not a member of the power elite, whatever that might be. I know more about social and economic abuse than you'll ever be able to comprehend as a mere, big-mouth academic. How dare you associate me or any member of my team with oppressive forces in this country! There are no oppressive forces in this country. . . ."

"Mr. Cates, I'll warn you this one last time . . ."

"Excuse me your honor. . . . Thank you, Dr. Briscoe," Cates said in a dry, weary voice so full of contempt it was barely audible.

That night Lowell received a call from the father of Frank Thomas inviting him to a late, impromptu supper at their little house off La Cienega near LAX. The Thomases had also invited Mrs. Carter, Mrs. Franklyn, and Mrs. Smith, telling them that he wanted "Dr. Briscoe to know how grateful we all are for his honesty and integrity, and how sorry we are for his injuries." The Thomases had also asked Josephine and Mitchel Barker, the couple who had rescued Lowell from the mob, to come over, hoping to make Lowell feel more at home. It was a tense encounter. The Thomas home was elegantly tidy. The Thomases' four daughters, all under ten, thought Lowell to be something of a curiosity and watched his every move all evening. The families were all "completely frazzled and sleepless," as Mrs. Carter explained while the Thomases served Lowell KFC takeout chicken instead of homemade. Lowell tried to be charming but felt diffident and uncomfortable. Supper was eaten to polite banter. Everyone left before nine. Unfortunately, a reporter from a local radio show who'd been assigned to Mrs. Franklyn followed her to the Thomas house, as he often had. And this night his surveillance paid off. He saw Lowell go into the Thomas house and emerge two hours later in a warm, if formal, embrace of all the families of the defendants. The reporter thought he had a scoop. And, indeed, he had. A talk radio jockey on his station that morning reported Lowell was seen "hanging out with his pals who just happened to be the parents of his accused attackers." Front-page stories the next morning implied that Lowell and the families had colluded to "throw the trial," despite Lowell's vehement denials. These speculations, which were at the heart of the news stories, were based on extensive interviews with D.A. Cates.

Several days later, just before the verdict, Lowell wrote in his journal, "I don't really know what I've done here. I can't decide if I was defiant of authority or trying to please those young men and their families. Or was I trying to become a hero in their eyes, or make them feel really ashamed of the rotten way they treated such a nice guy as me, or was I truly liberating myself from the opinions of others? I can't decipher my motives. I feel empty headed. I don't think my testimony helped them anyway. I'm sure they'll be convicted. The evidence against them even convinces me. And I'm so completely baffled now that I really don't know what I know. I think they probably did beat me up. What the hell am I doing? Did I really feel a twinge of social conscience? Am I really trying to prevent another riot? It seems that way to me, but I don't trust myself. But I know I don't want another riot because of *me*. I've got to comport myself in such a way that I do nothing to trigger another one. At the same time, though, I really do feel caught between two absurd versions of reality, two hallucinations—that of the established and that of the wretched. I belong to neither reality. And I loathe the stench of cynicism rising from them both. And as far as the press and Mr. Cates are concerned, I hope they rot in hell. I hope I can make them seem to be the swine they really are. . . ."

SOS

1 June 1949

Thea Dear,

I write you seldom these days, but I need very much to see you for a short talk perhaps over lunch downtown, away from the North Valley. I suppose I could have used someone's phone to call you, but even my current distress couldn't make me use one of those misbegotten devices. I say "distress" because I believe I might not be seeing things for what they really are. I need to check with you and compare realities. This is an SOS only in the sense of an alert. I am not sinking, only perplexed. The gist is this—I'm sensing that "certain people," some of them are my oldest and closest friends, think, somehow, that I've become odd, perhaps even dangerously so. I'm frightened by these suspicions, but not hysterical or depressed. Please, could we meet for luncheon soon?

Love as always,
[signed] Your Hana

* * *

1 June 1949

Dear George,

SOS old friend. This sailor is a bit at sea and would like mucho to talk con tu over coffee or lunch downtown sometime soon. Nothing in the way of disasters, just a general uneasiness about what "some people" might be thinking, if you know what I mean. And you *do*, I know, know what I mean, and WHO I mean. I need to check with you to see if I'm being silly or very prophetic. Cassandra the Sailor, here. Send love to Miss Betty,

[signed] Your Hana

* * *

1 June 1949

Juliet my dear,

Let's revive our mental repasts next Tuesday, not here but at the Alvarado instead. I know it's a big change, but I don't feel very comfortable at Gloriamaris at the moment. Which is one of the things I'd like to discuss—the nature of perception and misperception.

How is Lowell? Is he strong enough for a visit from me? *Where* is he?

With love and eager anticipation,
[signed] Hana

Thea Has Her Say

Lowell had not seen Thea since well before what everyone had described as his "breakdown," but he knew the warmth he had once felt for her had always been returned in kind and that she would be glad, if somewhat startled, to see him. Lowell rode the five miles to her house that morning as slowly as he could, needing time to compose himself and prepare the proper face. He was dressed in a sports coat, blue pants, brown shoes, with the collar of his shirt spread out over the coat lapels. He'd scrubbed his face until his cheeks were rosy, and had combed his hair with Wildroot Creme Oil, so it was plastered smartly in place. Thea liked children to feign formality; it made their silliness all the more delightfully extreme.

Lowell loved the ride from Griegos farmland to the downtown neighborhood, pedaling under the shade of the giant cottonwoods along Rio Grande Boulevard. He then turned up Mountain Road. When he walked his bike down 13th Street he began to get that feeling he liked so much of being surrounded by normal people who wore clean underwear everyday, cut their toenails straight across, and lavished care on their violets and miniature dogs. They were whole milk people who lived in those shipshape Midwestern houses, sausage patty people. He knew every one of them would have taken him in off the street and treated him to breakfast and funny papers if he'd given them a chance. To him, their lives were good and their troubles had never materialized.

As he rounded the corner of 12th and Marquette he saw the familiar, venerable mansion of Thea Pound. Though neat as the rest of the houses along the way, Thea's two-story Victorian possessed none of their wholesomeness. It was built of dark brick and darker wood. Tall dark pines, wet greens, shadows, and moss made it seem as if Thea's house was the residence of a troll who was liked and coddled by her neighbors but not of their species. Thea was "so verdant," as Juliet was once heard to say.

Lowell scuffed through elm leaves up the path to the front door. It was a lovely, dark-stained wooden door, with a big piece of heavily beveled, leaded glass engraved with a woodland scene of two bucks about to slam their heads together. Lowell knocked on the door, waited, and knocked again, and then heard the padding of Thea's carpet slippers as she tried to scurry down the entrance hall, slipping every now and then on the Persian-looking runner. Great hugs mixed with wet kisses and the smell of cookies in the oven greeted Lowell as she folded him into her billowy bosom and the smoothness of her fresh starched apron.

Thea's welcome took Lowell by surprise. It was as if nothing had happened except that they hadn't seen each other in ages and she was glad they were together again. Lowell dawdled around her kitchen as she put the fresh, hot cookies on a gold-rimmed plate, poured two glasses of milk, and set them on the kitchen table. The room was oppressively warm, but the milk was ice cold.

She asked Lowell how he was feeling and if he had fully recovered. He answered awkwardly and they chatted dutifully back and forth until they had worked their way into a discomforting silence, which Thea finally broke by asking Lowell why he had come all that way by himself just to see her. Lowell told her it was because he had missed her and considered her one of his best friends and that he had been deeply troubled by what he had heard about Hana and hoped Thea might be able to help him understand what happened better.

"Hana was my best friend, Thea, my very best friend. And now she's gone and I don't know why. Will you help me understand?" Lowell told her, sounding as if he were close to tears.

Lowell had gone to Thea's house like a spy, expecting to find the arch accomplice, but found himself, instead, feeling glad, and more secure than before, in her presence.

Thea eyed Lowell with kindly suspicion, offered him more cookies and milk, but wouldn't say a thing about Hana. Finally, on the brink of another discomforting silence, Lowell blurted that he knew quite a lot about Hana's "disappearance." He took another bite of cookie then rambled, in extreme agitation, about his talks with Juliet and George Devon, about the strange differences in their stories, about the killing of the animals, about Hana's apparent anger at her circumstances.

Lowell then asked Thea point blank if she had been part of a plot to "get" Hana, and if she had, why?

Thea was flabbergasted. She paced the kitchen in a dither, turning to Lowell every few seconds and saying emphatically, "No, I am not a conspirator. No, no, no, you see. Not a plotter, either."

"How could you think that of me," she finally declared. "I'm your friend, you say. Is that a lie? Do you hate me? Have you come here to kill me, to eat my cookies and do me in?" Thea seemed torn between humor and impending horror.

"I just want the truth, the truth, that's all I want," Lowell said feigning nonchalance, popping another cookie in his mouth.

"Answer me first," Thea demanded. "Tell me if you hate me or if you'll give me a chance to prove myself?"

Lowell told her he didn't hate her. "But my heart is breaking. Please don't let me down. Please don't lie to me. Tell me what you know, all of it, please."

Thea regained her motherly distance. "Well, seeing as how you 'know so much,'" she said with an ironic upswing in her voice, "I guess it won't hurt you to hear the rest. But please, please remember there is nothing to be done now. We can only pray, do you see, that Hana gets better and forgives us all when she returns. It all happened before any one of us knew it, and we did what we had to do."

She passed Lowell a cookie and wiped the perspiration from her chubby chin and brow. "That part of my life is gone now. I've closed myself to it, see, turned off my hearing aid as my mother used to say. We did the best we could. Forgiveness—forgiving yourself—is important if you mean to survive."

Thea asked Lowell if he understood how a person could be so detached from herself and at the same time so close that she could "be different from who she was and thus forgive her errors, while being also quite the same person altogether?"

Lowell did understand and replied, "Maybe you can think of me as not only myself but as who I will be when I'm older, me as a grown up. And maybe you can pretend I'm older and tell me what you know, while you're still telling everything to a little kid who can't hurt you. You know, I'd be your real friend if I was older."

Thea looked at him, took another cookie, leaned back in her chair, laughed lightly to herself, and said, "Remember, old man this is very, very real. There is a real danger in this world. Little people can be cut down just like big people can, you see, no matter what kind of game we are playing. It's so strange you should be here today," she said thoughtfully, the ominous tone lifting from her voice. "This is the first Sunday in months and months that I haven't visited Hana."

"You visit her?" Lowell asked with astonishment.

"Yes, religiously, religiously."

"Well, why didn't you visit her today?"

"Because it means nothing to her at all," she said. "I just have to accept it. It's like talking to a piece of bread. She just sits there. Just sits. . . ."

Thea gulped the rest of her glass of milk, bit into another cookie, and lit a cigarette. Lowell was beginning to lose his patience, and started to fidget and drum his fingers. But then Thea leaned forward, her elbows on the table, took a couple of deep drags from her Herbert Tareyton, and told him.

"I am going to talk to you like an adult, Lowell. If you don't understand, it's your own fault, OK?"

"OK."

"You see, there's been lots of tension and animosity building up inside our little group for many years. We all tried to talk about it from time to time, but nothing came of the discussions. As near as I can tell, it was nothing really more than people who had known each other for years starting, slowly, to drift apart, whose lives were changing, whose needs were changing, and who felt more and more alone among people who were supposed to be friends," Thea said with empathic irony. "Do you see what I mean?"

"I think so."

"We all grew disappointed with each other, Lowell, do you see? Our ideals were replaced with realities," Thea said wearily. "Hana, Nola, and I were never really best friends or anything like that; none of us were the kind of people who had best friends. We were all too strange, really. Both Nola and I were one-man women. And we didn't like other people much, you see. But we had all known each other for a very long time and respected each other for various reasons. Hana was the stand-out, of course. Both Nola and I looked up to her for moral support, and she served as an excellent example. We both admired her courage and the stamina it took to live the way she did, to run her own place, to help so many, many people, and to try to keep up her scholarship, though I was never quite sure what she was a scholar of. I used to think that Hana and I were sisters, but that didn't last very long. She was hard to know. We were close to each other but didn't really know much about each other, do you see?"

Lowell thought to himself silently, "She's lying to me, or to herself. I've seen it otherwise. They loved each other."

By this time, Thea had almost forgotten Lowell was in the room. She was talking to herself, as if she were looking at a bathroom mirror.

"About five or six years ago, something changed between Hana and me. We began to deepen to one another. It wasn't anything like real rapport—who has that with anyone?—but we came, I think, to genuinely like each other. Of course, I was too awed by her to pry into her life or burden her with anything important or personal. But we did like animals, and that was our common ground. Hana considered me some sort of expert, her 'child shaman' she called me, whatever that means. For some reason, I could cure almost anything her animals got, which really wasn't all that much because they were so extravagantly well cared for, healthy and cheerful. . . . Well, to make a long story short," Thea said waving her hand away from her forehead as if brushing off bad thoughts, "in the long run Nola got miffed, do you see, that's all I can really point to, she got jealous or hurt and thought we were cutting her out, or joining in league against her. Utter nonsense, of course."

Thea stopped talking long enough to focus on Lowell's serious face. She reached across the table, patted his cheek, blew him a little kiss, and went right back to her rambling. "It was a minor hurt for Nola, I'm sure, minor, minor . . . like having your best girl friend in school make another friend . . . a very minor hurt, indeed. Trouble is, you see, it grew in intensity along with the deepening and entrenching of Nola's own peculiar brand of strangeness, which happens to everyone—becomes visible, that is, when people become a little too old to disguise it anymore. It happened to me, as you can see. It happened to Hana, and God knows Nola went nutty as a fruit cake, but very slowly and very subtly. These are all things, do you see, that no one really ever talks about."

She looked at Lowell and searched for some kind of recognition in his eyes. "Am I making any sense, dear?"

"Yes. Go on, please," Lowell said, learning across the table and kissing her on the cheek.

"Ahhh, thank you, sweetie. Where was I? Nola always did have a tendency to be puritanical. But Hana was something more, and as time went on, something increasingly and obviously 'more' than the rest of us, if you see what I mean . . . more strange, do you see. Well, I wasn't aware of what was happening until it just happened. First there was Thanksgiving dinner, then the blow up at the play, then you got into a brutal fight with that nasty little grandson of hers, then Hana's long depressions, her refusal to see people, her withdrawal, then the whole incident before you got sick."

"What whole incident?" Lowell asked, his adrenaline surging. "What do you mean?"

Thea sputtered a bit, looked flustered, saying "That will come later, be patient, but I always knew," she said with a long sigh, and a longer pause, "I always knew that you were more than the rest of us too, Lowell, and that Hana would find something in you that she hadn't found in anyone else, even Juliet, you poor dear."

Lowell felt distinctly the sensation of darkness closing in around the kitchen. The wind stopped. Everything turned deathly still. He was listening to Thea as if his ear were pressed to one end of a long narrow tube with her lips at the other end, sending the words down the darkness so that they bounded off the walls of the tunnel, rumbling like a lopsided ball, and slamming into his ear drums with incredible force.

Thea continued, talking more excitedly now, with more conviction and interest, in a gossipy, illicit tone. "It was her insane politics, as much as anything, that got me to thinking something was wrong. This is a dangerous time. Anyone with a grain of sense knows to keep a low profile, to zip their lip. But Hana went babbling on about McCarthy and what a monster he was, as if she knew something the rest of us didn't know. As if she knew she was right. She became so fierce, so outspoken, that she seemed, do you see, hysterical. I know judges and bankers, do you see. And I became afraid that I might become associated with Hana in their minds, if they were listening. . . ."

"How could they be listening?" Lowell asked in evident puzzlement. "Were you talking about McCarthy in the bank?"

"Well, no. No. In any case, the day it all came to a head, I had just returned from shopping. I hadn't seen Nola or Hana or your sister, for that matter, since the Christmas play, being busy with my own life in a pottering and happy sort of way. Suddenly, about a week after you were put in the hospital, Nola comes to my house all lathered up, saying she just had to speak with me about Hana and the terrible trouble she was getting into. Nola was very cool about it, if you can be cool and lathered up all at once. She told me bluntly that she was worried that Hana was going mad. She actually used that word, *mad*. She said that she'd consulted with Dr. Barrows, and he concurred with her:

paranoid delusions, delusions of grandeur, persecution complex, something like that. Nola told me that Hana wasn't eating, wasn't speaking, was depressed, furiously grumpy, and living more and more every day in a reality all her own and that, along with her political delusions, one of the main reasons might have been that she was devastated by your breakdown and hospitalization."

"Devastated?!" Lowell said incredulously.

"Yes, Lowell." Thea was pointed and serious now. "Yes, Nola told me, quite frankly, that Hana had been driven crazy by . . . guilt, that she had 'enticed' you and 'polluted' you, so that you 'committed horrible acts,' yes physical acts," Thea almost whispered, "physical acts, Lowell, and that they had plunged you over the edge."

Lowell sat straight in his chair, then stood up, then walked around the table, bent down and stared into Thea's eyes. With the sternest and most mature and angry voice he could muster, he responded "That's crazy talk, Thea. You know that. There's no way anything like that could ever happen. Nola's the one who's crazy. Can't you see that? Hana would never have done that kind of stuff to me, and I would never have done anything like that to her. Don't you see how crazy that is for Nola to say something like that and believe it herself? You're supposed to be my friend, Hana's friend. You certainly don't believe this stuff, do you? How could you? It's just plain nuts, just nuts!" Lowell was yelling now.

"Shhhhh, child. Don't yell. I'm just telling you what Nola said. I don't necessarily believe it. She got mixed up herself from time to time, lathered up as she was. Once she let it slip, do you see, that *you* had polluted Hana, but then took it back. I don't necessarily believe any of it. But Nola is very persuasive. And I had come to the conclusion myself, quite frankly, do you see, that Hana's politics were borderline lunatic, even in a free country. Be that as it may, Nola told me that Hana was in desperate need of psychiatric help, it was either that or someone might want to take legal action against her for what she had done to you . . . presuming she had done something, of course. As I've said, Nola can be very, very persuasive. She said that Hana wouldn't do anything for herself, that she just sat there in her house all day long, dead still, her mouth wide open, her eyes glazed, lifeless almost, until one time when Nola came by her Gloriamaris to check on her when Hana threw Nola out, accusing her of causing your sickness."

"My sickness?! Well, that's a lot truer than the rest of Nola's story. This is weirder than I ever imagined," Lowell said in disbelief, sitting back down at the table.

"This all came to me in a horrible gust, Lowell. Nola was cogent and scientific and teacherly. She seemed to know exactly what she was talking about and trotted out Dr. Barrow's opinions, do you see, at every turn. It all hit me so fast, I was quite bamboozled; I hadn't been able to make the transition from the grocery store yet. There I was in my hat and coat, do you see, with chops under my arm, being lectured by some sort of lathered-up professor, telling me my best friend was insane."

"But didn't you just say that you and Hana weren't very good friends at all?"

"I didn't mean that, and I don't mean for you to think that. Of course we were chums, wonderful pals, sisters really, best buddies and all that. Of course, of course . . . it's just that we'd grown apart a bit, didn't see each other very often, got distant. And I didn't know why. My feelings were hurt. Doesn't that happen to you?"

Lowell nodded, not wanting to interrupt Thea's train of thought.

"I really didn't think even once about being suspicious of Nola. I thought to myself, do you see, 'Ah, that's why I haven't seen her in such a long time.' It made sense to me, Lowell, until I started thinking about it. And besides, Nola told me she'd met with George and Betty and your sister and that they agreed with her assessment, though Nola did say that Juliet was 'reluctant,' to use Nola's word."

Thea gobbled down more cookies like a fat-cheeked monkey hoarding everything for herself.

"Nola told me she would take responsibility, full responsibility, and have Hana put in a hospital temporarily, where she could get some help, and that George and Betty would take care of her animals until Hana returned. And you know the ghastly tragedy there, don't you?"

"Yes."

"All I needed to do, Nola assured me, was to appear before a magistrate and Hana would be taken care of. I agreed to go downtown with Nola to the county courthouse the following day. Hana had already been detained, taken into custody, you see, two days before, as near as I can figure out. Well, Nola took me to the courthouse. It terrified me. I hate those places. I cuddled up to Nola for protection. When we got inside, it turned out to be an empty room."

"What turned out to be an empty room?"

"Where we were, where we were, do you see. An empty room, with only the judge, some attorneys, Nola's lawyer, the Devons, Dr. Barrows, Nola, and me. Hana was there, of course, dressed in what I remember as a gray smock. There was a nice older nurse beside her. It was a sanity hearing, Lowell, do you see? A sanity hearing. Do you know what that means? Well, of course you do, don't you? Whatever. . . . I was ready to leave the minute I walked into the room, but Nola and the Devons held me back."

"Where was Juliet?" Lowell said, asking for reassurance.

"Nowhere to be seen, as far as I remember. Maybe she'd just washed her hands of the whole thing. In any case, Hana was sitting at a little table, the matronly nurse beside her. Hana's big gray head was bowed, her hands clasped together. She never said a word. Not a single solitary word all through the hearing, even when she was asked questions. She was like a zombie. It was like she was somewhere else entirely. She looked at me, you see, as if she was out of her mind with anger, with disbelief, with disillusion, with crushing sadness. They asked me some questions about her, as they had asked the others, and, I'm not kidding you, I don't remember one of them. But I answered yes to each one. Dr. Barrows was decisive. He and the judge were both transplanted New Yorkers. Eventually, the judged ruled something, a temporary period of observation in a sanatorium, I think. And Hana was taken away as docile as a child. She didn't appear to recognize a single one of us . . . dear, dear, dear, dear," Thea said sobbing and shaking her head. "Nola drove me home. I went inside, petted Herman and Snyder and Tarzan, poured myself a nice big sherry, and bawled my heart out."

Light fringed the kitchen; the dark tunnel was disintegrating. "But you did suspect something, didn't you? You did suspect something was wrong. And it was wrong, wasn't it?" Lowell shouted, pounding the table with the flat of his hand.

Thea reached over the table and grabbed Lowell's wrist like a stern old grandmother, squeezing it with fury and frustration. "Yes, something was wrong, but not what you think. Don't be an arrogant brat. You're unbecoming enough as it is in this role of inquisitor! Lord God, how I've agonized over this, over and over again. Juliet came to me, you see, and told me of her meeting with Hana in jail and she told me what Hana said about her being, well, detained without her consent. . . . I won't use the real word she used."

"Why not?" growled Lowell.

"It was the madness talking. Juliet actually accused me of doing Nola's dirt, of being in cahoots with Nola. I tried to explain myself but she wouldn't hear a word of it and stalked right out of the house like a pompous angel. But what Juliet told me rattled my old head enough to remember all the arguments Hana and Nola had, those bitter, bitter philosophical and political squabbles, all those hours of arguing about God and communism and witch hunts and social responsibility and the freedom of the artist. And then when George told me that all Hana's animals were not given away or put to good homes but killed, do you see, I started to feel terrible guilt and began to suspect that I'd been taken in somehow. Why hadn't I offered to take in some of the animals? I berated myself endlessly over that question. Well, you see, I didn't know anything about it until they were carried off to the pound. It was a blitzkrieg, Lowell, a veritable blitzkrieg."

Thea was ranting now, so caught up in the rolling logic of her story, she couldn't be stopped, like a log tumbling through rapids.

"I went to Nola, Lowell, yes, I did, you see, I did. I confronted her as best I could. I have to confess to you that I've always been a little afraid of her, you see, just a little, but always enough to allow her to intimidate me and, as a consequence, I've never been able to be truly honest with her. Nola did her best to dispel my doubts and went into high gear all over again. It was then that I learned where Hana had been taken, Nola let it slip. I should have guessed anyway. It's the sanitarium out on north Edith. And, as I've told you, I've gone there every Sunday since, on the vague hope, you see, that Hana would have revived and would be ready to leave, and if I were there she could tell me, and I could start agitating to have her released. Nola goes there, too, every week. God knows what their meetings are like. But Hana has never recognized me during one of those visits, never once, you see, as I've said. She just sits there waiting for me to leave, and I always do at the first sign of anger spreading across her face. More evidence, do you see, that Nola and Dr. Barrows were right."

Lowell got up and walked slowly around the kitchen, dragging his fingers along the counters, looking out the window over the sink. He sighed, he sniffed, he sighed again.

"Everyone has doubts, Lowell," Thea said turning her body to look at him. "I spoke to George and Betty too. They seemed puzzled and sad and didn't know what to do. I don't know what to think anymore, do you see? So, I've stopped thinking about it at all. I'm not a crazy old lady, you know. But I am all alone, and I do have to watch out for myself. If anything fishy were going on, I had to make sure it didn't go in my direction too. Do you see what I'm saying? Besides, Hana was *non compos mentis*. Period. Like a brick, like a squash."

"All right, all right, I get it, Thea. I do."

"It did cross my mind that Nola, or Dr. Barrows, had pulled off some hideous crime right under our noses with our help, that Nola was criminally insane herself and managed to dupe us all, or scare all of us without knowing it, or something. It's not beyond reason to think that she's the devil incarnate and did it to get Hana's land and fortune. Well, what about my land and fortune, do you see. I had to think of such things. I had to. . . . In any case, I came to the point where I had to say to myself, Thea, what's done is done, put it out of your mind, do you see. And I've done just that for quite some time, though, mind you, I knew all along, knew that you would come calling. I have dreaded it, don't you think I haven't. I've dreaded you. I knew Juliet would tell you awful things, that she didn't agree with any of this, and that you'd be furious and blame me, and that I couldn't really defend myself from blame. I knew that you'd come over here, do you see, and stir up the whole mess again, and make me feel like a criminal."

With that, Thea stood up and walked to the kitchen sink and asked Lowell if he could "use another cookie and some really cold milk."

Lowell scraped his chair loudly as he stood up. "Noooo," he erupted. "Don't leave me like this. Tell me. I won't blame you. I've got to know what you really think, once and for all."

Thea sat down again, looking somewhat cowed, but adopting a mothering tone. It crossed Lowell's mind that Thea might think that he was about to go berserk, too, right there in her kitchen. He wondered for a moment if that would help him pry new information out of her. But Thea regained control, treating him like a beautiful, but poisonous, snake.

"Are you all right, my darling?" she purred. "There's never any need to raise your voice with me, you know. I'm listening to you all the time. I'm keen on you, darling. I want to know everything on your mind. You don't need to shout to get my attention. You must be in terrible distress."

Lowell tried to make an apology so he could ask more questions, but Thea preempted him. "I know you think I'm not telling you the whole truth. But I am. It doesn't make any sense, I know that. Life rarely does, do you see? Think of the war, Lowell. Did that make any sense? No, it did not. Millions and millions of people cut down by the grim reaper as if they were so many weeds. Is that rational? Does that sound like God's plan in action? Hardly! This will never make any sense to you, or to me. And certainly never to Hana, no matter how 'diabolical' she thinks it might be." Thea frowned, wiggled in her seat, took a bite from a cookie, and said in a low, and somewhat desperate tone, "Lowell, you must promise me that you will do nothing, nothing at all to stir this all up again. You must promise me that. It's all settled down, like ash from a volcano. We're all used to it now. We don't need to cloud everything up again. Do you understand?" she said in the utmost seriousness. "Let sleeping dogs lie, Lowell. I've told you everything I know. I don't know any more, do you see. I just don't. I've cut myself off completely from Nola, George and Betty, Juliet, and I've changed doctors. I'll never go to Dr. Barrows again," she said with melodramatic exaggeration. "I see no one anymore. I'm afraid of them, frankly. And I'm getting afraid of you. I wish you could have seen yourself a few moments ago, shouting like that. Quite unbecoming. It scared the wits out of me. I almost choked on my cookie. I don't like that look in your eyes, Lowell. I don't like it at all. Not at all. Come here and give old Thea a hug. I can't stand it that you'd not love me. Let's be pals again. You could come here, if you wanted, like you used to go to Hana's. I'd give you milk and cookies every week. I promise I won't tell anyone you've been here. Just give me a smile. Come on, give a big smile and a kiss and a hug," Thea said throwing open her arms. "Let's forgive and forget, forgive and forget."

Lowell got up, put on his biggest smile, trying as hard as he could to contain the terrible frustrations he was feeling. He mustered his gentlest tones, his kindest looks, his softest voice, hugged her, kissed her cheek, and then her lips lightly, and thanked her for being so honest.

"I really understand now that you don't know who did what to who. I understand, Thea. You don't have to be afraid of me. I can tell you don't know anything about Miss Nola and Dr. Hal. I know you don't know if they did something they should be punished for or not."

Thea looked at him quizzically. And then, with an angry shine in her eye, bored into him. "And who's going to make them pay if it just so happens that they 'owe'? Will it be you, Lowell, a sickly little boy who tips over at the slightest trauma, will it be you? How foolish. How absurd. Can you say you're completely right in the noggin? Can you say you're without blame? Can you be so sure you didn't drive poor Hana crazy like Nola says you did? Can you be so sure?"

Thea's face had become more pudding-like, and her eyes squinted as if she were looking directly into the sun. She'd become a creamy white custard with fangs. "Can you say you didn't just destroy her? Can you? Can you? I know if you'd done something like that to me, I'd have gone mad, you cavorting around in masks and feathers and nothing else."

"Feathers?" Lowell asked in furious astonishment.

"You know what I mean! My God! You're a little animal, you know! Don't look so shocked. Don't you see? She saw you. She knew all along there was something wrong between you and Hana. She knew, she knew. It was an unnatural affection. Why should a woman like Hana, a great civilized being of towering conscience and moral control, have you for a little friend? All the children in her other plays were good kids, a little tattered maybe, but good kids, normal children. Not you. Not you, oh, no. Not you, the avenging angel, the child who falls into comas."

It was then that a terrible idea crossed Lowell's mind for the first time. Nola was confusing Juliet with Hana. She must have sensed something with her inquisitorial intuition, but she mixed the people up, pinning his relationship with Juliet onto Hana. "No, no, too complicated. I can't . . . ," Lowell said to himself, unable to bear the implications.

Lowell was ready to rear up and defend Hana, denying everything. But he caught himself and stopped short. Thea had put him on the defensive, and that was not acceptable. It was his turn to attack. "Oh, so she told you everything, did she? Saw it all, did she? Knew something was wrong between us, did she? She's a Goddamn stinking liar. She saw nothing. She knows nothing. She's making it all up, she's made up a great big fib to hurt me, to hurt everyone. What if I told you that Dr. Hal gave me shots to knock me out, to keep out of the way?"

"What? What do you mean?"

"What if I told you that? Would you run away? I bet you would! I bet you would!" Lowell's voice rose in intensity with each word, until he was shrieking.

Then he stopped, put his head on the table, and began to moan and cry with all his heart, pounding the table with his fists. Just as Thea was about to stand up and either comfort him or throw him out of the house, Lowell stood up, wiped his eyes, and spoke with grave menace, "You've told me all I need to know, Thea Pound. You people have hurt me, and I won't ever forget it, ever, ever." Whereupon he wheeled around and stalked off to the front door, with Thea skittering behind. She grabbed him before he stepped outside, a terrified expression on her face, her deep eyes pooling and yellow.

"What are you going to do?" she squealed.

"Nothing for you to worry about right now, Thea Pound," Lowell said with finality, kissing her brusquely on the cheek as one might hurriedly pat the head of an old cat. "Thanks for the cookies, but you won't be seeing me again."

"Lowell, Lowell, Lowell, be good, be a good boy, see, be a good boy. Don't stir it up," she pleaded. "I never believed her. No, I didn't. No, not for a minute. Come back for cookies next week, OK? OK? Forgiveness, Lowell, it's the great defense. Dear God, I loved her too," Lowell heard her say as he reached the end of her walk, jumped on his bike, turned the corner and headed down Marquette for Old Town and the river. "No, no, no, no, no, no, no, no," Lowell sobbed, pedaling as fast as he could.

— —

From Lowell Briscoe's "A Nest of Hells."

A Second SOS

Monday

Dearest Thea,

I'm not trying to pester you, and I know you're very busy. But I really do need to see you soon, away from the North Valley, down-town, so we can be alone for a while. It's not like me to worry, but I am wondering why you haven't answered the SOS letter I wrote last week. Are you upset with me, afraid of me for some reason, or just too busy? Or did you just forget? I know this may sound strange coming from me, an urgency in needing to talk, me who's so rigorous and intent on keeping her time clear so her mind can be clear. And I'm not being the judge here, blaming you for not responding. But I feel as if I'm in something of a pinch and really do need to see if you think I'm being silly or not. You must have guessed what it's about—Nola and her "Dr. Hal."

I'm sensing something, something ominous. Please drop me a line, won't you.

Your difficult but enduring friend,
[signed] Hana

Thea's Reply

Thursday

My Dearest Hana,

I'm a forgetful and giddy ol' gal, aren't I? I send heartfelt sorries for not writing back to your first letter. I couldn't even find it when I searched my stacks of stuff. It must be buried in newspapers.

Let's meet at the Alvarado on Friday next, usual time. This should reach you the Saturday before, right?

Nola and Dr. Hal, huh? Let me guess, they're worried about you, right? Well, they're "worried" about me, too. They think it's unhealthy that I'm living alone and "preoccupied" with my health and social causes. I think they're worried about everyone. Perhaps it's the "tie that binds" them together. Worry warts of a feather. . . . Need I say more? Well, probably. I'll say more when we ensconce ourselves for lunch amid Mildred, Joanne, and the other Harvey girls.

SOSs are always all right with me. And you're never a bother.

Much love to you, dearest Hana,

[signed] T. P.

Just So Much Fool's Gold

Now Lowell had only Nola's stony skull to storm. As he brooded over strategies of attack, it came to him that Nola had kept him at bay for so long because she had made him afraid of her—and for no good reason. "I can outrun her anytime I want," Lowell reasoned. "The only person she could really hurt is Juliet. She's the adult." Fear was Nola's great weapon. To get what he wanted, Lowell had to find some way to make her afraid of him, but in such a way that she'd be helpless to retaliate. He thought he would conceal the source of her fear at first, then gradually make her aware that it was he. Fear, perhaps, would inspire guilt, and guilt might inspire disclosure, or so his reasoning went.

He partially dismembered a rose blossom and nailed it to one of the tires of Nola's car, scattered the petals like drops of blood. He cut her garden hoses, threw rocks at her bedroom window late at night, wrote obscene things on her front steps, and collected dog, horse, and cattle droppings and put them on her stoop. He even took a dead toad he'd found squashed by a truck on the ditch, wrapped it in black crepe paper, and left it on her doorstep with the name of one of Hana's dogs printed out on a Christmas tag attached to the paper.

Lowell thought for sure Nola would connect him with the vandalism, but she never confronted Juliet and never mentioned it to him. His plan was an absolute failure. In fact, since the screaming match in the grocery store parking lot, Nola considered him extinct, refusing to admit he even existed. He never really wanted to hurt her physically, just grab her attention and force her out into the open so he could corner her. But he was getting nowhere, so he decided to drop all pretenses and go to Nola and confront her openly. It took him two days hiding out in the bosque to summon enough courage to go to her house. And when he did, he marched up the front steps, held his breath, and pounded forthrightly on the door.

Lowell felt just then like he'd spent half his childhood waiting terrified at doors. He knocked again. And waited, thinking all the time that Nola was about to pounce down the steps, kick him in the face, and send him tumbling into a thicket of cactus.

Finally, a little window in the front door opened and Nola's face peered through the iron bars. When she saw who it was, her eyes rolled up in disgust and she was about to slam the window shut when Lowell said in an angry whisper, "I know Nola, I know what you've done. I know all about it. And I'm going to tell everyone, everyone I can find that you've murdered Hana."

Lowell couldn't be sure how much she heard, as she closed the little window almost immediately after she'd seen him. Afraid she'd open the big door and bash him with it, Lowell leapt to the front path and waited, expecting each second to be doused with scalding oil or shot with barbed arrows. But nothing happened, she didn't appear. She treated Lowell contemptuously as if he were an insect, as if his existence had no consequence.

His consternation was crushing. He pounded on the door repeatedly and futilely. He finally scuffed off down Griegos Road, retreating back to the cottonwood forest by the river. Now what would he do? Then, a week later, right out of the blue, one of those turns of fortune occurred for which we spend the rest of our lives in amazement and gratitude. Nola's grandson, daughter, and son-in-law were killed in a head-on collision on a barren stretch of New Mexico 44 south of San Ysidro. There was nothing bizarre about the deaths. It was just one of a thousand accidents in the world that day. The driver might have fallen asleep at the wheel, he might have been drunk, but whatever he was, the deaths he caused were a miraculous boon for Lowell.

Funeral services were to be held at the Queen of Heaven Chapel downtown and were arranged by the husband's family. The bodies were to be interred at the Sunset Gardens cemetery on Edith and Menaul. Lowell was amazed that Juliet wasn't going to go to the funeral. He'd always thought that death put a kind of truce on things. But Juliet scolded him when he asked her about her refusal to attend. "I will never go near that woman again, in life or death, as long as I live. Do you hear me? As long as I live."

Of all the strange and unaccountable turns of events! Lowell felt a thrill of curiosity and optimism about the funeral and decided that he would go himself, Juliet in tow or not. He put on his Thanksgiving suit and a tie, caught the Fourth Street bus, and arrived at the cemetery just as the priest was saying the blessing over the caskets. Lowell was off to one side of a small crowd of acquaintances and friends of the family of her daughter's husband. Not one of Nola's old friends were there—not

Thea, not the Devons, no one but Lowell, the one person she apparently hated the most. He didn't want her to see him, so he hid behind a tree. It wasn't that he was afraid of her anymore; he somehow didn't want to make things more difficult for her than they already were. He couldn't quite explain why. It was about a week before Christmas, and Lowell was well aware that now Nola would be as alone as he would be without Hana, and as alone as Hana was without her own life. The glaring absence of Nola's friends offended his sense of propriety. It struck Lowell as almost indecent to let someone suffer like that alone, to be so blatant about one's disrespect in a time of sorrow. Why weren't Thea and the Devons there, Lowell wondered. He concluded that it must mean that they knew Nola had used them, that what they did to Hana was wrong. What else could it be?

Seeing Nola there looking tiny and defenseless made Lowell feel compelled to make some gesture toward her. Lowell worried, too, that if she saw him lurking behind the tree she'd immediately think he was up to something, some trick to profane her grief. So Lowell came very quietly to stand beside her, as the minister eulogized her family. He halfway expected her to brush him aside or scream. But Nola only looked at him and made a tiny grimace of recognition. When the minister finished, Lowell turned to Nola and said in the smallest voice he could find, "I'm sorry you're all alone now," and then turned around and slowly walked away.

The wind was up. The sky was graying. Lowell wanted to get home as fast as he could. He was about a block from the cemetery feeling slightly disgusted with himself for being so generous with the ogre, so kind, when a rented limousine pulled up beside him and a harsh, plaintive voice called out, "Get in, will you. Get in." Lowell almost broke and ran. But he contained himself, turned slowly around, looking as defiant and independent as he could appear, and approached the car. Through the reflection of trees in the window, he could see Nola sitting stiffly inside, frail and subdued. Her head turned toward him as if someone had cranked it around. Her eyes looked into him as she opened the door. When he stepped inside, she scooted over to the far side of the limo, telling the driver to "hurry, hurry."

They sat in muddled silence. Lowell's head felt too heavy for him to support. His veins were throbbing. His feet were expanding in his shoes. Nola didn't say a word. "If only I could get out of the car without getting killed," he said to himself.

It was now or never. Lowell could feel himself shrink in panic. "This is it," he thought. He had to speak. He would never have this chance again. But what should he say? Lowell's adrenaline was pumping full steam when the silence was blasted open by Nola's quivering, shrill voice. "You loathe me, don't you? You'd like to see me dead or arrested, wouldn't you? I would if I were you. You think I betrayed Hana. You think I did something terribly wrong, something I should pay for, something I'm perhaps paying for right now? If you hate me so much, why are you here? No one else is here. No one but you who hate me so much. No one else." The shrillness of her voice had left, now it was muttering, almost changing each word and causing the next, as if her brain had nothing to do with what she was saying.

Lowell looked at her. She seemed as horrible to him as ever, but sad now, too; something pitiful was going on in her face. Her eyes looked, if not dead, then fake, like bad glass eyes, too real, too perfect. Lowell told her he didn't hate her, nor did he want her dead "any more."

"I don't know why I'm here either, you've been so mean to me for so long," he told her matter of factly. "Yes, I do know what you did to Hana. I just don't know why you did it." Lowell tried to find something ingeniously cruel to say. God knows he was capable of bestowing tremendous pain, but not now, not when he thought he needed that ability the most. He was helpless in the face of her grief. But then he asked her, "Why wasn't anyone else there but me today? Do they hate you, too?"

The limousine stopped at Nola's adobe on Griegos. She ordered Lowell into the house. And he obeyed. He couldn't believe that he was marching behind her like a little butler at her beck and call. But he was, though all the time wondering what she was going to do to him. Would she poison him? he wondered. Would she use him as Juliet did, to soothe her nerves? The thought horrified him.

When Nola opened the front door to her house, a strange smell of camphor, chicken soup, and cooked cabbage rose up from the carpets. Lowell imagined a little pile of chicken skin smoldering in a pit in the middle of her kitchen, covered with rubber gloves and nylon stockings.

Nola ordered Lowell to wait in the living room. He sat in a straight-backed chair padded with cushions embroidered with roses. Pretty soon the smell of furniture polish overcame the camphor and chicken. The room seemed like the burrow of an animal with nothing to do but clean and decorate—a forest of floor lamps spit-shined and dazzling, doilies on every gleaming surface, gold curtains that looked like ball gowns, crystal bowls filled with hard candy, wall mirrors in extravagant frames, a few landscapes by Taos painters, and some fine Indian pots and old kachinas that looked so out of place that they must have been gifts from Hana.

When Nola reappeared, she was still dressed in black, but had exchanged her black pumps for pink slippers. Her face was so pinched and dry that it seemed pushed in on itself, flattened out and bundled in a nest of curly gray hair. Her lips were almost bone white. Her eyes seemed like finger prints or dirty smudges. Her legs were too thin for her stockings. She wore one of her furry, white, hand-knitted sweaters, and her arms were wrapped around her.

She spoke in a voice that sounded as if she were drowning. "Isn't it odd, monstrous even, that you and I would be here together today of all days, today at this time of my most terrible grief and doubt? You, a person I have found odious beyond belief, here you are with me—you, the cripple who wouldn't heal; you, who are so, so . . . grotesque." Nola spoke as if she were preparing a lecture, trying out phrases and possible constructions. "You with me, at this time. Why? Why? Why were you the only person from my circle at the funeral? You, the pitiful child and dupe of corruption. Why would you be kind to me? Are you here to finish me off when I'm helpless, alone, without hope, kill me off symbolically, make me confess to things I haven't done? Now is the time to do it, if you are. Now is the time to twist me into terror, to break me in two. Now is the time for your foul retribution," she said dropping her words like chloroform through cheesecloth.

Nola brushed her hair out of her eyes with the back of her hand. She sat down in an overstuffed chair with crocheted antimacassars on the arms and, trembling slightly, gazed at the wall. "You've drained all my vim, young man. Look at you, sitting there like a choirboy! You've robbed me of all my pizzazz, ruined my roses, you've plagued me, you've driven my dearest friend stark raving mad, you've caused all my friends to desert me, you've corrupted and mangled my own life. And you're only a little boy, only a little, little boy! Why are you here? Why have I let you into my house? What," she screamed at the top of her lungs, "what are you doing here?!!!"

Lowell raised himself like a stork from his chair, walked across the room to the big front windows shaded by a tangle of ancient pyrocantha, folded his arms and said methodically, like a teacher controlling her temper, "Nola, settle down. Keep a lid on it, dear. You're going wiggy. Straighten up. It's not me, Nola, it's you. You're the one who's ruined lives. You're the one who's ruined my life, Hana's life, and probably Juliet's and Thea's and the Devons'. It's you, old girl. Not me. Not me, not me, not me, not me, not me, not me," Lowell yelled in crescendo. "It's you, you who are the foulest, dirtiest, most disgusting, steaming sack of shit on earth. It's you! And I don't know why I'm here." Lowell stalked back to his chair. Silence stuffed the room.

Then Nola said, "Would you like some sherbet?" And Lowell said he would.

She went to the kitchen and started talking again, talking as if she were sitting down and staring Lowell straight in the face. He had to chase after her to hear what she said. "Are you sure? Are you so sure? Are you sure it was me and not you, not you, are you so sure? Are you sure it was me and not you, not you, are you sure?" she mused, scooping orange sherbet into pressed glass cups.

"Yes, yes, I am," Lowell said, as if counting beans or bales of hay. "Yes, I am sure. I sure am."

They walked back to the living room, spooning up dabs of the orange ice.

Lowell huddled in his chair not knowing what to say next. Then he heard a crisp little chuckle from where Nola was sitting. She was shaking her head. "I must be going mad myself. Surely, I ought to be impounded, too. I feel so dirty. My brain feels dusty, covered with grit. You know, young man, you've made me into an old fool, an old fool who doubts herself, herself!"

Lowell looked up at her with a frown of interest. He felt giddy, like someone who knows he's about to laugh at road kill or find mashed potatoes suddenly hysterical beyond all reason.

"No, no," she sighed. "It's not only you that's breaking my heart. It's this Christmas. *This* Christmas. One year ago, that's all it was, one year ago, one year since everything that's holy was dragged through the filth of ego; this year it will be sullied by silence. Everything's gone wrong, horribly wrong, wrong and evil and sick for me, since I. . . ."

"Since what?" said Lowell with his voice rising. "Since you murdered Hana, right? Since you executed her, right? Since you had her dragged away by the cops, right? Since you had her animals slaughtered, right?

Since you stole her land and locked the Kiva, right?" Lowell was sighting his sword over the horns of the bull, on tiptoes ready to thrust for the heart, an immediate kill.

Nola looked up with an expression at once tortured and amused, shook her head, wound her fingers around one another and answered. "Do you really believe that of me?" She was squirming now, Lowell thought. She looked like a person whose moral girdle had just ridden up a bit too high. "Do you really think all that? My God! Do you actually think. . . . I had no idea you *could* think, little Lowell, only moan and wiggle and exhibit yourself," she said with elegant and disdainful understatement. "Can you really think? Or is that what evil, squalid, little Juliet put in your pinhead? No, that's too smart for her. She's too absorbed in her Hollywood literary image, in her drink, her debauched values, in her sens-u-al-ity," Nola said with a swagger. "I suppose you really can think, after all. But what could possibly go on in that pencil-sharpener brain of yours?" she laughed under her breath. "Do you really imagine I'm that horrid, as horrid as you? Is that how I seem through your bloodshot woozy eyes? Is that why you're here?"

Lowell felt like a cat pretending to be asleep. "I've talked with everyone, Nola," he said. "I know. It's not me who's the mad one, who had dust all over her tongue, whose brain is covered with mold. I can see perfectly clear, clear through you, clear through your dirty, mangy heart. You're so guilty you're purple. Everyone else knows it, too."

"Purple?"

"Whatever."

"You squealing little pig," Nola said with relish as she now fully joined the fray. "You smarmy little worm. I've lost everything, all my friends, apparently, my family, everything I hold dear. And now you're trying to take away my reason, trying to make me doubt if I can tell right from wrong. You, a snake in the grass, a viper in diapers, accusing *me* of wrongdoing? You idiot. Right from wrong. Right from wrong. Only fools are certain they can tell. Only fools."

"Well, I can tell," Lowell said triumphantly. "And you're going straight to hell. They'll make pork chops of you down there."

Lowell was ready to plunge his rhetorical sword right through her heart when she screamed as if someone had shoved a real knife in her back. It was a shuddering scream that turned into a wail and then into moaning. She fell to the floor, writhing, holding her knees to her chest. "Please, please, please," she groaned. "Keep still, keep still." Her face was bloated red and sweating, almost on purpose Lowell thought, like someone who's held their breath just a little bit too long.

Her scream ended the game. Lowell could take no pleasure in this. He knew he was right. She didn't have to say another word. He could learn nothing more, he thought. He felt exhausted, completely drained. He stood to leave, walked to the front door without saying a word, opened it, and took in the fresh afternoon air. He was just about to tumble out into the street when he heard Nola's sad little voice make more sounds. "Please don't go. Don't. I can't stand it. I couldn't bear it if you left. Don't go. Be damned if you do."

Lowell slammed the door, marched back into the living room and said loudly, "That does it, God damn it! Don't you ever talk to me that way again! 'Damned if I do,' huh? I can do any Goddamned thing I want to do. Any Goddamned thing. I am not the guilty one. Don't you ever talk to me that way again!"

Nola had risen from the floor and was now sitting in her chair, her head held high, tears wiped away, posed as if for a portrait of dignified and accomplished old age. She didn't say a word. Lowell sat down and waited. Nola didn't open her mouth for a full five minutes. She appeared to be in a trance, a kind of mental cocoon. Lowell became hypnotized by the tension. Finally, his impatience becoming unbearable, he stood up to leave again. "Sit down," Nola said, "I won't have you thinking such things about me. I won't have a person like you accuse a person like me. It's unthinkable. Who do you think you are? I won't have it." Lowell didn't say a thing. Nola had regained her old self for a moment. It was a fascinating performance.

"Oh yes," she said with an air of wisdom, "I've had my doubts. That will please you, I'm sure. Oh, yes. Even goodness has doubts. What did you expect—that I was so sure of myself, so perfect, that I was some sort of arch fiend? Have you ever spent time with someone who was destroying themselves? Have you ever felt responsible for someone else? Have you ever loved someone so much that you actually thought more about them than you do about yourself? Have you ever felt as if you were your sister's keeper?"

Lowell laughed out loud at that. Nola frowned quizzically, and kept on talking. "Sometimes you have to make decisions that are simply impossible to make. Sometimes you make them even when everything inside you says 'no.' You have to follow your conscience, Lowell. Do you know what that is? I scarcely think you do. I sought help. I consulted professionals. Dr. Barrows was most helpful and supportive. So were my 'friends,'" she said with sudden pointedness. "It was never meant to turn out like this. It was all supposed to be temporary and helpful." She shook her head, bit her lip in consternation. "And when everyone slowly stopped seeing me but Dr. Hal, I did begin to wonder, of course. Were they afraid of me? I asked myself. Did they feel guilty? Did they come to hate me? They all agreed to help me help Hana. They all agreed with me," she said almost plaintively.

"But it was your idea, wasn't it?"

"Yes,, yes. It was. And Hal's too. Terribly botched, no doubt. Terribly. But whose fault was that? Whose?"

"Yours?" Lowell asked quietly with one eyebrow raised.

"The consequences matter, not the cause," Nola said with vainglorious logic.

"You can't have one without the other, can you?" Lowell said softly.

Nola moved right on. "What really hurt the most was when I visited Hana. She wouldn't look at me, she turned her head. She wouldn't acknowledge my presence at all. This is a woman who is my best friend, whom I consider a sister, my deepest . . . she never spoke to me. I didn't exist—until that last time when I saw her face, when she thrust that face into mine. I almost died. I can't think about it even now. She was punishing me with that savage silence and demonic expression. She wouldn't deal with me as a friend, let alone acknowledge what I'd suffered on her behalf, and when she got worse and worse, more and more withdrawn, when she froze up completely, I felt vindicated somehow and utterly crestfallen, as if I were the victim, as if she were taking her revenge on me, as if I had done her some terrible disservice. Of course I lamented the death of her animals and pets. I told her, I told her to come to her senses quickly because no one could take care of such a menagerie without her. She heard not a word. That they all died was, of course, a lamentable error. Of course it was. I didn't like them, never did, but I did not have them slaughtered. It was a mistake. I left them in the hands of uncaring people. Was that my fault? Was I too trusting of strangers? Yes, I have my doubts.

"No one came to the funeral. No one. George and Betty sent flowers. Thea sent a nice little note. Juliet, Juliet . . . no wonder you're the monster that you are. And you, you're so crazy you'd think God, himself, told fibs. Do you have any notion of what it means to be hated? When you can think of nothing that you've done wrong?"

Lowell told her that he did, indeed, understand. But Nola heard not a word.

"What I can't understand, what worries me the most," she said, "is why my family was taken away from me and why you and I have been brought together—unbearable grief and unendurable torture all in one day." Her composure began to crumble again. Her hands squeezed each other until they were blotched with white and red. "Have I done something horrible without knowing it? Was I tricked into being bad? Am I being punished for taking responsibility? Why has God, in His majesty, robbed me of all I own, of all that's mine, of all I love? Sweet Jesus, I don't understand. Here I am," and now she was shrieking, "in this very room where we all used to play, the babies and I, here I am with a mad boy, with her accomplice, with the very demon who shoved her over the edge of guilt, insanity, and corruption, with this poor baby who, in her dementia, she so brutally and vilely used for her own dark practices. Why? Why?" Her scream seemed to pierce through the front window and blast into the piñon tree.

Lowell remained silent. He felt like bursting into laughter, smiling her to death, shattering her fury and despair with a single giggle. But she was dissolving, and all he had to do was wait and watch.

Nola took a deep breath, pulled gently on her ear lobes, brushed a wisp of hair from her eyes. "Hana, you know, was so unique," she said softly. "So strange. She didn't used to be. She used to be my friend. Then she became so foreign, so funny. I got so I was embarrassed to be seen in her presence. Her house embarrassed me. She became so childish, so full of fancies. When old friends of hers and mine would ask me how she was, I'd just crumble with embarrassment and make up stories to cover for her. She became so queer. The clothes she wore, the way she did her hair, the way she talked at me and argued with me all the time. The way she would smile at me, as if she thought me inferior somehow, or someone who needed to be indulged, put up with, encouraged to do better. How dare she? She became so strange, we came to have nothing in common at all. And then she did get sick, fall into these bouts of staring and depression and seclusion. She was becoming a manic depressive with delusions of grandeur. Hal was afraid of suicide. Suicide!" She had the air of someone trying to explain the impossible to people who can afford only to be skeptical.

"I did what I had to do," Nola said like a soldier. "She would have destroyed herself if I hadn't. I did the right thing, stemmed the tide, caught her in the nick of time. When you became ill, the last vestige of Hana as we knew her simply disappeared."

"That's simply not so," Lowell said sounding like an attorney. "I got sick because I knew you had been a peeping Tom, and saw things that were none of your business. I think you and Dr. Hal had me drugged so I'd be out of the way and you could steal her land. Everybody's told me that you lied about what you saw. You told them that I'd danced naked. How could you lie like that? How could you? I gave Hana a present, I gave Hana my love, and you made it dirty. I hate you for that more than I've ever hated anything or anybody in my life. And I always will. And then you made me sick. You poisoned me. You knocked me out. You must have done the same thing to her, told lies about her, terrible lies, poisoned her, gave her shots. Why would you want her land so much? You've got enough. Or was it Dr. Hal, your lover, who wanted the land. That's it!! That's it. And that's what I'm going to tell everyone. That's it!" Lowell said with glee and with as much detestation in his voice as he could find. "How a nothing like you, a busybody nobody, how a stinky little old lady like you could have gotten the upper hand on Hana! I'll never understand."

"Think what you like, don't understand if you don't wish to. But lie about me, and about Dr. Barrows, and I'll tell the police about you, *all* about you, and you'll end up in a foster home somewhere, a little orphan on a slow boat to jail," she bellowed. Then her voice got menacing and soft. "Don't you ever lie about me. Don't you dare. Don't you dare. You . . . will . . . pay for it if you do. Here's the truth, if a broken, sick little monster like you could understand it. The truth is that Hana simply folded up when I told her what I'd seen. Yes, I did see it! I did! When I told her, she just looked at me and shook her head and told me to leave, in the same tone of voice one would use with a bothersome salesman. That's how queer she was, how sick she'd become. I went right to work. I could stand it no longer. Poor woman! I went to my lawyer and filed a suit in district court. Eventually, Judge Hanratty agreed with our contentions. I told them the utter truth. Dr. Barrows, Thea, the Devons, even Juliet, in her own timid, fruitless way, supported me. Hana had gone temporarily insane, I said. We worried for her safety. There was no one to help her, no relatives. I told the court that I, as her oldest and dearest friend, the one who looked after her investments, I was the only person she had to turn to. I felt responsible, I said, and told him I would indeed take full responsibility. I took care of all her finances anyway. It was her deteriorating relationship with children, her nudity in the garden, her twisted politics, and Dr. Hal's diagnosis of chronic depression that convinced the court, not to mention Hana's complete silence.

"I thought of going to Hana that evening after I'd filed suit," Nola continued, "to tell her what I thought about her condition and what I had taken it upon myself to do for her. But I was fearful she'd become enraged, that she might actually hit me and drive me from her house, screaming obscenities. And I worried that she might take off to the hills and escape. But Judge Hanratty had already issued a warrant. The poor dear woman had just gone out of her mind. And don't you feel proud, Mr. Lowell Briscoe? See what you're a part of. She's gone over the edge. And, you know, I think she knew it herself. At what they called the 'sanity hearing,' in that awful dark little court room—I felt so sorry for her having to be in such a place—she didn't say a word, and she even smiled at me during the recess, smiled a silly little-girl kind of smile at me and then made an awful face at me, a really terrible naughty grimace. When Judge Hanratty asked her if she had anything to say in her own behalf, and if she understood what was happening to her, she didn't even nod her head. She just sat there, as if someone had removed her brain. I knew right then that I was right. The judge made me her temporary legal guardian, you know. And gave me power of attorney. I have so much responsibility now, so much, so, so much. . . ." her voice trailed off. It seemed to Lowell that she was falling asleep.

Lowell had drained everything out of her. He walked wearily over to her chair and whispered in her ear, "There, there. You're a sweet little thing . . . for a murderess." Relaxed, sure of himself, he moved again for the door.

Nola jumped up, rebounding, and like a staggering drunk, reeled in Lowell's direction, shouting, "She's not dead, you idiot. She's not dead. She's sick, sick and getting sicker. She's a zombie, just sits there, just sits. . . . She'll never get better. Maybe I am. . . ."

Nola's voice faded off into sleepiness again, became a sobbing little mumble that came to sound more like a grumbling snore. She lay down on the carpet, breathing heavily. Lowell had the most powerful and shameless urge just to kick her head from her body and watch it sail into her clean, golden curtains.

She looked up at Lowell and smiled. "Go home now, little boy. Nola's got to nap. Go home, go home," she slurred.

Lowell felt a sudden rush of hate and nausea fill his torso. He couldn't control it. He doubled up and vomited all over the rug, the hall cabinet, the grandfather clock, the hat rack, umbrellas, canes, puking on the doorsill, retching until he practically drowned. Gasping for air, his lips puffy, his throat burning with bile, he shot one final glance at Nola's body on the floor near the edge of the divan and ran out into the chilly late afternoon, leaving the front door wide open. He heard two ravens gnawing the air from the limb of one of the front cottonwoods. He hoped he might see them fly into Nola's house. When their caws turned to laughter, Lowell started laughing too. But when he saw one of the ravens hop up the front steps and come close to the front door, he chased it away and carefully shut the door, weeping a pure, raw-hearted sorrow he thought would kill him.

➤ ➤

From Lowell Briscoe's "A Nest of Hells."

Immediately Absorbed

[JOURNALS OF HANA NICHOLAS]
14 April 1946

I love everything about my life. Everything. I wake up every morning immediately absorbed by projects and the unbelievable beauty of my surroundings. Such gratitude I feel! I'm fifty-one years old. In perfect health, except for my famous feet, lower back pains, and hot flashes (which keep me warm in winter). I can still do the work of a couple of strong teenage boys. I feel closer to the Earth, to the gods, all of them, than I ever thought possible. The estrangement, the alienation of so much of my life is lifting. I'm not exactly sunny, but I'm not falling into those crushing depressions from which it takes me weeks to decompress. Even my nosy friends don't bother me this morning. I belong to my life. I belong to my town, my neighborhood, my land, my house, my critters. Here I am in my thinking room, in my big chair, wrapped in a warm robe, a strong cup of coffee by my side. It's 5:00 a.m. I'm reading about Athena and archetypal psychology, in my own fortress adobe, the same house I've lived in for twenty-three years. Gloriamaris, a little ship of a place, anchored in an ocean of land, by a ditch that might be a thousand years old, that waters my trees and crops twice a week. I'm less than a mile from the river and bosque. My trees surround my land like an impenetrable wall, they're so thick and lush and foreboding. And in between them are my coyote fence and its hedge of pyracantha and lethal ocotillo. I have trumpet vines and honeysuckle growing over everything. Catalpa trees spring up in my gardens spontaneously each spring. Ravens drop apple seeds in my victory garden and every year or so I transplant my tiny orchards into bigger orchards of bigger trees. I grow vast tomato plants. My garden canals are lined with thousands of sweet garlic plants from Tomé. My squash and beans and chile are so fruitful I give away three-quarters of my yield every year. I have superb neighbors: the amiable, hardworking Luceros, the Archibeques and their four sweet sons. We help each other all the time. We feel like family. We cook for each other. We work each other's projects. And they leave me alone! They don't pry like some people. They are there when I need them. And I am there for them. Best of all, we never talk politics or religion. It's all crops, weather, family, food, and animals. I know nothing of their scandals, presuming they have them like everyone else, and they know nothing of mine.

This morning I'm going to make myself some wonderful toast from my own bread, cover it with Ruth Lucero's orange marmalade, cook up some of my own eggs, fry up onions, toss them in potatoes, cover everything with Domingo red, the hottest, richest chile on earth. I'm going to sit at my kitchen table, look out over my garden, and feel completely safe.

How supremely lucky I am. Every little thing is right, from the comfort of my bed and its spring quilt to the books I read and the pens I use. All my animals are healthy. All the "babies," even little Godwin's ancient brown body here in my lap seems stronger than ever despite his hundred-plus cat years. Nothing is too much work anymore. I can spend three or four days at a time, studying, writing, gardening, working the land, tending animals, and never even know I haven't seen a soul. I'm starting to really master Greek after all these years, and have enough Latin to read Apuleius in the original. I'm working on translating the Homeric Hymns to Hermes and Demeter right now as well. Thanks be to the Muses, especially Erato. How can life be so wonderful? And in about two hours, I'll take my daily five miles on the Duranes lateral, down the Griegos drain, up the clear ditch to the western bosque and down back through the fields past Chavez Road, past La Quinta and Los Poblanos to home. Oh, how I love that walk. I've taken it every morning, snow or sun, for more than seventeen years, with work ahead of me or not. . . . My heavens, it's 5:45. . . .

Nothing from Nothing

[JOURNALS OF LOWELL BRISCOE]

I'm writing this on a plane to Chicago a week after I scandalized L.A. and the nation, I guess, by failing to identify the Normandy Four as the guys who beat my brains out. I'm on my way to give a lecture on "Truth Telling and the Media" at . . . where? . . . the University of Illinois at Chicago, wherever that is. . . . What do I know about the truth? The whole truth? So help me God, I don't know. I don't know a damn thing. I know it's true that I want to be a good person and do the right thing. But so much of the time I don't know what that is. I read and reread sagacious formulas for behaving well, but my life has been lived in contexts where the formulas generally don't apply.

So little in my life makes sense to me still. I'm always winging it, always just barely surviving. Everything for me seems like an endless series of catastrophes and malevolent surprises. Joel and Alice, Juliet, Hana, all those murders, the beating, me as I was, me as I am. I will never know what happened to Hana. I'll never really know what happened to me. Hana's journals, Nola's letters and diaries, all that material and solid data, and I still know nothing. So, I'm tempted just to say that sometimes the logic boards go bad, the irrational wins, the great forces of nature sweep everyone in their wake, fear being the human equivalent of drought or the plague. I know absolutely that fear-induced ignorance and fear-induced madness are the most lethal things on earth. Fear is tragedy's Petrie dish.

That makes sense, but everything else seems unaccountable, an accident of happenstance, an unseen cliff, a dark stair, an uplift in the sidewalk, a crack in a pipe that lets weeds clog the sewer. Movement stops. You crash to the ground. Nothing works. We're all faced with the unaccountable. Seventy million dead in WWII, sixty thousand nuke warheads around the world, genocide as a response to stress, Stalin, Hitler, Mao, Pol Pot, Pinochet, the KKK, Wounded Knee. Who knows? Asteroids crashing into the earth, car accidents, bashing your head on the bedstead as you flop back with a sigh of pleasure and going bonkers and blurry for weeks, losing your glasses, your wallet, your car in Macy's garage.

Maybe we're not supposed to make sense of it, just ride it out, keep the flow going, keep the faith, keep going, keep going, try to give to the world what it needs from us, the only thing it needs from us: our love and respect, not our fear, not our disillusion, not our despair, not our cynicism. Love will do. But it's very hard *to* do. Even Hana wasn't inherently strong enough, wasn't a good enough natural spiritual jock to survive her own fears. It's more than that, I think, but I'm only able to say that the hardest thing of all is to believe the preposterous has happened to you, and when you do believe it, it's either too much to take and you escape, or you're so stunned you can't respond. I think of poor Leo Frank, lynched for a crime he didn't commit, dancing on the end of the rope to the jeers of Jew haters. I can't even stand to think about it. The thought of Hana in there all those years, locked up, alone, her whole beautiful life erased as if it had never happened.

I only have one regret anymore. And that's Hal.

The Seduction

Lowell's anger was choking him. After he left Nola's house he walked for hours on the ditches. What satisfaction he'd felt watching Nola dissolve and leaving the contents of his stomach all over her house was a passing release. Even though everyone had told him what he knew to be the truth, he was still convinced he was no closer to reality than he was before. Only one person remained, Dr. Harold Barrows. How could he get that pillar of rectitude to crack and crumble as Nola had? How could he torture the truth out of him?

Lowell knew enough about the world to suspect that Dr. Hal had many secrets. He was too nosy not to. And despite his relationship with Nola, he lived alone. Lowell imagined that neither Nola nor Hal was sexually inclined toward the other. What did Hal desire? What made him vulnerable? Lowell thought and thought. "It might be me. No. That's too simple. It's something else. It isn't really Hana's land either, though somebody's got it, or is going to get it," Lowell said to himself.

The impossible question remained. "Did I really have a breakdown? Or did they all do something to me? What do I know? What do I really know? I know when I saw Nola at the door with Juliet I thought she'd spied on me, found out about my love for Hana, that she knew about Juliet and me, and was going to get me, blackmail Juliet and Hana, and send me to an orphanage. I was scared that she'd use me against Hana, that she'd call the police and scare Hana to death. . . . I don't know what I was scared of, but I was scared. I had too many secrets. But did I collapse, go into a coma, whatever that is, and stay out cold for months? That can't be. I've never done that · before. Never. They must have done something to me. They must have secrets too. But what are they?" he shouted the question aloud into the afternoon air. "What are they?"

He was never going to get anywhere merely thinking about it. He ditched school that Monday, contrived to phone Dr. Barrows at his office demanding that the nurse let him talk to the doctor in person. He told Barrows that he'd remembered something from the time he was in his "coma," something he didn't understand, and that he absolutely had to talk to the doctor about it. And no one must know he was coming. Dr. Hal had sounded brusque and annoyed before Lowell spoke, but mellowed quickly and told Lowell to come by the office after school at around 4:30.

When Hal let Lowell into his office and locked the door behind him, Lowell began to get giddy and frightened. Hal seemed puffy and stale. He was clearly uncomfortable. When Lowell sat down across the desk from him, Hal looked into him as if he were drilling holes and said imperiously "Well?"

Lowell covered his face with his hands and began to sob convincingly. "I'm so lonesome. I feel so bad, so bad," Lowell coughed and cried. "I'm scared. I'm scared. Juliet's drunk, so drunk she can hardly walk. Nola threatened to put me in an orphanage. I'm all alone. Thea hates me. George and Betty think I'm a crazy boy. I don't know what to do. I don't know what to do? What happened to me? I'm really scared. . . . Could I come and stay with you?"

"What do you mean," Dr. Hal said with an astonished frown.

"I'm alone. I'm scared. You're a doctor. I trust you. Take care of me. OK? Take care of me. I don't know what else to do."

Hal leaned back in his chair, ran his fingers through his hair, turned his head toward Lowell, and said, "You know, you're very, very good at this. I know you've talked to everyone. And everyone's told you all they know. But they don't know it all. And neither will you. I suggest you leave."

Lowell looked at him with horror and fury. He stared and stared.

"Young man, I will not be intimidated by a child. I will not be seduced. I will not be interrogated. And if you know what's good for you, I suggest you get up and walk out that door and forget everything. And I do mean everything. If you don't . . . you know full well how vulnerable you are. You know very well."

Lowell couldn't believe his ears. This was the man. Hal was the one. He didn't know why, but he knew it was Hal.

"Dr. Barrows," Lowell said with mock respect, "you scare the hell out of me. And I don't like being scared. I'm going to leave now. But don't you forget for a moment that I know your secret. I know it."

"And what secret is that," Barrows said with contempt.

"What's the worst thing you can think of, the worst thing that I could accuse you of?" Lowell asked menacingly. "What is it?"

"What do you mean?" Barrows said dryly.

"You know what I mean. I've already told Juliet. It didn't surprise her a bit."

"Told her what?"

"Come on. Wake up. You threatened me. You tried to scare me. You drugged me. Do you think I'd come to you without protecting myself? I told Thea and George Devon too. George was shocked, I'll tell you that. What would it take to make them talk?"

"What did you tell them?" Barrows asked squinting and cold.

"Tell me what you did to Hana and why you did it, and I'll tell you what I told them."

"You didn't tell them anything, did you? Because there's nothing to tell. Nothing."

"Oh, Dr. Hal. You know that doesn't matter, doesn't matter a bit."

Dr. Barrows stood up, rolled down his sleeves, and buttoned his cuffs. "Well, let's go talk to all these people that you told something to. Let's see what they have to say."

"Get serious," Lowell said with a sneer.

"No, young man, let's go right now. I have nothing to fear."

"Except your good name."

"What do you mean?" Barrows said, his voice rising.

"Do you think Juliet will come clean to you when she has something on you now? She hates you. All you need is one of them to believe me. Just one. And one already does. Maybe they all do. Get serious, you big tub," Lowell said laughing. "Get serious. You don't have to tell me anything. I know that. But you touch a hair on my head, and they'll be putting you in a real nasty dark place for a real long time."

"What did you tell them, for God sakes? What did you tell them?"

"Use your head, dummy."

"You little bastard. You slimy little bastard. I should have given you. . . ."

"What? An overdose?"

"Don't be absurd. But you better watch your step or you'll find yourself in a very unpleasant place. One word from me to the court. . . ."

"I'm warning you. Don't you ever threaten me again. Do you understand? Juliet knows Ralph Caxton. Do you know who he is? He's the editor of the paper. They know each other real, real well. Do you know what I mean?"

Barrows looked at Lowell now with a quizzical sense of recognition. "And why are you telling me that?"

There was no answer.

Barrows closed his eyes. Took a deep breath. Sat tall in his chair. "What do you want?"

"You know what I want."

"No I don't."

"Guess."

"I can't."

"After you let Hana out, then I want you to. . . ."

"Get out of here, young man. Get out before I come over there and. . . . Do you understand? Get the hell out of here! Get out! And if you ever repeat the terrible things you've said about me, I'll. . . ."

"You'll what? You chickenshit asshole. You'll what?"

"Get out, get out," Barrows said clenching his teeth. "Out!"

Lowell knew he had touched Hal Barrows's core of fear. But he didn't know how much.

From Lowell Briscoe's "A Nest of Hells."

Soren and Epicurus

[Journals of Hana Nicholas]
6 February 1949

Soren Kierkegaard's own brother, Peder Christian the minister, gave a lecture condemning him as "unrealistic, ecstatic, eccentric." Poor devil. But what a compliment! If Soren had any humor left in the bottom of his soul, he must have rejoiced at being so excommunicated by such a realistic, sodden, and predictable fellow as his odious sibling. Soren and Epicurus might agree that despair over the maliciousness of other people's insecurity is a uselessly painful folly, one that merely compounds the discomfort of the victim of attacks. Despair can lead to suicide as an alternative to being somehow despoiled or symbolically or actually murdered. Suicide, I must remember, is never warranted, and is always a waste in the eyes of Epicurus, because even in the most miserable and disappointing and mangling of circumstances there is the possibility of pleasure. What kind of pleasure is that, I wonder? Moral pleasure? Aesthetic pleasure? That must be it. In this case it would be a refusal to be tempted to fall into despair over "meaning," to keep one's faith in meaning itself despite the seeming total lack of it. And there must be some way to keep the pleasure of humor, to even cultivate it under extreme circumstances. There must be a way to do this. What did William James call it? The religion of "healthy mindedness." Am I healthy enough upstairs to resist hopelessness and move through this time of troubles, move through and let it just pass by me patiently?

The Jell-O Was So Nice

Lucian Duran was introduced to Hana by his Auntie Rosalie in the day room of the state hospital for the mentally ill in Las Vegas, New Mexico. "She's such a nice aviator, Lucianito, such a good flier," Rosalie Duran told her nephew. "We go everywhere together. Even went up there to Roy and down to Stanley. The Jell-O was real nice down there."

"Jell-O?"

"Jell-O's everywhere. We're walking on Jell-O right now. If you're not careful, cherry Jell-O can smother you when you go outside."

"Uh huh. . . . What's wrong with *her*, Tía?"

"Who? Hana?"

"Yeah, her."

"There's nothin' wrong with her. The wind just changed when she was cross-eyed, that's all."

"Oh."

"See, Hana here and I know all about the cold water, the icy cold sheets. The ice cube baths. We've flown over the North Pole many times. Oh, yes, oh yes, we do, we do, don't we, Miss Hana? Oh, yes we do, we do, we do, we do, we do, do, do, do, do, do, we do. Yes sir, we do. We do, do, do. . . . Now, Lucianito, you know I'm nuts. Everybody's always said so. I've been crazy since the day I was born. Crazy happy. Crazy sad. But Hana here, the lady with the windy face, she used to be strange, that's it, just strange. This place made her crazy. God made me crazy. This place made *her* crazy. God made me crazy. This place made her crazy. God made me. . . ."

"OK, OK. I see. How about a little walk?"

"Can we go out there to London? Hana told me all about *that* place."

"Sure, Tía, let's go."

"No, I'm scared. Let's nap right here."

"Come on, Auntie Rosalie. The walk will do you good."

"Do you have a gun? You know what they do to you out there!"

"No, but I have a lollypop, and that works just as well."

"OK."

The two moved through the glass doors into the sunlight. Hana sat still in her chair, thinking to herself, "Rosalie knows, all right. She's not too crazy. . . . What a beautiful day. Maybe tomorrow I'll go outside. Go to Paris. . . . Maybe next month. . . . Maybe sometime. Maybe when I wake up. What a nightmare. I've been asleep for such a long, long time. Why can't I wake up? Doesn't anyone hear me moaning? Why won't someone shake me awake? Poor Lowell. . . . Poor Lowell. . . . He made me stir, but I couldn't find the strength. Nola always did put me deeper asleep than ever. Good thing. . . . What a fine day! . . . I'm Rip van Winkle, aren't I? Yep, old gal, you sure are. . . . And what's wrong with my face anyway? You have to be invisible, wear the hat of Hermes. Am I fading into view again? No, no, no. . . . This place is such a church. Such a back-alley church. . . . Where are they? Where did they go? Where did they take them? They could have left me one, just one . . . one cat. . . . I can't keep praying like this forever. . . . But I have to. This is the cloister. My skull is the cloister. The catacombs . . . buried alive? Buried. I could go really nuts, really cashews, really Almond Joy, if I think like this. . . . No, nonono. Keep thinking of the possibilities. This *is*. Nothing else is. A life of prayer. What an opportunity. Keep polishing the mountain. It won't take long if you do. Maybe just ten thousand more prayers. Then I'll become visible. Then I'll go outside, go with Rosalie to London. . . . OK, that's a deal. . . . Polish the mountain. Deep breath, deep, deep breath: let it out, let it go . . . one . . . one . . . one. . . . Count and breathe. . . . One . . . one . . . one . . . one . . . one . . ."

Sometime in the spring of 1957, a few months before Hana Nicholas died of congestive heart disease complicated by pneumonia, August 31, at age sixty-two.

The Rabid Mole Escaped

[JOURNALS OF LOWELL BRISCOE]
Summer 1992

Melinda Tuttle asked me yesterday what happened to Dr. Hal. I had a hard time telling her, not because it was sad or I felt guilty or anything like that, but because he frightened me so much that I eventually let him go. He was alive when I left for Yale. He was alive when Nola died. Of all the people who should have been polished off, it was he. And for a long time I did think of killing him, as much out of self-defense as anything. But he didn't die a suspicious death, at least as far as I can tell. He was, of course, the only one in town when everyone was killed, I believe; at least he lived in Albuquerque all that time. It's entirely plausible that he did get Hana's land, subdivided it, made a mint, and killed off all the witnesses, including giving Nola and Hana fatal doses. That's certainly one way a whodunit could be solved. But the world doesn't work like that necessarily. Though it's certainly in its nature to spring on us whole lifetimes of evil circumstance, malign psyches, and horrible, bad joke catastrophes. The world is usually more obtuse. And more surprising. What if Hal and Nola and Hana were in some kind of love triangle that went wrong? That's preposterous of course. I wish I had more details. All I can dredge up is that look of his, that pasty, superior, sheepish, "help-me-I'm-a-fat-boy-from-upstate-New York" look. He looked like a killer who needed mothering. His hands, I remember them. Juliet had him take care of me. His hands disgusted me. They were very, very soft; they looked like they'd never touched a shovel; soft and cold and humid all at once. He would peer at you as if you were a specimen, wrinkling up his nose when he touched you.

He was a fat kid grown up. His glasses were too big and they didn't seem to work well. That's just being petty. Maybe I'm just being a bully. But he did ask me lots and lots of questions about Hana and Juliet. I knew what he was doing, so I didn't tell him anything. I heard that he was also in the military, which is hard to believe.

I've thought so much about that last meeting with him. His anger chilled me to the bone, even if I was the aggressor and scared the wits out of him. Hal. I know he died sometime in 1967. My god! That's right. Oh, man. . . . Did the rabid mole escape?

"Doctor Found Dead at Home"

[dated February 23, 1967]

Albuquerque (AP) — Harold Barrows, a prominent Albuquerque physician, was found dead in his North Valley home on Griegos NW Wednesday morning with a gunshot wound to the head.

Martin Anaya, of the Bernalillo County Sheriff's Department, said it was "an apparent suicide," though no note was found.

Dr. Barrows, a general practitioner, served in the Office of Strategic Services during World War II, in Army Intelligence in the Korean War, and worked as a civilian with the National Security Agency in Los Alamos and at Sandia Base. His brother Carl Barrows, of Flushing, N.Y., said yesterday that Barrows "was always interested in foreign languages, applied physics, and human behavior. He loved people, though war really took its toll on his peace of mind."

Dr. Barrows was awarded the Bronze Star in World War II for his role in the Africa campaign. He retired from the armed services in 1953 with the rank of major.

Lowell's half-sister Juliet was found strangled to death in her kitchen in early 1967. The man convicted of Juliet's murder, Mark Spindle, died of complications of liver disease in the New Mexico penitentiary in Santa Fe, N.M. in 1971.

The Riot of 1992
The Possibilities

In his summation to the jury, D.A. Cates dismissed "Dr. Briscoe's testimony" as being that of a man "obviously still unsure of himself and badly disoriented after the savage attack on his person by the four men at the defendants' table. They beat him so viciously, and with such inhuman brutality, as the video tapes have demonstrated to the world, that a man of wide experience, unimpeachable reputation, and superior intelligence like Dr. Briscoe cannot even make up his own mind about what happened that day. Rest assured that Dr. Briscoe is a highly moral and compassionate man who does not want to contribute to a miscarriage of justice. I have no doubt of that, and I apologize to Dr. Briscoe for impolitic and insensitive remarks made in haste and in anger recently to the press. I do not really think that he 'colluded' with the families of the defendants for 'some misguided, liberal, bleeding-heart motive that no rational person would condone,' as the press reported I said. I do not think he changed his testimony at the most dramatic moment in the trial according to some prearranged deal with the defendants' parents. Of course not. No. I choose to believe Dr. Briscoe's account of an innocent, spur-of-the-moment dinner to which he was invited by grateful family members. But no matter how pleasant, how sweet, how upstanding the Franklyns, the Carters, the Thomases, and the Smiths might be, and very well are, their children on trial in this courtroom behaved like monsters, as the evidence shows beyond the shadow of a doubt. This case is not a matter of interracial equity, not a matter of so-called economic or social justice, and certainly not a matter of trading off the acquittal of police officers in the case of Rodney King with the acquittal of these defendants in the case of Lowell Patrick Briscoe. Finding these defendants guilty is the only righteous, the only sane thing to do, with or without Dr. Briscoe's corroboration of our evidence. We have showed you the ninety-three horrifying seconds of his sadistic pummeling on videotape and you have heard the testimony of twenty-seven other witnesses who have sworn under oath and threat of perjury that the defendants are guilty as charged. Dr. Briscoe's incompetence in this trial has been profoundly sad to behold, if not pathetic to watch. His sense of conscience and responsibility are, of course, in the best traditions of noble idealism, but I am certain he is not in full possession of his senses even yet. He is a beloved and respected citizen of this city who has spent many years in poor neighborhoods working for the disadvantaged. And his beating at the hands of thugs and gangsters is the thanks he gets! Yet do not be swayed by the defense when they say that Dr. Briscoe's uncertainty, his moral reserve, casts reasonable doubt on the guilt of these defendants. The videotape and testimony leave no doubt whatsoever about the nature of their misconduct that first day of the riot. None whatsoever. They became savage animals, slavering beasts preying on the white people who wandered into their grasp."

Lowell, who was sitting in the back of the courtroom, took out a piece of paper from his breast pocket, and wrote, "Call lawyer Jack . . . 'incompetence,' 'pathetic,' 'not in full possession of his senses' . . . slander??? Stuff Cates in the trash!!!"

It took the jury less than eight hours to convict each defendant on all counts. As the verdicts were read, the family members in the courtroom began to sob. Some even cried out in desperate sorrow, some in desperate rage. Newspaper accounts reported that "the defendants' faces showed no emotion." But Lowell, from the back of the room, saw their necks tense, and one of them make movements as if he were trying to stop from crying.

"What a terrible mess it was. It felt emotionally like The Raft of the Medusa in there; the suffering was terminal," Lowell wrote in his journal. "I don't know if my behavior created unrealistic expectations that led to such crushing disappointment. I don't really understand, either, how the Smiths, Carters, or anyone (they are all reasonable people) could imagine their sons wouldn't get convicted, no matter what I'd said. The evidence was overwhelming. And even Cates is partially right: The cry for a kind of distributive justice (you let off the cops, you can let off my kid) struck a chord with no one outside their community.

"I hope the interview I gave helped a little. It probably didn't. I was, and I still am, terrified that a new riot will erupt and that somehow I will get caught up in it again, or that the friends of the Normandy Four will track me down and finish the job. Well, they won't do that now, I don't think. Paranoia, paranoia, paranoia. Was I so craven as to commit perjury just to make friends with my enemies so they wouldn't hurt me anymore? Could I be that stupid? I honestly don't think I connected my duplicity in the courtroom with my fear of retribution, though safety is a nice by-product. Ultimately, I know in my heart that I couldn't stand the thought of wasting more lives. I'm not confused about that. Those kids were inflamed by injustice. So am I."

As he left the courtroom, Lowell was dogged by a pack of reporters and photographers. To shake them loose, he gave a ten-second impromptu press conference in which it is reported that he said, "I really have nothing to say, except that justice is blind and can be led anywhere, if you can attach a rope to the ring in its nose."

Norman Gin, a columnist in a small, radical California political weekly, noted that "Briscoe was beaten senseless in the riot, and beaten black and blue in the courtroom by the prosecution. But his plight as a likable, twice victimized, dazed and, yes, slightly 'pathetic,' though morally clearheaded person, did have a calming effect on the violence that was so near the surface just after the verdict. Despite his often mystifying metaphors and occasional descent into sarcasm, Briscoe is a man who's hard to hate, even for professional hate mongers. He's open, and he's candid about his feelings that most things in the world outside his office are 'disagreeable.' Best of all, he has a disarming sense of humor. How terrible to torture a man like that!"

Lowell's private feelings about Gin's column are evident in these remarks from his journal, "'Morally clear headed'? If someone could see the whole picture of my life, of anyone's life, all the details public and private, could anyone be called 'morally clear headed' consistently throughout their lives? Not even St. Augustine could avoid making 'confessions' about the past. I'm glad people think I'm morally accept-able. As long as I haven't killed anyone or done someone terrible damage maliciously, I have to take a neutral view of myself, if I can . . . neither inflated nor deflated. I like praise, but I don't take it in. I detest judgment and accusation because I internalize it immediately. At least I can say this for myself, I'm not afraid to get my hands dirty. I am not afraid of taking risks when it comes to integrity. But if integrity implies a line not to be crossed, nor to be forced across, then my line is very, very far away. It gives me a huge field of moral latitude. Cates tried to push me across that line. Nola did too. They couldn't. But never Juliet, and certainly never Hana. They never pushed like that."

* * *

Dr. Tuttle was particularly crisp and cool after the verdict, not hostile or distant, but dominant, as if she were trying to reestablish her professional authority, or so Lowell thought. But he refused to be deflected.

"Now that it's over, the verdict I mean, do you have any regrets working with me all these months, Melinda?"

"Of course not, Lowell. Why do you think I would? Are you still afraid I might have been working for the district attorney's office secretly all along? I hope not."

"No, I may be paranoid, but I am not a total idiot." Lowell laughed. He went on at great length praising Tuttle for her kindness to him, and for the sense of security he felt in her presence. "Still," he said, "I feel as if I've been under surveillance for years and years. What if your public image, your persona, is so out of synch with what you consider to be your inner life, or whole self, that you feel as if you could never explain yourself to anyone, and that if anyone could see your total life all at once, as if under a microscope, its inconsistencies and contradictions would be considered suspicious by even the most tolerant of people? That's the way I've always felt. I've always had secrets, secrets that were dangerous in an ultimate sort of way. And I've always felt guilty about my secrets, not a stabbing kind of guilt but a guilt that settled over my life like a thin, yellow wash, coloring everything, and making me suspect everyone and everything, mostly myself. I felt as if I were an inquisitor, popping up in my life unexpectedly and rudely. 'You don't expect the Spanish Inquisition,' as Monty Python would say. I was terrified of that aspect of myself; terrified of my own puritanism, my own self-denunciation, my own passing of judgment on myself, cruel judgment, a judgment against standards that I normally do not hold, which, in fact, I normally disown as fascist and completely deplorable and would never apply to others."

"What kind of standards do you mean?"

"Standards of perfection, of my own perfection derived from some amorphous soup of 'shoulds' made up by children when they become convinced they've heard voices from God, old children who judge others for their own crimes. Don't you notice that? That the most damning judges of others always display the qualities they condemn? Well, what if that judge is yourself? That's why I think I'm paranoid."

"I'm not quite sure what you mean."

"Well, I've felt guilty and under surveillance for hating my father, for loving my mother in erotic ways, for sleeping with my half-sister, guilty for sleeping with her without a sense of guilt; guilty for hating Nola, for hating the Devons, for hating Thea, for hating Juliet, guilty for their deaths, guilty that I might somehow, by simply being who I am, with no intention, in complete innocence, have betrayed Hana, or caused her to betray herself, or have been an unwitting catalyst; guilty for most of my relationships, for not being good enough to make them last, for being too needy, too distracted, too easily enticed; guilty for getting beaten, for somehow being a reason Los Angeles is so racially tense and racially suicidal at the moment; guilty for lying twice to the D.A., twice, lying to gain the upper hand, to defend myself, to not become a victim of his authority, of normalcy, of the expectations of the mass mind, to use Hana's phrase. And then guilty because guilt inevitably is linked to anger. For years I was furious at Hana for not defending herself in court, at her sanity hearing. I was furious that she let herself be destroyed without a fight. I couldn't understand it. I could make no sense of it. It infuriated me and caused me the most awful doubts about her and about her sanity—her sanity, which I held onto like the grail, as it was the touchstone for my own. And I feel guilty now that I am proud, proud that I did defend myself, that I defended myself against the monsters, that I didn't offer my neck, that I didn't go slack, that I did what I had to do, that I used my wiliness, the wiles of Odysseus. I somehow prevailed, and in saying that I become terrified that the forces of the universe will think me proud and will strike me down with another catastrophe, another glimpse of hell on earth, another domestic inferno, and still, terror aside, I am proud I defended myself, I preserved my integrity even if it took deceit to do it, even if it took a secret, a lie, several lies, to pull it off."

"Are you saying that you lied on the witness stand, that you per-jured yourself, that you really did believe those young men were your attackers?"

"Are you going to break confidentially and turn me in?"

"Of course not."

"Yes and no. Yes and no. I did think they were, and I didn't. Can I trust you? Can I? OK. I lied. I did. I do think they did it. And I said I didn't. I wanted to take control of my own defense, of my own con-science, of my own integrity. And that was the only way to do it, the only way to stop being railroaded, to put my motives to the forefront. I was worried far more about becoming a symbol for a white backlash and a black vendetta in Los Angeles than I was, in the long run, about getting judicial vengeance for myself. Though I'd be a thoroughgoing hypocrite if I didn't say that I have deep contradictory feelings about revenge—I do want it, but I can't have it, and to get it in court, participating in the basically racist values of the prosecution and the established order, could have meant more violence, and I couldn't have lived with that. So I took the other side. There's a wonderful line by Auden that says 'Alienation from the collective is always a duty,' but I wasn't behaving ideologically, I don't think. I was sacrificing temporary and debatable self-interest for two greater goods—my own self-respect and the safety of the city. It doesn't matter anyway, does it? They were convicted. Still. . . ."

"Sounds like a load of rationalization to me, if you pardon me saying so. I know just saying that might put a breach in our therapeutic relationship. But my integrity demands it. I don't really think I can be your therapist anymore. I can't support your motives or your methods. I know you're working actively for a retrial, aren't you, based on your inability to identify them? And you just told me you can identify them. That's bald-faced lying. What gives you the right to take history in your hands like this, going against the truth? Isn't that hubris? Isn't that what the gods destroy?"

"Could be."

"Just come out and say it. You're fucking the system, aren't you? Pardon my language."

"Your language is just fine. Yes, I am. I'm fucking the system."

"It's the system that you think took Hana, isn't it?"

"Is it? It must be. . . ."

"Of course it is!" Dr. Tuttle said angrily. "You're getting even with the system by undermining the trial that would punish your attackers and, I fervently believe, would give other potential rioters a clear message about society's view of mob violence, providing the penalties were harsh enough."

"You're not one of those who want them strung up, are you?"

"No, but what they did to you, and possibly others, demands many, many years in prison, many, many years. It could have been me; it could have been any one of our friends or family members. Don't you realize you're undermining the legitimacy of the law, the legal structure which keeps our society from collapse?"

"Come on, Melinda, the only thing that keeps our culture from collapse is money. Justice doesn't have a thing to do with it, because,

because . . . there is none. And besides, what good will it do those young men to waste away for years in prison? What will they learn? What could they give back to help their world from their experience?"

"I can't deal with you anymore."

"Good. You just did the unpardonable anyway."

"Excuse me? Just what do you mean?"

"You, you ethical creature you, you *professional* of high integrity, too ethically glorious and elevated to deal anymore with bottom feeders like me, you of supremely ponderous arrogance, you suckered me into a 'confession,' into vulnerable candor and then used what I told you against me, to judge me and punish me. That's unforgivable. That's a thousand times worse than anything I chose to do in the courtroom. I won't forget it. You're a charlatan, a conformist in philosopher's clothing. You and your talk about 'personal culture'! What a hypocrite! You'd probably be one of those 'helping professionals' who'd put Hana away for her untidy views. . . ."

"Well, you know, Dr. Briscoe, it is possible that she was quite insane, if you're her protégé, and she's your mentor," said a smiling, suddenly Olympianly prim Dr. Tuttle. "Oh my, time's up."

"What a fabulous reversal, doctor. I come in looking like a shmuck and I leave with you looking like a sphincter—tight-assed, inscrutable, and toxic, if you get my meaning. Bye, bye."

"So you're the 'beloved Lowell Patrick Briscoe' are you? What a revelation!" Dr. Tuttle muttered audibly as Lowell closed her office door behind him.

* * *

After many months of effort, and the expenditure of tens of thousands of his own dollars, Lowell was instrumental in securing a retrial for the four young men accused of his beating, as well as securing their release into the custody of their parents. The Los Angeles press was critical of the courts, and disappointed in Lowell, if remaining solidly deferential. In the poorer parts of Los Angeles, however, Lowell Briscoe was lionized wherever he went. He ate breakfast and lunch in cafes in South Central and East Los Angeles every day. He gave talks at elementary schools and middle schools about racism and the "dominant culture's reflex suspicion" of people of color. He felt safer and more relaxed in the barrios and the hoods than in his own beachfront neighborhood. And he even contemplated moving into a small house on Olympic Boulevard just east of La Cienega. He noted in his journal that he felt at home for the first time of his life.

During the struggle for a retrial, Lowell waged a media campaign of great skill and persistence, appearing on talk shows and news interviews for months and managing to keep the issue in the papers and the public eye, characterizing the conviction of the Normandy Four as a racially motivated miscarriage of justice. And he spoke with ferocious eloquence against mob violence. The press paid more attention to his presence than to his philosophy. At one point, he was quoted as saying to a group of "reformed gang members" that "the truth is a tool of those with power. They squeeze the truth out of you and use it against you. Values are relative to power and the lack of it." When he read the quotation in the *L.A. Times* he wrote in his journal "I better not ever run for public office. That quote would hound me wherever I went. Do you believe it, yourself? Not entirely. There is a truth beyond interpretation; it's just that we can't tell which interpretation is true."

All through this period, Lowell appeared to be virtually angelic, almost saintly, and completely believable in his encounters with the press. As he began to take on the public persona of a compassionate martyr, he came to be disliked more and more by conservative politicians and the business community. The district attorney's office publicly attacked him. Conservative columnists called him a "moral relativist" and a "misguided promoter of race hatred." Lowell was about the most visible person in Los Angeles for weeks on end. His shortcropped white hair, which had a tendency to stand on end like a flattop of cowlicks, his long, gaunt face, the scars on his forehead and cheeks, his full white beard with a great patch scarred out of it on his right jaw, his proclivity for regimental striped ties and an Ivy League appearance made any efforts at evading notice impossible. And he really didn't want to become invisible anyway. "I'm in the public eye for a moment. I have a purpose to serve. Eventually, I'll recede into the background and disappear, like a pygmy, impoverished Howard Hughes," he wrote.

The night before the Normandy Four were to be released into the custody of their parents, Lowell was dining at the Smiths' house, which was crowded with family, activists, political supporters, and the legal team that had secured their release.

Lowell had written earlier in his journal that he was worried about meeting the young men face to face, fearful that he might "suddenly burst out in uncontrollable rage and go for their throats, unable to contain or hide my desire to kick the shit out of them, to teach them how it feels to be me. But maybe I can do that over the years, one on one with each of them, gently, with purpose, help them to come to terms with their own anger and feel *something*, anything really, for someone else. Maybe they'll eventually come to like me and feel bad about what they did, admit it, face up to it, and get it behind them. As much as part of me would like to kill them, I think this is what Hana would have tried to do."

His journal continued, "I'll meet these boys in the bosom of their families. And they'll know I know they did it, they'll sense it, feel it as something haunting that they can't quite put their finger on. Eventually, maybe many years from now, one of them will ask me something that will give me an in to explain what I did for them and why I did it. Someone will say something. I only hope I have the courage and the brains left to tell them. Maybe it won't happen until they are old and I am very old and they know better. Maybe they won't have very long to live at all. Maybe I'll have to help them purge themselves on their deathbeds. I don't know. Just give me the strength to do what is right to do."

After supper at the Smiths', Lowell and Mr. Thomas, whom Lowell had described earlier in his journal as "a man with a beautiful intellect and a passionate social conscience," went for a stroll around the neighborhood to walk off dinner and the double helpings of apple pie that Mrs. Thomas made sure they devoured. They were talking, no doubt, about what tomorrow would bring. Perhaps Lowell even told him something elusive about his misgivings. Police reports detail the events that followed. An "unknown vehicle" with "unknown occupants" opened up with, apparently, two assault rifles, spraying as many as fifty rounds of ammunition in the direction of Lowell and Mr. Thomas, cutting them down and killing Thomas instantly. When the bodies were found it was apparent that Lowell had lived long enough to wriggle through his own and Thomas's blood to reach the body of his friend. His head rested on Thomas's left calf, his hand on Thomas's back.

In the weeks of coverage that followed the assassination, one interview with Mrs. Thomas was the most revealing. Mrs. Thomas recalled the conversation around the dinner table an hour before the shooting. She said that Lowell and her husband were "smiling like kids, eating apple pie and talking about 'the possibilities,' and about how important it was to keep faith in what might happen next." "You never know what saving grace is just around the corner," she quoted Lowell as saying. The last thing she heard her husband say as he and Lowell walked out the door was "you've created possibilities we never could have imagined or hoped for."

—— ——

Lowell Briscoe and a friend were assassinated on December 13, 1995.

Postscript

After working four years to make sense of the historical and metaphoric circumstances described in this book, I have come to the conclusion that there is no clear path of blame. In fact, it seems to me now that the intellectual fallout of this story, and Lowell Briscoe's fanatic search for understanding, is that there is rarely, if ever, any clear, reliable, one-to-one blame relationship to be found in anyone's behavior and motivation. Certainly, crimes are committed and blame can be affixed to specific persons. But the cause-and-effect chains of events and circumstances that led to their actions, and perhaps determined them, are not open to our capacity for knowledge. Every effect, it seems, is the result of a tangle of causes that no one can unravel. If we cannot find cause and affix blame for situations, they appear to us to be meaningless. The mystery of meaninglessness torments us all. Why should meaning be so difficult to find? And why does the misery of our Odyssey toward meaning often lead to a greater sense of compassion and solidarity with others? The latter question has an almost self-evident answer. The one thing we all have in common is the condition of being subject to random, personal situations of indecipherable cause. No cause, no meaning: That seems to be the rule. As far as Lowell Briscoe's frustration of the will to meaning is concerned, his confusions were vast and intricate.

I've struggled to submerge in the text my overwhelming respect for Dr. Briscoe. I have long admired his work with abused and impoverished children around the world. His consistent stance against political violence, and his belief that misogyny is its grossest form, has been an inspiration to young women of my generation. That he was also a deeply flawed and troubled man makes his politics all the more admirable. But it's his classic Christmas fable, "The Witch and the Star," that I've appreciated the most, from the first time the story was read to me when I was six to my rereading of it again with my own children. It is, in my opinion, the most caring and yet unsentimental affirmation of the Christmas spirit I have read. I had no notion, until I began my research, that the heroine of the fable, Auntie Ana, was a real person transformed into a saint of childhood. Hana Nicholas was that real person, and the tormented childhood that was transformed into a blessing was Lowell Briscoe's. I am elated that Auntie Ana, my own childhood hero, embodying as a *free woman* all the compassionate nobility of the human race, was not wholly a fictional character, but was rather based on a real woman's life and deeds, a real person who lived in my own hometown for most of her adult life and, as it turns out, just blocks away from my own childhood home on Los Griegos Road. In the 1960s I played in the streets of the little subdivision that now occupies the site of Hana Nicholas's sprawling farm and magnificent old adobe that she called "Gloriamaris." I am sure I have walked hundreds of times over the very spot where she held her Christmas plays for the children of the neighborhood. I could well have been one of Hana Nicholas's "Christmas children," as Lowell Briscoe was in 1948. The more I have learned about this real person, the more I, too, have become convinced she was a saint of sorts. And since I have been writing this book and trying to solve the painful and often horrendous mysteries of her life, I have felt her presence around me, watching me and directing my gaze.

I have felt liberated when I have written in the voices of the characters in this book, trying if not to imitate them then at least to reflect the structure and tone of their thought. Speaking in the voice of Hana Nicholas, I have found in myself a tolerance that I have only associated in the past with my grandparents and mother in Ribera in San Miguel County, New Mexico. That Hana Nicholas was an Anglo whose temperament and character allowed her to internalize the values she found in New Mexico makes her eccentricity and integrity all the more valuable to me. When I speak in the voice of Lowell Briscoe, I discover in myself the language of anger and of cunning that allowed him to survive the gothic nature of his upbringing. It is an anger and cunning that I know of firsthand, in my own way, as a Catholic Latina struggling to succeed in Anglo male-dominated universities and media conglomerates.

Even after four years of researching and writing this book, during which I became painfully aware of the foibles and disagreeable traits of everyone involved, my admiration for Hana Nicholas—and for the Auntie Ana in Lowell Briscoe's Christmas fable—has never abated. She is the archetypal feminist pioneer, a female human being who would not be chained by the requirements of insidious conformity and "nice appearance" any more than Lowell Briscoe would be forced into